"Desires ar[...] Valerian said. "The more you deny them, the stronger they become, until they are all you can think about, all you can see."

"Stop right there." Her voice shook, and he knew she was deeply affected by what he'd said. "Don't try to engage me in a conversation about desires, okay? I'm not interested."

He grabbed her wrist, closing his fingers around her delicate bones with soothing finesse. He tugged her in front of him. A surprised gasp slipped from her.

"You're right," he said. "We should not talk about it. I should *show* you."

Suddenly panicked, Shaye leaped away from him and to the wall, where she grabbed one of the smaller swords. She held it in front of her, looking very much like the warrior queen she so vehemently denied being. "I just helped you, so you owe me a favor. And I'm asking that you not touch me tonight. Do you understand?"

He froze in place, a blank shield shuttering his expression. "Very well," he said. "Tonight is yours. I will not touch you."

"Thank you."

They stared at each other, locked in a silent battle. "Tomorrow, however, belongs to me...."

Gena Showalter

the Nymph King

Recycling programs
for this product may
not exist in your area.

ISBN 13: 978-0-373-77535-4

THE NYMPH KING

Printed in U.S.A.

Dear Reader,

I gave you a peek at Valerian, King of the Nymphs, in *Jewel of Atlantis*...but I didn't intend to tell his story. Well, I did—just not right away. There were several more books that I planned to write first. Bad little boy that he is, Valerian insisted I concentrate on him. (Picture me shaking my head and muttering, "Typical Nymph behavior.") I tried to say no. Really, I did. But...

I couldn't resist him. Neither can Shaye Holling, though she gives it her best shot. She's the woman Valerian is determined to claim. Like me, Shaye finds herself up against the greatest lover of all time. A mesmerizing and seductive force unlike any other. A rogue. A fantasy come to life.

Anyone else shivering?

I hope you enjoy reading their story as much as I enjoyed writing it. For more information about Atlantis and all the creatures and humans who reside there, visit my website at www.genashowalter.com.

Warmest regards,

Gena Showalter

To Leigh Michelle Heldermon and Shelly Mykal. Cousins. Extraordinary women. Angels (a long time ago I might have added "fallen" before that last one, but that's neither here nor there).

To Jill Monroe. You had me at hello, and now you complete me. You are the wind beneath my wings. I am nothing without you.

the Nymph King

CHAPTER ONE

Atlantis

UPON AWAKENING, Valerian, King of the Nymphs, untangled himself from the naked, slumbering woman beside him...only to discover his legs were entwined with two other naked, slumbering women.

With a sleep-rough chuckle, he fell back onto the softness of the bed, dark strands of feminine hair cascading atop his shoulder. Silky red tendrils floated over his stomach, intertwining prettily with another woman's blond tresses. Satisfaction hummed inside him.

There were only four females in residence, and all four were deliciously human. Utterly sexual. Captivating. A few weeks ago, right after his army had taken control of this fortress, the women had accidentally entered through a portal leading from the surface world. The gods must have been smiling upon him last eve because three of them had found their way into his bed.

He grinned slowly, and his gaze traveled over the sated beauties sleeping so peacefully around him. Tall, rounded and sun-kissed they were, with faces ranging from daringly bold to endearingly plain.

Whatever they looked like, he didn't care. Quite

simply, he loved women. He loved his power over them and wasn't ashamed of it. Wasn't repentant. Oh, no. He enjoyed. Relished. Savored.

Devoured.

Though none in particular had ever been more to him than a passing fancy, he adored every luscious inch of them. Their sweet softness, their breathy moans. Their decadent flavors. He loved the way their legs tightened around his waist (or head) and welcomed him into paradise, allowing him a gentle slide or a rough pounding—whichever he happened to prefer at the time.

As he lay there, light uncoiled slender fingers from the crystal ceiling above, caressing everything it touched and bathing his companions in a haze of glittery shadow and shimmery illumination. Desire scented the air, nearly palpable in its headiness. Heat radiated from each of the female bodies, weaving a dangerously seductive cocoon around them.

Yes, he led a sweet, sweet life.

Women had only to look at Valerian to crave him. Smell his erotically seductive Nymph fragrance to ready themselves for his pleasure. Hear his husky, wine-rich voice to strip for him. Feel a single caress of his fingertips to erupt into peak after delicious peak and beg for more. He was not boastful about this; it was simply fact.

Just then the female with the raven hair stirred and rested her small, delicate hand on his chest. Janet? Gail? He wasn't sure of her name. Couldn't recall *any* of their names, really. They were bodies, in a long line of well-pleasured bodies in which he found succor; females who had chosen to eagerly allow him inside.

"Valerian," the dark-headed one breathed, an exquisite prayer. Her expression remained soft from sleep, but her hand began a slow, downward glide and wrapped around his cock, stroking up and down, awakening it from slumber.

Without sparing her a glance, he reached down and clasped her palm to his, stilling her movement and bringing her fingers to his lips for a chaste kiss. She shivered, and he felt her nipples harden against his side.

"Not this morning, sweet," he said, speaking in her native tongue. It had taken him the entire length of the past two weeks, but he'd finally mastered her oddly fluid language. Once he'd figured it out, it was as if some part of him had always known it. "In a few moments, I must be on my way. I'm needed elsewhere."

As much as he would love to stay and lose himself in another hour (or two) of such delicious debauchery, his men awaited him in the training arena. There, he would help them hone their sword skills and vanquish the frustration plaguing them so fiercely all these many days. Hopefully their ever-present carnal needs would be forgotten as they prepared for the war he knew waited on the horizon.

War. He sighed. Since his army had conquered this palace and stolen it from dragons—dragons already weakened from a previous battle with humans—war had been inevitable. He accepted that. But now *his* men were weakened. Not from battle, though. They were weakened from lack of sex. And that was *un*acceptable.

Sexual contact helped their minds and bodies retain strength. Such was the way of the nymphs. Perhaps he should have brought the nymph females with them to this palace. But to keep them safe, he'd forced them to remain behind. He had not anticipated being separated from them this long.

Since the initial battle was over, he *had* summoned their females here. Unfortunately, they had not arrived and there was no trace of them in the Inner or Outer cities. Concern grew inside him daily. He'd sent a battalion of men to search for them—with an order to kill anyone who might have hurt them. Woe to that enemy, for a nymph's wrath was a terrible thing.

Despite his concern, he would not doubt if the females—who needed sex as desperately as the males—had stumbled upon a group of men and had yet to end their orgy. That didn't help his men, however.

"Hmm, you feel good," the dark-haired woman beside him whispered. "Being near you is better than making love with any other man."

"I know, sweet," Valerian uttered distractedly.

With no end in sight to his army's abstinence, he should have felt guilty for his excess last night. And he would have felt guilty, if he'd been the one to summon the women here. But they had followed him, tearing at his clothes and tracing their tongues over every inch of his flesh before he stepped a single foot into the room.

Truly, he had tried to peel them off and send them to his men, but the women had attacked him all the harder. What else could he have done but give in? Any other man—with a fully functioning cock, that is— would have done the same.

Perhaps, after the training session, he would suggest once again that these delectable morsels find other lovers.

"I know you have to leave, but…I'm dying to touch

you, Valerian." Black lashes fluttered coyly, and the raven-haired female dipped her lips into a pouty frown. She eased to her elbow, placing her lush breasts in his direct line of vision. "Don't tell me no," she beseeched, tracing a fingertip around his nipple. "You took such good care of me last night. Let me take care of you now."

On his other side, his other companions stirred.

"Mmm," the one with the fiery curls breathed. "Morning."

The other stretched like a contented kitten, uttering a low, throaty purr. As she inched into a sitting position, her disheveled golden locks tumbled onto her shoulders. When she spied him, she smiled slowly, seductively. "Good morning," she drawled, sleep clinging to her voice.

"You were amazing," the redhead said, her pale blue eyes wide with remembered satisfaction.

"As were you…sweet." Again he tried to remember her name, but couldn't. He shrugged. It wasn't important, anyway. They were all *sweet* to him. "Morning has arrived, and it's time for everyone to go about their duties."

"Don't send us away. Not yet," the dark-haired one said. Her warm breath fanned his ear a moment before her tongue flicked out and traced the curve of his left cheek. "Let us have another—" she kissed his jaw "—taste of—" nibbled his throat "—you."

Three sets of hands and breasts were suddenly all over him. Hot, greedy mouths sucked at him. Wet, needy female cores rubbed against him. The scent of new desire wafted from the bed, enveloping him.

"Just being near you makes me desperate to come," one gasped.

"You always know what I want even before I know," another panted. "I can't get enough of you."

"I'm addicted to you," the third breathed. "I'll die without you."

Moans and cries of pleasure echoed in his ears, the women's insatiable lust making them frantic for his touch. A fiery heat ignited in his own blood, strengthening him as only sex could. At times, when the need came upon him, he was reduced to an animalistic state, taking his lovers with a savage intensity better suited for the battlefield.

Now was one of those times.

With a growl, he opened his mouth and accepted someone's kiss, his hands tangling in hair and sweetly fragranced skin. Perhaps he'd join his men for lunch….

CLANG. WHOOSH. CLANG.

Sweat trickled down Valerian's bare chest, riding the ropes of muscle and pooling in his navel as he swung his sword, slamming the heavy metal into his opponent's upraised weapon.

Broderick stumbled backward and fell on his ass, flinging dirt in every direction. Some of it sprinkled on Valerian's freshly polished boots.

"Get up, man," he commanded when Broderick remained prone.

"Can't," his friend panted.

Valerian frowned. That was the fourth time Broderick had hit the ground during this training session, and they'd only been practicing an hour. Usually as stalwart and powerful as Valerian himself, Broderick's weakness today was disconcerting.

The guilt he'd managed to deny earlier roared to life. He should have sent the women on their way last eve, should have resisted them more determinedly this morning. While he was stronger than ever, these battle-hardened warriors were reduced to *this*.

"Damn it all," Broderick muttered, his voice strained. Still he remained on the ground, head bent and held in his upraised hands, golden hair shielding his eyes. "I'm not sure how much more of this I can take."

"What about the rest of you?" Valerian slashed his sword's tip into the sand, a tip that had been shaped and honed into the image of an elongated, lethal skull—a tip that inflicted irreparable damage. He'd aptly named it The Skull.

His gaze traveled the ranks of his army. Some were sitting on a bench, sharpening their blades, while others leaned against a silver-and-white stone wall, expressions lost, far away. Only Theophilus appeared ready for anything more than a nap. And only Theophilus paid him the least bit of notice.

Well, that was not quite true. Joachim was hunched over, elbows resting on his knees, his head tilted to the side as he gazed up at Valerian with undeniable sparks of fury.

What was his cousin angry about now? "Line up," Valerian commanded the entire group. "Now." The sharpness of his tone finally snagged their attention.

Slowly they ambled into a clumsy line, only a few of them trying to appear alert. His frown deepened. They were tall and well-muscled, his men, with bronzed skin and perfectly chiseled features. The force of their beauty sometimes caused grown women to weep. But right now they sported lines of tension around their eyes and mouths, shaky grips and unsteady legs.

"I need you strong and capable, but you're as weak as babes, every one of you." At any moment Darius, King of the Dragons, would learn Valerian had taken this palace, defeating everyone inside, and attack. How quickly these warriors would fall if they were challenged today.

His hands fisted at his sides. Defeat was not something he allowed. Ever. No, he would rather die. A warrior won. Always. No exceptions.

Broderick sighed and scrubbed a hand down his face, his expression grim. "We need sex, Valerian, and we need it now."

"I know." Unfortunately, the three exhausted humans sleeping in his bed would never be able to handle all of these lust-hungry nymphs at once.

He could send a handful of soldiers into the Outer City to capture sirens—a race of women who reveled in sex just as the nymphs did. Dangerous women, yes. Women who lured, seduced and killed. Well, tried to kill. But they were wonderfully satisfying to tumble, completely worth the risk.

However, the few times his men had entered the city in these past weeks, females of every race had remained well hidden, avoiding the nymphs as if they were hideous, foul-smelling demons. None wanted to find themselves enslaved to a nymph's dark, sexual hunger, losing their very identity, wishing only to please their lover. An inevitable outcome. Even for mates. *Those* females, whomever they happened to be, wherever they happened to be found, were treasured, but they were still enslaved.

"I can smell the humans on you, and it's making my own need all the more intense," Dorian said. With his obsidian hair, godlike features and mischievous sense of humor, women of every race usually flocked to him. There was nothing mischievous about him now, though. He radiated jealousy and resentment. "I'd kill you if I had the strength."

More guilt swept through Valerian. He had to make this right. As much as he hated to admit it, there was only one true solution to this predicament.

"Do you still wish to travel through the portal?" he asked, bracing his hands behind his back. Since discovering the strange, upright pool in the caves beneath this palace—the very pool the women had used to travel from the surface world to Atlantis—his men had begged to enter it so many times he'd lost count. Each time his answer had been the same: Gods, no. His friend Layel, King of the Vampires, had told him that Atlanteans could not survive on the surface for long periods of time.

Besides, he needed his men here, ready to fight and defend. But weak as they were now, these warriors would not obtain a victory over a tail-chasing griffin, much less a brutally savage fire-breather.

If there was a chance they could find more human women, traveling to the surface would be worth the risk, he realized.

"Well?" he said.

Nearly all of his men smiled and closed around him. A chorus of "Yes" burst from their mouths. Only Theophilus remained quiet, but then, he had no need to visit the surface. He was mated to the fourth human female in residence.

Mated. Valerian tried not to cringe. When a nymph mated, he mated for life. No matter his age, no matter his circumstances, when he found the woman destined to live at his side, his body would crave no other; his heart would beat only for one. *The* one. He'd been told a nymph would know this "one" the moment he scented her, and she would, in turn, recognize him, choosing him above all others.

Valerian, as well as many of his men, lived in fear of finding his mate, for too well did he enjoy his freedom. He couldn't imagine desiring only one woman. He couldn't imagine one woman being able to hold his interest and sate all of his passions for longer than a single night.

Perhaps he was not destined to take a mate. A man could hope, anyway.

"Will we travel through the portal?" someone asked, cutting into his thoughts.

"Yes," he said. He splayed his arms wide in surrender. "At last, my friends, I relent."

"How soon can we leave?" Broderick.

"Thank you, great king." Shivawn.

"Gods, my cock needs some female attention." Dorian.

Relief dripped from their voices. Already lust burned white-hot in their eyes, strengthening them. He didn't blame them for their eagerness to leave the palace. *He* would have been reduced to a snarling beast had he been forced to go without a woman's sweetness for as long as they had. But that was something he, as king, had never had to endure. And *would* never have to endure, he was sure.

His carnal appeal was greater than any other's, and

quite simply, no woman could resist him. A fact his men had long since accepted—and he himself enjoyed. "Most of you will have to remain here, guarding the palace," he informed them. "And those who go cannot stay long. No more than an hour, mayhap two. We'll bring back as many as we can, then decide who gets whom."

"We should have gone days ago," Joachim grumbled.

Valerian chose to ignore him. He knew frustration spoke for his cousin.

"Why do we need to return so quickly?" Dorian asked, frown returning. "I want to enjoy a lover or two before coming home."

"We know nothing of the surface, their people or their weapons, but more than that we do not know when the dragons will attack us. We must go in, grab the women we want and hurry back."

Broderick's sandy brows arched. "We?"

"I will lead you, of course." He wouldn't send his men into uncharted territory without him. "But do not worry. I won't be taking a woman for myself. The three happily sated and sleeping females in my room provide enough stimulation for me." For now. "I'll leave the claiming to you."

CHAPTER TWO

A FLORIDA WEDDING. Complete with wide expanse of glistening beach, crashing cerulean waves, magical pink-gold sunset and warm, sultry breezes. White rose petals were scattered along the fine-grained sand, dancing and twirling with every gentle wind. The couple even now pledging their undying love stared deeply into each other's eyes, their hands clutched together, their lips softly parted in expectation of the coming kiss.

Was there anything sweeter? Anything more romantic?

Was there anything more gagworthy?

Shaye Holling expelled a frustrated breath and gazed down at her seashell bikini top and grass skirt. Who picked this kind of crap for bridesmaids? Someone who wanted them to look like hideous beast monsters, that's who. The uglier the bridesmaids, the prettier the bride.

God, she was afraid to ponder what the richly dressed crowd of onlookers thought of her let-me-give-you-a-lap-dance hula outfit. *I probably resemble one of the slutty undead.*

Pale, that was Shaye. Pale skin, pale hair. More than one person had teased her throughout the years, calling her Casper, Snow Queen, Vampire, Albino. The esteem-crushing list went on and on. The only color she possessed came from her eyes; they were a deep, rich brown and were, in her opinion, her one redeeming feature.

She could have used the self-tanner her mom had sent her for this event, but the consequences from the last time she'd tried that type of product were still too fresh in her mind: frighteningly orange skin; diseased-looking, spotty hands and horrified stares. Maybe she should have spent a few hours in a tanning bed. They might blister her from head to toe, but at least she'd have some color. Fire-truck red, of course, but it *was* a color.

As she stood there, a new idea for her business, Anti-Cards, popped into her mind. *I must admit you brought religion into my life,* she thought, gazing at the bride, who also happened to be her mother. *I finally believe in hell.*

She sighed. The long length of her silvery-white hair dusted her shoulder, a perfect mimic of the creamy satin slip dress billowing at her mom's ankles. Was there anyone more beautiful than Tamara soon-to-be Waddell? Anyone more surgically enhanced? Anyone else who went through men like sexual Kleenex?

This was what? Her mom's sixth marriage?

At that moment, her mom looked over at her and frowned. "Back straight," she mouthed. "Smile."

As always, Shaye pretended not to notice the *helpful* commands. She focused her attention on the minister.

"To love, honor and cherish…" he was saying, his smooth baritone drifting through the waning sunlight. Mostly, Shaye heard *blah, blah, blah* before she blocked his voice altogether.

Love. How she despised the word. People used love

as an excuse to do ridiculous things. *He cheated on me, but I'm going to stay with him because I love him. He hit me, but I'm going to stay with him because I love him. He stole every penny from my savings, but I'm not going to press charges because I love him.* How many times had her mother uttered those very words?

How many times had her mother's boyfriends groped Shaye herself, claiming they'd only done it because they had fallen out of love with her mom and into love with her? Her, a mere child at the time. Perverts.

Shaye's father was another prime example of such "love is all that matters" idiocy. *I have to leave your mom because I've fallen in love with someone else.* Apparently he'd fallen in love with several someone elses.

After his last wife had cheated on him and then divorced him, Shaye had sent him an "I'm so sorry" card. What she had really wanted to send was a "Finally getting what you deserve sucks big-time, doesn't it" card. Of course, none had been available—which was the reason she'd started making her own. Anti-Card business was booming. Seemed there were a lot of people out there who wanted to tell someone to fuck off—in a roundabout way.

She worked eighty hours a week, but it was worth it. Thanks to popular cards like "I'm so miserable without you, it's almost like you're here" and "You can do more with a kind word and a gun than with just a kind word," she provided jobs for twenty-three like-minded women and made more money than she'd ever dreamed possible.

Life, for the weird-looking little girl who'd never met her parents' expectations, was finally good.

"You may now kiss the bride," the pastor said.

Thank God. Shaye expelled a relieved rush of breath, her shoulders slumping as her tension melted away. Soon she'd be on a plane, flying home to Cincinnati and her quiet little apartment. No signs of romance to irritate her there. Not even a cat to bother her.

Amid joyous applause, the brow-lifted, cheek-implanted groom laid a sloppy wet one on Shaye's mom. The glowing couple turned and strolled down the aisle, the lyrical thrums of a harp echoing behind them. Shaye inched closer to the water, away from the masses, escape within her grasp now that everyone was filing toward the reception tent.

She'd done her daughterly duty (again), and there was no more reason to stay. Besides, she wanted out of the chafing shell bra and itchy grass skirt ASAP.

"Where are you going, silly?" one of the other bridesmaids said, latching on to her arm with a surprisingly iron grip. "We're supposed to take pictures and serve the guests."

So, the torture wasn't over yet. She groaned.

After an hour of posing for a photographer who finally gave up trying to make her smile, she found herself serving cake to a line of champagne-guzzling guests. Most of them ignored her, merely swiping up their cake and ambling away. Some tried to talk to her, but (she was guessing) found her too abrupt and quickly retreated.

When will this end? I just want to go home. But the line had stopped moving, prolonging her torment. *Grrr.* She glanced up. A man had claimed his dessert, but hadn't stepped out of the way. Instead he watched her, studied her.

"Can I help you?" she asked.

"I'll take a little slice of you if you're serving it," he replied, balancing the plate in one hand and swirling his champagne with the other. His green eyes twinkled with merriment.

He wore a white shirt unbuttoned at the collar, a loosened black bow tie, and formfitting black slacks. His sandy hair was perfectly cut, not a strand out of place. A groomsman, she recalled.

"Sir, you're holding up the line." She forced a hard tone and severe expression as she returned to slicing cake and scooping it onto plates. She'd learned at an early age that it was best to keep people at a distance from the very first. And if she had to make them hate her to do so, so be it, because she could not allow herself the slightest inkling of softer emotion, the very thing that led to disappointment, rejection and heartbreak. "Move. Now."

The man didn't walk away as she'd hoped. "I think perhaps I need to—"

"Shaye, darling," her mother called airily. The expensive scent of her perfume wafted from her, blending with the aroma of sugar and spice as she floated to Shaye's side. "I'm so glad you've met your new stepbrother, Preston."

Stepbrother? *Not another one.* Showed exactly how much contact Shaye had had with her mom these past few years. She hadn't known that groom number six had children. Actually, she hadn't even met her newest daddy until an hour before the wedding.

Shaye glanced at Preston. "I've never played well with others," she said to smooth the edge of her earlier rudeness. But that was it, nothing more.

"So I hear," he said, chuckling.

He was even more handsome when he laughed like that. Looking away, she gathered two plates and passed them to the people behind him. "It was nice meeting you, Preston, but I really need to finish serving the guests."

The band chose that moment to break into a soft, romantic ballad. Preston still didn't take the hint and move away. "I never thought I'd say this, but would you like to dance with me, little sister? After you're finished here, of course."

She opened her mouth to say no, but no sound emerged. She wanted to say yes, Shaye realized. Even though her stepbrothers and sisters changed more frequently than her clothing and she'd most likely never see this man again, she wanted to say yes. Not because she was attracted to Preston or anything like that, but because he represented everything she'd always denied herself. *And need to keep denying yourself. Safer that way.*

"No," she said. "Just…no." Once again she turned her attention to the cake.

Her mother uttered a strained laugh. "There's no reason to be rude, Shaye. One dance won't kill you."

"I said no, Mother."

There was a heavy pause, then, "You," her mom said, voice suddenly hard. She pointed to one of the other horrendously clad bridesmaids. "Take over the cake. Shaye, come with me."

Strong fingers curled around Shaye's wrist. A second later she was being dragged out of the reception tent to the edge of the beach. *Here we go again….* She sighed. This always happened. Whenever she and her mom were forced to share the same space, Tamara always erupted, and Shaye always left reminded of what a disappointment she was.

God, I don't need this. Sand squished between her sandaled toes as a warm, salty breeze wrapped itself around her, swishing her grass skirt over her knees. Slivers of ethereal moonlight illuminated their path. Waves sang a gentle, soothing song.

Her mom's velvety brown eyes—eyes exactly like her own—narrowed slightly. She dropped Shaye's hand as if touching it could cause premature wrinkles. "You're treating my guests as if they're diseased."

Shaye wrapped her arms around her middle. "If you knew me at all," she said softly, "you'd know I treat everyone like that."

"I don't care how you treat everyone else! You will treat everyone here, including Preston—no, *especially* Preston—with respect. Do you understand me? Just—" she shoved a wisp of hair from her face "—pretend you have a heart for a few hours."

That stung. Badly. But Shaye forced herself to smile. "Why don't you go find your new husband and let him calm you down? This kind of upset will only cause you to shrivel up like a raisin."

Gasping in horror, her mom patted the skin around her eyes, feeling for crow's feet. "I just had Botox. I shouldn't have a single line or crease. Do you see a wrinkle? Do you see a goddamn wrinkle? I can't lift my brows to find out—the muscles won't work."

Shaye rolled her eyes. "Are we done here?"

Her mom stomped her foot and ground out, "I've finally found the love of my life. Why can't you understand that and be happy for me?"

"Uh, hello. This is the *sixth* love of your life."

"So the hell what? I've made mistakes in the past. That's better than cutting myself off from relationships like you've done, just to avoid getting hurt." She paused, raised her chin. "You spurn everything male, Shaye. You never date."

No, she didn't. Not anymore. She'd always been leery of the roads she would have to travel to obtain the fabled happily-ever-after. At one point, however, she *had* tried the dating thing. She'd quickly discovered that men never called when they said they were going to call. They weren't interested in her as a person; they were interested in getting her out of her clothing. They admired other women when they were supposed to woo her.

They lied, they used, they cheated. And they weren't worth the trouble.

Shaye twirled a strand of grass around her finger. "I wish you all the best with your new husband, Mother." No reason to rehash everything. Again. "Now, I'm going home."

"You're not going anywhere until you've apologized to Preston." A finger was shoved in her face. "You treated him shabbily, and I won't have it. I won't have it, do you hear me?"

She *had* treated him shabbily, and she felt bad for it. But she wouldn't apologize. That would invite conversation. Conversation would invite friendship, and friendship would invite emotion. Emotion, ultimately, would invite everything she'd worked so hard to avoid. "Do you truly expect me to obey a parental command from you? Now? After a childhood of being raised by nannies?"

"Well, yes" was the hesitant response.

"You're forgetting something. I'm the Ice Princess of Bitterslovakia, the Grand Duchess of Bitterstonia and the Queen of Bitterland. Isn't that what you've called me over the years?"

A gentle roll of waves splashed in the distance.

"I should have known you'd act this way," her mom snapped. With an angry flip of her wrist, she tossed a dark tress over her shoulder and glared out at the water. "All I've ever wanted was a nice, normal daughter. Instead I'm stuck with you. You won't be happy until you've ruined my wedding."

"Which one?" Shaye asked dryly, pushing aside her hurt. She much preferred the icy numbness she usually surrounded herself with. That numbness had saved her during childhood, sweeping her away from depression and desolation and into a life of satisfaction, if not contentment.

"All of them, damn it." Tamara didn't face her, but continued to stare out at the pristine water. Another splash sounded, this one closer. "You're jealous of me, and because of that you've never wanted me to be happy. Every time I'm close, you do something to hurt me."

Of all the things her mother had said, that cut the most. After all, Shaye was here because she wanted her mom to be happy. She'd never shoved the woman from her life, because, despite everything, she did care. It was something she'd fought against and hated, but there it was. The girl who wouldn't let herself care for anything or anyone else still wanted her mommy's approval. *Ugh.* "Don't blame me for your misery. You alone are responsible."

"Conner and I wanted this day to be perf—"

Tamara's eyes widened, glazing with lust as her words jammed to an abrupt halt. "Perfect." She sighed dreamily. "Hmm. So perfect."

The way her voice dropped to a husky purr, as if she wanted to peel off her dress and dance naked in the moonlight, had Shaye blinking in confusion. "Um, hello. Arguing here."

"Man." There was a hypnotized quality to the word, an entrancement that spoke of passion and secret fantasies. "My man."

"What are you talking about?" Shaye dragged her gaze to the ocean. Her mouth fell open in shock.

There, rising from the water like primitive sea gods, were six gloriously tall and muscled barbarians. The moon settled reverently behind them, enveloping them in a golden halo. Each of them carried a sword, an honest to God, I'll-slice-you-into-a-million-pieces sword, but she couldn't seem to make herself care. They also carried unconscious scuba-clad men, some anchored under their arms, others draped over their backs. Again, she couldn't make herself care.

The warriors were shirtless, and all of them possessed sinewy washboard abs, skin so tanned it resembled liquid gold poured over steel, and faces any male supermodel would have envied. Only better. So much better.

Unbelievable…surreal…magnificent.

Shaye gulped, and her heart skipped a beat. Heated air snagged in her lungs, burning and licking her with white-hot flames. All six of the warriors were suddenly looking at her as if she'd make a tasty meal, no silverware required. Strangely enough, she wanted to splay herself on a table, naked, offering her body as the dinner buffet. All you can eat. No charge.

She moistened her lips, her mouth watering, her skin tingling, her stomach clenching. *I'm turned on. Why the hell am I turned on?* More important, why wasn't she running?

Closer and closer they came. So close now she could see the silvery water droplets sliding down their hairless chests and gathering in their sexy navels. The water slid lower, lower still....

Snap out of this, dummy, she thought dazedly. Her gaze snagged on the man in the middle, and for a moment she forgot to move. Forgot to breathe. *Dangerous,* her mind supplied. *Lethal.* He was taller than the rest, his dark-blond hair hanging in a wet tangle around his wickedly mesmerizing features. His eyes... Oh, Lord. His eyes. They were blue-green, neither color blending with the other but standing alone, and so erotically seductive she felt the pull of his gaze all the way to her bones. Her nipples hardened, and an ache throbbed between her legs.

There was something wild about him, something untamed and savage, a deceptively calm glint in his expression that said he did whatever the hell he pleased, whenever the hell he wanted. And as she stared at him, he stared at her. He studied her face, searing arousal flickering in those magnificent eyes of his, deepening and mixing the blue-green to a smoldering turquoise. But the arousal was quickly followed by a glint of anger.

Anger? Was he mad? At her?

"Mine," her mom said on a wispy catch of breath, still lost in some sort of trance. "All mine."

Never ceasing their confident swaggers, the warriors exited the water and dropped the still-unconscious scuba-men on the beach. Arms now free, the warrior in the middle cocked his finger, beckoning Shaye over to him. Shivering, drowning in his maleness, she somehow managed to shake her head no. *Go to him,* her naughty mind beseeched. She shook her head again, violently this time.

The man's smooth chin canted to the side, and he frowned. "Come here," he said, his voice a husky whisper that drifted over the small distance, as intoxicating and heady as an erotic caress.

Another shiver slipped down her spine, so intense she almost fell to her knees. What would happen if he actually touched her? What would happen if he trailed those luscious pink lips along her every curve and hollow?

Stop, Shaye, a small, rational voice inside her commanded. *Just stop.*

"Come here," he repeated.

"Yes," her mom said, already stepping toward them. The dreamy glaze in her eyes darkened with eagerness. "I need to touch you. *Please* let me touch you."

The part of Shaye that acknowledged these men were dangerous also acknowledged there was something wrong with her mom—and with herself—but she still couldn't seem to care. A stunningly intense sensual fog was weaving through her mind, and nothing else mattered.

"Fight this," she told herself. "Fight this, whatever it is." Waging a mental war, she kicked and shoved at the sudden images of herself and that man, naked and straining together, his mouth on her breasts, his fingers slipping inside her, her legs parting, giving him better access....

"No. No!" she ground out. Even as she spoke, a blanket of calm settled over her thoughts. A familiar, icy wall encased her emotions, pushing away everything but the need to escape.

These men, whoever—*whatever*—they were, were dangerous, their intentions obviously malicious. They had *swords,* for God's sake, and they radiated lust. Blood lust, sexual lust, she didn't know.

They were almost upon her.

Scowling, fear cresting, she reached out and latched on to her mom's arm, jerking Tamara to a halt. "Don't go near them."

"Must…touch."

"We have to get help, warn the others. Something!"

"Let me go." She struggled against Shaye's hold, desperate to free herself. "I have to—"

"*We* have to go back to the tent. Now move!" Dragging her flailing mother behind her, Shaye raced toward the reception area, toward the laughing voices, soft music and unsuspecting guests.

As she ran, she dared a glance behind her. The men hadn't slowed, hadn't turned away. Lust and hunger intensified in their features as they followed her.

"Help us," she shouted, kicking sand with every step. She swept the curtain aside and entered the tent. "Someone call 911!"

No one heard her. They were too busy dancing and drinking themselves into oblivion, thanks to the open bar.

"Let me go," her mom continued to shout. When that failed to gain her freedom, she sank her sharp little teeth into Shaye's arm.

"Goddamn it!" Shaye did the only thing she could

think of: she hooked her foot behind her mom's ankles and pushed, sending the bride hurling backward into the dessert table. Food and platters crashed to the ground, but at least her mom remained horizontal, trying to catch her breath.

Several people glanced at Shaye, then at the fallen bride. Their eyes widened, some in confusion, some in horror, but mostly in amusement.

"There are men—" Shaye pointed "—out there. Dangerous men. They have swords. Does anyone have a gun? Did someone call 911?"

Reoriented, her mom jolted to her feet, unconcerned that red-and-white frosting now streaked her ten-thousand-dollar dress. She elbowed her way past the guests. "I need him. Let me go back to him."

"Tamara?" her new husband asked, incredulous. He rushed toward his bride and locked her in his arms, his expression concerned as she struggled to break free. "What's wrong with you, kitten?"

"I need...*him*." The last word was uttered on a relieved, happy sigh.

The six sea gods had jerked back the tent flap. They stepped inside, consuming every inch of breathable space and blocking the only exit. Immediately the music screeched to a halt. The male guests cowered, as if death had just arrived, and the females gasped in bliss, already moving toward the warriors, reaching out, eager to touch them.

"Get out of here," Shaye growled. "We have weapons. Guns...and...and other menacing stuff."

All six sets of eyes scanned the crowd, drinking in every detail...searching...searching...and then locking on her. She trembled, dizzying warmth spearing her. Naked images tried to rush through her again. Sweaty skin, flushed, pink with arousal...

Not again! She forced her mind to remain blank.

Who were these men? How did they do that? How did they make her long to forget who and what she was and simply enjoy the pleasures she somehow knew they could give her?

Fighting a wave of panic, Shaye quickly grabbed the cake knife from the ground and held it in front of her. Icing smeared her hand; her heart thumped erratically in her chest. In high school she'd picked a few fights with her stepsiblings. Yes, it had been her misguided attempt to keep them at a distance so she wouldn't begin to like them only to lose them a few months later, but she'd actually managed to win some of those fights. Not that any of her brothers and sisters had carried knives or sported more muscles than two body builders fused together.

The warrior in the middle, the exquisitely formed blond giant who had beckoned her over to him on the beach, motioned her over once more. There was still a hint of anger in his eyes, still a too-sensual pull about him. Now, however, he seemed all the more predatory. Sexual. In the well-lit tent, she could see the silver hoop winking at his nipple.

"Come," he said.

Everything inside her might scream to obey, to go to him, to suck that hoop into her mouth while she ground herself against his erection, but she gulped and shook her head. "No." Erection. God. She hadn't even looked there. But she knew, as if the knowledge was imprinted on her every cell, that he *was* aroused.

His kissable, lickable lips lifted in a slow, wicked smile, as though he'd wanted her to deny him. "I will delight in showing you the error of your ways."

Yep. He'd wanted.

CHAPTER THREE

MY MATE, VALERIAN thought, incredulous. He'd found his mate.

He hadn't been looking, hadn't wanted to find her, but found her he had. As legend claimed, he'd caught the scent of her and had known. Known beyond any doubt. *Mine.* His every cell had awakened for her, responded to her.

When he and his men had first exited the portal, human sea-warriors clad in strange, tight, black garments had attacked them and tried to drag them onto boats that waited above. There had been a struggle, but the nymphs ultimately won, disposing of both the men and the boats. After that, the nymphs hadn't cared about the scenery of this surface world they'd only dreamed about. They simply wanted to find some women and sweep them to Atlantis.

One female in particular had caught and held his gaze. She was tall and slender, yet beautifully curved, her stomach flat, her hips slightly rounded. Her legs were long and tapered and climbed straight to the new center of his world.

Her angelic face boasted a luscious little chin, glowing cheeks and a daintily sloped nose. Her eyes were big and brown, a rich brown, almost gold, filled with striking vulnerability and undeniable determination, offset stunningly by pale, gloriously long lashes.

He'd never seen skin as fair and luminous as hers, not even on a vampire. Like the very moon he'd seen shining in the heavens, she was soft and radiant. Ethereal. His hands itched to reach out and caress her slowly, lingering and savoring, making sure she wouldn't shimmer away, an unattainable dream.

As to the clothing she wore, well, he vowed to keep her dressed exactly so for the rest of her life. The many strips of green grass hanging from her waist parted with her every breath, revealing succulent glimpses of her thighs. No, he hadn't wanted to find his mate—and a human, no less—and he was angry that he had. But beneath the anger was a possessive hunger he couldn't deny. Didn't want to deny.

He'd been pleasured by women (many, many women) for so many years he'd forgotten what it felt like to desire one on his own. To simply look and crave. Already his blood heated with a seemingly un-quenchable fire, and his skin tightened. *Mine.* His muscles hardened. *Mine.*

Obviously she hadn't yet recognized him as her mate. In fact, she seemed to want only his disappearance. Humans, he inwardly scoffed. Standing as she was, she appeared untouchable, this mate of his, but touch her he would. He would die if he didn't.

Valerian paused, blinked, the words echoing through his mind. *He would die if he didn't.* How many times had a woman said something similar to him? That she would die if he didn't touch her? That she would die if he didn't fuck her? He'd never understood that until just now, this moment, studying the little moonbeam.

She was essential to his being. Hate that fact, he might, but there it was.

As he drank her in, her lips parted slightly, as if she couldn't decide whether to suck in a breath or belt out a scream. Valerian wanted her to do both. Wanted to hear his name roll from her tongue as she panted and screamed in climax.

She was his mate—his woman—and he would prove it to anyone who said otherwise. Even her. Oh, yes. His every cell knew it, knew she belonged to him. Never again would he be able to enjoy another woman. Enjoy? he thought. He almost laughed. Had he ever truly enjoyed a woman until now?

He wanted the moonbeam, with her ghostly hair and frosty skin. The moment he had seen her, bathed so prettily by the moonlight, he'd wanted her. The world around him had faded, and he'd seen only her. She radiated an untouchable veneer his every warrior instinct responded to and relished.

Gods, he wanted her. Just looking at her now, his body forgot about the day's excesses. He was starved for a taste of her.

But she had told him no. Several times. She'd run from him, too. Valerian hadn't yet tamped down his shock over that fact. Or his arousal. The warrior in him delighted in the challenge of changing her mind and making her desperate to have him.

His gaze flicked to the small dagger she held, upraised and ready, and the corners of his mouth twitched. Did she really think to keep him from her with such a puny blade?

Oh, but she had a lot to learn about a determined nymph warrior.

"Gather all the unmated females," he told his men, speaking in his native tongue, never taking his gaze from the object of his fascination.

She retreated a step. When she realized what she'd done, she stilled. She straightened her shoulders, raised the blade higher and stepped back into place. Ah, a woman of courage. One who would fight to the death. He grinned, desiring her all the more.

"What do you want with us?" she demanded, using the same language the other surface females had used.

He barely heard her words; he was too entranced by the way her soft-as-petals lips moved so sensuously. By the pink little tongue he'd glimpsed inside. His cock jerked in reaction.

A female suddenly brushed her fingertips over his arm. He tore his gaze from the moonbeam—surely one of the most difficult things he'd ever done—and glanced down. Not just one female, he noticed, but several surrounded him. They had already worked their way to him and his men and were running their hands over them, oohing and aahing, some even rubbing their breasts against them.

Valerian bit back a gasp of shock when he noticed one of the human *males* trying to kiss Dorian. Dorian wore an expression of utter horror and pushed the determined male away.

"Only the unmated ones?" Broderick asked, his eyes closing in surrender as a pretty brunette licked his collarbone.

"Only the unmated ones," he confirmed. The nymphs would be able to smell another man on the women, and those women with permanent lovers would be left here. If the pale little moonbeam who held him so enraptured had already been mated, he would have taken her anyway. Without reservation. But he knew from her sweet, entrancing scent that she belonged to no man save himself.

Not needing any more encouragement, his men leaped into action, beckoning the unmated females to line up. Of course, these women obeyed without hesitation, their feminine instincts instructing them to obey a nymph's every edict. The mated ones cried in distress because they weren't chosen and tried to shove their way into the line, anyway. Even the male who desired Dorian tried to take a place in line.

When a human man protested the happenings, he was quickly subdued: a hard fist to the temple that swept him straight into slumber. Most were too frightened to do anything and remained hunched and shaking at the edges of the tent. What puny men, Valerian thought. Had they never engaged in battle before? He could not imagine acting in such a way.

He returned his attention to the moonbeam. "Do you know who I am?" he asked her.

"What do you want with us?" she demanded a second time, ignoring his question.

He grinned his most debauched grin. "What any man wants from you. Your body. You will belong to me. Now, come."

Instead of obeying, she bared her teeth in a scowl, revealing a white row of perfection. Why wasn't she entranced by him? Why wasn't she begging for his touch? The mystery intrigued him.

"You can't do this," she spat. "Get out of here before the police arrive and you're arrested."

Police? Arrested? Valerian frowned. "You will change your mind about my possession of you, this I swear." He maneuvered around the women still vying for his attention and closed the distance between himself and the moonbeam. Her dark eyes widened with his every step. The closer he came, the more her delectable fragrance drew him like an invisible chain. Except…

One of his warriors reached her first, his strong arms wrapping around her from behind and swooping her into his arms. She screamed and kicked, fighting like an enraged vampire famished for blood.

A feral growl rose in Valerian's throat, and he bit back a wave of utter fury. Fury over her torment; fury over his intense sense of possessiveness. *Mine. She belongs to me.* He'd never experienced a moment's jealousy in his life. He and his men shared women all the time. But the sight of another man holding his little moonbeam nearly undid him.

"Mine," he barked. Even though he wanted to rip the warrior's arms away from her, he remained still. "She's mine."

Shivawn paused, the beads in his hair clanging together. The moonbeam continued to fight in his arms, pounding her fists into his face, making him bleed and grimace.

If he dropped her and hurt her, Valerian seethed, he would die.

"But, my king, you said you didn't want any of these surface women. You said they were for us."

He had, Valerian realized. The reminder sent another

wave of dark fury pounding through him. He'd never broken his word to his warriors before; they would expect him to keep his promise today, and rightly so. Which meant one of his men would expect to claim this woman, *his* mate, for his own, stripping her, pleasuring her, watching her climax.

He couldn't allow that.

Every instinct he possessed demanded he do something, anything, to prevent it from happening. Yet there was nothing he could do now and he knew it. Eyes narrowing and hands clenching at his sides, he said, "*I* will carry her," an edge of steel to the words.

Shivawn regarded him silently for a protracted moment, then shrugged, handing her over. "She's a wild one. Be careful of her legs, for she'll try to kick your manhood." The moment his hands were free, Shivawn grasped another woman, a dark-haired beauty who looked less than pleased by the happenings around her.

Hmm. Very odd. Another unhappy one. What was wrong with these surface females?

Valerian forgot about her, however, as he gently clasped the moonbeam in his arms. She stilled, delicious little bumps breaking out over her skin. She kept her face away from him and wrapped her hands over her stomach. Unable to resist, he burrowed his nose into her neck, breathing in her fragrance of…snow and wild flowers—yes, that's what her scent was—relishing the softness of her pale skin.

"Do you smell my scent?" he asked her.

"N-no. Should I?"

His shoulders slumped with disappointment.

"If you don't put me down," she said stiffly, as if

each word were forced from her throat, "I'm going to claw out your eyes and eat them in front of you."

He chuckled, disappointment forgotten. She had a sweet face and a bloodthirsty nature. What a delicious contradiction. "Why are you not begging for me to pleasure you?"

"Are you kidding me?" she gasped out. "Someone needs to check into Egos Anonymous, I see. Now put me down!"

"You did not answer my question."

"And I'm not going to. For God's sake, put me down!"

"I want to hold you. Forever."

A muscle ticked in her jaw, but this time she didn't reply.

"I wish I could give you what you ask," he said, "but too well do I like where you are." The side of her body was pressed into his chest, and everywhere their skin touched, he burned. "Perhaps, though, I would be willing to bargain with you. Perhaps you could convince me to grant your request."

Finally she cast her glance in his direction. When their gazes met, blue against golden brown, he sucked in a breath. Awareness sizzled inside him, stronger than before. Such beauty. His nostrils flared, and he knew his pupils dilated. His body hardened painfully.

She gulped, and her already pale skin became pallid. "No bargaining. Just put me down. Or do you and your steroid goon squad plan to rape us?"

"Rape?" he asked, unfamiliar with the word. Judging by her tone, it was not favorable. "Explain this rape to me."

She did. And in the most disgusted voice he'd ever heard.

He chuckled again. Unconcerned male pig? Unwilling female? "Sweet moonbeam, how you amuse me. I've never forced a woman in my life, and I will never have to. No, when I get you into my bed, you will be desperate for it. Desperate for me."

CHAPTER FOUR

WHEN I GET YOU INTO BED, you will be desperate for it. Desperate for me.

To Shaye, the utter confidence in his voice was more frightening than if he'd screamed the words. As it was, a delicious heat wove through her blood. A heat that begged her to stop resisting and enjoy every stolen touch, every caress of the man's breath on her skin.

Never mind that the other women in the tent were petting the warrior as if he were an innocent house cat. Make that an innocent blow-up doll. They were begging—yes, begging—him to make love with them. Moaning, even, and groaning. Sounds of rapture continually wafted to her ears.

Give in, her body beseeched. *Taste him. One taste won't hurt you.*

Panicked by her weakening will, Shaye slammed her palm into her captor's nose. His head whipped backward, and blood trickled onto his lip. "Why did you do that?" he demanded after a shocked pause.

Thankfully, his hold on her had loosened. Shaye bowed her back, and he struggled to maintain his grip on her. She managed to squirm free and tumble to her feet. *Get out of here!* common sense shouted, drowning out her body's ever-growing wails for her to stay. She stepped forward, dragging her wild gaze in every direction, scanning for her mom. Her breath emerged in shallow, ragged pants.

She saw Preston, lying unconscious on the floor. When he'd protested the warrior's actions, one of them had hit him. She saw Conner, her mom's new husband, frantically searching the crowd. But there was no sign of her mom. Damn it! Where was she? They might have a rocky relationship, but Shaye couldn't— wouldn't—leave her behind.

Shaye stepped forward, intending to follow Conner's lead and push through the masses, but the warrior behind her seized her wrist in a viselike clamp. Her blood ran hot from the sensual touch, then cold from fear.

He'd asked her if she smelled him, and she'd said no. Well, she'd lied. She inhaled his erotic, virile fragrance every time he was near, and it fired her hormones into a frenzy. Now was no different.

"You hit me," he said. Undiluted shock layered his words, as if no one had ever dared raise a hand to him before. "Why did you do that?"

Silent, Shaye turned around and kneed him in the balls. Just lifted her leg and *boom*. Contact. He doubled over, a strained wheeze gasping from his throat.

"Not so hot for my body now, are you?" she mumbled, never stopping her search.

"That…hurt," he gritted out.

"Of course it did, and there's more where that came from if you grab me again."

Without another word, she darted away, still looking…looking… There! Finally. In the corner, her new stepdad had his arms wrapped around her mom, locking a struggling Tamara in place.

Shaye jumped over fallen chairs and skirted around upturned tables, slipping and sliding along a river of red punch. Someone snaked an arm around her waist and hauled her against a stone wall of a chest—and it wasn't *her* warrior. This man's scent was different, not quite as exotic. Even his skin felt different, not quite as hot. His arms possessed a faint dusting of dark hair.

She screamed and slammed her head backward, hitting him in the chin. Her entire body vibrated with the force of the blow. He growled something, and she didn't have to know his language to know he was cursing. His arms fell away; she whirled on him, ready to fight.

She never should have come here, never should have gotten on the plane. Nothing good ever came of her mom's weddings. Only pain and suffering, and *this* was the worst of all.

The he-man regarded her through wide blue eyes. "I only meant to kiss you," he said, in English this time, his voice so heavily accented she had trouble deciphering the words. When her frantic mind finally deduced his meaning, she slapped him.

"Ow!"

"No kissing." What was it with the Steroid Squad and their carnal obsessions? *Let me pleasure you. You'll be desperate for me.* No, no and no! Except for the leader. Or the one she assumed was the leader. Earlier, when they'd first entered the tent, he'd spoken in that strange language and all the men had rushed into action. Him, she foolishly desired.

Her eyes narrowed. His ethereal, beautiful face

formed in her mind. Fuck-me eyes, fuck-me lips. I'll-fuck-*you* body. She bit the inside of her cheek until she tasted blood. How did he wield such a heady, seductive power? Even now, she sizzled and ached and yearned.

An obviously gay wedding guest dressed in a pink sequined top and black velvet pants approached the warrior in front of her. Without asking permission, the man wrapped his lithe arms around the warrior's middle and kissed his sun-bronzed shoulder.

The warrior stiffened, and his mouth pulled into a scowl. "I told you to stop. Do. Not. Touch. Me. You are a man. Act like one!"

Shaye didn't hang around to hear the rest of the conversation. She leapt around her would-be captor, closing the rest of the distance between herself and her mom. "Come on, we have to get out of here," she said at the same time Tamara said, "If you don't let me go, Conner, I'll stab you while you're sleeping and cut out your heart!"

Lines of strain bracketed the groom's too-thin lips. Concern and fear gleamed in his eyes. "What should I do?" he asked, looking to Shaye.

Urgency pounded through her. "Just throw her over your shoulder fireman-style and get the hell out of here. Before it's too late."

"It *is* too late," she heard behind her.

The familiar, husky voice made her shiver. Made her muscles clench, ready for sublime satisfaction. She melted. No, she stiffened. One of the leader's hands slid around her bare stomach, tanned and hard against her pale softness. Goose bumps broke over her skin. His other hand glided down her shoulder, along her collarbone and anchored on her seashell-covered breast. Both arms tugged her gently backward and locked her against him, muscled chest to welcoming back. That delicious scent of virility and dark, moonlit nights wafted to her.

She should protest. At the very least scold him for such daring. The words refused to leave her mouth, however, and she counted her blessings that she didn't lean her head against his shoulder.

"No more fighting." His warm breath kissed the hollow of her ear, shooting dangerous sparks across her nerve endings. "My nose still hurts," he added sulkily, "as does my co—manhood. Perhaps the first thing I need to teach you is how to properly treat the aforementioned manhood."

Oh, God. Sinking…sinking…deeper under his spell. If it hadn't been for the shell barrier of her bra, his fingers would have surrounded her nipple, probably pinched and rolled it. Her knees almost crumbled. Ohmygod, ohmygod, oh…my…exquisite. Absolutely exquisite. The long, hard length of his erection pressed into the crevice of her lower back, and he rubbed it against her.

Her eyes drifted closed in surrender, a strange weakness invading her limbs. She'd always thought herself immune to lust. On all the dates she'd been on, no one had ever affected her like this. Not even the ones that ended in a kiss. Those seemed paltry now, utterly unexciting.

Men annoyed her, she reminded herself, and this one annoyed her more than any other. *Keep thinking it and maybe you'll believe it.*

To her horror—cough, total enjoyment, cough—he

brought his other hand into play, cupping her other breast. "Paradise," he whispered. "Are you sure you do not smell me?"

Why did he want her to smell him so badly? "I'm sure."

Pause. Then, "Imagine when I have you naked, how intense the sensations will be."

Yes, he annoyed her. And she wanted to be annoyed for the rest of her life. "Please," she managed to gasp out. Sadly, she didn't know exactly what she was begging for. Freedom? Or more of him?

"Please what?" Showing her no mercy, he purred the words straight into her ear. His soft lips brushed the outer edge; his tongue darted inside, only to quickly retreat and leave her shaking for more. "Please take you to my home? Please give you untold pleasure? Say the words, and I will do it."

Oh, God.

Around her, excited twitters and breathy moans of passion reigned as other couples stole a moment to embrace. No matter that no one paid her the slightest bit of attention. These people could see her, could see where her captor had his hands positioned.

If she didn't stop him soon, he would slide his fingers past her skirt and into the very heat of her. She knew it, *felt* it in the taut strain of his hold. "Please. Let us go. Just leave us alone."

"I'm afraid that's the one thing I cannot do for you." He squeezed her breasts. "I need to be inside you too badly."

She gulped. *Don't think about his words, don't think about his words.* "I'll give you nothing but trouble. I'm mean and cranky, and most people can't stand to be around me."

"Soon I'll have you so well sated all you'll be able to do is smile."

"Sate *me*," her mom said, finally ripping free of Conner's clasp. She curled herself around the warrior's ankles, kissing his feet. "Sate me, I beg you."

"Get up," Shaye demanded. Seeing her newly married mother humble herself snapped her out of the sensual spell. "Run. Escape!"

He ignored Tamara, saying, "What's your name, swee—love?" The question emerged as calmly as if it were an everyday occurrence to have someone slobbering all over his boots.

"I'm Tamara," her mom answered before Shaye could speak, "but you can call me anything you want."

Sighing, he bent down, lifted Tamara up with one hand, and thrust her at Conner. His hold on Shaye never loosened. "What is your name?" he repeated, having to speak over Tamara's sudden sobs.

Mutinous, Shaye pressed her lips in a thin line and forced herself to ignore the heady, seductive fire tingling through her. What could she do to force her mother to listen? To rip the foolish woman out of her enchantment?

"I will bargain with you. I will tell you my name, and then you will tell me yours." He paused. When she didn't respond, he continued, "I am Valerian, leader of the nymphs. You may call me Oh, God. That is what the other surface dwellers have preferred to call me."

Valerian. The name whispered along every corridor and hollow of her mind. He—wait. Had he said *surface dwellers?* "I'd prefer to call you Person Whose Ass I'm Going To Kick, and what do you mean, surface dwellers?"

A pause, thick and heavy and tense, fell over them like a curtain. Then, "You surprise me," he said, the honeyed timbre rich with confusion. "I expected my mate—"

A string of foreign words cut him off.

Stiffening, Valerian faced the speaker. Shaye did the same. The man was nearly as tall as the one holding her, but his hair was black and his eyes were green as emeralds. He, too, wore only pants and boots, his bronzed, bare chest on ample display. He said something else.

Valerian responded in the same, clipped language.

What were they saying?

When he next spoke, the dark-headed man motioned to Shaye with a tilt of his chin.

Whatever Valerian's reply, it was not nice. His tone was hard, utterly unbending. Dripping with command. The warrior paused only a moment, shrugged and strode away.

"What was that about?" Trying not to panic again, Shaye angled her head and stared up at Valerian.

That proved to be a mistake. A big, fat chocolate-covered mistake. The moment their gazes locked, a wave of sexual energy sparked between them, stronger than before, undeniable and irresistible. He ate her up with his eyes, bit by devastating bit, mentally stripping her, already riding her. Hard. Fast.

Look away. Look away, damn it! Any more of that piercing, heady gaze and she'd come. Then and there, no physical stimulation required. Need coiled between her legs, pooling hot and wet, spiraling through her stomach, her nipples.

"Oh, God," she gasped out. *Look away!* The intense ache was too much. "What was that conversation about?" She didn't mean to shout, but the question ripped from her as she jerked her gaze to the ground.

"I am taking you to your new home," he answered. "You will live with me and see to my every need. Will you come willingly?"

"Hell, no." Her eyes narrowed on her sandals as she fought the urge to face him again. "I'm staying here. Do you hear me? I'm staying!"

He leaned down, his mouth teasing her ear. "I'm glad you said that, for now I get to carry you." Without another word, he spun her around and hefted her onto his shoulder as if she weighed nothing more than a bag of feathers.

"Idiot! Jackass! Moron!" She fought and kicked with all her might, and her knee slammed into his stomach. "Put me down. I'll make you miserable. I'll never stop fighting you. I won't see to your needs."

"You, love, will make me a well-satisfied man," he gritted out. "That I promise you." He strode past the line of women.

Even through her struggles, Shaye held her mom's watery stare until the tent flap was swept aside and Valerian carried her into the night. At least her mom wouldn't be forced to endure…whatever these men were going to make her and the others endure.

The rest of the men fell into pace beside Valerian. The young, single women followed blithely, happily, behind them. From inside the tent, the sound of feminine sobs echoed. "Take me with you," several called. "Please. I'm begging."

Shaye stilled. She rubbed her eyes, pinched the bridge of her nose. *This is not happening.* Surely this big, brawny, sinfully gorgeous warrior was not carrying her over his shoulder, striding toward the ocean, determined to take her to his home. Wherever that might be. What should she do? What *could* she do?

Valerian hesitated for a moment, as did the others. "Beautiful," he whispered, gazing at the velvety night sky, the pinpricks of starlight. "So beautiful." He spoke in English—for her benefit? "Now that we have our women, we can enjoy the sights."

"The heavens seem to go on forever," another said, awed. He, too, spoke in her native tongue, following Valerian's lead.

"I'd dreamed of this land, but never imagined such majesty."

"Are you sure we cannot stay here, my king? We could bring the rest of the army here and—"

Valerian shook his head, and the silky tendrils of his hair brushed her bare back. She shivered. "I am sure," he said. "Layel was very clear. To remain on the surface is to die on the surface. Let us tarry no longer." He started forward, expecting everyone to follow. They did.

"For the last time, put me down!" Shaye shouted. She slapped his butt. "Now!"

He slapped her butt in return, then surprised and excited her by massaging away the sting. His hand lingered and savored the feel of her backside. If her grass skirt parted any more...

She snarled low in her throat. Angry at him, angry at herself. Remaining cool and emotionless was not an option. "This is illegal. You're going to get caught.

Criminals always get caught. At your trial I'm going to request the death penalty."

"As long as I have tasted you, I can die a happy man."

"Is that supposed to make me shut up?" She beat her fists into his back, watching sand kick at his feet. The echo of churning waves filled her ears. "Is it supposed to make me happy that you've got me trussed up like a sack of potatoes? And why the hell are you walking toward the water?"

"I told you. We are going to my home." His gait easy, he stepped over several of the scuba-clad men who were still lying motionless on the beach.

"Did you kill those men?" she demanded. "Who are they?"

"They were waiting at the portal and attacked, so I did not stop to seek an introduction. And no, we did not kill them. We simply made them sleep." Valerian entered the ocean. Cool waves lapped at his ankles…his knees…thighs. Salty droplets sprayed over her face, burning her eyes.

A gasp slipped from her lips. "Stop! Stop this instant. Put me down."

He kept moving, sinking deeper and deeper into the water.

"Idiot! What are you doing? You're going to drown me."

"I will never allow harm to befall you, little moonbeam." Still, he continued into the water. The other women followed merrily, each wearing a giddy smile. As if frolicking to their deaths was perfectly acceptable. Even fun.

Wait. No, not every woman followed happily. The

one with dark curls was fighting her captor, struggling for freedom.

Shaye's heart pounded in her chest, an erratic drumbeat. A war beat. "You're going to kill us all, you overgrown G.I. Joe. You're going—umph." She swallowed a mouthful of salty water, and the next thing she knew, she was completely submerged. Her eyes burned. Her throat constricted. Hair floated around her face like strands of ivory ribbon.

The idiot man kept his strong arms locked around her, one at the bend of her knees, one at the small of her back. His palms were hot, so hot, a startling contrast against the chilly liquid. Silver-white hair continued to dance around her. Colorful fish swam past her line of vision. She wanted to scream. Oh, how she wanted to scream. But every time she opened her mouth, she swallowed more water.

Deeper, deeper he sank. She needed to breathe, damn it! Any minute her lungs were going to burst. Valerian was insane. A drowning murderer on a suicide mission.

She fought against his hold with all her strength, kicking, beating, scratching. Finally the ocean became so deep he couldn't remain upright. They tilted forward, and he began using his powerful legs to swim them even deeper. Deeper still.

I'm going to die, she realized. *Truly die.* Terror beat through her. Already her lungs shrieked for air. There were so many things she wanted to do, and dying wasn't one of them. She wanted to write a book, maybe a sappy romance where the heroine experienced the love Shaye had always denied herself. She wanted to get another tattoo, maybe a pretty flower this time. Her first tattoo, a skull and crossbones on her lower back, was something she'd gotten in an attempt to make her parents notice her.

Her mom had definitely noticed and still mailed her tattoo-removal coupons every few weeks. The coupons amused her, actually made her feel liked— if not loved.

Another thought tried to form, but her mind blanked, cutting it off and becoming as dark as the water. *Breathe,* she mentally shouted. *Breathe before you pass out.*

Suddenly the water cleared, so glassy she could see as perfectly as if she were on land. Even the salt dissipated, soothing her irritated eyes. Valerian tugged her forward until they were eye-to-eye. Automatically she tried to push herself away from him, but he held tight.

Maybe that was for the best. She didn't want to lose her single connection with life. And right now, Valerian was her only solid anchor—psychotic though he was.

Yes, at the moment he was both destroyer and savior.

"Breathe," she mouthed. Her body verged on spasming, on forcing her to attempt to suck in air. No matter that water still surrounded her.

"Soon," he, too, mouthed. He motioned with his head, and she squelched her panic enough to turn and look. Her eyes widened when she saw the swirling, gelatinous whirlpool looming ahead. What the hell was that thing? And why was Valerian swimming straight into it?

Had to…stop him. With a shaky arm, she reached out to block his forward momentum. Her fingertip brushed the whirlpool. Instantly the aquatic world crumbled into dark nothingness, an abyss welcoming her with open arms. A thousand screams ripped through her ears, violent, intense. Needles jabbed at her every pore, the pain nearly too much to bear.

A stream of bright light erupted and whizzed past her, then disappeared altogether. Wind gusted, spinning her round and round. Where was Valerian? He, too, had disappeared. Dizziness consumed her as she continued to twirl. Alone. Frightened. No end in sight.

Falling…falling…

CHAPTER FIVE

"I'VE GOT YOU, MOON."

Strong arms wrapped around Shaye's waist, and she gratefully buried her face in the hollow of Valerian's neck. In that moment she didn't care who was holding her, she was simply happy that someone was. She even wrapped her legs around his waist, strengthening her grip on him. She could finally breathe, she just couldn't stop falling.

"Don't let go," she cried.

"Never."

She'd never held on to anyone with such force, such need. That Valerian held on to her just as tightly was…comforting, something she'd craved for many years before convincing herself she didn't need or want such a thing. And she would believe it again—tomorrow.

They were spinning faster and faster, left and right, tumbling toward the unknown. Nausea churned in her stomach. She didn't understand what was happening; she only knew the water had disappeared as if it had never been, leaving only this spiraling black tunnel that stretched for eternity.

"Valerian," she panted. "What's happening?"

"Don't worry, love. It will be over in a moment."

Did he speak of death?

Zipping lights once again blazed past her ears, firefly flickers extinguished all too soon and replaced by that thick, oppressive darkness. The bevy of screams increased in volume and shattered her fragile hold on calm. No. *No!* Her temples hammered with a sharp ache. Her blood froze, yet sweat beaded over her skin. Fear clutched her in a painful grip.

As a little girl, her favorite fairytale had been *Alice in Wonderland.* Over and over she'd read about Alice falling down the rabbit hole, and had wanted to fall into that hole herself. Not now. Now that she felt like Alice, plummeting into the unfamiliar, she didn't like it.

Alice had landed in a whole new world—and that thought scared Shaye more than never landing at all.

"I'm not sure…how much more…I can take," she gasped out.

Then, suddenly, Valerian hit a solid foundation. His knees bent, absorbing the impact, and the vibration trembled through her. His arms tightened around her waist, holding her up with his determined strength.

"Take a moment to breathe." He slid her down his body inch by gradual inch. "Breathe for me, love. I don't feel your chest moving."

In. Out. Air filled and left her lungs. In. Out. Surprisingly, she *did* calm. She could smell his scent, salty, sultry. Could feel his heat, his strength.

"Good, good. But you are pale," Valerian said, a hint of concern in his voice.

"I'm always pale," she muttered. Her eyes were squeezed tightly shut, she realized, slowly forcing them to open.

They had entered a cave. She gulped. How had they

entered a cave? The walls were bleak and rocky, silver stones splashed with crimson. A metallic tang layered the cold, cold air, and that cold, cold air continued to wrap around Shaye's soaked, nearly bare body, chasing away Valerian's warmth. That frigid breeze ruffled her wet skirt and hair, and she shivered.

She slowly turned, taking in every detail. One by one, the other warriors were walking out of a clear, jellylike pool that swirled mysteriously. They were clasping as many frightened, trembling women as they could hold. Mist curled all around them and drifted to the ceiling. The entire scene was like something found in a movie. *Where am I?*

Trembling, Shaye faced her captor once again. Her gaze traveled over him, starting at his booted feet, moving up his muscled legs, skipping over his male…parts to his chest. Droplets of water trickled over his tiny brown nipples, through his silver nipple ring, and pooled in his navel. He had no chest hair; not a strand dared mar his perfection. Rope after rope of tantalizing muscle banded his bronzed stomach.

How could one person be so utterly flawless?

Up her gaze went again, finally hitting his face. His savagely, amazingly perfect face. Perfect sandy brows, perfect crystalline eyes, perfect nose. Perfect lips, lush and pink. Of course, he now sported bruises under his eyes because she'd punched him in the nose. Even with the bruises, however, he was the most sensually erotic creature she'd ever seen. He wore confidence like a cloak; he radiated primal ferocity.

Reaching up, he gently traced his fingertips over her forehead, nose and chin, wiping away the water. She

wanted to pull away, but couldn't summon the
strength. His touch reverberated through her like a live
wire. Hot. Scorching.

"Welcome to your new home, little moonbeam."
Desire coated his words—as if he had felt the sparks,
as well. "Welcome to Atlantis."

Atlantis. She blinked once, twice. Atlantis…the city
buried under the ocean? Like the ocean she'd just
exited? Her mouth went dry. No way. No damn way.
"Please tell me you meant to say Atlanta, as in Georgia,
and your accent screwed it up."

His brow puckered. "I know not this Georgia. You
heard me correctly. You have entered Atlantis, city of
the gods' finest creations. Home to nymphs, vampires,
demons and many others that do not bear mentioning,
for they are unimportant."

No, no, no. Hell, no. She shook her head, her mind
valiantly trying to discredit such an explanation.
Atlantis was a myth. It couldn't possibly be real. The
creatures he'd named were also myths. They, too,
couldn't possibly be real. For God's sake, vampires?
Demons? In nightmares, perhaps, but not reality.

Welcome to Wonderland, Alice.

No, no, no, she thought again. There had to be
another explanation. And yet…she could think of
nothing else. She'd entered the sea, fallen into a dark
tunnel, and now stood in a cave. A cave found below
the water, not above it.

Atlantis whispered across her mind. She gulped, tightening her hold on disbelief, unwilling to relinquish it even
for a moment. To do so meant accepting the craziness of
Valerian's claim—the claim of a deranged kidnapper.

"So I drowned, and I'm in hell." Eyes slitted, she tilted her chin stubbornly. "Obviously, you're the devil."

"We shall see. Men," Valerian called, a harsh growl. His penetrating stare never left her face. "Take the women and gather the rest of my army in the dining hall. The choosing will soon begin."

With an air of eager anticipation, the warriors leapt into action. One of them tried to grab her arm, but Valerian stopped him with a feral, "I will bring this one," even as she slapped at the offender's hand.

"As you wish, my king."

King? King! They pounded up a coarse, wooden staircase, the women close on their heels. Most of the men were grinning and clapping each other on the back. "Who will you choose?" she heard one of them say. Another responded with a hearty, "I want the redhead. Her breasts are…" Their chatter faded away.

A single man remained behind. Or perhaps he'd been waiting here in the cave. He wasn't wet like everyone else. He wore a white shirt with a deep V-neck that almost reached his navel and tight black pants.

Valerian finally released her from his stare and turned to the remaining warrior. "How are the prisoners?" he asked.

Prisoners? Shaye's eyes widened, and she clutched at her throat. Dear God.

The man gave a brusque answer in that odd language she'd heard Valerian use earlier, but Valerian shook his head. "Speak in the human tongue."

"Alive," the man said with a frown.

Wait. *Human* tongue? What did that make Valerian's dialect? *In*human?

"Have they given you any trouble?" Valerian asked.

"None at all, my king."

"Very good. Continue to see to their needs." He waved in dismissal, scowled, then called the man back. "Has there been any word about our females?"

"None."

"Very well," he said, his disappointment clear. "On with you."

The man nodded and clomped off, his boots beating into the rocky ground.

"What prisoners?" Shaye found herself asking on a trembling breath.

"Beasts. Killers." He turned toward her and she was once again hit by the full majesty of him. Icy air at her back, pure heat in front. "Do not fear, for they will not be allowed near you. Some are to be a present to my friend, Layel, and some are to be used to bargain."

How ominous both plans sounded. What did the man have planned for *her,* then? Was she to be a present for one of his friends? Was she to be used as a bargaining tool?

He watched her with a frighteningly possessive intensity. The water in his hair was already drying, lightening the locks to a rich, honey gold. Several of those amber strands fell over his forehead and trickled tiny, lingering droplets onto his cheeks.

"I see the disbelief in your beautiful eyes," he said, leaning one shoulder against the jagged silver wall, "and I will do my best to prove my claim that this is Atlantis. The faster you accept the truth, the faster you will accept me."

Before she could respond, he reached out and applied pressure to the boulder behind her. His hand brushed her bare skin, shooting those electric shocks through her blood. She twisted, seeing one of the huge rocks embedded in the wall slide backward and sink deeply. As it descended, a secret doorway revealed itself. Rocks creaked and grumbled as they parted. Inch by inch, smooth, glassy crystal was exposed.

Her mouth fell open in an imitation of the doorway. Unbidden, her feet walked her to the edge. Water swirled behind the enclosure, and sand swayed at the sea's bottom. Pink coral and multicolored fish danced a lazy waltz. Emerald plants rose proudly.

"That's the bottom of the ocean," she said, awed and shocked. "That's the freaking bottom of the ocean."

"I know. I discovered this wall only a few days ago and have spent many hours down here. Breathtaking, isn't it?"

A gentle hum echoed in her ears when she flattened her palm against the crystal. The coolness and vibrations of the water assured her this was no hallucination. *My God. Atlantis.* As she peered out, trying to come to grips with what she was seeing, a gorgeous, dark-haired woman swam up to the crystal. No, not a woman. Shaye's brow furrowed in shock. A mermaid. A bare-chested, tail-wagging mermaid.

Curiosity gleamed in its—her—green eyes. She stretched out a dainty arm and placed her hand exactly where Shaye's rested. Gasping, Shaye jerked away. Shock pounded through her, and her hand fell to her side. Her mouth dried. Her knees shook. The creature frowned…until her gaze latched on Valerian. She smiled, pleasure gleaming in her eyes, and waved.

"You know her?" Shaye managed.

He nodded, but didn't elaborate.

The woman…mermaid…*whatever,* had the face of an angel, innocent and more lovely than a long-awaited sunrise. Long black hair curled around her delicate shoulders and lush breasts. Her tail shone like spun glass, an irradiance of violets, yellows, greens and pinks, each scale a kaleidoscope of colors. Naked desire adorned her features as she stared at Valerian.

"Do you believe me now?" he asked.

"Yes." The admission left Shaye on a ragged breath. Part of her wanted to sink to the twig-laden floor, curl into a ball and cry. *I've been abducted by an Atlantean and carted to a city under the sea.* The other part of her wanted to—she didn't know what.

Another mermaid joined the brunette, a symphony of curves and colors, pressing herself against the crystal and smiling seductively at Valerian. Passion glazed her amethyst eyes. Shaye had no doubt what the two women were thinking: three-way.

"You said this is the home of the gods' finest creations," she said softly. Without facing him, she asked, "What kind of creature are you?" He'd already mentioned that he wasn't human.

"I am a nymph." His tone reeked of pride. "*The* nymph, actually. King of my people. Leader. Warrior." He hesitated. "Lover."

A nymph. Another so-called myth. A sexual being. Seductive. Irresistible. Able to give pleasure with a glance, a word. Beauty personified. Valerian fit the description perfectly, and that frightened her so much more than if he'd said he was a soul-sucking demon from the deepest depths of hell.

"I thought nymphs were…" Obsessed with sex—

check. Continuously naked—close. Willing to sleep with anything that moved—probably. "Female," she ended lamely.

He snorted and stepped closer to her. "There are females, yes, but mostly we are males."

God, she had to get out of there. His nearness disturbed her sense of peace and reduced her to a trembling, sex-starved hormone. Already her nipples had hardened. Her stomach quivered. "Take me home, Valerian. I don't belong here."

He didn't reply. The wall began to close, gradually shutting out the view of water, gradually shutting out the now infuriated mermaids banging on the crystal. Shaye covered her mouth with a shaky hand. "Please take me home."

"Love, *this* is your home now. I swear to you, you will soon come to adore it as I do."

How beguiling he sounded. His husky tone promised endless nights of passion and days of wild abandon.

Resist. Flee. More than ever, she needed the safety of numbness. She squared her shoulders and raised her chin. She would feel nothing for this man; she would be rude, completely unlikable. Sometimes that was the only way to keep someone at a distance. "I'm going home," she said, determined. "With or without your permission."

Before he had time to respond, she jolted into motion and sprinted toward the whirlpool. Her sandals dug into rocks and twigs. Breath caught in her throat, burning, urging her on. Almost there…just another step…

Valerian grabbed her by the arm and twirled her around.

"No!" she shouted, kicking backward.

"If you enter the portal without me, you will die." The words held an unmistakable edge of fury. His hand tightened on her. "You will never be able to swim the length of the water alone. Do you understand? You will die out there, your body nothing more than nourishment for the fish."

She stilled, the blood chilling in her veins. The water…how could she have forgotten the water? As if he'd shackled her wrists and ankles to the wall, she was trapped. Leave and die. Stay and…what? It didn't matter, really. Living here held no appeal—not when she had King Pleasure to contend with.

"*You* can swim the distance," she said, using her haughtiest tone. "I command you to take me home."

"It is my greatest pleasure to give you anything and everything you request, but I cannot give you that. Anything else you desire will be yours." He released his grip on her arm and traced his fingertip along her collarbone. "One day soon I hope it will be me that you desire."

Red alert, red alert. She had to get away from him, had to escape that tempting wish. How? Where could she go?

"At least tell me your name," he cajoled.

"Up yours." The words emerged breathless, rather than insulting as she'd intended. Exquisite fire trailed the same path as his fingers, then journeyed the length of her spine. Dangerous.

A heavy pause stretched between them. All the while, Valerian radiated a sense of amusement, sadness and anger. Sadness? She frowned. Surely not. Hulking he-man warriors were never sad. Were they?

His arm curved around her waist, an impenetrable force. "Come then, Up Yours, and I will show you the palace." He ushered her up that long, winding staircase, coarse and crudely built.

Not knowing what else to do, she followed without protest. Really, what could she say? *Leave me in this cold, dank cave to rot?* God, what kind of nightmare had she entered? Every second that passed became more surreal and damning than the last.

There had to be another way home; she had only to find it. Shaye studied the markings on the wall. The higher she stepped, the less jagged the rocks became. They appeared to be dusted with glitter, sparkling and inviting her to touch. Unable to resist, she brushed her fingertip over the smooth surface.

Valerian stopped abruptly. She bumped into his back and gasped at the fiery, full-body contact. As she hastily backed away, he spun around and faced her. He pushed her against the cold wall, his frown fierce, his turquoise eyes gleaming with purpose.

"Close your eyes," he commanded.

His imposing stance didn't frighten her. No, she struggled against a surge of excitement. Heady, blissful excitement. "Hell, no," she said.

"That was not a request, love. That was a demand."

"You should have taken me home when you had the chance. I'll never do anything you say. I told you that before."

One of his brows arched. "Keep your eyes open, then."

She smirked. "Nice try."

He pushed out a frustrated breath. "I do not want you to know the way back to the portal. Do not force me to blindfold you."

"*Force* you? Please." Her smirk became a glare. "I

seriously doubt I could force you to do anything you
didn't already want to do. The same holds true for me.
I don't like you, I don't trust you and you'll never be
able to bend me to your will."

"I could have lied to you." As he spoke, he closed
the small distance between them, crowding her, eating
up her personal space. But he didn't touch her. No, he
left her craving it. "I could have told you that you would
go blind if you looked at the rocks. You would not have
known the difference. But there will be only truth
between us. No matter how harsh, I will always tell you
the truth."

Her defiance drained, and fear claimed center
stage—past the kernels of desire fighting for life. His
tone was so final. He truly expected her to remain here.
He truly expected her to obey him. To trust him.

Valerian had said before that he and his men wanted
her and the others for their bodies. Translation: sex.
Were they to be sex slaves? Was *she* to be *Valerian's*
slave? Shaye's eyes narrowed to tiny slits. She'd die
first—and kill every male within reach in the process.
She'd spent her childhood a slave to her parents' edicts.
*Kiss your new daddy, Shaye. Give that woman my phone
number, Shaye. Don't you dare use profanity, Shaye.*

She'd fought hard for her independence and would
relinquish it to no one.

"Did the other women have to close their eyes?" she
asked.

He ran his tongue over his teeth. "No."

"Well, there's your answer."

He leaned his face close to hers, cutting away the remaining distance inch by precious inch. His warm

breath caressed her face, but still he didn't touch her. His male scent wafted deliciously. "Unlike you, the others will not try to escape."

"I don't know about that. The one with the curly black hair didn't look happy to be here."

Something dark settled over his expression.

Don't infuriate the man. No telling what he'll do. "What if I promise not to try and escape?" She didn't plan to try, she planned to succeed.

"I would laugh at such a blatant untruth and then scold you for lying to your man."

"You are not my man!"

"Not yet." *But I will be* echoed between them, unsaid, yet powerful nonetheless.

"Not ever," she said through clenched teeth.

His brow puckered, confusion settling over his beautiful features. "You continue to amaze me. How are you able to resist me with such fervor?"

Was she resisting him? She didn't know. She'd never felt so…needy. Even now, when defiance beat hard fists through her, her heart pounded, her skin stretched too tight. His heat slithered over her, inside her, shattering and chipping away at the ice she prized. Her nipples still reached for him. Her legs parted slightly, inviting an intimate glide, a hard press. Just…inviting.

His nostrils flared as if he sensed her growing arousal. If he moved another inch, he'd mesh himself fully against her. Finally. Part of her screamed in protest, part of her trembled in welcome.

"I want to touch you and kiss you, love, and feel—"

"No!" she shouted. "No kissing. No touching. And

for God's sake, stop calling me 'love.'" But, oh, the thought of his lips feasting on hers was heady. "I don't know you, and like I said, I damn sure don't like you. You abducted me. You deserve jail time, not a make-out session."

"I can make you like me." He braced his palms on each side of her head, trapping her in a hard, muscled circle, touching her hair but not her skin. "Oh, I can make you."

The truth of his claim shimmered between them unmercifully. Because deep down, she admitted that with every second that passed, she liked him more. She wanted him more. Wanted that skin-to-skin contact he was denying her. Was he doing it on purpose? Making her desperate for something she couldn't have?

Idiot! Shaye didn't need a lot of experience with men to know she dangled on a precarious edge. If he pushed, she would crumble. She would take the momentary pleasure he offered and be glad for it. But in the taking, she would be no better than the others, forgetting his atrocious crime and throwing herself at his sexy feet.

She'd be one of those pathetic creatures who did anything for pleasure, everything for love. Just like her mom.

Make him despise you. Hurt him. Now! Determined, she jerked up her knee. He anticipated the action and jumped backward, out of striking distance. His mouth thinned and firmed.

"I warn you now." He met her gaze, otherworldly blue against plain brown. Determination against determination. "Fight me if you must, but do not attempt escape. I will punish you, have no doubt."

She forced herself to snort. "I haven't begun to fight.

And what the hell do you mean, you'll punish me?" The fury she didn't have to force. It increased with every word she uttered. "A little while ago you said you could never hurt me."

"There are ways to punish a woman that will not physically hurt her."

"And I bet you know every one of them, you sick pervert."

He released a long, frustrated sigh. "We have not the time to fight right now. Come. I will show you Atlantis before we meet with the others." Reaching out, he offered her his hand.

She stared at his blunt-tipped fingers, at the calluses and scars slashed across his palm, a contrast to his perfect beauty. As she stared, her anger drained. Total strength lay there, dormant now, but ready to kill at any moment. Except...he could have crushed her with those hands at any time. He'd shown her nothing but gentleness.

Foolish woman, she chided, placing her hand in his. *Of course he hasn't hurt you. He needs a healthy sex slave.* His fingers intertwined with hers. At the moment of contact, dark, erotic pulses tingled through her. They'd touched before, and each time had elicited sparks. But this time...it was more intense. A deeper awareness in this skin-to-skin contact she'd wanted so badly but hadn't wanted to want. Gasping, she tried to tug away from him, to sever the connection. He held tight.

"Mine," he said.

She bit the inside of her cheek against the pleasure that one declaration wrought. "I don't understand any of this. I don't understand you."

"You will. In time."

The dire words—warning? promise?—rang in her head as she climbed the rest of the wooden stairs. At the top, two gleaming crystal doors were held open by giant rubies. Jeweled doorstops?

Curiosity got the better of her. "Why do you have the entrance propped open like that?"

"A dragon medallion is needed to open and close the doorways, and I do not wish to wear anything belonging to a dragon." He spat the word *dragon* as if it was a foul curse.

What kind of response could she offer to that?

He tossed a frown over his shoulder. "And you had better not try to search for a medallion. If you do, you will be punished."

"Will I be punished for breathing?" she snapped. He seemed to be looking for an excuse to punish her.

"If it is done in the direction of another man, yes." The warning was serious, though the tone lacked true heat.

"Pig."

"Lover."

"Bastard."

He flicked another glance over his shoulder. This time his lips were curled in a wicked half smile, and knowing intent sizzled in his eyes like blue fire. "Say that while we're naked. I dare you."

She gulped and tore her attention away from him. A smart woman would have been memorizing her surroundings for possible escape routes instead of antagonizing (aka drooling over) her captor.

Shaye forced herself to act like a smart woman. Down a long, winding hallway they strode, the walls jagged once again and completely barren, offering no distinguishing marks to help her find her way back. They turned left. Left again. Right. Left. Right. They bypassed several open doorways, but they moved so quickly she had no chance to peek inside. The sound of their footsteps echoed throughout the hall.

"Where are we going?" she asked.

"My bedchamber."

"Your what?" Mouth opening and closing, she dug her sandy, squishy sandals into the marble floor. "Hell, no. Hell. No."

He could have dragged her along, but he stopped and faced her. His luscious mouth twitched in amusement. "We will not make love tonight unless you beg me for it. Does that appease this sudden fear you have of my room?"

"No," she gritted out.

"I wish only to show you the Outer City from my window." He sighed another of those long, drawn-out exhalations. "Unfortunately there is not time for anything more."

Glaring, she anchored her hands on her hips. "You're lying. Your kind always has time for sex."

"My kind?" The smile quickly faded from his face. "By that I hope you mean the honest kind. I vowed never to lie to you, and I will not. My honor demands nothing less. I said I will not touch you tonight until you beg for it, so that is the way it will be."

Shaye didn't allow his fervent vow to sway her. Even if he kept his word and kept his hands to himself, they would be near a bed. Most likely a decadent, made-for-sin bed. What if she saw it, lost her will to resist, and made a pass at *him?* "Your honor doesn't mean shit to me. I'm not going to your bedroom."

A muscle ticked in his jaw. An inferno blazed in his eyes, a churning tempest of blues. From cerulean to azure to the palest violet. "Very well," he said, each syllable precise. "We will not steal a moment for ourselves. We will join the others. I can only hope your prudish nature will prevent my men from choosing you."

"Choosing me for what?" she bit out, ignoring the "prudish" comment. She suspected the answer, and she almost screamed when it came.

His brows arched, and his lips dipped downward. "For their bedmate, of course."

CHAPTER SIX

VALERIAN HAD TO CARRY his intended mate to the dining hall. Something he enjoyed immensely, even though she kicked and shouted profanities the entire way. Her breasts pressed into his back, her legs draped over his stomach.

He grinned. Oh, but he liked this woman's spirit. How amusing she was. He only wished he knew her name. Up Yours, indeed. She refused to tell him the truth, and that he *didn't* like. He hadn't cared before, with other women, but knowing this one's name seemed necessary for his survival.

"I will not be your sex slave, and I will not be your army's sex slave. Do you understand me? I won't!"

No, she would be his lover. His mate. *His.* And only his. Earlier he had seen the way his men glanced at her, the way their gazes had trailed over the curve of her waist, awaiting glimpses of the pale skin beneath her grass skirt.

Perhaps he would not keep her dressed that way, as he'd first thought. Perhaps he would drape her in thick, dark cloth from head to toe. As it was, one of his warriors would probably try to select her. What man could resist the fire burning beneath the cool facade, begging for release?

Valerian would kill before he allowed another man to have her.

He'd told her that his honor would not allow him to lie, but really, honor meant nothing in the face of losing her. He'd lie, he'd cheat, he'd do whatever was necessary to ensure that no other man tried to claim her.

As he turned a corner, Valerian wished the little moonbeam would have let him take her to his room. He would have shown her the city view as promised, yes, but he also would have utilized the stolen time to the fullest. He would have tempted and tantalized her until she thought only of him. A forbidden caress, a lingering, heated glance. His men would have seen how much she desired him, only him, and would have been less inclined to choose her.

Now he would have to think of something else.

"Take me back to the beach," she said, beating her fists against his buttocks. "Right now, damn it! I'm through playing nice. Do you hear me?"

"I am not sure how many different ways I can tell you that *this* is your home and you are staying here forever." Perhaps it was best they hadn't gone to his room. Now he could get the selection process over with. Now he could prove she belonged to him. Now his men could concentrate on *their* chosen.

He, of course, could then concentrate on…Up Yours. "What is your name?" he asked. While her continued defiance was amusing, it was also frustrating.

"When the cops hear about this you'll…you'll…this is kidnapping, you bastard."

That she didn't want him and would have been happiest if he'd left her on the surface world was as humbling as it was shocking. "You are frightened," he rationalized. "I am sorry for that."

"Frightened? Ha! I'm pissed."

Despite her denial, he knew she was scared. Her heartbeat drummed erratically against his back, and he could feel the shallow exhalations of her breath against his skin. She fought the emotion, however, showing only fury. His admiration for her increased.

Gods, he wanted—nay, needed—her. To kiss her. To know the taste of her tongue. He'd come close to kissing her in the cave. But one touch of her sweet little tongue, and he would not have been able to stop. One touch and he would have needed a second and a third. He knew it. He would have spread her legs, laved his tongue through her heat, then pounded inside her to the hilt. So deep she would only have been able to gasp his name.

He knew women and knew this one would be violent with her passions. Look at the way she reacted to anger and fear, like a hissing, scratching wildcat. Her sexual desire would be no different. Once she unleashed her inner fire, she would erupt into flames, burning her lover to sated ashes.

That passion belonged to him, he mused darkly.

Frowning, he came to a halt. "Will you attack any man who attempts to claim you?" With a gentle tug, he moved her body down his. Slowly, so slowly. Their naked stomachs brushed, and she sucked in a breath. His muscles jumped in excited reaction.

She might deny it, but she was aware of him in a very sexual way.

"Will you attack them?" he repeated. He'd plant the suggestion in her mind, if necessary.

"Damn right I will." Her eyes glared amber fire at him, daring him to contradict her or threaten to punish her. "I'll fight to the death. *Their* deaths."

As if he would punish her for something he wanted desperately. His lips edged into a contented smile. Since he could not make her admit her desire for him—yet—this was the next best thing.

Get this over with. Urgency filling him, he intertwined their fingers and pulled her behind him. They quickly bypassed the training arena, as well as the kitchens. "Do you like the palace?" he asked before she could begin protesting again. *See the beauty,* he silently commanded. Sconces decorated the walls, flames flickering inside and illuminating the path.

Her eyes locked on the murals, murals so vivid they almost looked alive. Sensual multihued scenes, all, where naked men, women and creatures of every race writhed in different stages of orgasm. He and his men had painted the scenes to make the palace theirs, not the dragons'.

Nymphs were natural wanderers, flittering from one location to the other, always searching for the next sexual conquest. They'd never cared where they resided. But Valerian had grown weary of that type of existence. He'd wanted more for himself, more for his people. He could not pinpoint exactly what had made him feel this way; he only knew that a sense of restlessness had been growing inside of him for months and that the thought of wandering had no longer held any appeal.

When he learned a mere hatchling of a dragon had been left in charge of this palace, he'd decided to take it. Quickly. Easily.

And so he had.

He did not regret the decision. Once he'd entered the palace, his restlessness had been replaced by rightness. Valerian tilted his head as a thought occurred to him. Perhaps he needed to take the woman at his side the same way he'd taken the dragon palace. With cunning. With precision. With an absolute lack of mercy.

Oh, yes. Slowly his lips lifted in a grin. She would soon find herself on the receiving end of a full-scale, irresistible attack. He could hardly wait to begin.

"Do you like the palace?" he asked again.

She hesitated before saying, "I'll be honest. Your home…the walls, remind me of you."

Our home, little moonbeam, our home. "Thank you."

Frowning, she slapped at his hand, trying to force him to release his hold. "That wasn't a compliment."

"Being told pictures of sex make you think of me is not a compliment?"

Her mouth fell open, but she snapped it closed. "That's not how I meant it, and you know it."

He chuckled. "Deny it all you want, but every time you look at me you think of naked flesh and writhing pleasure."

"Don't forget the gag and rope," she growled. "Let me go."

"I like the sound of the rope."

"You would, you dirty pervert."

The air was heavy with anticipation and excitement as he stepped into the dining hall. Up Yours stilled, gasped. He stopped and wrapped an arm around her waist. For once, she didn't protest. Didn't fight. Shock probably held her captive.

"We have arrived," he announced. A contingent of

warriors lined one side of the room. A sweet-smelling cluster of females lined the other. And a large wooden table etched with fierce dragon heads separated them.

He'd meant to destroy the table, for he wanted no dragon possession in *his* home. But he'd found no other table large enough for his men.

Perhaps he'd keep it and love his woman on it.

The walls were plain onyx and ivory. Before, sapphires and emeralds, diamonds and rubies had glittered from the wide expanse, but they had been removed by human soldiers months ago. Those humans had been slaughtered by dragons, providing the opportunity Valerian needed to sneak his men inside and conquer.

Usually nymphs only attacked when provoked, keeping their bestial natures under strict control. Yet dragons were enemy to the only ally they possessed: the vampires. Unlike every other race in Atlantis, the vampires did not curse the nymphs for their power over women; they did not seethe with jealousy. Layel, the king, found it amusing.

Wiggling at Valerian's side, his mate said, "I'm not placing myself on the menu of this—this smorgasbord." Her elbow slammed into his stomach, almost knocking the air from his lungs.

"Be still, woman."

"Die, bastard."

His men watched them with varying expressions of horror. He'd taught each of them the surface language, for he believed knowledge equaled power, so they knew exactly what the little moonbeam had said to him. Women simply did not act that way. Not with Valerian, at least. Women loved and worshipped him. They fought for his notice. They begged for his touch.

They did not command him to die!

He was not embarrassed by this display, however. No, he was elated. If Valerian, the most desired of the nymphs, failed to woo her, his men would know that they were destined to fail with her, as well. And by choosing her and failing, they would be forced to sleep alone this night, something they would hope to avoid. For right now, they wanted sex. Not love, not a mate. Just sex.

Valerian had to force himself to frown when he tapped her bottom, knowing it would encourage her antics all the more.

She screeched. "Did you just spank me? Tell me you didn't just spank me, Valerian, before I introduce your nose to my fist. Again."

Ah, he loved hearing his name from her soft, pink lips. Because her face was so pale, the color of her lips stood out like a beacon, lush and begging to be sampled.

"I'm waiting," she growled.

"No. You're beautiful."

At first her expression softened and he was given a glimpse of a sweet and vulnerable female. He almost kissed her, unable to help himself. Then fury sparked in her eyes, driving away the heart-melting image. "Don't talk to me like that. I don't like it."

He blinked. She would rather he utter mean things? Interesting. Confusing and odd, as well, but something to ponder. Why would a woman want such a thing? Was it a defense against him?

"My king," Broderick prompted. "We are ready. We

have instructed the women to remain in line until they are chosen."

A quick count revealed more men than women. "My elite will pick first," Valerian said. They had fought in more wars, were stronger, faster, and needed sex more than an average solider.

The elite cheered. The others groaned in disappointment.

"Stay quiet," he said to his woman, knowing very well she would do the opposite. "And stay in this line. My men need a good look at you."

To his utter delight, she retorted, "Like hell. No matter how eager everyone else might be, I will not quietly accept this T-and-A pageant. I will not passively stand here."

Except…she didn't bolt. No, she pressed into his side, allowing him to surround her with his strength, though she still wouldn't face him. Her shoulder brushed his chest, and several strands of her silky hair caught in his nipple loop. He could hear the erratic beat of her heart, could feel the warmth of her soft, soft skin.

He splayed his fingers over her rib cage, and she shivered.

He had to see her face, had to see what emotions lingered there. Helpless, he cupped her chin and forced her to look at him. Their gazes clashed and held. The rest of the world faded away, as it always seemed to do when he looked at her. Her eyes were dark velvet, rich and warm, absolutely riveting in her pale face.

"What is your name?" he found himself asking again.

"There's no reason for you to know," she said breathlessly. She licked her lips, then ran the plump bottom between her teeth. His cock jumped in reaction. "I'm leaving soon. *Very* soon."

As if he would ever allow this delicious morsel to leave him. "If I promise to help you drive these men away," he whispered, "will you tell me?"

"I—maybe." Her eyelids slitted, and the length of her lashes cast spiky shadows over her cheeks. "Why would you help me?"

Why indeed. The answer should be obvious to her. "I want to keep you for myself." He stated the words as baldly as possible, smiling slowly, eagerly. He needed an extreme reaction from her. Anything to appall his men further.

As he'd hoped, she began struggling against him. "I am not a piece of meat. This is not a buffet. You should be ashamed of yourself."

Valerian forced himself to sigh. "If you will not remain in line, I will be obligated to hold you here." A wave of triumph swept through him. Things were working out just as he'd hoped. "Broderick," he called.

"Yes, my king." Broderick stepped forward, his color high.

"As second-in-command and leader of the elite, you may have first choice." Valerian loosened his hold on his captive so that her movements were more obvious. She squirmed all the harder, her pants and grunts filling the air. The actions, the sounds, aroused him.

Broderick grinned and approached the females, starting at the far end. Feminine twitters and purrs echoed throughout the spacious enclosure. "Pick me, pick me," erupted.

Relishing his role, the warrior slowly edged his way

down the line, stopping here and there to unzip a woman's dress and peek at her breasts. For a joyous few, he also sampled a taste of their nipples. Unfortunately, he had not made his selection by the time he reached the little moonbeam, and he studied her with desire in his emerald eyes.

Valerian's jaw clenched. *Mine,* he thought again, tightening his grip.

Broderick reached out to part the woman's grass skirt.

"I'm Shaye," she said in a rush, the words almost a screech. "My name is Shaye Octavia Holling."

Valerian knew immediately what she wanted from him. *I'll help you drive the men away if you tell me your name,* he'd promised her. Promised Shaye. *Shaye.* He rolled the name over his tongue, savoring. Relishing. The name fit her. Seemingly cool, aloof, yet utterly sensual.

"Kick him," he breathed into her ear. "Hard."

She did so without hesitation, bringing up her leg and slamming her foot into Broderick's stomach. The stunned warrior propelled backward, tripped over his own feet and tumbled to the ground. The rest of the army burst into gales of laughter. Broderick popped to a stand, frowning at Shaye in confusion.

Valerian bit back a grin. His second-in-command quickly selected a pretty, sedate brunette. They rushed from the dining hall without a backward glance. One down…

"Dorian." Valerian nodded to the black-haired man, whose muscled body emitted a palpable air of eagerness. "You are next." To Shaye—ah, he couldn't get enough of her name, as delicate and lovely as the woman herself—he whispered, "When he approaches you, ignore him. Do not even look at him."

"Are you sure?" Shaye couldn't believe she was relying on Valerian to get her out of this mess. He was the one responsible for it! But she could think of no alternative. Letting one of these barbarians "claim" her, then drag her away and do God knows what to her, held no appeal. "Won't ignoring him bring out all his caveman instincts?"

"Not with this man." He sounded amused.

Dorian had onyx hair and irises so blue they rivaled the ocean in purity. His mouthwatering beauty was something out of a fairy tale. Somehow, his features were even more perfect than Valerian's. He didn't make her ache, however. *He* didn't fill her mind with X-rated images of naked, straining bodies.

Shaye's stomach churned with nervousness as the man followed Broderick's example and considered every woman in line. He looked, he tasted, he enjoyed a little too much. Shaye was offended for the women. How dare he treat them so casually? It didn't matter that they seemed to love it. Didn't matter that they asked for more.

When he reached her, he remained out of striking distance and crossed his arms over his massive chest. He studied her, his intense gaze lingering on her every curve. Several seconds ticked by and Valerian stiffened.

"Remove the shells," Dorian finally said. "I would see your breasts."

Ignore him had been Valerian's advice. She turned her chin away from Dorian and studied her cuticles. If he tried to remove the bra himself, he'd walk away with a bloody stump in place of his hand.

"Did you not hear me, woman? I said, remove the shells."

She yawned—a nearly impossible feat. With Valerian's strong arms banded around her, she was foolishly turned on. Not bored. Despite every other emotion— fear, anger, affront—her desire had remained. Grown. She didn't feel like her normal self around the vain, ego-tistical giant. She felt like a sexual being whose only purpose was pleasure. Giving and receiving it.

Why had she not felt this way on any of the dates she'd gone on? Why now? Why this man?

Dorian expelled a frustrated breath. He tangled a hand through his silky hair and eyed his boss. "Valerian, make her look at me."

Valerian lifted his shoulders in a shrug. "I cannot force her eyes to you."

"But—"

"Is she the one you want or not?" The words lashed from him, abrupt, harsh. Filled with impatience. "The others are waiting for their turn."

A scowl darkened Dorian's features. He spun away from Shaye and stalked to the only redhead in the group. "I choose you."

The degrading debacle continued for half an hour. Only one other woman seemed upset by the happen-ings, the same woman who'd been as unwilling as Shaye to blithely walk into the water with the nymphs. She was a tiny thing and very pretty, with dark, curly hair, wide, dark eyes and a button nose. And, despite her innocent, school-girl features, she radiated dark, wild sensuality.

Unfortunately, she was selected by a tall warrior

with beads in his sandy-colored hair. One of the men still in line—she couldn't see which—slammed his fist into the wall, the force of it reverberating through the room. "I wanted that one," he growled.

"Too bad for you, Joachim," was the smug reply. "She's now mine." Beaded Hair clasped Nervous's hand and tugged her from the line.

She dragged her heels, but didn't utter a word in protest.

Obviously puzzled, he glanced over his shoulder and frowned. "Do not be afraid. I will not hurt you."

The girl chewed on her bottom lip, tears in her eyes.

"Let her go," Shaye shouted. She'd seen enough. "Let her go right now! She doesn't want to leave with you."

His frown deepened, and he glanced at Valerian in confusion. "But…I chose her."

The girl leveled a frightened, watery gaze on Shaye. Still she didn't speak, just continued to bite her bottom lip.

"Valerian." Shaye latched on to his wrist and squeezed. "You have to do something about this. She doesn't want to leave with him."

Seconds passed in absolute silence. "What will you give me in return?" he finally replied. "If I do something as you've so sweetly *asked,* my men will think me odd. But if I was to receive compensation, I would be willing to risk their displeasure."

"I'll allow you to live," she said through clenched teeth. "That should be payment enough."

He chuckled, a husky, sensual sound of pure enjoyment.

Damn him and his amusement!

"I'll be nice to you. For a little while," she grumbled.

He didn't hesitate. "Do you wish to be chosen by another warrior?" he asked the woman.

Her eyes roved over the remaining, eager men. She shrank back, gulped. Then she slowly shook her head.

"Take her, Shivawn, but do not touch her unless you have her permission. And do not force her to give permission," he added as an afterthought. He paused. "Does that satisfy you, Shaye?"

The way he said her name…she shivered and forced her mind to the matter at hand. No, it didn't satisfy her. But she knew he would not let the girl return to the beach. "Can Shivawn be trusted to obey your command?"

"All of my men obey me." There was a good amount of affront in his tone. "Go," Valerian told the couple.

Shivawn hurried the girl from the room before Shaye could utter another protest. Another man, the one who had hit the wall, swore under his breath.

And on the "selection" continued.

Every time a soldier approached her, Valerian told her exactly what to do. Spit, curse, faint. Thankfully, no one selected her. The line dwindled significantly, until only Shaye and a few others remained. Everyone else had adjourned to their rooms.

Later, when this was over, she suspected Valerian would demand some sort of reward for his aid. More than just her promise to be "nice." He copped a feel when attention was diverted from them, tracing his fingers over the curve of her hip. Dipping his thumb into her navel. Her nerve endings were on fire, clamoring for more of him.

Oddly, his possessive manner thrilled a secret part of her. A part she hadn't known existed. When someone approached her, he stiffened. A few times, he even growled low in his throat, as if he had withstood all that he could.

"It's almost over," he whispered. His breath fanned her ear as he trailed a fingertip along the bumps of her spine.

She almost slumped into a boneless heap. Only the sudden, unexpected feeling of being watched strengthened her resolve to appear unaffected. She felt a heated gaze boring into her, laden with purpose and determination. Eerie goose bumps broke over her as her eyes darted across the remaining men—and collided with a handsome brunet.

His heavy-lidded, come-to-my-bed stare slammed into her, and she stiffened. He scared her. There was menace in his eyes.

"Lean on me if your feet hurt," Valerian said, mistaking her reaction.

She pulled her attention from the dark-haired man. "I'm fine," she said, nearly breathless. Then she frowned; she'd meant to snap at him.

Her captor kept throwing her off guard with his sweet, let-me-care-for-you comments. He was treating her like a precious treasure, seeing to her comforts. She didn't like it. It made her vulnerable, made it harder to resist him.

There had to be something she could do to make him hate her. But what? He laughed at her insults, ignored her taunts. *Keep trying until you succeed, damn it.* If he continued to be nice to her, she would soften toward him. He might just melt the ice she so desperately needed to survive. What would happen to her then? Love? Would she lose herself to a man who could never return the depth of her feelings? God, no. No, no, no.

With all of her strength she attempted to pull from Valerian's hold, to at last put distance between their bodies. He locked his grip, cutting off her breath and shackling her in place.

"Be still, moon. Already my body hungers for yours, and I'm not sure how much more I can tolerate. We are almost done here."

She stilled, not wanting to arouse him further. But damn this! Why did she have to feel so safe in his arms? Safe and wonderful and aroused? He was dangerous to the solitary life she had built—and wanted—for herself.

"Joachim," Valerian called. "Your turn has arrived." He lowered his voice, murmuring in her ear, "Your scent is amazing. I want you so much. I want—"

"That one," a male voice said. Joachim—the current "picker," the angry-looking brunet who had been staring at her, stepped forward.

Valerian froze. Shaye gasped. She'd been so sure she'd scared everyone away…but he had… Dear Lord. Ice chilled her blood.

"What did you say?" Valerian gritted out. His fingers, wrapped so tightly around her waist, dug into her skin.

"I want the pale one, the girl in your arms." Joachim braced his legs apart, his expression stern and smug. Ready. He looked like a man who craved war. "Give her to me. She is mine."

CHAPTER SEVEN

"VALERIAN," SHAYE SAID, her voice shaky. As shaky as her body. "Help me."

"I will take care of this. Worry not." All at once, Valerian felt infuriated that someone would dare try to take Shaye from him, overjoyed that Shaye felt safest with him and frightened that he might actually lose her.

And to his cousin, no less.

They didn't share an easy camaraderie, for Joachim's thirst for power made him rebellious. Wild. How Valerian was going to change the soldier's mind, he didn't know.

"There are two other females in line," Valerian said. "Are you sure you would not prefer one of them?"

Joachim nodded, never once glancing toward the women in question. Determination filled his eyes. Determination...and lust. For Valerian's head? Or Shaye's body? Either way, Valerian would not give up easily.

Nor would Joachim, apparently. "I want her," the man said firmly.

Shaye's soft body pressed into the hardness of Valerian's. Her frosty scent enveloped him, fueling his own sense of determination.

"I will challenge you for her." Valerian pinned his

cousin with a hard stare. "I will give you the opportunity to defeat your king." Joachim could not take the throne that way, but there was much honor in fighting the king. Even if—when!—Joachim lost, he would be lauded for participating in such a rare occurrence.

For a moment, an all-too-short flash of time, Joachim considered the offer. He even began to nod but stopped himself. He shook his head instead. "Unacceptable." Frowning, he gripped the hilt of his sword. "Last night, you had female flesh in excess, making you strong. I have been neglected for weeks. We are not on equal ground."

Valerian's jaw clenched painfully. Did his cousin hope for a night with Shaye, *then* a fight with the king? "You may spend the night with the three women who pleasured me. They will ensure you are strengthened. We can fight for Shaye on the morrow."

Joachim's black brows arched, and something—an unreadable emotion—brightened his blue eyes. "You said you would not claim another surface woman, yet there you stand, attempting to do just that."

"Wait." Shaye held up her hands. "Hold everything. You slept with three women at the same time, Valerian?" Had she been facing him, he felt certain she would have slapped him. "What, do you expect me to join the love train? You're disgusting! All of you are."

"Do you want them or not?" he asked Joachim, ignoring her.

Lips curling in a smile, Joachim pointed to Shaye. "I want that one. As is my right."

"She will cause you nothing but trouble." His teeth were clenched so tightly, he had trouble getting out the words.

"That's right." Shaye nodded, tufts of white hair dancing over her shoulders. "I'll stab you while you sleep. I'll cut off your balls and use them for earrings. I'll…I'll—"

Color faded from Joachim's cheeks, and he swallowed. At least her threats to Joachim were more violent, Valerian mused. She'd only wanted to cut out *his* eyes.

"I want her still," Joachim said, though he did not sound as confident.

His cousin would not relent. Frustrated, infuriated, Valerian gave an animalistic growl. He'd never lied to his men, never gone back on his word. His father had died when Valerian was only a boy, leaving Valerian to take over the nymph army. He'd had to prove himself worthy and capable over and over again. And he had.

"Honor them," had been his father's dying words. "Lead them. Protect them. You are ultimately responsible for their fate."

He could take Shaye, and no one could naysay him. Grumble about his lack of honor, yes, even curse him to everlasting Hades. But not naysay him.

While he had told himself he could surrender his honor to possess Shaye, he realized now that he could not. How could he expect her to fall in love—and love him she would—with a dishonorable man?

"I have said I would not claim the females brought here, and I will not," he said.

Shaye stiffened. She closed her hands over his arms, which were still wrapped around her, and dug her fingernails into his skin.

"I will not," he continued, switching to his native tongue so Shaye would not understand the rest of the conversation, "without reaching amicable terms. Allow me to buy her from you."

Once more, Joachim shook his head. "No."

Damn the man! "What can I do, cousin? The woman—" he stopped, pressed his lips together "—the woman is my mate."

Joachim's nostrils flared, and he bared his teeth. He took a menacing step forward. "She does not seem to think so. She has not accepted you as such."

"She is human. Their reactions must be different from ours."

"You would say anything to keep her."

"In this, I do not lie. If you take her, she can never love you. She will never be able to give her heart to you. In her soul, she will always belong to me." They both knew the ways of mates and nymphs. Love was love. That Shaye was human made no difference. He had to make Joachim understand. "When you take her to your bed, it will always be my face she pictures. My body she craves. Can your pride stand such a thing?"

Dark, heavy silence greeted his pronouncement. His cousin paled, his jaw clenched.

"What did you say to him?" Shaye looked from him to Joachim, Joachim to him.

Joachim's gaze narrowed on Valerian. "I must think on what you have said. Let us both stay away from her this night and discuss her ownership in the morning."

Since he'd spoken in the surface language, Shaye understood. "Ownership?" she gasped.

Stay away from her this night? Valerian's body jerked at the horror. Since the first moment he'd seen her, he'd thought only of possessing her. Denying himself would, perhaps, be the most difficult thing he'd ever done.

"I am in…agreement." At least his cousin would not be allowed to touch her, either.

"Well, I'm *not* in agreement." Shaye stomped her foot, determined to be acknowledged.

He tightened his hold on her, hoping to silence her. Of course, it didn't work.

"Let me save you both a lot of trouble," she said. "I don't want either of you. Now, I'm a reasonable—"

Valerian snorted.

"Reasonable woman," she finished, glaring at him over her shoulder. "And I'm willing to forget this entire episode of *The Male Whores of Atlantis* if someone will. Just. Take. Me. Home."

Ignoring her, Joachim crossed his arms over his chest. "Where will she stay tonight?"

"I will place her in the chamber next to mine. We will both guard her door."

His cousin paused for a moment, running the idea through his mind. He nodded. "Very well."

Valerian dropped his arms from Shaye, instantly mourning the loss of her softness, her heat. She must have felt the same loss, whether she would admit it or not, because she laced her arms over her middle and shivered.

"Damn it." She drummed her fingers against her sides. "Will someone pay attention to me and tell me who's taking me home?"

"I am," Valerian answered before Joachim could respond. "I am taking you home."

On a startled gasp, she spun and faced him. "Really? You'll take me home? Now?"

He drank her in, struck anew by the beauty of her. How could one woman make him ache so intensely? Make him forget everyone who had come before her until only she existed?

Reaching out, he held his palm face-up. "Will you come with me willingly?"

Suspicion suddenly blanketed her features. But even that did not detract from her beauty. "You're not lying to me?"

"Never."

For a long while, she did nothing. Then, she tentatively placed her hand in his. Their fingers intertwined, a perfect fit.

He knew she'd misunderstood his intentions; *this* was her new home. But he said nothing. Not yet.

Joachim growled and held out his own hand to Shaye. Seconds ticked by as she stared at it. Every muscle in Valerian's body clenched. If she took Joachim's hand, she would encourage the man's attentions. She would disprove the validity of Valerian's declaration.

One heartbeat passed. Then another.

She leveled Valerian with an exasperated glance. "Well. What are you waiting for? Let's go. If we hurry, I'll be able to make my flight back to Cincinnati."

Flight? She could fly? Surely not. He pushed away his confusion and concentrated on his surprise. She'd ignored Joachim and his proffered hand as if they didn't exist. But him, she asked for aid. Inside, Valerian howled with triumph.

"Crosse," he called to one of the remaining men. "Prepare the room next to mine." Hopefully, the loyal man would know what he truly desired—the removal of all traces of the human women he'd pleasured last eve. Unfortunately, they hadn't limited themselves to the main chamber. Shaye erupted at the slightest hint of carnality, and he did not want her upset.

Crosse nodded, cast a wistful glance at the two remaining women and rushed to obey.

Joachim, who hadn't moved, at last dropped his arm to his side. "Best you be cautious, woman, and treat me with care." His voice was low, gritty. "I might change my mind and choose to take you now."

"At odds already." Valerian *tsked* under his tongue, though he really wanted to attack.

"Why don't both of you go to hell and save me the trouble of sending you there?" Shaye said, radiating absolute innocence. Total sweetness. "Now, be a good boy and take me home like you promised, Valerian."

He glimpsed Joachim's astonished gaze and fought a grin. That sharp tongue of Shaye's just might save them. He turned back to the others. "Terran, Aeson, you may choose between the final two." As they cheered, he faced Shaye and said, "This way." He led her into the hallway.

A few of the warriors, he noticed, had not made it to their rooms. Some were in the process of making love to their new women right there in the hall, while others had simply pushed their lovers against the wall and were feasting between their legs. Moans, purrs and groans of delight echoed.

"My God," Shaye gasped out.

Such a sight was common in a nymph household, but he did not mention that to Shaye.

With her close on his heels, and Joachim close on

hers, he ushered her past the kitchens, past the training arena, past the warriors' barracks—where more moans and purrs abounded.

"Do they ever stop?" Shaye muttered darkly.

Shock and—was that desire?—laced her voice. Yes, he realized. Yes, it was. The shock amused him. The desire excited him on a primal level. If she were his, he would have vanquished the first and leisurely explored the second right then and there. Soon, he swore. Soon.

His chambers were situated in a hall away from the rest of the palace. Each room was spacious, with a large bathing pool, an immense bed and a panoramic wall of windows that offered a breathtaking view of the Outer City below.

"Thank you for agreeing to take me back," Shaye said. "I know you don't want to, and I'm grateful."

He'd never heard such a gentle, tender tone from her. She even wore an expression of genuine gratitude, the sweetness of it softening her features and gifting her with bright radiance. He could not allow her to wallow in false assumptions any longer. "I'm not taking you back to your world, moon. I'm taking you to your home. Your new home."

She hissed in a stream of air; her nails dug into his flesh. "You knew what I thought, you misleading bastard."

"Does she always speak this way?" Joachim asked, voicing his first doubt.

"Always," Valerian and Shaye snapped in unison.

"I'm not staying in your room," she growled to Valerian. "I told you that already."

He had to drag her (gently, of course) the rest of the way. Joachim watched the interaction with an unreadable expression. Finally they reached the outskirts of Valerian's rooms.

Crosse exited the main doorway, swishing the wispy material that hung there. His features were flushed with pleasure; his eyes were closed in surrender as he blindly felt his way out.

Having caught his scent, the three naked human women chased after him and trapped him in a circle. Instantly their hands were all over him, touching and caressing his back as they moaned in eagerness. In impatience.

Seeing them, a plan sprouted thick roots inside Valerian's mind—and it irritated him that he was reduced to planning and scheming to have a woman who should, by all rights, be panting for him. He was a king. A leader. His word was law. "Take whichever woman you desire, Crosse, and go to bed."

The warrior's eyelids popped open in surprise. "My king," he said. One of the women cupped his testicles, and he moaned. "May I have all three?"

Valerian rolled his eyes. "No. Two are needed…elsewhere."

Shaye's mouth flailed open and closed, each time emitting a strangling sound. "You're treating those women like objects, and what do you mean *elsewhere?*" She pointed a finger at Crosse, but her gaze remained on Valerian. "What if the woman he picks doesn't want to leave with him? What then?"

"You have doubt of their willingness?" Valerian motioned to the writhing foursome with a tilt of his chin. "They are eating him alive even now."

Her eyes narrowed on them, and she *humphed.* "Well, you still sound like a pimp," she muttered. Then, louder, "Stand up for yourselves, girls. Tell these men you won't take part in their debauchery."

In lieu of a response, all three ran their tongues over Crosse's bare chest and back. The man whimpered in unadulterated bliss. Shaye pinched the bridge of her nose and shook her head.

"Take your woman, Crosse, and go."

"Thank you, my king." Crosse grabbed the brunette, who was even then trying to slip her hand into his pants, and raced away with her. Her giggles echoed behind her.

The other two groaned at the loss of their lover… until they spied Valerian. They clapped and laughed in renewed delight. He backed away. He even thrust Shaye in front of him as a shield.

"I am mated," he told them. Mated nymphs did not usually draw females with the same potency and fever as unmated ones. These women might want him still, but they would never again want him beyond reason. Beyond all sense of self.

Perhaps humans did not know that was the way of things, for they sauntered toward him, undeterred.

"Back off, ladies," Shaye suddenly barked. They obeyed instantly, their features crumbling in a pout.

Valerian blinked in surprise. Had that been jealousy in Shaye's tone? Possessiveness? Dare he hope? "Joachim is in need of a lover," he said, pointing.

Their gazes slid to the warrior in question—whose eyes were widening in suspicion. And anticipation. Both women grinned slowly and sashayed to him without question.

"You are so big," the blonde cooed.

"And strong," added the redhead.

Joachim backed away, determined to resist. "I have made a choice?" he said, but the words were a question rather than a statement. "The…the pale one is to be my next bed partner, and I must guard her door this night. For that reason, you…can…not… touch…me. *Touch me.*" The last was an unrestrained moan of helpless capitulation.

They'd reached him, and their hands were already on him, stroking. Their warm breath was probably bathing his skin; their eager scent likely filling his nose. Valerian almost grinned. *Perhaps I have already lost my honor,* he thought, even as he said, "Shaye will not mind if you do not stand guard at her door this night. A man has needs, and she knows that."

"Needs," the lost-in-a-passion-haze warrior repeated, dazed.

"I want your naked skin sliding against mine," the blonde said, breathless.

"I want you, hot in my mouth."

Joachim audibly swallowed. "Valerian," he began.

"Go. I will see you in the morning."

"The pale one—"

"Will remain untouched." Tonight. "I have given you my word."

"I trust you." Joachim strode away then, a sexually charged woman on each arm. Valerian doubted they would make it to a room. Most likely, Joachim was already naked and inside one, pinning her against the wall—

A woman's ecstatic cry of pleasure rang out.

Valerian finally allowed his grin to peek through.

Joachim was occupied, and he had Shaye alone. But he couldn't taste her or caress her body, he reminded himself. He'd given his word, after all, and his cousin trusted him. He lost his smile.

"Unbelievable," Shaye muttered.

He gripped her shoulders and twisted her around, letting her see his frown. "Just what do you find so unbelievable?"

"The amount of communal sex to be had, of course. Haven't you people heard of diseases?"

She looked so lovely standing there in her pique. So surreal, like the moonbeam he called her. Lust coiled strong fingers through his blood. He'd touched the softness of her skin today, but had yet to taste her. He'd held her, but had yet to make love to her.

The sounds of loving echoed from every corridor of the palace, audible even in this remote hideaway. Shaye's cheeks pinkened. How he would have loved to taste that color in her cheeks, to see if it was as pure as it appeared. His cock hardened painfully.

Now that they were alone, his body wanted only to learn hers. To strip her. To sink into her. To pound, hard and fast, a never-ending rhythm. She looked at him, as if she herself had just realized they were finally alone, and her nostrils flared. In desire?

He had to have her, honor be damned. Had to— He fisted his hands at his sides to keep himself from reaching out.

"Shaye, listen to me very closely." The words were nothing more than a growl of barely restrained need. "I want you, but I cannot have you. If you do not go inside that room right now, I'm going to forget that I'm not supposed to have you. I'm going to take you. I'll rip away your clothes and taste every inch of you."

As he spoke, she inched away from him. Her eyes widened, impossibly round, velvet-brown with sparks of, dare he say, need?

"The cloth behind you covers the only doorway. If you cross it, even once, I will view it as an invitation to take what I so desperately crave."

The total conviction in his voice must have frightened her. Pallid, she spun around and sprinted into the room, pale hair drifting behind her like a cluster of falling stars.

For a long while, the cloth hanging in the doorway rippled, daring him to enter. Finally it stilled, and Valerian covered his face with a shaky hand. Having a mate was going to be hell on his body, it seemed, for he foresaw a long, painful night ahead.

With no real end in sight.

CHAPTER EIGHT

SHAYE'S HEART THUNDERED in her chest, pounding so hard she feared her ribs would crack; her ears rang loudly, and she covered them with her hands to block out the awful sound. She sank onto the edge of a decadent made-for-sex bed of red silk and velvet.

Not daring to breathe, she stared at the sheer, white lace in place of the door.

She remained in that exact position for over an hour, fearful—and, damn it, anticipatory—of Valerian following her inside the room. That look in his eyes when she'd left him...she'd never encountered anything quite so scorching. So blistering. If she'd reached out, the heat from his gaze would have burned her skin.

She gulped. Seeing him like that, she'd felt as if she'd traveled too close to the sun, ready to combust into flames at any moment. A part of her had *wanted* to combust.

On Earth, or rather the *surface,* she didn't have to worry about that sort of thing. Desire, thankfully, wasn't a part of her life. Her employees were female; she'd purposefully kept the office testosterone-free to avoid temptation.

"Relationships," she muttered. Ugh. It wasn't that

she'd watched her mother devour men like candy or that she'd witnessed her father plow through women like a linebacker. It wasn't the stepdads who had tried to sneak into her room, forcing her to hide in shadowy corners just to get a little sleep. It wasn't even the charmingly sly men she'd dated in that brief, curious period of her life.

It was the fear that she would turn out to be just like them, a slave to her own desires. A fool for love. Accepting of whatever crap the object of her fascination dished. Shaye sighed.

Sure, she'd had more adventure in the last few hours than she'd had in her entire life. She hadn't experienced a moment of loneliness, hadn't had to pretend everything was okay. But up there, the men she pushed away *stayed* away. If someone asked her out and she said no, they left her alone. Most wanted nothing to do with her, to be honest, finding her too…prickly. Too cold.

Not Valerian. There was no getting rid of him, it seemed.

She rested her head against the bedpost, which was intricately carved with frolicking dragons and naked females. So far Valerian had proven himself a man of his word and had not entered. He hadn't even peeked at her through the wisp of lace. She knew he stood guard just beyond the curtain, though. She heard him shift from one foot to the other.

I have to escape before morning.

"I'm not a trophy," she muttered. "I am not a prize for Valerian and his Sex Squad to fight over."

"Yes, you are," the man of the hour said.

The sound of his husky, sexy voice gave her a jolt

of pure pleasure. Made her heart skip a beat and heat coast over her skin. She jumped to her feet, gaze scanning the room for an exit. All she saw was the large tub that was filled with hot water. Tendrils of steam curled to the vaulted crystal ceiling, which showcased the now turbulent ocean above. Waves churned and swirled, leaving wisps of foam behind. No horny mermaids in sight, thank God. Multicolored gowns— togas?—hung in the closet.

The room looked as if it had been taken from the set of a movie. A period piece with a dash of modern. Glamorous, expensive, surreal. While the vanity was made of ivory, the chair in front of it was composed of diamonds, the cushion layered with vivid violet silks from the palest lilac to the darkest amethyst.

True to Valerian's word, there was no other doorway. No other—wait! Biting her lip with the force of her excitement, she raced to a lavender veil hanging over the far wall and shoved it aside.

The sight that greeted her was not what she expected, but it made her gasp all the same. Her eyes widened. "Dear God."

"Magnificent, is it not?" Valerian said through the curtain, as if he could see through her eyes. Pride dripped from his words. "We call it the Outer City."

She stood in front of a wall of windows. A lush green view greeted her. Thick, dew-kissed trees, some as bright as emeralds, others as white as snow, circled the landscape. Clear waterfalls tumbled into pristine rivers. Rainbow-colored birds soared overhead.

In the heart of it all was a crowded, pulsing-with-life city. Buildings of stone and wood created a maze of winding streets. Streaks of light emanated from the dome above, murky and dim, as twilight gave way to night. Light from a crystal instead of a sun, Shaye mused.

She would have loved to visit, to stand in the midst of such spectacular beauty and simply bask in it. "I'm as close as I'll ever get to heaven," she breathed. She stared down the cliffs, amazed by the creatures she suddenly noticed. Okay, maybe not heaven. There were bull-faced men, women with horse-bodies, lions with wings, and— "Holy shit!" She slapped a hand over her mouth, shocked by what she saw.

A deep, throaty chuckle greeted her ears. "We must work on your language, Shaye."

The sound of that chuckle washed over her erotically. The sound of her name on his lips, however, proved more stimulating. *Be rude. Make him dislike you.* A heartbeat of time passed, and she didn't say anything. *I don't want to be rude,* some part of her whined. She gnashed her teeth. *Just do it!* "Well…you can just blow me, Valerian."

"Thank you. I will."

She shook her head in frustration. The man simply couldn't take an insult the way it was intended. A horde of harpies—the very thing that had so shocked her a moment ago—took flight, their huge breasts jiggling as they ascended into the air. Long, sharp talons stretched from their hands and feet. Their faces were hideous with beak noses and evil, black eyes.

"There was no need to travel to the beach, Valerian," she said, trying again. "Your perfect mate was right here in your own city all along."

"Only you would do, love."

Her stomach tightened at his words. Forcing her at-

tention away from the fantastical metropolis, she studied
the windows. They were made of the same crystal as the
dome, only smoother, with no cracks, no seams. Translation: no way to open. She stomped her foot. So what
that she couldn't have scaled the walls outside. So what
that she was high up, and falling to her death would be
the most likely outcome. A girl needed options.

"Perhaps you should use this time to come to terms
with your fate instead of finding a way to escape,"
Valerian suggested from his post.

"Perhaps *you* should shut up."

Another husky chuckle rumbled from him, and she
scowled at the dark, drugging sensuality of it. It was
more potent this time. Beguiling. Quietly beseeching
her to join him in his merriment.

"Why do you find my insults so humorous?" Most
people ran as fast as they could to get away from her.

"You do not really mean what you say," he explained
patiently. "I suspect you want just the opposite, in fact."

A tremble moved through her. Shock—yes. More
than ever before. Awe—certainly. No one, not even her
family, had ever suspected the truth. She did not enjoy
hurting people; she simply wasn't brave enough to risk
making a friend. How did he know? She cleared her
throat, striving for a hard tone. "You don't know me
well enough to judge what I mean and what I don't."

"But I would like to."

As he spoke, his face swam before her mind. Perfect
masculinity, rugged and untamed. If she dared touch
him, his hair would be silky soft, and the gold strands
would tickle her palms. She knew it.

"Will you let me know you, Shaye?" he asked quietly.

She could make out the shadowed outline of his body, just beyond the doorway. She watched his strong fingers trace the lace separating them. Was he imagining the cloth was her body? Imagining those fingertips circling her nipples, trekking down her stomach, past her panties and— A shiver racked her, and she frowned.

This type of reaction was unacceptable.

"No," she said. "There will be no getting to know each other." Already she wanted him. What would happen if she actually learned what made him tick?

She valued her independence, her solitariness, and being with a nymph would strip those things away layer by precious layer. So many times now, she'd seen women become mindless around them, forgetting everything except sex. Shaye refused to allow the same fate to befall her.

"I need *something* from you, little Shaye, and I am willing to deal with you. Bargain," Valerian said, interrupting her thoughts. "Negotiate."

Her eyes narrowed on his large silhouette. "For what, exactly?"

"I will be silent for the rest of the night if you agree to give me your affections."

She snorted. "You're not getting my affection."

"Compliments, then. Will you give me compliments?"

"No. Absolutely not."

He sighed with regret. "Won't you give me *something?*"

"I'm giving you grief, aren't I?"

He paused, chuckled. "So you are."

Stop talking to him and find a way out of here, her mind shouted. Steps clipped, she approached the far, jewel-encrusted wall. In the hall and dining area, the walls had been bare, as if someone had stolen the gems. Here, wealth abounded. Maybe… She brightened. Maybe one of the jewels was actually a latch that would open a door into some sort of corridor.

"I wish to become your slave, Shaye. I wish to cater to your every desire, to see to your every pleasure." Valerian's voice was smooth, mesmerizing. "Do you not desire such things from me?"

She struggled to harden herself against him, to retain the wall of ice around her emotions. If she ever decided to—God forbid—enter into a relationship, it would not be with a nymph (aka male whore). No matter how irresistible. Shaye knew herself well enough to know she despised sharing. She'd shared her parents with their ever-changing lovers. She'd shared her childhood with sometimes cruel, rarely caring stepsisters and brothers, with loneliness and disappointment.

If ever she gave herself to someone, it would be to a man who wanted her and only her. A man who would give up his life to make her happy. She, in turn, would do the same.

Was she asking and offering too much? Absolutely. But it was what she wanted, and she wouldn't settle for less—even though she knew it was an impossible dream. Perhaps that was why she wanted it in the first place. If she couldn't have it, she didn't have to worry about heartbreak.

Valerian talked a good talk, and God knows he could probably walk a delectable, mind-shattering walk all over her body, but he'd do the same for any and every woman who caught his fancy. He wanted "now" from her, a momentary dalliance, no ties afterward.

No, thank you.

She could have had that on the surface.

Silently she worked the room for two hours, feeling every ounce of wall and floor she could reach. To her vast disappointment, frustration and fury, she found no hidden latch. She was stuck here. If she were home, she would be peacefully tucked in bed right now. Alone. *And lonely,* her mind piped up.

"Shut up, you stupid brain," she muttered. Lonely was good. Besides, she had a fulfilling life. She would have woken up in the morning, had coffee with her assistant and discussed the day's events. She would have presented a new card idea, probably something along the lines of *Congratulations on your new promotion. Before you go, would you mind taking the knife out of my back? You'll probably need it again.* Her assistant would have laughed, the rest of the staff would have laughed, and she would have felt like a smart, appreciated person. Not like a confused, horny teenager.

"Go to sleep, moon," Valerian said, cutting into her thoughts. "I sense you're upset. Since I cannot comfort you as I would like…"

"Well, you're responsible for it." She tangled a hand through her hair, nearly ripping out the strands. "Please, Valerian. Take me back to the beach."

A pause. Heavy. Thick. "What is so important there that you must return to it?"

"My home." Paid in full. "My job." Her only real source of accomplishment.

"What was your job?"

He'd used past tense. She made sure to use present. "I make anti-greeting cards," she said proudly.

"Tell me of these anti-cards," he beseeched.

It was a subject she embraced. "There are many companies that produce sappy *I love you, I miss you* type salutations. Not mine. They say just the opposite."

"I am not surprised," he said, chuckling. "Can you not make such cards here?"

She could, but she didn't want to, so she ignored his question. God, how was she going to get out of here?

"I notice you do not mention friends and family," he said a short while later.

Knowing exactly where this conversation was headed, she should have stopped it then. Should have told him to get lost and leave her alone. But for some reason, she didn't. Couldn't. "That's right," she found herself saying.

"Why?"

She leaned her forehead against the cool wall and squeezed her eyes closed. *Lie. Make him feel guilty.* "I don't have many friends," she admitted instead, the truth a tangible entity that refused to be denied, "and I don't get along with my family."

"Why?" he repeated.

Why, indeed. "You might have noticed I don't have the sweetest of personalities."

He barked a quick laugh. "Yes, perhaps I did notice."

"That tends to drive people away." The way she intended. Her hands slid up the glittering stone and anchored beside her head. Telling him about her life was dangerous, giving him ammunition against her, but she couldn't seem to end it. He called to something deep inside her. Something…primitive.

"You have not driven me away," he said quietly.

"No, I haven't." She sighed. Why hadn't she? Why hadn't he run from her? Run as fast as his feet could carry him?

"What is so important about your home and job that you cannot stay here with me? *I* can be your family. I can be your friend. You can sell the cards to me."

"I worked hard for my home. It's mine. I worked hard to make my job a success. I have nothing here."

"But you could." He was still speaking in that soft, tender voice. *Let me give you everything,* his words implied.

A hot ache squeezed at her chest. She needed to fortify herself against this man, she reminded herself. "Why are you doing this to me? You could have any of the other women. They would eagerly come to you and do anything you asked of them."

"They are not you."

A simple sentence, yes, but it rocked her to the core. Scowling, she straightened. "What's so special about me, hmm? I defy you to name one thing."

For a long while he didn't reply, and that both elated and defeated her. *Stupid,* she chastised herself, *to crave praise from him.* The goal was to convince him he didn't want her. Right? "Well?"

Still nothing. Not a single remark or declaration.

"I didn't think so," she finally muttered. She turned her back to the door and stomped toward the bed, battling despair. She needed to think, to consider all her options. Chatting it up with her abductor wasted valuable time.

She'd stay awake all night if she had to, but she wasn't giving up. She *would* find a way home. She wouldn't sleep, even though she needed the rest. In slumber, she would become even more vulnerable to Valerian. He would be able to sneak into the room and do whatever he wanted to her—and she would have no idea.

But deep down, she knew that was a lie. A defense against him. When that man pleasured a woman, the woman would know it. Even in sleep, she would know. Her body would sing and weep with pleasure.

The man was a menace.

A menace who couldn't name one thing about her that he liked. Bastard.

"Don't come inside this room," she barked. "Do you hear me? And don't speak to me again. I need silence."

"Shaye."

His guttural growling of her name froze her in place. He'd sounded like he was in pain, like he was about to fall down a long, dark, never-ending pit. "What?" She hoped for a waspish tone, but the question emerged as nothing more than a wisp of air. Was he hurt?

"You are the woman of my heart. The one I have been awaiting the whole of my life, though I didn't know it until I spied you. There isn't one thing that makes you special to me, but all things. Now sleep. Tomorrow promises to be a day ripe with unpleasantness."

Just like that, her knees buckled. She would have fallen flat on her face if she hadn't grabbed the edge of the bed and held herself upright. Dear God. Those words. No one—not her mother, not her father, not brother or sisters or an endless string of nannies—had ever spoken to her like that. Made her feel so important, so *necessary*.

She barely knew Valerian. In their short time

together, she'd railed at him, desired him, cursed him and hit him. Now, with a few words, he made her long to throw herself at him. To destroy every wall she'd ever built, melt every piece of ice she'd ever surrounded herself with, and just throw herself at him.

"Dear God," she whispered, horrified. Everything she'd ever secretly dreamed of hearing had just come from Valerian's lips. How was she going to resist him now?

CHAPTER NINE

VALERIAN SPENT the entire night posted at Shaye's door. She'd finally obeyed him, had at last slipped into sleep. Stubborn girl that she was, she had fought it until the end.

He was hyperaware of her every movement. Every sound she made. For hours she'd searched for a way out of the room, then she'd paced and muttered under her breath about "stupid men," "stupid emotions" and "stupid mystical cities coming to life." But her steps had eventually slowed, her curses eventually ceased. He'd heard her drift into unconsciousness with a soft sigh. A quick peek had confirmed that she did indeed sleep, sprawled on the cold, hard floor, her hair spilling around her like a snowy curtain.

He suspected she'd avoided the bed on purpose, and he was still frowning about that fact. Did she think he would not take her if she was not on a bed? Silly woman. He would take her wherever, however he could get her.

Gods, he wanted so badly to touch her.

Just one touch… Such a heady thought. Surely there was nothing wrong with placing her on the bed. He was her man, after all, and it was his duty to see to her comfort.

He shouldn't—he knew he shouldn't—but he allowed himself to enter the room. He swept aside the lace that covered the doorway. Much as he might crave sexual contact with her, he would not touch her in that way. *That* had been his promise to Joachim…and to Shaye. And he would keep that promise. Gods help him, he would keep it.

His steps quiet, he moved toward her. She still lay on the ground, on her back, one hand over her head, the other next to her ear. He sucked in a breath.

She looked like a winter goddess, a snow nymph, lovelier than Aphrodite herself. That pale hair ribboned around her delicate frame, the strands so silky they glistened as if they'd been sprinkled with starlight. Her eyelashes were light, only a shade darker than her hair. Her lips, those soft, lush, all-your-dreams-come-true lips were parted, begging to be kissed.

Resist, he commanded himself. *Resist her allure.*

Too late.

She uttered a breathy, sleep-rich sigh. His inexhaustible desire clamored to instant life, reaching for her. Frantic for her. He wanted that sigh in his ears, on his chest—lower still—her breath warm and caressing. If only she didn't appear so soft and vulnerable, so ripe for the taking….

She was to be his greatest satisfaction, his greatest pleasure.

Damn Joachim to Hades, wanting something—someone—that belonged to Valerian! As the curse echoed through his mind, he found his lips lifting in wry humor. Could he blame the man for coveting such an enchanting morsel as Shaye?

Hades, yes! he decided in the next instant. He scowled. She was meant for no man save himself, and those who thought otherwise deserved a painful death. Valerian had never wanted anything as much as he wanted Shaye, and not being able to have her immediately was…difficult. Hard—literally.

Bending down, he scooped her into his arms. She was as light as he remembered. As soft. As warm. As lovely. "I will have you yet," he told her. "Say nothing if you agree with me."

Of course she made no reply.

He was grinning, his humor restored, as he carried her to the bed. Gently he placed her on the mattress, his arms already protesting her loss. He removed her sandals and traced his finger over her coral-painted toes. As he straightened, he smoothed the hair from her face and reveled in the feel of her glorious skin. As cool as she looked, she was surprisingly, wondrously hot.

"Dream of me, moon," he whispered.

The pink tip of her tongue emerged and swept over her lips. A wave of desire swept through him as he imagined himself meeting her tongue with his own. Twining. Dueling. Tasting.

Sucking.

"I'll dream of you, I have no doubt." Lingering a moment more, he traced his fingertip over the seam of her lips. She sighed breathily again. His stomach clenched; every muscle in his body hardened.

He couldn't tear his eyes from her, but he knew he had to leave her soon, or he wouldn't be able to do so at all. The longer he stayed, the more his control would slip. Already it clung precariously to a sense of honor he wasn't sure he possessed anymore. A sense of honor he truly despised for the first time in his existence.

One look at Shaye and she was all he thought about, all he craved, wanted. Needed.

Leave! Now. Slowly, so slowly, he backed out of the room. His gaze remained on her heavenly form for as long as possible. When the lace finally blocked his view, his hands tightened into fists. He leaned his forehead against the cool wall.

I have to win her. I cannot let another have her.

Straightening, he paced the length of the antechamber, skirting around lounge chairs and armor. The thick soles of his boots thumped against the onyx floor. For the first time in weeks, not a single member of his army had approached him during these twilight hours. They were locked in their rooms—or in the halls beyond—floating on the clouds of ecstasy found only in a woman's sweet arms.

Even Joachim had stayed away.

Valerian prayed his cousin became so enamored of his current lovers that he forgot all about Shaye. If not…well, Valerian would just have to think of something Joachim would find irresistible. Something he'd place above the importance of a bedmate. What?

Joachim was a good man (at times), a strong warrior, with a (slightly) loyal heart. What were the man's weaknesses? Women? Beyond a doubt. Women were the weakness of all nymphs. Power? Definitely. Weapons? Most surely. Joachim collected them. From every warrior he'd killed or bested, he had taken their weapons and hung them on his bedchamber wall.

Valerian's gaze strayed to his own blade, resting against an onyx chest. The Skull. Large, sharp. Lethal. One of the finest swords ever made. No, *the* finest ever made. Crafted by Hepaesteus, blacksmith of the gods. The weapon had slayed many of his enemies, rending them with unmendable injuries. It was the only one of its kind. Its twisted frame and elongated skull tip were envied by every soldier who spied it.

He hated to give it up, but his mate held much more importance to him. Even a mate who wanted nothing to do with him. Would Joachim accept it?

He sighed, the answer remaining a mystery. As much a mystery as how to win Shaye's well-guarded heart. Jewels? Pretty clothing? If he thought, even for a moment, that she valued those things, he would sweep her up that very second and take her into the Outer City. He would buy her everything she desired. But so far she had seemed unimpressed by his wealth, wanting only to return home.

Did she have enemies in need of slaying? If so, he would gladly lay their lifeless bodies at her feet.

He pushed a hand through his hair. Uncertainty about a female was foreign and horrible and challenging and exciting. Winning her—defeating Joachim and overcoming Shaye's own resistance—awakened his deepest warrior instincts. He'd gladly present Hades with his soul and live forever damned, just to be with Shaye.

"She will be mine," he vowed to the heavens. "She will be mine."

THREADS OF LIGHT flowed from the crystal dome above, gradually brightening the room. Different-colored shards shot in every direction, a lovely rainbow spray. Blues, pinks, purples, greens. Shaye tore her tired gaze from them and stared directly above the—she gasped.

The ceiling above her was composed of glass, not crystal, and she was given a full view of her reflection.

She was splayed atop a bed of red silk sheets, her pale hair and skin a startling contrast. Her eyes were at half-mast, heavy and slumberous, with dark circles under them. One of her arms rested at her side; the other was raised and bent at her temple. Still wearing her seashell bra and grass skirt, she could have been taken straight from the pages of *Beach Bunny* magazine.

She looked ready and eager for a man.

Not just any man, though....

She gulped and rolled to her side. She shouldn't be on this bed, she thought, recalling how her knees had given out and she'd tumbled to the floor, too exhausted to get up.

Her gaze narrowed on the door. Had Valerian entered without her knowledge? Had he carried her here? Seen her like this? *Posed* her like this? That...that... *Calm down. Nothing you can do about it now.*

At least he hadn't woken her up and tried to seduce her. Not that she would have had the strength to send him on his way. Not last night. Not after the things he'd said to her.

She hadn't meant to fall asleep, damn it. She should have been searching for a way out, not dreaming of her sexy captor. Of his hands on her, tracing the arch and planes of her lips, holding her to his chest. Cherishing her.

"Diabolical man," she muttered. Surprisingly, she wasn't stiff or sore as she eased up. She yawned and rubbed the sleep from her eyes, then scanned the room, hoping the way out would reveal itself in the light of day. The bathing pool still steamed with hot water, like a natural spring. Cloth still draped the windows. Columns still rose to the ceiling with Roman majesty.

Except for the lace-covered doorway, no exit magically presented itself.

I have to get out of here, she thought, suddenly urgent, *before* he *comes to get me.*

He. Valerian. Unbidden, his image rose in her mind. Strong, proud. Sexual. A hedonist to the extreme, with skin that looked like dark, lickable cream, hair as radiant as spun gold, and eyes… God, his eyes. They beckoned. They teased. They *promised.* His turquoise irises were as mesmerizing as a turbulent ocean and just as deep. Those long, dark lashes acted as the perfect frame, the perfect contrast.

What are you doing mooning over him? Dummy! It's time to leave. Fighting a rush of desire, she lumbered to her feet—and tripped over her sandals. So. He'd taken off her shoes. She should be grateful that was all he'd removed.

Shaye used the surprisingly modern bathroom and washed her face, hoping the water would also wash away her unwanted feelings. Then she circled the room, seeing everything she'd seen the night before—a prison.

There might not be a secret exit, she thought then, but there *was* a way out. The front door. Was Valerian still guarding it?

As quietly as possible, she tiptoed toward the lace. The closer she came, the stronger Valerian's masculine scent became, a heady mixture of aroused man and determined warrior. Her skin prickled with delight. She tried to hold her nose, to fight the scent's allure and the weakening effect it had on her.

Once at the doorway, she clasped the material and inched it to the side. All the while, her heart drummed a staccato rhythm. *Da-dum da-dum da-dum.* Would he be there, awake and waiting? Or had he thankfully, blessedly, fallen asleep?

"Good morning, Shaye."

She gasped. Valerian stood just in front of her, arms crossed over his massive chest, legs braced apart. Their gazes linked, clashed. Her treacherous heart lost its rhythm and skipped a beat. He looked as unbelievably mouthwatering as before. Shirtless. His body roped with the tightest abs she'd ever seen. Golden hair tumbled onto his forehead and shoulders.

She licked her lips. "What are you doing here?"

His blue gaze raked over her, peeling away the shells, parting the grass. "Waiting for you, of course."

A shiver tripped along her spine. Oh, his voice. How could she have forgotten that take-no-prisoners voice? Pure temptation. Utter decadence. She mentally reinforced the icy walls around her. *He's a lecherous abductor. Dangerous in every way.*

Yes, she'd wanted to throw herself at him last night. Now, in the light of day, she told herself that had been a moment of impaired judgment. A moment of exhaustion and insanity.

"Did you dream of me?" he asked.

"Yes," she admitted grudgingly. She had. She'd dreamed of his hands caressing her, of his mouth devouring her.

His lush lips inched into a surprised but pleased smile.

"You were naked," she told him.

His grin spread; his eyes gleamed with satisfaction.

"And tied up…"

He arched his eyebrows in smug expectation. "I did not know the idea of bondage would please you."

"Oh, I love the idea of tying you up." She paused dramatically. "Just like in my dream, you'll be secured to an anthill and the little things will eat you alive."

His grin faded completely, but the twinkle in his eyes did not diminish. "Cruel woman." He propped his shoulder on the side wall, a pose of carnal relaxation. *Sink into my arms,* his posture proclaimed. *I'll catch you.* "I dreamed of you, too. Naked."

Suddenly light-headed, she backed up a step.

He showed no mercy, and stepped toward her. "You were splayed for my enjoyment." His eyes were heavy-lidded now, wicked. Intent. "And enjoy you I did. Twice."

She dropped the curtain in place, cutting the sexy man from her view. Breathe, she had to breathe. The oxygen she did manage to draw in burned her throat, singed her lungs. He had only to speak, and his words began to paint a picture in her mind. A terribly beautiful picture.

His rich chuckle floated across the small distance, wrapping her in a decadent shiver. "There are robes in the closet if you wish to change," he said. "The shells look…uncomfortable."

That hadn't been the word he'd wanted to say, she knew. There had been a wicked inflection in his voice, as if he'd meant to say "easily removable" or "exquisite." So, change? Hell, yes. "Will you take me home today?" Her voice trembled.

"You *are* home."

She flipped him off, taking a small amount of satisfaction from the action, even though he couldn't see it.

Then, with nothing else to do, she trudged to the closet. She'd given the gowns inside only a cursory inspection last night. Changing clothes *would* be nice.

Feminine dresses abounded, a sea of colors and silks. They were long and flowing, barely there scarves held together by sheer luck. One in particular drew and held her attention. It was a drapery of ivory, threaded with gold. Both the hem and leg slit were twined with amber leaves and emerald flowers. Jewels sparkled from the deep vee in the bodice.

"Once you have bathed and dressed, Shaye, we will have breakfast."

She snorted. "I'm not bathing until there's a lock on the door."

"A lock would not keep me out if I wanted in."

He was right, she realized with frustration.

"You will feel better after a bath."

"I'll feel better once I'm home," she told him darkly.

"Must I state the obvious?" He sighed. "Again?"

Her teeth ground together, causing her jaw to ache. "What about that warrior? Joachim?"

"We will deal with him when he awakens." The words growled from low in Valerian's chest.

Her fingers tightened over the ivory fabric; it was cool and soft against her fingertips. *Do not think about Joachim. You'll only drive yourself to panic.* The dresses, she'd think about the dresses. Once more, her gaze slid over the one she held. She had never worn anything so feminine. Never *owned* anything so feminine, for that matter. This was something an ancient Greek or Roman queen would have worn. Luscious and exquisite. Not a stitch out of place or a flaw to be seen.

"Whose room is this?" she asked. Valerian had said it was his—hadn't he?—but surely he would not own this many gowns.

"The room is mine," was his answer.

She faced the door. His silhouette paced back and forth, a large slash of black. A phantom. "Do you often wear women's clothing, Valerian?"

"Gods, no!"

She grinned at the affront in his voice. "Then why do you have all these robes?" The answer slammed into her, and she lost her grin. They were for his women. His too-numerous-to-count conquests.

"Shaye," he said warily.

To wear the gowns was to imply *she* was one of his women. "I do not belong to you, and I will not dress as if I do." She turned away from the closet, from the lovely ivory silk she wanted so badly to slip over her head. She'd suffer in her shells and grass skirt, thank you very much, rather than proclaim herself Valerian's lover. Even in so small a way.

Tiny allowances like that one could open the door to other, more severe allowances. Like giving in to his expert touch.

"We could bargain," he cajoled.

What was with the man and his bargaining? "I wear one of the gowns and you'll…what?"

"Kiss you?"

She gulped and had to blank her mind against the passionate images trying to force their way inside. "You really need to work on your bargaining skills. They suck." Had her voice shaken?

"I would like to," he muttered. "Suck you, that is."

Her cheeks fused with heat, and a tremor stole over her. "I don't want your kisses." There. Finally, at long last, she knew she sounded convincing.

"A fake protest, if I've ever heard one."

"Offer something else!" she demanded, before she pounded out of the room and slapped him.

"Such as? And do not mention taking you to the surface, for you know I will not negotiate on that point."

"I don't know why I'm even talking to you." She huffed out a hot breath. "Stubborn, that's what you are."

"Do not change if that is your desire. I am not forcing you, moon. I like seeing your skin. I see it, and I imagine myself licking it."

O-kay. So. She couldn't stay dressed in the shells and grass, after all.

Shivering, with molten lava running through her veins, she gazed around the room. Valerian's room, he'd said. She remembered seeing *male* clothing when she'd searched the place last night. Where…where…the vanity! She grinned as she raced to the thick, intricately carved marble beauty. The drawers slid out easily. Inside the top one lay stack upon stack of shirts. They were huge and would swim on her, but at least they would cover her (apparently lickable) skin.

With a quick glance at the doorway, she tore off the hated shells and tossed them on the floor with relief. She tugged on a shirt, and the black, buttery-soft material made her sigh in delight. The second drawer held pants, all leather, all black. The fact that they were folded so neatly struck her as…odd. Domestic.

These nymphs were anything but domesticated.

She wouldn't have doubted if the women she'd seen

leaving the room last night were responsible. Caring for all of Valerian's needs, even his laundry.

A spark of jealousy burned inside of her. "No, that's not true. I am not jealous," she muttered in a futile attempt to convince herself. Motions clipped, she unwound the grass from her waist, letting it pool on the ground, then tugged on the pants. She had long legs, but even so the panels of material dwarfed her. She had to roll the hem numerous times and belt the waist with a scarf from one of the gowns in the closet. She slipped on her sandals.

There were no mirrors (unless she counted the ones above the bed), so she had to guess how she looked. Ridiculous, she was sure. Sloppy. And that, to her way of thinking, was perfect. She wanted that too-intense Joachim guy to find her completely unattractive.

Valerian, too, she reminded herself.

As she stood there, deciding what to do next, Valerian's masculine scent wafted to her, filling her nostrils. Strong, spicy. So arousing her nipples hardened, abrading the shirt she now wore. Why was she smelling him? She wasn't by the door, wasn't even close.

She twisted and turned, only then realizing the heady fragrance curled from the clothes. Her eyes widened. Wretched clothes! Wonderful clothes. Had he worn them? Had they touched his body? An ache throbbed between her legs.

She'd never been a sexual creature, and these new, continued sensations rocked her. How long could she deny them? How long could she resist? She'd wondered before, but the answer suddenly seemed imminent. She almost ripped the shirt and pants off. She did moan, the sound raw and needy.

"What are you doing in there?" Valerian asked, his voice tight, drawn.

Did he know she was aroused? He couldn't know. *Please, don't let him know.* "I was—I'm just hungry."

For several seconds he didn't speak. She used the time to calm herself down, to recite math equations in her mind. If he knew just how vulnerable she was to him, he'd pounce without mercy.

"Come, moon," he said evenly. "I will feed you."

She swallowed past the sudden lump in her throat. She'd eat breakfast with him because she needed out of this room and needed to keep up her strength. Then she could escape him and search the palace for a way out. A way home. She couldn't stay here. Couldn't stay with this potent man a moment longer than necessary.

"Let's get this over with," she muttered.

CHAPTER TEN

JOACHIM LAY IN HIS BED, his arms propped under his head. Scowling, he stared up at the glistening crystal, wishing he could take comfort in the plethora of colors shooting from the jagged shards. Pink, like a woman's nipples. White, like a woman's skin. Russet, like a woman's soulful eyes.

Alas, he took no comfort.

Night had long passed, and morning was here. Through it all, his thoughts remained black and refused to settle. He shifted and eyed the wall of weapons he'd acquired over the years. A weapon for every man he'd slain. Their numbers were so vast, he'd long ago lost count. He was not ashamed of that. No, he reveled in his victories.

That was why his behavior last night cut his pride so deeply.

After leaving Valerian and Shaye, he had brought the two females to his room. He'd been about to enter one; he'd held his cock in his hand, poised, ready. She'd been willing, so willing, writhing in passion, opening herself wider. And he'd stopped. Stopped!

As he had stared down at her, the sense of all-consuming need had abandoned him. There one moment, gone the next. An image of the dark-headed witch he'd wanted so badly at the selection ceremony, the one with the curly hair and ripe little body, had flashed through his mind. Suddenly he'd wanted her. Only her. He'd pictured her in Shivawn's arms, moaning, mindless with pleasure, and a terrible rage had overcome him.

Joachim's two bed partners had tried their hardest to excite him after that, but they'd failed. He should have taken them anyway. He needed to sate himself and regain his strength. Yet…he'd sent them away to find another lover and pleasured himself instead.

Still. He was as weak as before. But at least Valerian, too, would be weakened this day, having gone without a woman's touch. His mate's touch, if he were to be believed. Mate. How Joachim wanted to find his, that one woman who would love him above all others.

He sighed. He didn't want to take the pale woman from Valerian. She did not excite him. Not really. Not like the dark-headed one with her sensual, lush curves, her innocent and wild contradictions. What was her name? She hadn't said. Hadn't spoken at all. He wondered what her voice would be like. Low and husky? Sweet and soft? If he'd had the opportunity to choose her, the night would have ended differently. Damn Shivawn for taking her and forcing him to change his plan.

As his friend had led the lovely witch from the room, Joachim had decided to console himself by taking Valerian's crown.

He liked and admired his cousin, but he liked and admired power more.

Joachim did not enjoy being told what to do. He never had. *He* preferred to give the orders, to have others do *his* bidding. Even his women. He was master. He was commander.

His cousin ruled with an iron fist, expecting total and complete obedience. It was time to change that. It was time for Joachim to rule.

Valerian had offered to fight him, true, but Joachim could not become king that way. No, Valerian had to willingly *agree* to surrender his throne. Would he? Valerian had had a night to consider his options, to realize there was only one thing to be done to keep the pale woman.

"The crown will be mine," Joachim snarled.

Some men were meant for greatness. Some were…not. And Valerian had made many foolish mistakes lately. The first and most important was leaving the nymph females behind to take this palace. The women were now lost, no trace of them to be found in either the Inner or Outer City. Yes, Valerian had a contingent of men searching for them even now. But that wasn't enough. They would not need finding if the king had brought them along in the first place.

The second and most unforgivable mistake Valerian had made was not letting the men travel to the surface until yesterday, when their strength was nearly drained. The palace needed guarding, true, but the men could not guard if they were weak.

I would not have allowed such things to happen. His eyes narrowed. The pale woman was simply a means to an end. He'd seen the way Valerian hovered over her, protecting her, silently willing the warriors away from her. So Joachim had chosen her, hoping his cousin would do *anything* to keep her.

His hope had paid off.

And perhaps, when he became sovereign, he would simply take the dark-haired witch from Shivawn. He grinned at the thought.

Oh, he was going to like being king.

When Shaye brushed aside the door cloth and stepped toward him, Valerian's breath caught in his throat, burning like the hottest fire.

Would she always affect him this way?

She wore *his* shirt, *his* pants, and even though they bagged on her slight frame, she was the most beautiful sight he'd ever beheld. The dome's rainbow flecks glistened over her cheeks. Like a siren she was, luring him, tempting him. He would willingly go to his death for her.

"If you're going to tell me to change," she said, challenge in her voice, "save your breath."

Tell her to change? Never. "I like you just as you are."

Surprise darkened her eyes, making the brown velvet swirl with black.

He held out his hand, not touching her, but needing to. So badly he wanted her to accept him. He wanted her willing. Wanted her to find joy in each and every moment of contact they shared, as he did.

That glorious gaze of hers flicked to his palm. Slowly the color abandoned her cheeks. So pale now, he thought. She could have been a dream, a ghost. A phantom come to torment him.

A flicker of something blanketed her expression.

Pain? Panic? "No. No touching." She shook her head, punctuating the words. She even whipped her hands behind her back, as if to remove temptation.

Hearing her rejection, he decided to push her—to see how far she would *allow* him to push her, really. He wanted her touch too much to admit defeat so early in the game. "Sweet moonbeam, why won't you acquiesce over something so small? I am not asking for more than a touch." Yet.

"Please. I'm not stupid. One touch will lead to one kiss. One kiss will lead—" She flushed, returning that heavenly, rosy glow to her skin. She cleared her throat. "You get the picture." Chin high, she sailed past him. But she stopped abruptly at the fork of doorways. She didn't turn to face him. "Which way is breakfast?"

"What if I told you *I* was the main course?" He watched her back stiffen, watched her hands clench at her sides. However long it took, he'd chip at her resistance until she caved. *I'll have you begging for me, love.* "Would you be so eager to leave then?"

Waves of anger and frustration radiated from her. "Which way?" she ground out.

He paused a moment before responding, drinking in the vision of her pale hair tumbling down her back. Some of the ends curled, some of them fell straight. What he would have given to sift his fingers through the thick mass. His home? His life?

His soul?

Yes, all of those things. The need was sharp inside him, yet so unattainable at the moment. "I will show you the way," he said, his voice deep, nearly a croak.

He closed the distance between them, his long legs quickly eating up the short space, and brushed past her, purposefully caressing his arm against hers.

Gasping, she jumped away from him as if he'd shoved her. She even glared at him with suspicion. His lips twitched in amusement and victory. *Oh, yes. She will be mine.* Her awareness of him—for that's what this reaction was, whether she denied it or not—would ultimately be her downfall.

She might not have accepted him as her mate, but her body recognized him. Desired him. And when the physical body desired something, or someone, it did whatever was necessary to convince the mind to seize it. People could not help themselves. They wanted what they wanted, bad for them or not.

Shaye would be no different.

Soon, he thought. *Soon.*

"Don't you ever wear a shirt?" she grumbled, turning away her gaze.

"I saw how you looked at my chest and decided it was in my best interest to never wear a shirt again."

Her lips compressed into a thin line. "I was staring in horror."

"Who are you trying to convince? Me? Or yourself?"

She bared her teeth in a scowl.

He had made his point, so he let the subject drop. For now. "Breakfast is this way." He clasped her hand (without permission) and led her out of his quarters, down the winding hallway of his army's barracks. Several couples had decided to camp there, even when the loving was done. They lay naked and intertwined in the open. Unlike the chaotic moans of last night, all was now silent. Most likely everyone was exhausted from their long night of sexual gratification and debauchery.

How he would have liked to be in their numbers, to have experienced that same satisfaction.

Perhaps tonight…

"So, what are we going to do about Joachim?" Shaye asked. "I'm not going to be his slave. No matter what. And don't tell me we'll deal with him when he wakes up. Give me an answer this time. I hate not knowing."

We, she'd said. Not I. Not you. *We.* He liked the sound of that, liked that she did not reject the thought of his aid. Liked that she saw them as partners in this. "Worry not. I will do whatever is necessary to keep you with me."

"Would you—" she gulped "—kill him?"

"If necessary." He answered without hesitation.

She uttered a frustrated groan. "If you would just take me to the beach, he couldn't have me and you wouldn't have to commit murder."

"If I took you back, I couldn't have you, either."

"Exactly."

"Your plan—what is it you told me about my bargaining skills?—sucks. Yes, your plan sucks."

He kicked a pile of clothing out of their way and turned a corner. Finally the dining hall came into view. A fresh, warm scent wafted to him. The male centaurs and minotaurs he'd acquired from the city had prepared the usual breakfast of fish, fruits and nuts.

Beside him Shaye purred, "Mmm." Her stomach growled.

Usually at this time of the morning warriors surrounded the table, devouring every morsel of food. Now he and Shaye were alone, the servants having already retreated to the kitchen for their own meal, his men still sleeping and recovering from the night's pleasures.

Without a word, Shaye commandeered the chair at the head of the table. As she did so, she eyed him, expecting him to balk, he was sure. When he didn't, she shrugged and piled a plate high with food.

She swallowed a bite of coconut cream, and her eyes closed in sweet surrender. "Who prepared this? Surely not your army. They may look life beefcake, but I doubt they know how to cook it."

"As if I would allow my men to cook," he said, filling his plate.

"Hey, there's nothing wrong with a man knowing how to prepare a meal." She popped a grape into her mouth.

He eased onto the bench beside her. "Warriors battle. Warriors kill. Warriors seduce. They do not cook. That is a servant's job."

"What if all your servants get sick and can't work? What if all your servants are stolen? What will all your big, strong warriors do then, huh?"

He blinked, the idea never having occurred to him. Who would be foolish enough to steal from a nymph? "We would acquire new servants."

"Typical," she said dryly. Her gaze traveled the room.

Looking for a way out? he wondered. He wouldn't doubt if she'd engaged him in this conversation about servants just to distract him. He let her do it, though. Talking with her excited him. "How is such a thing typical?" He leaned back and bit into a strawberry. How he would have loved to trace the berry over her lips and lick the juice away.

"In my experience, men such as yourself are—"

"Men such as myself?" he interjected.

"Yes."

"What kind of man is that?"

Her gaze returned to him, and she seemed to forget her search. "Arrogant. Bossy. Chauvinistic. Pigheaded. Stubborn. Half-witted. Spoiled. Demanding. Self-absorbed. Morally corrupt."

When she paused for breath, he grumbled, "Is that all?"

"No. Horny. Overbearing. Mean." She paused, tapped a finger against her lips, then nodded. "That's all. Anyway, as I was saying. Men are—"

"'Mean'?" He frowned. "I have been the epitome of *nice* to you, catering to your every need. Have I not clothed you? Fed you? Kept you safe and warm? Refrained from making love to you?"

She pursed her lips. "Did you not steal me from everything I hold dear? Have you not refused over and over again to let me go?"

Unconcerned, he waved a hand through the air. "One day you will thank me for my refusal. Now, please continue with your explanation of my 'typical' male behavior."

"Fine." She raised her chin, looking down at him. "But you won't like it."

"Nevertheless. I will listen. Because I am *nice*."

"Nice? Really? To save your male pride from doing something you consider beneath you, you would rather steal someone from their home and their family so they can do it for you." She bit into a strawberry of her own, white teeth sinking into the fruit. Droplets of juice trickled down her chin. "I'm living proof."

His body tensed. Once again he was overcome with the desire to lick juice off of her lips and chin, perhaps cover the rest of her with strawberry juice, as well, and lick that, too. Several sweetly tart droplets would pool in her navel, of course, before dripping to the pale, silvery hair between her legs. She would writhe when his tongue followed the liquid. She would tunnel her hands in his hair. Her knees would squeeze his temples.

The fantasy came to a halt when she wiped the naughty juice away and scowled over at him. "You're staring at me, and I don't like it. Stop."

Her voice held a strangled edge, as if she fought a wave of anger—or desire.

"Yes, I'm staring," he said. "You are a beautiful woman." He popped another grape into his mouth and relished her dismayed shock. Normally he ate his share of fish, as well as the fruit, but right now he hungered only for Shaye. His woman. His mate.

"Do you have no reaction to my words, then?" She shifted uncomfortably in her seat. "I all but called you dishonorable."

"Why should I react to your words? They are true. I *would* rather steal someone from their home than cook for myself."

Her mouth fell open, forming a delightful *O*.

He arched a brow. "My easy admission surprises you, I see."

"Well, yeah." She regarded him warily.

"I have only ever taken those in need of a better life, Shaye, or those I thought I could give an easier life, whether they thought they needed it or not. The men who prepared this meal were slaves to the demons before I stole them. They were forced to steal, kill and destroy, and would have one day become the main course of a demon meal. Believe me, they are grateful that I took them." He leaned back on the bench, stretching out the long length of his legs, watching her, gauging. "Perhaps, though, you will help me see the error of my ways. I am more than willing to let you try to convince me of my terrible deeds—over and over again. I listen best when the speaker is naked."

As he watched her, a flush of pink suffused her cheeks. Another blush. The hedonistic women of his acquaintance were as comfortable with sex and erotic banter as he was. That Shaye found the topic risqué enough to blush excited him. Mesmerized him.

He had to touch her.

He was just leaning toward her, outstretching his hand to see if that blush of hers gave off any heat and perhaps spread to her breasts, when two of his warriors strode into the room. Disappointed, he fell back into his chair.

Both men wore wide, toothy smiles of sheer bliss. Their faces were completely relaxed, utterly radiant. Power emanated from them. Each wore gilded breastplates, black pants and jewel-studded armbands. After their night of loving, they were ready to train.

"Good morning, great king," Broderick said. His voice had never sounded so joyful.

"This is the best of days, is it not?" Dorian sighed happily.

They whistled as they circled the table and heaped their plates with food. They must have worked up hearty appetites during the long hours of the night. Valerian glared at them. He had yet to sample Shaye's sweetness—yes, he knew she would taste sweet—so no, this was not the best of days.

A few seconds later, Shivawn entered. He wasn't smiling, wasn't relaxed. No, he was stiff and glowered at everyone. He slammed himself onto the bench beside Valerian, hair beads rattling, and silently filled his plate with the food in front of him. He didn't bother to reach for anything more.

Had his woman denied him? Valerian wondered. He and Shivawn probably wore the same expression. "Where is your chosen?"

"Sleeping," Broderick and Dorian replied in unison, as if he'd asked the question of them. Their grins grew wider, and they slapped each other on the backs.

"Flying through the gates of Olympus," Dorian added.

"Did you stop and make sure the women were willing before you bedded them?" Shaye asked, her tone dripping with loathing.

Dorian blinked at her, the question foreign to him.

Broderick chuckled. "Your woman is amusing," he said to Valerian.

"Amusing?" She popped to her feet with an angry growl. "I am not amusing when discussing rape."

At least she hadn't denied the fact that she belonged to him, Valerian thought, pleased.

"As if a woman would turn me down," Broderick said.

"Believe me, it happens," Shivawn muttered. He swiped up his plate and stalked from the room without another word.

Everyone watched him leave, each with a different

reaction. Broderick—laughter. Dorian—intensified confusion. Shaye—satisfaction.

"FYI, gentlemen," she said, drawing attention back to herself. "Just because your mojo entrances a woman doesn't mean she truly, deep in her soul, wants you."

"Mojo?" Having no more room on his plate, Dorian eased into the empty seat beside Valerian. "What is that?"

"Doesn't matter." Shaye crossed her arms over her chest, causing the neckline of her shirt to gape and reveal soft hints of her breasts. "What matters is this— if the women knew you, your personality, your likes, your dislikes, your past, your plans for the future, would they want you still?"

If a woman knew you echoed through Valerian's mind. Not an altogether welcome thought, either. He'd never taken the time to discuss his life—past, present or future—with any of his bedmates. He hadn't cared to discuss it, and they hadn't cared to ask. Still, the question intrigued him.

He wanted that with Shaye, he realized. He wanted to tell her about himself and watch her reaction, hear her thoughts. He wanted to listen to her tell him about her own life. Wanted to know what gave her joy. What she secretly desired with every ounce of her being.

Too, he found himself wondering what type of man she had favored in the past. Scholar? Warrior? How had these men treated her?

Had she loved them?

His hands clenched at his sides, one nearly snapping the bench arm in half. A need to maim, destroy, kill any man who'd once held this woman's affections consumed him. Searing. White-hot. Hotter than even a dragon's fire.

Perhaps it was hypocritical of him—all right, it *was* hypocritical, considering his own debauched past—but he didn't like the image of his woman splayed and open for anyone save himself. Her passion—his. Her heart—his. He didn't want her deepest desires awakened by anyone but him. Couldn't tolerate the thought.

He yearned to brand his very essence into her every cell. She'd know no scent but his own. Feel no touch but his own. Crave only him, as he craved only her.

"Well, I see my chosen has quenched one hunger," a male voice suddenly said from the doorway.

Valerian stiffened as his eyes narrowed on his cousin. Joachim, who obviously still thought to claim Shaye, stood poised, ready. He wasn't dressed for training, but for war. Silver armor etched with battle scenes covered him from head to toe.

Valerian didn't stand. If he did, he would have leapt over the table and attacked. Joachim wanted to war, so they would war. It was past time he showed his power-hungry cousin the error of his ways. Beginning now.

CHAPTER ELEVEN

TENSION AND TESTOSTERONE sparked around the room, hot enough that Shaye felt burned. Fury sizzled and snapped; a raging inferno, barely banked, burned in Valerian's turquoise eyes.

Shaye was used to being around emotional people. How many tirades, fits of jealous rage, had her mother thrown over the years? Countless. If a husband came home late, crystal china was thrown at his head—right along with accusations of infidelity. If a birthday was forgotten, tires were slashed.

Yet Shaye didn't know how to react to such potent fury from Valerian. Someone who, until this point, had shown only desire, amusement and patience. Well, he'd given glimpses of anger, but nothing like this.

The need to kill was there in his expression. His lips were thinned, his teeth bared like an animal's. He was cold, capable of any evil deed.

"I have a bargain for you, Joachim." Never had his voice sounded more brusque.

Joachim gave no outward reaction, though his eyes did bear traces of the same dissatisfied tension Valerian and Shivawn possessed. Seemingly unconcerned, he leaned against the towering door frame, a column of twisted gold filigree. "I am listening."

"I will give you my sword," Valerian said. "You may have it with my blessing, but you must renounce all claim to the girl."

"Unacceptable." Joachim removed his helmet and anchored it at his side. His black brows were winged arrogantly. "Make me king, and you can have her. She will be yours to do with what you will."

Shaye laid her palms on the table, looking back and forth between the men. She didn't know what to do, what to say. She felt as helpless now as she'd felt watching her parents fight as a child.

Tense, Valerian shook his head. "I cannot simply make you king. You know that. My men would never follow a man who had not proven himself worthy."

"True," Joachim allowed. "That is why I'm willing to prove myself worthy."

"And just how do you plan to do that?"

"Yesterday you were willing to fight me. Are you still?"

Valerian's hands clenched and unclenched. "Yes."

"But are you willing to give up your reign of leadership if I best you, thereby proving myself worthy?"

A predatory stillness came over Valerian. For a long while he didn't speak. Considering his options? Shaye wondered. Finally he said, "Such a thing has never been done," his tone careful, guarded.

Joachim's hand tightened over his sword hilt. "Yet such a thing has often *needed* to be done."

Shaye had thought tensions already high. With Joachim's last words, the room began to pulse with danger. More than ever, she didn't want these larger-than-life men fighting over her. With swords, for God's sake. She didn't want Valerian fighting, period. Strangely, the thought of him getting hurt unsettled her.

Only because you don't want to be stuck with someone else, someone less tolerant, she assured herself.

She eyed his opponent. Joachim appeared confident in his ability to win. He radiated the same arrogance as Valerian, yet at the same time he glowed with a blood-thirstiness that did not encompass the king.

"Why don't you fight me instead?" she found herself asking Joachim. The words slipped from her unbidden. "It would be my greatest pleasure to cut off your balls and feed them to you."

A muscle ticked in Joachim's jaw. Valerian's lips twitched as he fought back a…grin? A scowl? The two men at the table chuckled, thankfully relaxing.

"That I would like to see," the too-handsome-to-be-real one said. Black hair, violet eyes. If she remembered correctly, his name was Dorian.

"Shaye will not be fighting," Valerian said.

"As if a woman could best me," Joachim snorted. "Well, Valerian." He straightened, his armor clinking ominously. "What say you? Shall we fight, the winner made king with all rights to the woman?"

Slowly Valerian eased to his feet. "I accept. However, winner will *remain* king and *keep* the woman."

"Only time will tell," was Joachim's satisfied reply.

"Now wait just a minute." Shaye slapped the table, frustrated when the bowls failed to shake and the food and drink failed to spill. "You're acting like children. There's no reason to fight."

Valerian leveled her with a fierce gaze. At least she'd

gotten his attention. "In this, moon, you will not have your way. My cousin is in dire need of a lesson."

"He's your cousin?" She scrubbed a hand over her face. This was worse than she'd thought. "There were times I wanted to kill my family, Valerian, but you have to resist the temptation."

"You will not change your mind?" Joachim asked him, ignoring Shaye as if she were not even in the room. "When you lose?"

Dorian and Broderick snarled like animals at the insult to their king, then there was only silence. Wave after terrible wave of Valerian's fury wrapped around Shaye, and she was immensely grateful it was not directed at her.

"Are you. Calling me. A liar?" Each syllable seemed to be ripped from him.

Joachim's cheeks colored bright, vivid red. "My apologies. That was not my intent."

Only slightly mollified, Valerian splayed his arms, encompassing the room and everyone inside. "We have witnesses. Dorian and Broderick will hereby attest to my consent to this battle—and the outcome."

Panic unfurled sharp fists inside of Shaye, beating painfully. They were going to do it; they were going to fight. The knowledge was there, churning in their eyes.

"What is your weapon of choice?" Valerian asked his cousin, crossing his arms over his chest.

"Swords, of course," was the reply. "The weapon of a true warrior."

"To the death?"

Joachim considered the idea and frowned. "I do not want to kill you, Valerian. I do not hate you. We were friends once, as children, but I was born to rule. Commands should be mine to give, not receive."

For a long while the two men simply stared at each other. Finally Valerian nodded. "Go to the arena, Joachim. I will be there shortly."

"Another command." Joachim looked as if he meant to protest but ultimately nodded. He turned on his heel and strode away. Shaye was not given time to argue.

"Dorian," Valerian said, "gather the rest of the men. I want them to watch what happens to those who think to usurp my rule. Broderick, go and prepare my gear."

Chairs skidded backward. Footsteps pounded.

I can't believe this is happening, Shaye thought.

She'd been kidnapped from her mother's wedding— shrug. She'd been dragged underwater and into a lost city—yawn. She'd been chosen to be the king's mistress—could someone pass a nail file? All of that suddenly seemed paltry, dreamlike.

This battle, though…it was pure nightmare.

"I'm asking you not to do this," she said to Valerian. They were alone now, no one else in sight. "He obviously doesn't want me. He just wants to hurt you and take your crown."

Valerian sat down, leaned back in the bench and regarded her intently. "Do you fear for me, moon?"

She snorted. Inside, though, she trembled with fear. "I could care less about you, actually." Lie. Stupid of her, yes, but a lie all the same. His safety did matter to her, she admitted silently. He'd said all those nice things to her. His touch electrified her. And he was…sweet, damn it. "I just don't want to be pawned off on that Joachim jerk." Truth.

Casually, he popped a grape into his mouth. "I told

you I would do whatever was necessary to keep you and I meant it. Now I am not going to take offense at your lack of confidence in my skills as a warrior because you have yet to watch me fight. You do not truly know me."

"And I might not have a chance to know you. Not that I want to," she added quickly. "But still."

"I will, however," he continued as if she hadn't spoken, "take great offense if this lack of faith ever occurs again."

Her eyes focused on him with forced unconcern. "I'm shaking. Really."

His eyes rounded with incredulity, and he shook his head. "Have you no sense, woman? I've just warned you of my wrath and you mock me?"

"Two words—hell, yes."

Far from angering him, though, her words seemed to amuse him. "I like your wit, Shaye. I also like your courage. You please me, for you are a worthy mate. A worthy queen to my warriors."

Queen? Hardly. Look at the mess that her own life had become. Like she really needed to be in charge of other people. And as for the other, well, she didn't want Valerian to like her. Okay, she did. She just didn't *want* to want him to like her. The more he liked her, the more determined he'd be to keep her, the harder he'd pursue her and the tougher it would be to resist him, to remember who and what he was—and the less she would want to escape.

"Come. I have tarried enough, yet I was unable to resist stealing a moment alone with you." He pushed to his feet and held out his hand, palm up, a silent command for her to take it. "They are awaiting us in the arena."

She studied his palm, powerless to turn away. She

knew that if she intertwined her fingers with his, warmth would tingle up her arm. Such drugging warmth. Unwanted warmth. Dangerous warmth.

Her throat constricted. She stood, keeping her hands at her sides. "Lead the way."

He remained where he was, beckoning with a single wave of his fingers.

She crossed her arms over her chest.

His lips dipped into a disbelieving frown as he realized she was refusing him yet again. "I allowed you to refuse once. I will not allow you to do so now. I need your touch, Shaye. I need your strength. My victory depends upon it."

Ah, hell. Way to stick a knife in her. Their gazes locked in challenge. The lush length of his black lashes cast decadent shadows over his cheeks. How did a man with blond hair have such dark eyelashes? They should have been pale, like hers. "Sorry," she said. And she was.

"You are stubborn," he said. "And you want to be cold."

She raised her chin. "I assure you, I *am* cold. I'm a bitch."

"Given time," he added smoothly, "I will heat you. I will make you burn."

The words were laced with promise, dripping with determination, and drifting beneath them was a challenge: *every resistance will be met and conquered until you've soared over the sweet edge of surrender.*

She gulped, but still didn't allow herself to reach for him.

A muscle ticked in his jaw. "You have a choice. Take my hand or be carried in my arms."

"You didn't mention my third choice. Leaving."

She skidded around the chair and backed away, a single step.

"You? Leave?" He shook his head. "No, you are too brave. I will give you till the count of three to decide, then I will make the decision for you. One."

Another step backward.

"Two."

Yet another.

"Thr—"

She rushed forward and clamped onto his hand. At first contact, the warmth she'd feared speared her, spreading up, spreading out, overtaking her entire body. But if he had chased her and thrown her over his shoulder—and he would have—the sensations would have been so much worse. More potent.

She scowled up at him. Light banked his features, giving him a breathtaking radiance no one person should possess.

He grinned. "That was not so hard, was it?"

"Shut up. Just shut up."

He chuckled, but his laughter didn't last long. His expression grew serious. "I have your scent in my nostrils, moon, and can find you wherever you are. Wherever you go. Do not think to try and escape from me during the battle." With that, he turned on his heel and stalked out of the dining hall, dragging her with him.

Hissing a breath between her teeth, she fought to keep up with him, flying forward at neck-breaking speed. "Slow down. And what do you mean, you've got my smell in your nose?" She recalled yesterday, how obsessed he'd been with making her smell him.

"Just that your essence is branded into my every cell," he said, not bothering to face her. "As mine will soon be in yours."

"There will be no branding!"

"Actually, there will be no stopping the branding." Utter confidence cascaded from his voice.

Another promise.

Don't engage him. Don't encourage him. Her gaze snagged on the wall. White marble inlaid with silver stone, crumbled in bits and pieces. Scratch marks, as if someone had taken a tool to every inch. Changing the subject she said, "What happened here?"

"Humans invaded, is my understanding."

Her gaze whipped to his back. Hard muscle and sinew strained under bronzed velvet. "Humans know about Atlantis?"

"Some do."

Wow. People actually knew about this place, yet they'd managed to keep it a secret. "Have you always lived in this castle?"

"No. My army claimed the palace only a short time ago."

Claimed. Aka "stole," she was sure. "Who did it belong to before you?"

"The dragons."

She skidded to a stop, forcing him to stop, as well, or drag her prone body. "Dragons? Did you say dragons used to own this property? And you stole it from them?" That explained the dragon murals, the dragon etchings, the dragon medallion he'd told her about.

Slowly he faced her, his expression confused. "This upsets you. Why?"

"Dragons spew fire and eat humans as tasty snacks. They'll want their palace back."

"Yes."

Her eyes widened at his nonchalance. "And that doesn't bother you? The thought of battling such fierce creatures?"

"No. Why should it?" His chest seemed to expand before her eyes. "I am fiercer. I am stronger."

God save her from male arrogance. "Sorry I don't share your confidence," she said dryly.

He frowned. "If the thought of dragons scares you—"

"Terrifies me," she interjected.

"How will you react when I introduce you to the vampires?"

A strangled gasp wheezed from her throat, and she covered her mouth with a shaky hand. "I'm not meeting vampires."

"They are our friends."

He'd said *our*. He hadn't said *my*. But *our*, as if they were already a couple. "You told me those creatures were in Atlantis, but I never thought you'd make me interact with them! Vampires drink blood, Valerian."

"They will not drink yours."

Grrr. There was no arguing with him. He had a response for everything. "That's right, they won't. I'm not meeting them, and I'm not staying here."

"Vampires are our allies. You have nothing to fear from them. You have nothing to fear from anyone in this land. I will always protect you. With my own body, if necessary." His voice dipped with sexy, husky promise, once again flashing images of naked bodies, sweat-soaked skin and quivering pleasure through her mind. Grrr!

"You know, if you had any chance of convincing me to stay here—which you didn't—you blew it with talk of dragons and vampires."

He shook his head, his brow furrowed. "How you distract me, woman. Why are we discussing this now? I have a battle to win. A woman to claim," he said as he tugged her back into motion.

Crap. The battle. In the distance she could make out the sound of swords clanging together. Grunts. Male laughter. Excitement.

"I'm going to say this one more time. I don't want you to fight."

He lost his air of affection. He stopped, turned and took a menacing step toward her. Close enough that she felt the heat of his skin, the heady scent of it. Saw the flecks of blue and green in his eyes, brighter than the most precious jewels. He became utterly wrapped in malevolence.

"I warned you what would happen if you voiced such doubt in my ability again. I am powerful, a force to be feared, and I will have your faith."

If he expected her to apologize or back away, he did not get his wish. She stepped toward him, destroying even more of the open space between them. Where she attained such bravado, she didn't know. She only knew she could not let him in that ring. "And I told you I didn't give a shit about your warning."

Sconces blazed from the walls, their glow flickering over the contours of his face. Shadows and light fought for dominance, playing over his cheeks. He suddenly appeared even more harsh than he had a moment ago.

Tendrils of desire, the same consuming desire she'd

encountered when she'd first watched him stride from the ocean, glittered inside her.

"You will," he said, right before he tangled his fingers in her hair and jerked her to him. Instantly his lips slammed into hers with such force she gasped.

He used her open mouth to his advantage. His hot tongue pushed inside, past her teeth, past any thought of resistance. His big body engulfed her, set her on fire with ethereal flames. Flames that spread with dizzying speed. Wondrous speed. In mere seconds she went from cool, uncaring, untouchable Shaye to wild, aching, never-stop-touching Shaye. A woman who existed only for pleasure. For sex and debauchery. For *this* man.

He consumed her. Dark need consumed her. And she discovered that she liked being consumed.

His tongue worked hers with expert precision, causing her nerve endings to leap to blissful life. Her nipples hardened, her thighs ached, her stomach quivered. His taste was pure sexual heat, exotic, addictive. She shouldn't want to, knew she should pull away, but she found herself winding her arms around his neck and accepting him fully, demanding more.

A feral growl of satisfaction escaped him, raw, as if he couldn't hold it back.

"Do you want me?" he whispered fiercely.

As always the sound of his wine-rich voice excited her. More so than ever before. He'd been made for her, only her, his every action, every breath, existing simply to please her. The thought was intoxicating. Like the man himself. Heady and sultry and drugging.

"Do you want me?" he asked again.

"No," she forced out, then contradicted herself by

licking the seam of his lips. Who was this wanton woman she'd become?

Valerian's woman drifted across her mind.

His callused hands slid from her neck over each vertebra of her spine and settled softly on the curve of her hips. His fingers gradually scrunched up the hem of her shirt.

"*I* want *you*," he said fiercely. Warm breath fanned her cheek.

There was a reason she should push him away. Yes, there was definitely a reason. A reason she should...drag his mouth back to hers. Taste him again. Feel the strength of his chest straining against her, feel the barely leashed power humming through his blood. Her nipples beaded tighter and hurt, actually hurt, for contact.

He released her shirt and reached under it, his fingers tickling her skin. She gasped in wonder.

"Your nipples ache for me, I know it." His hot gaze lingered on the area in question, making them pearl all the more.

"No, they don't," she denied.

"It would be my pleasure to prove it to you. I could stand you in front of a mirror, slowly remove your top, baring your flesh inch by precious inch. I could cup your breasts in my hands, framing your nipples as they cry for me."

She should have been used to it, expected it even, but the picture he described tunneled into her mind. Valerian behind her, his arms reaching around her, kneading her breasts. One of his phantom hands began a slow, languid glide down her stomach, stopping at the pale curls between her legs.

"I hate that idea," she lied breathlessly. "Hate it." She brought her hands to his chest, her palms over *his* nipples. They were hard little points her tongue yearned to lick. To suck. As her fingertip curled in the steel loop anchored there, she wanted to lick and suck that, too.

He groaned. "I like the way you hate."

Oh, she did, too. Their breaths mingled together. Their gazes locked, a sultry clash of turquoise against brown, passion against passion.

"Hate me some more," he breathed.

She didn't think to resist. She rose on her tiptoes—her body seemed to have a mind of its own—placing her lips just in front of his. His hands tightened on her waist, the grip needy, hard, commanding. Not allowing escape. He urged the lower half of her closer to him, so close, until she nestled against the long, hard length of his erection.

A hot, raspy gasp shuddered from her. Spears of pleasure arced through her, spawning other bursts of sensation. Needed sensation. Welcome sensation.

"I want to hate you, too," he told her in that same soft tone. "I want to hate you hard and fast, the first time. Slow and tender, the second."

"My king," someone called.

Shaye heard the voice distantly and despised the interruption. *More kisses.* She wanted more kisses.

As if Valerian didn't notice the voice—or simply didn't care—his gaze slid to her mouth. Wicked intent gleamed in his eyes. So much desire blazed from him, she had trouble catching her breath. He was a man ready to give her as many kisses as she desired.

"My king," the voice said again, this time projecting equal measures of reverence, impatience and eagerness.

Valerian's fingers clenched at her waist. "I don't want to stop hating you," he said softly, a growl.

Saying "You must" almost killed her.

"Must hate you?"

"Must stop."

He ran his tongue over his teeth. His nostrils flared, as if her taste lingered there. "For now," he allowed.

"Forever." *What are you, stupid?* She gulped. She'd never been kissed with such passion. Such fervor. As if the man doing the kissing savored her. Would be destroyed without her. And she wanted like hell to experience that urgency again.

Dangerous, her mind whispered.

But totally worth it, her body responded.

"Don't ever hate me again," she forced out. She tugged from his embrace, turned away, suddenly cold and empty. Hollow, as she'd been through her entire childhood.

He gripped her shoulders and spun her around. His eyes were compressed to tiny slits, his thick lashes nearly intertwining top with bottom. "My greatest pleasure will be—what is it your people say?—making you eat your words."

"Valerian," another man called. Joachim, this time. She recognized the deep baritone. Impatient now. Valerian didn't face him. "The woman is not yours to kiss."

Shaye drew her arms over her middle, tamping down a tremor of dread. She glanced over her shoulder, only to see that the dark-haired man resembled an angel of death. Great. A sign?

"Yet," Valerian said, the single word more lethal than a sword. His eyes never left her face. "Yet."

CHAPTER TWELVE

AFTER ONE FINAL LOOK at Shaye, Valerian whipped around, facing his cousin and shoving the moonbeam behind him, his body acting as a shield. How dare his first kiss with Shaye, his mate, his one and only, be interrupted. And by *this* man! Fury seethed and bubbled through his blood, a rushing river of molten lava.

"May I recommend the two of you sit down and discuss your problems before you resort to bloodshed?" Shaye suggested primly. She tried to sidestep him. When that didn't work, she peeked around his shoulder.

"No." Joachim. Smug expectation colored his face. The man truly thought to win and become king.

"No," Valerian replied, even knowing Shaye didn't want him to fight. While he did not want to deny her anything, fight he would. Even though he was at a disadvantage. While Joachim had spent the night gaining strength thanks to his sexual conquests, Valerian had…not. He had not even self-pleasured.

Without looking behind him, Valerian reached back, palm extended, for Shaye to place her hand in his. She'd refused twice before and coercion had been necessary. He expected her to refuse once again. But he had to try, had to touch her once more before entering the arena.

Shock pounded through him when her fingers slowly laced with his. Her hand was soft and delicate, the bones fine, the skin smooth. He couldn't help himself. He stood in place, tracing his fingers over hers. Her nails felt perfectly rounded, and he knew they were painted the color of coral shells. More than anything, he wanted to suck them into his mouth.

She squeezed his hand, and his shock intensified. Did she offer him comfort? A silent warning? He didn't know, but he reveled in the action.

Was she coming to care for him?

She'd responded to his kiss so passionately, erupting from cool to blazing in seconds. She'd responded, and she'd wanted. Just as he had. He'd bedded many women over the years, more than he could count. Yet none had ever stirred his heart like she had. A simple kiss, and he'd burned for her uncontrollably. He hadn't wanted just her body. He'd wanted all she had to give.

Later, he promised himself. *Later.*

"I am waiting," Joachim said, impatient.

Valerian's eyes narrowed. "Come," he said to Shaye, ignoring his cousin. Anger fueled his steps as he ushered her down the rest of the hallway.

Joachim remained in place, watching them.

Valerian barreled past him, shoving the foolish man out of the way. No one would treat him with such disrespect. By the time their private war ended, anyone who harbored thoughts of taking his place would see the error of his ways.

Perhaps he should take Shaye to his room and place a guard at the door. He wasn't sure he wanted her to see his most vicious side, the animal inside him. An animal that maimed and conquered. Already she protested the confrontation.

Yet as much as he wanted to protect her from the beast inside him, he wanted her to see it, to know his strengths and know that he could take care of her. Whoever, whatever the enemy.

"Well, this is fun," Shaye said dryly.

"Wait until the battle actually begins," Valerian replied.

Joachim's gaze bored into his back, and he felt the heat of it as he strode forward. Sand flung from his boots. The arena overflowed with warriors, he noticed. They circled the walls, brimming with anticipation and eagerness. Good. He wanted all of his men to witness the coming event.

Several warriors had brought their women, and these females stood interspersed with the men. They were draped in Atlantean robes, violet and yellow and rose-colored scarves woven with silver thread. Sapphires, rubies and emeralds sparkled from the soft materials, and all of the scarves split at the bottom, offering glimpses of thigh. Fine, metal links looped around the women's waists, showcasing the shapely curves of some, the lean delicacy of others. They ranged in age, size and beauty, but each had her own appeal.

None of them, dressed as finely as they were, compared to Shaye. Not even close.

Valerian stopped in front of Broderick. "Is all ready?"

"I have taken care of every detail." Broderick grinned and wound his arm around his chosen, a pretty brunette. "Women and war in one day. The gods must be smiling upon us."

Smiling…or cursing. "Watch this little morsel for

me," Valerian said, gently thrusting Shaye at him. She *humphed.* "Guard her well and allow no one to touch her." He paused, considered Broderick's past liaisons, and added, "Not even yourself."

Broderick's grin faded, and he lost all traces of his enjoyment. "Keep her with me, but do not touch her? This is the wench who fought you. What if she tries to run away?"

"She won't." He turned his gaze on Shaye and met her rebellious eyes. "Will you?"

She studied her fingernails. "Whatever you say, big guy."

He expelled a hot breath. "I do not want to punish you, Shaye, but I will if you force me."

"If *I* force you?" She glared up at him. "Now there's Barbarian Mentality 101 if I've ever heard it. Perhaps I need to make a card for women who find themselves stuck with a Neanderthal. It could say something simple like, 'Got Razors'?"

He did not even pretend to understand what she had just said. "Promise me you will stay here. If I am worried about you, I cannot concentrate on the sword being swung at me."

She paled once again, a lovely ice queen. He drank in her snowy beauty.

"Promise me," he said again, tenderly this time.

Her expression softened ever so slightly. "Fine. I promise. But only for the fight. *The fight I don't want you to participate in.* After that…"

Satisfied, he looked to Broderick. "When I return, I want her in the same condition I have left her. Not a single bruise."

"As if I would ever hurt a woman," his friend grumbled.

"As if I would allow him to hurt me," Shaye said, her chin tilted stubbornly.

Broderick arched his brows, a who-is-this-woman expression on his face. Valerian fought a grin.

The brunette at Broderick's side pointed an accusing finger at Shaye. "I don't like you standing near Broderick."

Shaye rolled her eyes.

Broderick regained his amusement and grinned. "Rissa is possessive of me, what can I say?"

"Just make sure she keeps her hands off Shaye."

"I can take her," Shaye said. Her dark brown eyes glowed with challenge.

"I know you can, moon, but if you were to hurt her I would owe Broderick another woman." He clasped her delicate shoulders in his hands and rubbed her arms. Brave, sweet thing. "I would rather not have another battle on my hands."

Shaye's lips pressed in a mutinous line, and she peered down at the sands. At least she didn't offer another rejoinder.

He wanted to kiss her just then, to thrust his tongue into her mouth and feel her heat, her wetness. Taste her sweetness. He couldn't. Not yet. Not again. Not with Joachim's challenge hanging over their heads.

"Valerian!" a female squealed from behind his mate. "Valerian!"

His muscles stiffened. Damn it! Already Shaye resisted him, and she'd made her dislike of his past lusts very clear. Yet now, heading straight toward him, was one of the three women from the other night. She shoved her way through the crowd, swathes of red hair trailing behind her.

"My sweet king. I came to wish you well."

Shaye, too, stiffened—before she was shouldered out of the way. He scowled, was about to issue a stinging rebuke, but the redhead's hands were suddenly caressing his bare chest, lingering over every curve and hollow, pulling gently at his nipple ring, then riding the ridges of his abdomen and cupping his backside.

"I just heard about the fight, and wanted to cheer for you."

"Isn't this special," Shaye said, an airy breeze to her tone. "A Lust family reunion."

Eyeing the newcomer, Valerian said, "Our association is at an end, sweet." He kept his tone gentle, not wanting to inflict unnecessary hurt. He felt guilty for not learning her name. "Joachim is your lover now. Warm his bed this night, for he will need all the loving he can get."

Her pink lips dipped into a pout, and she traced her fingertip over his navel. "I don't want to warm his bed. Joachim didn't please me like you always do."

"Did. Always did. I have a mate now," he reminded her. His guilt increased.

"You can please more than one woman at a time, I know for a fact. The three of us can—"

"This conversation is boring." Shaye sighed, but the breathy exhalation held a sharp bite. "I believe your cousin is ready to cut your head off. You might want to hurry out there."

Jaw clenched, Valerian wrapped his hands around the clinging redhead's waist and handed her to one of his men. Whom, he didn't care. She opened her mouth to protest, but he held up his hand for silence. Instead of simply quieting her, everyone in the arena stopped speaking.

He did not want an audience for the conversation he needed to have with Shaye. "I will speak with you about this later," he said, his eyes only for her.

She shrugged as if she didn't care, but she couldn't hide the fire in her gaze.

He had to force back a chuckle of satisfaction. His woman did not like others to handle him. She might deny it, but he knew women very well. She was jealous.

Finally, something was going right in this seduction.

"Are you, at last, ready to begin?" Joachim demanded behind him.

With a final glance at Shaye, he turned. It was time. Joachim stood in the center of the sandy arena, swinging a spear over his head, loosening his muscles. The metal whistled and zinged in the air like a war cry. In his other hand, he held a silver shield. Except for the color, Valerian's shield was exactly the same, with two wings embossed on each side. In the center of both shields rested a sword.

Joachim replaced his helmet, covering his skull and ears. The movement caused his armor to glint.

Valerian held his hand out, and Broderick slapped a spear into his grip. He felt its familiar weight, nodded. Broderick then handed him a shield. He handed it right back. "Remove The Skull from the center and replace it with another sword," he commanded.

"But, my lord, you have never—"

"Do it." He had never used a sword other than his

own, but he did not want to inflict irreparable damage to his cousin, and that was what The Skull would do.

He didn't want Joachim to die. As Joachim had pronounced earlier, they *had* been friends as children. The best of friends. Then Valerian's father died and Valerian had to take control, become leader. That was when Joachim's resentment first sprouted.

Valerian wanted his cousin to live, forever an example of what happened to those who challenged the king.

"Any sword will do," he said. "Any save The Skull."

A pause, then the shield was taken out of his hands. Footsteps. The cool press of the shield's handle. His gold shield, yes, but his sword no longer lay inside of it. A plain, sharp-tipped blade now held the honor. He nodded in approval. This battle was not just about Shaye. Not anymore.

"Your helmet, my king," Broderick said.

"No." He kept his gaze on Joachim. "Not this time."

Broderick frowned. "What of your other armor?"

"No."

"I hope you pound each other to a bloody pulp," Shaye mumbled behind him. "This is stupid."

Her words elicited several male chuckles and several feminine gasps of horror. He suspected that her anger was merely a defense against something she feared. Losing him? He should be upset by her lack of faith, but he was strangely thrilled.

"How dare you say such a thing," the redhead said accusingly.

"She is allowed to say whatever she wants," Valerian informed everyone, "for she will one day be your queen." He tossed her a glance over his shoulder and saw that she now wore an expression of pique. "That doesn't mean I will always give in to her desires. This time, however, I will take great pleasure in granting part of her request."

"I, too, will enjoy granting part of her request," Joachim said.

Valerian scowled at him. He hefted the weight of his spear in one hand, his shield in the other, and stepped into the arena. Determined, he circled Joachim. The man watched him, never slowing his swinging lance. "Shall we begin?"

"We shall. I've wanted to be king for a long time," Joachim admitted.

"I know. But what makes you think you will be a better commander for my army? You are too war-happy, too ravenous for control."

"Such qualities should be lauded."

"Lauded? When the hunger will never be appeased? There will always be someone else to conquer. Were you to rule my army, you would lead them straight into war. In the end, I have every faith you would conquer Atlantis and all the kings and queens inside, but you would also destroy the entire city."

"Better to rule a decimated land than not to rule at all." With a roar, Joachim leapt at him.

Their spears clashed together midair. Immediately Valerian countered, ducking low, pivoting and slashing. He missed as Joachim sliced to the side. *Clang.* Their spears met again. In the next instant Joachim raised his lance and Valerian rammed it high. He spun, aiming for his cousin's neck.

Joachim darted out of the way with a grin.

"Getting slow, Valerian." He removed his helmet and tossed it aside.

Valerian stabbed forward, his spike and shield swinging simultaneously. Joachim quickly lost his smile as he was forced to duck. He stumbled backward. Valerian's spear nearly sank into his stomach, but Joachim blocked, swung. Thrust.

That low thrust grazed Valerian's thigh, slicing cloth rather than skin. Valerian dropped to one knee, absorbing the next blow with his shield. When he regained his footing, he lunged forward. The tip of his weapon whizzed past Joachim's side, taking a hunk of armor with it.

"Still think I'm slow?" Valerian asked.

Their fiery gazes met, blue against bluer, and Joachim scowled. He swung to the left, missed, then swung to the right. As the lance dipped toward the ground, Valerian leapt over its middle, trapping it between his legs and jamming his elbow into Joachim's nose. Blood squirted and Joachim howled as he tripped, falling away from striking distance and flinging dirt in every direction.

"Get up," Valerian commanded.

"You'll pay for that." His cousin jumped to his feet and ran straight at him, continuously stabbing forward.

Valerian circled quickly, shield blocking. His muscles began to burn, and sweat began to run down his face and chest in rivulets. Already his breath emerged in shallow pants. Damn this! At this rate, his strength would be quickly depleted. Lack of sex did that to a nymph.

Looking tired himself, Joachim arched high, intending to puncture his shoulder on the downward swing, but Valerian hit Joachim's wrist and his cousin dropped the spear. At a disadvantage, Joachim dove, rolled and reached for it. His fingers closed around the middle. Maintaining a fluid pace, he spun back to his feet. But Valerian was already there, stomping on the lance and snapping it in two.

Growling low in his throat, Joachim kicked up. His foot slammed into Valerian's wrist and Valerian, too, lost his spear. Both men sprang apart, unsheathing the swords from their shields.

As blood continued to drip down his face, Joachim launched forward, wildly swinging. Air whistled, zinged, just like it had before the battle began. Movements slower than normal, Valerian didn't duck in time. The blade sliced his forearm. He felt the sting of it, the burn of torn flesh.

He didn't give a reaction, didn't allow it to slow him further.

He stabbed low, then up, twisting before Joachim could counter. The tip of his sword whizzed by his cousin's face, and the man paled. He raised his shield and slammed it into Valerian's other arm, the sharp wings cutting skin. Valerian used the momentum to spin around and slice into Joachim's thigh.

His cousin shouted, and his knees buckled into the sand.

"Get up," Valerian snarled. "I'm not through with you."

Gritting his teeth, Joachim lumbered to his feet. He still clutched his weapon and shield. His eyes were dark with rage, his lips swollen with his thirst for power. "I am not through with you, either." He dropped his shield and slid a second dagger from his side.

Valerian hurled his shield aside, as well. He held out his free hand, and Broderick tossed him a second dagger. He easily caught the hilt. Two blades against two blades.

Instantly he and Joachim leapt for each other. One blade clashed, then the other, a lethal dance of dodge and slash. Valerian spun as he worked his blades, lunged and stabbed.

"I should have been born to your father. I should have been king," Joachim panted as he ducked.

"The gods did not think so." Stab, turn, stab.

"I was created to rule."

"You were created, yes, but not to rule. Verryn should be here, commanding us both, but he is gone. My father is gone. And that leaves me. It is well past time you accepted that." The first blade finally hit home, jabbing into Joachim's side.

His cousin screamed and dropped to his knees. Valerian's momentum kept him from drawing back his other weapon. He wasn't sure he would have, though, even if he could. But he did angle his arm, his second blade embedding in Joachim's shoulder, close to his heart, but not hitting directly. The silver glided smoothly through the links of armor. Joachim gasped for air as a trickle of blood ran from his mouth.

Total silence filled the arena.

Valerian straightened, panting.

"Why did…you let…me…live?" Joachim gurgled. "Should have…hit…my heart."

"You will live, and you will regret," Valerian said, unemotional and loud enough that everyone could hear. "If you ever again challenge my leadership, I will kill you without a thought. Without hesitation. Without mercy. No matter that we are family. No matter that we were once friends."

Joachim's chin fell to his chest, and his eyes closed. Dark shadows couched his blood-coated face. He tumbled into the dirt, unconscious. Grains of sand sprayed onto Valerian's boots.

He slammed the tip of his dagger beside his cousin's body and whipped around to eye the crowd of warriors who watched him in openmouthed shock. Perhaps they had expected him to kill his cousin. Perhaps they had expected him to deflect the final blow completely.

His gaze connected with Shaye's. *Mine,* his mind shouted. *Mine now.* No one could say otherwise.

Like his men, her face was darkened with shock. And horror? He knew he must look a sight, blood and sand covering his arms, legs and face. Strands of sweat-soaked hair clung to his temples.

Perhaps the surface dwellers did not fight quite so violently, but he couldn't force himself to regret what had been done. She belonged to him, would live *here* with him, so it was better for her to learn his way of life now.

Tearing his gaze from her, he looked at each of his men. "Is there anyone else who wishes to challenge my authority?"

After the echo of his voice settled, silence reigned. He paced in front of them. "Now is the time to issue such a challenge."

No one came forward.

He stilled, hands clenched at his sides. "Then I hereby claim Shaye Octavia Holling as my woman.

Mine. My mate. Your queen. He that questions this shall meet the steel of my sword."

Amid Shaye's choked squeaks, he moved in front of Broderick. He didn't look at Shaye again. Not yet. He wasn't ready to see what expression she now wore—rebellious? Furious? Disgusted? He wasn't ready to know her thoughts.

Broderick cleared his throat. "What should we do about Joachim?"

"Pray that Asclepius and his two daughters visit." The words were uttered out of habit, for when a nymph became injured, prayers were raised to those gods of healing, even though they had wanted nothing to do with the people of Atlantis for many, many years. No one knew why the gods had abandoned them, only that they had.

Valerian still did not want Joachim to die. He wanted him to suffer.

Valerian scanned the crowd of onlookers. "Is there a healer among you?"

After a pause, Shivawn's silent, black-haired wench stepped forward. There were tears in her eyes as she raised a tentative hand. He nodded at her and faced Broderick. "Take Joachim and the healer to the sick room. She is to bandage him up and nothing more. Make sure she does not touch him sexually." If she did, Joachim would heal quickly, his injuries forgotten all too soon. Before the fight, Valerian had thought to give his cousin a speedy recovery. Not so now. He did not have time for the trouble the man was sure to cause.

Broderick nodded.

Without another word, Valerian grabbed Shaye's hand and tugged her into the corridor.

Now she truly belonged to him—and it was time he proved it to her.

CHAPTER THIRTEEN

POSEIDON WAS BORED.

He was god of the sea, ruler of fish, merpeople and ocean waves, and he was bored. Lately even the storms and destruction he caused failed to amuse him. People screamed, people died, yada, yada, yada.

Maybe he'd care if the humans had not forgotten his existence. But they no longer served him; they no longer worshipped him—both of which were his due. After all, he'd helped create the ungrateful race.

He traced his fingers through the dappled liquid surrounding him. There had to be something to combat this constant sense of ennui. Create a hurricane or a tsunami—no. The last few had been yawners. Start a war—no. Too much effort for too little reward. Abandon the water and enter Olympus—no again. The other gods were selfish and greedy and he did not want to deal with them.

What could he do, what could he do? The only worlds he had dominion over were Earth and Atlantis, he thought, straightening. Oh, oh, oh. Was that…yes, it was. For the first time in what seemed an eternity, he experienced a flash of excitement.

He hadn't considered Atlantis and its people in years. He'd walked away from them, thinking—hoping, perhaps—that they'd destroy themselves so that he'd never again have to gaze upon what he considered an abomination. Instead they'd thrived and he'd let them, because they had obeyed the laws he'd set in place. More than that, he'd been completely caught up in his humans and had forgotten about the races of creatures made before the formula of Man had been perfected.

Yes, it was past time he checked on Atlantis and its citizens.

Poseidon couldn't help himself. He grinned.

SHAYE STARED at Valerian's back as he led her through the palace, following the same path they'd taken earlier. She didn't protest. Muscles strained and bunched in his bare shoulders. Blood blended with sand, and both were splattered all over him, forming lines and circles on his skin.

He'd very nearly killed a man. His own cousin, no less. Might have, actually, if Joachim's wounds became infected. He had done this without hesitation. Without remorse. She'd watched him do it and hadn't flinched.

She'd been too relieved that *he* was the winner and would live.

The fight had unfolded like something out of a movie. Valerian had moved with grace and fluidity, each intricate step as beautiful as it was dangerous. A menacing ballet. Her heart had drummed erratically in her chest, then stopped altogether when Valerian was injured. She'd been unprepared for the anger she'd felt toward Joachim in that moment.

She'd been unprepared for the fright she'd felt for Valerian.

She could have run away and escaped the madness.

But she hadn't. She'd stayed. Not because she had promised Valerian—a promise made under duress wasn't really a promise, to her way of thinking—but because knowing the outcome of the battle had seemed vital to her own survival.

I hereby claim Shaye Octavia Holling as my woman. My mate, my queen, he had said.

His words drifted through her mind, making her shiver now as they had in the arena. He'd said them, and they hadn't bothered her as much as they should have. They hadn't bothered her at all, really. She'd actually experienced a tremor of—she growled, just remembering—contentment.

Just then Valerian stumbled over his own feet. He quickly righted himself, but the action brought her to the present. "You're injured," she said, as if he didn't already know. Her concern for him doubled. "You need a doctor."

He didn't turn to face her. "*You* will act as my healer."

The thought was as appealing as it was disturbing. "I know nothing about wound care."

"I trust you."

Why? She didn't trust herself. Not around him. "I might do more harm than good."

"Shaye," he said, clearly exasperated. "You are the only person I want touching me in any way."

Put like that… "Fine. But when you die, you can tell God I warned you."

His shoulders shook, and she heard the rumbling purr of his laughter. Unbidden, her lips inched into a half smile and she forgot her concerns. She liked his amusement.

"Were you trying to save him," she asked, "or did you accidentally miss his heart?"

The question made him stiffen. "I never miss an intended target."

Apparently male pride was the same for nymphs as it was for humans. "What if he challenges you again? And what if he cheats next time, hitting you unaware?"

"He will not."

"How can you be sure?" she persisted.

"Joachim lost. He was shown as the weaker warrior. Whether he kills me in the future or not, he will never be accepted as leader."

"Oh." She barely managed the one-syllable reply, so upset was she by the thought of Valerian dying.

"What's more," Valerian continued, unaware, "he did not need to die for you to become my woman, and *that* is the main reason I fought him."

A shiver rolled through her. "I am *not* your woman."

"Cease your protests, moon. They will only embarrass you when you at last admit your love for me."

She snorted, but quickly changed the subject. His words were a little too...prophetic. "Where are you taking me?" she said, studying the torch-lit hallway with its familiar nicked-and-scuffed walls. Recognizing the area, the answer hit her, and every molecule of air in her lungs froze. "No!"

A pause. A sigh. "My bedroom," he admitted reluctantly. "Yes."

Her stomach clenched against the sudden bombardment of erotic sensation. Valerian. Bed.

Hell. No.

She shivered again. "Are you going to lock me inside?" The question trembled from her.

"No." There was more determination in that one word than she'd heard in her entire life.

"Wh-what are you going to do to me?" Deep down, she already suspected the answer was going to be—

"Make love to you, moon. I am going to make love to you."

"No, no. No!" She dug her heels into the polished ebony floor, bringing them to an abrupt halt. "I refuse. Do you hear me? I refuse!"

Slowly he turned and faced her. He didn't release her hand. His lush lips were firm, his harsh expression etched in stone. "I have been injured," he said, as if she should know why that was important.

She scowled up at him. "I can see that you're injured. I even pointed it out to you. But you should know that you'll sustain more injuries if you try and take me to bed."

"I am injured," he repeated. "Sex strengthens me. I will heal faster once I have penetrated you."

A hot gasp bubbled in her throat, nearly choking her. "Uh, you can die for all I care. I'm not letting you—" she weaved a hand through the air "— penetrate me."

"You will find my lovemaking exquisite." The corners of his mouth edged into a deep frown. "I assure you."

"No."

"Shaye," he cajoled. "Sweet moonbeam."

"Valerian," she snapped. "Whoremonger."

A muscle twitched beside his eye. "I have turned away all other women for you. I have publicly vowed to make you my queen."

"I'm going on record right now saying I don't give a shit and my answer is no."

If she'd thought his expression hard before, she was now shown the error of such an assumption. His gaze became frosted with turquoise ice; his nostrils flared. His cheekbones looked cut from glass. "I can make you beg for it."

She quivered with trepidation but said, "I don't beg for anything."

He regarded her silently for a long while, then pushed a hand through his hair, causing several blond locks to fall over his eyes. A foreign part of her—a part that revealed itself more and more lately—urged her to reach up and caress those errant strands from his beautiful face. Yes, he could make her beg for it. There. She'd admitted it. His decadent flavor was still in her mouth, the press of his lips imprinted on her memory. But she had to resist him. She had to fight him.

And she had to, at last, escape him.

Before she could take a step, however, he moved toward her and licked his lips, as if he knew—*knew, damn him*—exactly what naughty memory played through her mind and planned to exploit it by whatever means necessary. All thoughts of escape vanished.

"I need you, Shaye. More than I've ever needed another."

Only Valerian spoke to her in that tone. Husky rich, honey warm. As if the thought of her ravishment was an exquisite bliss. As if, in his mind, she was already naked and he was already inside her. She had no response for him—not one she was comfortable giving.

Silence once again encompassed them; this time it was a knowing silence, a heavy silence. A tempting silence. He waited, letting her mind and body battle for

supremacy. *Stay strong. Be cold.* If he touched her...
Wait. He *was* touching her, and it felt good.

She ripped free from his clasp and inched backward,
not caring if the action was cowardly. "I'll clean your
wound, but that's it. Nothing more. Do you understand?"

He considered her words as he stared into her eyes,
gauging her inner resolve. "Are you resistant to me
because I almost killed a man?"

"No," she admitted.

"Then why? Some women abhor violence. Some
are titillated by it." Closer, closer he came to her.
"Which are you?"

"Neither," she said, and backed herself straight into
the wall. She gasped. "I just don't—" *say it, hurt him*
"— like you."

He stilled, popped his jaw. Maybe she had hurt him,
maybe she hadn't. She'd definitely hurt herself. Lying
like that caused her stomach to clench painfully and her
throat to constrict.

"Very well, then," he said, toneless. "I will allow you
to care for my wounds. Both of my arms need tending."

Be casual, unaffected. "Gee, thanks. You will *allow*
me." She snorted, hoping she appeared properly unimpressed. While she administered aid, would he "accidentally" touch her? Would he purr his warm breath
into her ears, over her skin, and let his white-hot gaze
devour her? "But there will be no...petting."

Because here was a better question: Would she be
able to resist him?

Already her resolve teetered on precarious ground.
Perhaps playing doctor wasn't so smart, after all. She
would have to be on full alert. Being with Valerian, she

suspected, would be like shooting herself full of heroin. Addictive, lethal and absolutely stupid. If she could resist taking that first, experimental taste, she wouldn't have to deal with withdrawal. And after she patched him up, she could leave him with a clear conscience.

You've already had a taste. Remember that white-hot kiss? Shut up!

"While you help me," he said, "I will not pet you. If, however, you change your mind and wish me to do so, you have only to say."

Not giving her time to respond, he grabbed her hand, pivoted and kicked back into motion. With his final words ringing in her ears, she was aware of every point of contact between them. Smoothness against rough calluses.

"Do you have any Neosporin?" she asked, hoping to get her mind off everything related to sex.

"I have no idea, as I do not know what that is."

When his hair was damp, it had a little curl to it, she realized. Then she scowled. Why did she care about his stupid hair? "It's medicine for your arms."

"I will gather everything that you need." They came to the room's entrance, and with his free hand, he swished aside the white lace.

He stepped inside; she followed on his heels. Though the room was located in the same corridor as the one she had slept in, it was more masculine than hers, a combination of battleground and leisure. A large bed occupied the far section, with rumpled violet-and-gold sheets and the imprint of a large male body. Gold armor and an arsenal of weapons hung on ruby hooks. Rainbow lights glistened from the walls, like diamonds trapped in glass.

To the side, steam curled from a bathing pool, twining around the flower petals that floated on the surface. That was a very feminine touch, and she knew Valerian was not responsible. One of his many lovers must have prepared the water.

"This is your main bedroom?" she asked.

"Yes." He released her hand.

Slowly she twirled around. "I noticed that some of the walls have holes, as if things have been scraped out of them. Jewels, right? Like these?"

"Yes," he repeated.

"Why is this room still intact? And the other room of yours, the one I slept in?"

"After I took possession, I made sure they were worthy of me."

He spoke with no hint of smugness, no hint of pride. Only truth. "You don't think too highly of yourself, I see."

Standing there, Valerian drank in the sight of his woman. Then he drank in the sight of the bed. Large, beckoning. Violet sheets with golden trim. He wanted Shaye there, splayed and open for his view. For his touch. Being inside his room, having a bed nearby and Shaye within reach, proved an intoxicating dilemma.

Why had he promised not to touch her sexually while she tended him?

He'd never had to seduce a woman before. They always desired him, no provocation needed. Shaye made him feel at a loss. While he hungered for every part of her, she continually pushed him away. And of all the women in the world, she should want him most.

How much longer could his body withstand the rejection?

Not much, he suspected.

He gathered clean rags, a basin of hot water, a jar of cleaning oil, and a vial of healing sand from the Forest of the Dragons. He placed all of them on a tray. His ears remained attuned to Shaye's every movement, lest she decide to bolt for the door. Surprisingly, she didn't. She remained exactly where he'd left her, in the center, gazing around.

Their eyes locked as he walked toward her. Gods, she was lovely. Her pale hair was pulled over her shoulders, an erotic curtain. *Kiss her.* Instead of placing the tray in her outstretched hands, he leaned down, slowly, giving her ample time to realize what he was doing.

He couldn't resist. He had to do this, was helpless to stop. *Not petting,* he rationalized.

His lips lightly brushed hers. A gentle kiss, no tongue, but arousing all the same. Her snow-sweet scent filled his nostrils as he captured her gasp in his mouth. "Thank you for tending me," he said, his voice as soft as his touch.

Her eyes had widened and now they glinted with a trace of fear. Of him? Or herself? "I'm not known for my gentleness," she warned. Her voice trembled. "So you might want to save your thanks."

He fought a smile and straightened. "Then what are you known for, little moonbeam?"

"Being a bitch." Biting her lip, she appropriated the tray from his grasp and spun on her heel.

"That is not a compliment, I take it?"

Her shoulders lifted in a shrug as she moved toward an amethyst chest. "Not to some." She anchored the tray on the surface.

After he explained what she needed to do with each item, he hefted the room's only chair—trying not to grimace—and placed it next to Shaye. "You like people to think you are cold and unfeeling. You have even tried your hardest to convince me of this. Several times. Why?"

Her lips pursed, and she motioned to the chair with a wave of her hand. "Just sit down and shut up. My mom made me see shrinks when I was a kid, so I don't need an amateur diagnosis right now."

"Tell me," he beseeched. He remained standing. She might think she wanted to be cold, but he saw the moments of warmth and softness she tried so hard to hide. He noticed the way she sometimes hesitated before she issued an insult, as if she had to force herself to say it. And when she spoke of her uncaring nature, there was wistfulness in her brown eyes, a neediness she hadn't yet accepted.

"There's nothing to tell, really. Over the years, I learned that emotions bring only pain and upset." She pushed on his shoulders. Her strength was no match for his, but he eased into the chair nonetheless.

With somewhat shaky fingers, she brushed the dark sand from his shoulder, careful to avoid his wound. He winced as sharp pain radiated from one corner of his body to the other.

He frowned. "I would not be suffering right now if you would simply accept the inevitable and make love with me."

"Don't be a baby. I warned you that I wasn't good at this sort of thing." She soaked one of the rags with oil. "This smells good. What is it?"

"Soap, I think your people call it."

"Our soap doesn't smell like this, like orchids and magical waterfalls."

His chin tilted to the side, and he eyed her. "You wish me to think you aloof and yet you enjoy pleasing your senses with delicious smells."

Scowling, she slapped the cloth against his wound. He laughed, for he was beginning to see a pattern to her bouts of anger. When her sense of detachment was most threatened, she reacted with waspishness.

As she gently rubbed the flesh around the wound, cleaning away sweat and dirt, she said grudgingly, "You did good out there."

His amusement died a quick death; shock pounded through him. A grunt of relief even gusted past his lips. Perhaps violence did not bother her as much as he'd feared. He was glad, for that meant she might more readily accept her life here, where wars constantly raged. "Are the men of the surface allowed to combat each other with swords?"

"No. Not without consequences."

"What do you mean?"

"If a man on the surface maims another man like you did today, he is hunted down and locked away. If his victim dies, he can be executed."

He rolled her explanation through his mind. "What if the man is protecting himself or those he loves?"

"There are still consequences, they simply aren't as severe. People in my world sue for the dumbest stuff imaginable. I heard about one case where a man broke into another man's house. The thief fell off the roof and sued the homeowner. He actually won the case, too. How dumb is that?"

"I do not think I would like living on the surface, then."

"Well, I like it," she said defensively.

He sighed.

"This cut is pretty deep," she muttered, probing the edge with her fingers. "I think you need stitches."

He bit his lip to hide his wince. He'd never had to deal with his wounds before. After a battle, he immediately made love to a woman and his wounds disappeared of their own accord. "What I need is sex." He tried for a seductive tone, but sounded reproachful. "With you."

She scowled, even as she tenderly dried the injury. "I'm more than willing to go get one of the other women for you."

As her words echoed between them, she pressed her lips together. A combination of rage and trepidation— that he would take her up on the offer?—flitted over her expression.

"Ah, little moonbeam. When will you learn that only you will do?"

She relaxed, her expression softening. "Yes, well, when will you learn that I don't sleep around?"

"Have I not already explained that you are my mate?" He did not want to listen to another of her denials, so he added, "Your protests are silly."

"A mate is a willing partner, right? I think we both know I'm not willing. Nor am I your partner. Or queen. I am *not* a queen."

Unable to help himself, he plucked the ends of her hair and sifted the silky strands through his fingers. He brought them to his nose and sniffed. Ah, sweet heaven. "You smell so good."

"I can't say the same for you."

He didn't take offense. "I am most definitely in need of a bath. Would you care to join me?"

A quiver raked her, and she dropped the rag to the floor. "Damn it. Stop saying stuff like that."

"Why? I want you. I am not one to deny my desires."

"Yeah. I get that." Bending down, she scooped up the rag and tossed it into the unlit hearth. She picked up a clean rag and scooped sand into a gaping pocket. "You do realize I'm about to put sand in an open sore, right?"

"Right."

"And you still want me to do it?"

His brow puckered. "Of course."

She shook her head, incredulous, then shrugged. "Whatever. It's your infection." But she hesitated a moment before smearing the grains into his injury.

He didn't speak for a long while. He concentrated on her breath, gently fanning his shoulder. He concentrated on her teeth, nibbling on her lower lip. His cock grew increasingly hard.

"Desires are a natural thing, moon," he said. "The more you deny them, the stronger they become, until they are all you can think about, all you can see."

"Stop right there." Her voice shook, and he knew she wasn't unaffected by what he'd said. Her nipples were hard little points against her shirt. "Don't try to engage me in a conversation about desires, okay? I'm not interested."

He grabbed her wrist, closing his fingers around her delicate bones with soothing finesse. *Still not petting,* he assured himself. He tugged her in front of him. Her gaze slid to his mouth, to his erection. A surprised gasp slipped from her.

"You're right," he said. He needed her so badly. "We

should not talk about it. I should *show* you. Tell me to show you, Shaye. Tell me."

Suddenly panicked, she leapt away from him and to the wall, where she grabbed one of the smaller swords. She held it in front of her, looking very much like the warrior queen she so vehemently denied being. "No. No! Do you understand?"

Shaye had been fighting a fierce desire for him since he'd first sat down, and every time he touched her, every time he looked at her, every time he spoke to her, her resistance crumbled a little more.

He froze in place, a blank shield shuttering over his expression. Only his eyes revealed any hint of emotion. They were blazing with need and rage and disappointment.

"Very well," he said. "Tonight is yours. I will not touch you."

No, her body wept. *Don't listen to me. Fight for me.*
"Thank you." She had to stay strong. She couldn't give in. The ramifications were simply too great.

They stared at each other, locked in a silent battle. "Tomorrow, however, belongs to me. There will be no more denying me. Do *you* understand?"

She gulped, didn't dare speak.

"If you attempt to leave this room, you will regret it." He stood and left her then, striding away without a backward glance.

CHAPTER FOURTEEN

DR. BRENNA JOHNSTON tied her black curls on top of her head with a thin strip of cloth. As always, a few of the shorter curls escaped confinement and cascaded down her temples.

How did I get myself into this situation?

She gazed down at the man lying unconscious on the bed of sapphire silk. His beautiful dark hair was spread over his large shoulders. His eyelashes etched shadows on his cheeks. His nose was slightly crooked, his lips lush.

He looked like a fallen angel.

A dying, bloody, pain-entrenched fallen angel.

Blood oozed from the thick gashes on his chest and thigh. His skin, she knew from seeing him earlier, was usually tanned. Now it was pale, tinted slightly blue because he'd gone into a mild form of shock. She was a surgeon, but she would have preferred *her* tools in *her* hospital with *her* nurses. Not the jars of oil and sand she'd been given, not the nonsterile environment, not the lughead standing guard at the door. Still, Brenna couldn't let her patient die. She wouldn't.

She had been terrified since she'd been taken by these giant, hulking beasts, but for the first time since entering this…whatever it was, she felt in control. Like herself. Confident and in her element.

Brenna motioned to the guard stationed at the door, and he approached her. She didn't back away, but forced herself to stand her ground as she signed what she needed.

His face scrunched with confusion, and he held up his hands, a command for her to be still. "I do not understand what you are doing. Can you not speak?"

She sighed inwardly. Her vocal cords had been severely damaged years ago. There weren't any scars on the outside; no, her scars were internal. She'd been attacked—a blurred, blackened, hated memory she could not allow herself to relive at the moment, not if she hoped to function—and while she could speak, her voice was…ugly.

"Needle," she croaked. "Thread." Primitive that he obviously was, he probably wouldn't know a scalpel from a butter knife. "Operating tools."

He cringed at the rough, broken sound, but nodded and raced off. When he returned a short while later, he handed her a lumpy black satchel. She unrolled it, finding a bronze scalpel, long, thin hooks and several iron needles.

"Fire," she said. "Hot water."

Understanding, he grabbed a lit sconce from the wall and tossed it into the hearth. The logs inside quickly caught flame, crackling and burning. After he had gathered the bowl of water, she heated the instruments over the fire.

Once everything was as sterilized as she could get it, her hands scrubbed clean, she at last approached her patient, ready to act. He had yet to move, had yet to make a single sound. His features were relaxed, unaffected.

That both elated and worried her. At least he wouldn't feel the pain of her needle. But such a deep sleep… Brenna squared her shoulders and got to work. She cut off his pants, cleaned the gaping wounds on his legs and chest, and did her best to repair the torn tissue—which was in better shape than she'd dared hope. Sounded easy, sounded quick, but she was by his side for several hours and sweat beaded over her skin. Toward the end, fatigue shook her arms and back.

That will have to do. She would have liked to give him a transfusion but knew such a thing was impossible here. The man who had chosen her last night, Shivawn, had attempted to ease her distress by explaining where she was and why she'd been brought here. Of course, his explanation had only intensified her fear.

Nymphs. Atlantis. Sex. At first she hadn't wanted to believe him. However, after everything she'd witnessed today, she no longer had the luxury of disbelief. Sword fights and bejeweled walls. Silk pillows lining every wall and warriors having sex atop them. Mermaids and a crystal ceiling that produced light. Women going mad, becoming sex starved.

Shivawn had expected the same easy (and enthusiastic) response from her. How surprised he'd been to be met with slaps and kicks and, she was ashamed to say, sobbing. But he'd finally left her alone. He'd been oddly…sweet about the entire situation. Surprisingly protective.

Still, he regretted his choice already; he had to. This morning she'd caught glimpses of other warriors (naked) in bed with their chosen (also naked). Some of them hadn't been sleeping. Shivawn had to want that for himself, but she couldn't give it to him. She simply couldn't.

Brenna had only allowed him to pick her so that she would be taken away from the large group of men. One warrior she could (possibly) fight. But all of them? No way.

She sighed. For the next several hours, she remained seated beside the unconscious man—Joachim was his name, she recalled—sponging a warm, wet rag over his forehead and doing everything in her power to make him comfortable and keep him from getting cold. As much blood as he'd lost, he was susceptible to hypothermia.

"Brenna," she suddenly heard Shivawn say from the door. He sounded hopeful. "It is time I took you to my chamber."

Her heart kicked into overdrive. *Remain calm.* Bit by bit she turned to face him. He stood beside the guard, who was pretending to study the wall. Shivawn was a handsome man, with brown hair and green eyes, and a part of her wished she was a normal woman who could enjoy someone like him. Truly, just looking at him made her feel…achy inside. But she shook her head.

His shoulders slumped, and his lips compressed into a thin line. "Why do you continue to deny me? Have I hurt you in any way?"

She shook her head a second time. He hadn't, and that still shocked her.

He stepped forward. "I only wish to give you pleasure."

Again, a shake. "I stay."

He'd heard her voice before, so he didn't cringe this

time as he had at first. Would her continued refusal cause Shivawn to erupt? Would he try to force her? Morph from nice guy to beast? A terrible trembling began in her limbs and spread to her stomach, twisting and turning.

His expression softened as he peered at her. "You do not understand the ways of the nymphs, Brenna. We must be with women or we grow weak," he explained patiently, as he would to a child. "*I* am growing weak, while the others become strong."

"No." When she finally decided to be with a man, it would be with one far less...intimidating. Someone who couldn't snap her neck with a flick of his wrist. Besides, she had a job to do. She pointed to her patient. "Needs me."

Shivawn regarded her for a long while, a play of different emotions on his face. Disappointment. Regret. Resolve. He spun on his heel and stalked away. She breathed a sigh of relief and, shockingly, disappointment.

Get back to work, Johnston. She rotated back to the injured warrior and smoothed a hand over his too-cold brow. Would he survive? He'd lost so much blood.

He was bigger than Shivawn. Probably stronger. More dangerous, surely. But she found herself leaning forward, as if pulled by a power stronger than herself. She placed a soft kiss on his lips, willing him to get better. She hated to see anyone suffer. No one knew better than she how it felt to lie in bed, broken, beaten. Near death.

His eyes blinked open, as if that one action had given him the strength he'd needed to awaken. He spied her hovering over him and frowned, confused. She quickly straightened.

"Did I die, then?" she heard him say.

His voice was weak, strained. Still…she had to force herself to remain in place. *He's feeble. He can't hurt you.* Hand shaking, she again touched his brow. His eyes were opened only slightly, but she could see the pain-ripe gleam of his sapphire irises.

"Did I enter Olympus?"

She shook her head.

His gaze darted around the room. "Why are you here? Why am I—" His words ground to a halt. "Valerian," he gritted out. "The fight. Lost. I lost." He tried to sit up.

She gently pushed him down and smoothed his hair from his face, trying to soothe him and defuse his anger. Brenna didn't know what she'd do if he decided to fight her. Surprisingly enough, her touch seemed to appease him. He relaxed.

Drawing in a deep breath, he reached up and wrapped his fingers around her wrist. *Remain calm, remain calm, remain calm.* She tried to pull away but he held tight.

"What are you doing here, Shivawn's woman?"

Her pulse hammered in her neck as she pointed to his bandaged wounds.

His brows drew together as he studied her. "You are a healer?"

Brenna nodded and once more tried to free herself, but his grip remained strong. He should have been weak as a baby.

"Can you not speak?" he asked.

"Broken," she said, motioning to her neck with her free hand.

He didn't flinch at the sound of her voice, and amazement filled her. He released her hand and raised his own to her neck, where the pulse still fluttered wildly. His fingers brushed the soft skin, as if searching for an injury. She shivered, both appalled and needy. What was wrong with her? She hadn't reacted to a man in years, yet she'd responded to two today.

"How?"

People always asked, as if they were inquiring about the weather or about where she bought her shoes. In the beginning, the question had thrown her, brought back the horrible memories of being pinned down and choked by her enraged, jealous boyfriend. Now she always answered with a casual, "car accident," but she doubted this archaic warrior would understand what that meant.

Brenna bit her lip and leaned toward him. Tentative, she wrapped one of her hands gently around his neck and shook, then pointed to her own neck with the other.

His eyes narrowed, and his hands closed over her wrists, far more gently than before. "Someone choked you?"

Nod.

"A man?" The words were so quiet she barely heard them.

Again she nodded.

"No touching," the man in the doorway said, probably just noticing. "The king's orders. Release her, Joachim."

She'd forgotten about him.

Joachim's eyes darted to the guard, and he scowled. The two men engaged in a heated conversation in a language she didn't understand. During it all, Joachim retained that gentle grip on her.

She finally managed to jerk herself free, though. Relief swept through her, and she rubbed her wrist. Where he'd touched, the skin was warm. Sensitive. The man was frightening, volatile, *violent;* qualities she abhorred. She should not like his touch.

"Would you like me to kill him for you?" Joachim asked, surprising her.

She blinked in confusion and pointed to the sentinel at the door.

"No. The one who hurt you."

She hesitated a moment, then shook her head.

"Power is good," he said, his voice suddenly growing weak. "Hurting a woman is not." His eyelids drifted closed, but he pried them open.

She didn't know whether he believed what he'd said or not. Either way, he struck her as one of those people who could not control their actions when they were enraged. After today's sword fight...

"What's your name?" he asked.

"Brenna."

"Brenna," he said, the name like a treat savored on his tongue. But in the next instant, his mouth pulled tight in a grim line. Fury darkened his eyes, churning like a violent sea. "Where is Shivawn?"

She found herself rising from the bed, trembling. In the blink of an eye, he'd become angry. Why? What had she done?

He frowned as his eyelids dipped shut once more. "Why are you backing away from me, woman? Are you going back to your lover?" The last was sneered.

Before he could rise from the bed and grab her, she turned and fled the room, unsure where to go. Only knowing she had to leave this place. Had to leave *him*.

JOACHIM FORCED his eyelids to open and cursed long after Brenna had gone. He'd never felt so powerless, and the feeling infuriated him. He didn't want her to go to Shivawn. He wanted her to stay. With him. Wanted her to talk to him.

Had he been able, he would have vaulted from the bed and forced her to return. *He* was master here. But he couldn't even comfort her or thank her properly for taking care of him. Instead, Shivawn had the privilege. Not that the man would thank Brenna for helping *him*.

"Follow her, damn you," he commanded Broderick, who stood in the doorway. "Make sure she arrives at her destination safely."

"You had best watch who you order about," the warrior growled before taking off after Brenna.

Joachim wanted to blame Valerian for this predicament, but he couldn't. He'd issued the challenge, and his cousin had beaten him fairly. As a man who valued power and control above all else, he respected Valerian's win. And, at the moment, he understood his cousin's need for the pale woman, his willingness to do anything to keep her.

Joachim would have done anything just then to have Brenna.

CHAPTER FIFTEEN

HIS OWN WOMAN wanted him to stay away from her so badly that she'd held a weapon on him, Valerian thought as he stormed into the dining hall. "My own mate," he grumbled. "Refusing to pleasure me. Refusing to let me pleasure her."

Sadly, he knew not what to do about the situation.

Except, perhaps, drink himself into oblivion.

He halted abruptly when he spied Shivawn at the table, a different flask in each hand. The man already had red, glassy eyes and was wobbling in his chair.

Shivawn was young, nearing one hundred years of age. A babe, really, compared to Valerian's six hundred. Shivawn was a strong warrior, though, and swift on his feet. He did not hesitate to render a death blow to his foes. In fact, if an enemy needed torturing, Shivawn would volunteer for the job.

Good man, that.

However, Shivawn was impulsive, led by his emotions. Perhaps he was that way because his father had been staid, a rule follower in the extreme. Never deviating. Like Valerian's own father. Neither of them wanted to end up like their sires. Both men had died battling demons. Demons who had claimed to be allies, only to change their minds during a peace talk and slaughter every nymph present.

Such was the way with demons. Valerian, of course, had gathered the men, babe that he'd been, and attacked their camp the very next day. Much blood had spilled during the ensuing battle. Demon blood. It had been his first victory—the first of many.

Where was his victory now? He could defeat an army of demons, but not one small wisp of a woman.

"Women," Shivawn groused.

"Women," Valerian agreed. He plopped beside the warrior and grabbed one of the flasks. Only half of the liquid remained. He drained the contents in one gulp. Unfortunately, he found no comfort in the river burning to his stomach.

"My bedmate doesn't want me," Shivawn said bitterly. "How is that possible? I am a nymph."

"As am I. I am king. I rule this place. My word is law."

"Maybe—maybe Brenna only likes other women."

"Ha! Her sexual preference doesn't matter. All women like nymphs. They adore us."

Shivawn's shoulders slumped. "I do not understand her. She actually fears me. Fears *me,* as if I am a monster who wants only to hurt her. I have never hurt a woman, Valerian. Never. All women worship me. Desire me." He sighed heavily.

"Why are you complaining? Your woman did not hold you at sword's length." Valerian confiscated the other flask and drained it. "Besides, Brenna is not your mate. Why do you not find another lover?" Oh, that he could take his own advice. He should find another since Shaye did not want him.

No, that wasn't true. She wanted him. He'd seen the desire in her eyes, heard it in her voice, watched the way her nipples beaded. She just didn't *want* to want him, and so fought him every step of the way.

Their kiss, though…

She'd erupted, come alive. A living spark. She hadn't hidden her desire then. She'd reveled in it. Her body had burned for his, desperate for him to quench the seemingly unstoppable need.

Why do you not find another? drifted again through his mind. His hands clenched around the empty flasks, and he slammed them onto the tabletop. He didn't want another woman. Couldn't abide the thought of having another in his bed, actually. His arms craved Shaye. His legs craved Shaye. His *cock* craved Shaye. She exuded a special scent, and every part of him recognized other women as imitations. Imposters.

Shaye had wrapped him in a terrible and wonderful and hated and loved…lust. Consuming lust. How could he win her? She'd said she craved her home and her job. Well, he could not give her the first, but he could give her the second. Anti-cards, she'd said. She liked to write, she'd said. First thing in the morning he would deliver canvas and writing stones.

Would that melt her resistance?

He could only hope.

Aside from winning her affections, he wanted to know everything about her. Her past, her present, her future. What had made her the woman that she was? While he wanted to ram her defenses into the ground, just plow right through them, he suspected she would need gentle wooing. He sighed.

"…can't find them," Shivawn said.

"I am sorry. I was thinking of Shaye. What did you say?"

Frowning, Shivawn plucked a crumb from the table and tossed it aside. "The only women without lovers are the three surface women who came here first. I cannot find them. And believe me, I have searched."

"They are around here somewhere." He rubbed his jaw. "They will show up sometime, I am sure. You can claim one and give your black-haired wench to another warrior."

"Women," Shivawn said again. He stood, stalked to the kitchens and returned with an armful of bejeweled flasks.

"Women," Valerian agreed. He quickly drained two of them, the contents no longer burning. "I have told Shaye how much pleasure I can give her, but she does not listen."

"Perhaps she needs to hear a few testimonials from your former lovers."

He blinked. In his current state, that didn't seem like such a bad idea. She could assume his profession was nothing more than pride, but she would have to believe the women who'd actually experienced the bliss of his touch. Wouldn't she? Nothing else had convinced her.

"I do not think Brenna would care about testimonials." Shivawn's voice was a little slurred. "I think she would still fear me. Women," he growled. "We don't need them."

"Don't need them," Valerian parroted, raising yet another flask. But the declaration tasted foul in his mouth. His survival depended on Shaye, so yes, he needed her.

"I'm becoming weak as a babe," Shivawn admitted.

"Earlier, I tripped and fell in the hall like a clumsy dragon hatchling."

"The gods surely cursed us when they bound us to sex."

"Before coming here I would have said they blessed us. I would have said we were obviously their favored."

Neither of them had that illusion at the moment.

"Much longer," Shivawn added, "and not even self-pleasuring will help me."

"Don't our women know we have needs?"

For a long while, neither man spoke. Shivawn finally said, "I don't think I ever want to find my mate. Perhaps I will wander all of Atlantis, servicing every woman I encounter."

"The danger in that, my friend, is that many women will become enslaved to you. And since there will be no other nymphs with you, you will have to see to their needs. *All* of their needs, on your own. They will become resentful of the time you spend with the others—and if they left behind a spurned lover, that lover will hunt you down for vengeance."

Shivawn glared at him. "Thank you for destroying my dream," he said dryly.

"You are welcome."

"Theophilus's human mate isn't giving him problems. Why is that, do you think? What is he doing that we are not?"

Valerian linked his fingers behind his neck and leaned back, casting his eyes to the ceiling. He blinked in surprise. Two mermaids had their breasts, hands and faces pressed to the crystal, gazing down at him and Shivawn.

When they realized he'd spotted them, they smiled prettily and waved. He returned the greeting, but he was groaning inside. He pinched the bridge of his nose—a gesture he'd caught Shaye making a few times. These girls wanted him, would have welcomed him eagerly if he but asked (and even if he didn't). Why wouldn't Shaye?

Shivawn slapped his arm to gain his attention. "Do you not have an answer?"

"I have forgotten your question," he said, looking away from the mermaids. "Sorry."

"You are distracted." A statement, not a question.

"Yes."

"I wish to know why Theophilus's human mate gives him no trouble."

Valerian, too, would have liked to know the answer to that. He pictured the woman in question. She was a timid little bird. Plain, yet possessing a deliciously plump body made for a man's hands. She had put up no fight whatsoever. Had simply taken one look at Theophilus and offered herself to him.

Next he pictured Shaye, who wanted the world to think of her as arctic and untouchable. Who would not speak of her family. Whose loveliness blinded him to all others. "Perhaps our women have secrets—sad, painful secrets. Secrets that allow them to hold themselves away from us and remain unaffected."

He knew Shaye had secrets.

Unlocking them was becoming an obsession. A necessity. Like breathing. Like sex. If she again refused to tell him, well, he might be reduced to plying her with drink. One way or another, he *would* learn the truth about her.

She would tell him every detail of her life. And in

the telling, perhaps he would find the key to softening her and winning her heart.

Shivawn jerked a hand through his dark hair, and the beads clanged together. "I will try and divine Brenna's secrets, and see if she will have me afterward," he said, parroting Valerian's thoughts. He paused. "This…working to win a woman. It is not fun."

"No."

"I have learned I do not like challenges."

"As have I."

"Women," Shivawn grumbled.

"Women," Valerian agreed.

They clinked their flasks together and drank deeply.

SHAYE LAY ON THE BED, wondering where Valerian was, what he was doing. *Who* he was doing.

Was he with another woman?

He'd been aroused when he left her. Painfully, utterly aroused. He professed to want no woman but her, but men often changed their minds. Especially when they were aroused and one woman told them no.

She wadded the silk sheets in her hands. She was mad at herself. Since Valerian had stormed out, she hadn't tried to escape. No, she'd bathed. She'd thought of Valerian. She'd tried on the pretty gowns in the closet. She'd thought of Valerian. She'd lain down for a nap.

She'd wanted Valerian.

She'd…missed him.

She dreamed of him when she closed her eyes and desired him when she opened them. There was no escaping the man's appeal.

The day had passed. Night had come and gone, and

morning had once more appeared. Neither offered her any relief. Today, she decided, she was going home. There could be no more lingering. No more distractions. She'd come too close, too damn close, to giving in and stripping for him. To allowing Valerian to take her—body and soul.

He was too dangerous. Too potent.

"Come."

Shaye nearly jumped out of her skin, startled as she was by *his* voice. Slowly she sat up, dreading—anticipating—what she'd see. Her heart leapt inside her chest the moment she spied him. He stood in the doorway, holding the curtain out of the way. He was total masculinity, pure sex. He wore black pants, a black shirt that tied at the collar, and his hair was in complete disarray.

"Come," he repeated. There was no hint of emotion in his tone. His eyes were taut, his mouth thinned in…displeasure? Pain? He held out his hand and motioned for her with his fingers.

"Why?" Remaining in place, hesitant, she fingered the ends of her still-damp hair. "Where are you taking me?"

He again motioned with his fingers. "I am not going to pounce on you, if that is what you fear." How distant he was, so unlike his usual self.

Had he already given up on her? Did he now plan to take her back to the surface? Disappointment rocked her. *You should be thrilled, you big dummy!*

She gulped, but stood and walked to him. She clasped his proffered hand. He immediately turned and tugged her through the hallway. "What's going on?" she asked.

"I must practice with my men. To ensure you do not

cause mischief while I am preoccupied, you will stay in a room with the other women."

"Oh." He wasn't taking her back, and she was mad about that—really she was.

A few minutes later they reached the room in question. She didn't utter a single protest, even though she did not want to spend time with the lovesick, sex-crazed females from her mother's wedding. *Well, you can always use the time away from Valerian to escape. Like you freaking planned.*

Yes, that's exactly what she'd do. No more mooning over Valerian. No more crazy thoughts about staying.

Several men stood guard at the entrance. One held a bundle of paper and thin, colored rocks. Valerian scooped them up and handed them to her. "I thought you might enjoy writing some of your anti-cards."

A moment passed before his words registered, and her mouth fell open. With shaky hands, she clasped the bundle. How…sweet. He'd gathered these for her. Her stomach tightened with several different emotions—emotions she didn't want to name. He hadn't gone the easy route and given her flowers and candy. No, he'd searched for something she loved, something specific to her.

"Thank you," she said softly.

"My pleasure," he said, his voice rough. He pivoted to the men, saying, "I want two guards—no, *four* guards posted at this door at all times. No one is to enter or leave without my permission. Understood?"

Each of the warriors nodded.

Valerian turned back to her. "I must go."

Their eyes met, and she fought the urge to rise on

tiptoe and breathe in his scent, absorb his strength. *Kiss me,* she silently beseeched, hating herself for the desire but unable to stop it. In the end he didn't. He held back the curtain and gave her a gentle push inside the room.

"Until later," she heard him whisper. And then he was gone.

CHAPTER SIXTEEN

"I'VE NEVER, IN ALL MY LIFE, been pleasured like I was last night."

"Me, either."

"God, me, either."

Shaye gazed around the room. There was a couch, a thousand silk pillows, books that looked as if they were made from canvas rather than paper, needles and thread. A hobby room, she thought. Great. Women were everywhere, a sea of twitters and laughter. She'd never seen a better example of a harem.

Shaye's gaze strayed to the curtain-covered door, and she bit her lip. *Now is the time.* "Ladies," she said quietly. She clapped her hands until she'd gained everyone's attention. "It's time to think about getting out of here. There are enough of us to overtake the guards. We can look for a way home."

Someone laughed. "Why in the world would we want to do that?"

"I'm not leaving," someone else said.

"I'm staying."

"If you try to run, I'll scream for Valerian."

Shaye gritted her teeth in frustration and in irritation. "Why do you want to stay?" She said the words for herself, as well. "You mean nothing to these guys."

For over an hour the ladies lauded the sexual ecstasy they'd been given. For over an hour she countered with speeches of home and respect. Several women finally got tired of listening to her, and called for the guards. Much to her chagrin, Valerian was summoned.

It didn't take long for the king to respond. He strode into the room without preamble. He was sweaty and dirty. He didn't say anything, just pounded to her, wrapped her in his arms, and proceeded to kiss the breath right out of her.

The kiss lasted only a few moments, just enough to remind her of his taste and drive her crazy as it consumed all of her senses. When he pulled away, he was panting. Women were closing in on him, reaching for him…touching him.

Shaye scowled at them.

"Be good," he said, "and I will take you into the Outer City when I finish training." With that he left.

Oh, unfair, she thought, to issue such a promise.

Disappointed sighs filled the room. Trying to slow her erratic heartbeat and cool her heated skin, Shaye found an open corner and plopped onto a pillow. She couldn't help it; she really wanted to see the Outer City in person. The single glance she'd had wasn't nearly enough. From the moment she'd first spied it, she'd wanted to breathe its air and absorb its ambiance.

She would escape tomorrow.

I'm not relieved about this. I'm not happy to spend more time with Valerian. To distract herself, she used her new supplies to make anti-cards. Making the cards had always been a big stress reliever for her, and if she'd ever needed to de-stress, it was now. She already had a few good ones in mind.

"As the days go by, I'm so happy you're not here to ruin them for me."

"You want a piece of me? Oops, sorry. I already gave one to your brother."

A third card popped into her head, and it was so unlike the others that she blinked in surprise. "Some men aren't so bad. I guess."

Before she could ponder it, someone said, "I'm so jealous that you were chosen by Valerian, the hulking blond beefcake." In that moment all eyes focused on Shaye. "Was he as good as he looks?"

"He even fought over you." Another sighed dreamily. "How romantic is that? I'm Jaclyn, by the way."

"I'm Shelly," said an elegant, almost regal blonde. "I belong to Aeson."

"I'm Barrie," said a plain, soft-spoken brunette.

"Rissa," said the redhead who'd wanted to fight her for getting too close to Broderick. Now she appeared jovial, even affectionate.

On and on they introduced themselves. Though they'd been wedding guests and friends of her mother's—or maybe the new husband's—Shaye hadn't really met them until now. "Aren't we the luckiest girls in the world?" Jaclyn said.

Several squeals of delighted agreement erupted.

"Well, was Valerian good?" Barrie asked eagerly. "If he walks like a wet dream and talks like a wet dream…I bet the king fucks like an animal."

Shaye bet he did, too.

And she didn't like this woman wondering about Valerian, perhaps picturing him naked. A sense of possessiveness rose up inside her, hot and angry. It was a nail-baring, teeth-snarling possessiveness that surprised her with its undeniable force.

You don't want him, remember? You held him off with a sword. You had your chance with him and didn't take it, so let him go. She should be happy someone else wanted him. She should encourage Barrie to find out for herself if Valerian did indeed fuck like an animal.

She didn't, though.

She couldn't.

Something inside her, a greediness she hadn't known she possessed, said, *Mine. Only mine.* She hated the feeling, but there it was. It refused to leave.

Barrie and the others soon got tired of awaiting her answer. Actually they forgot about Shaye entirely, and resumed their conversation about their lovers as if it had never been interrupted.

Shaye stretched her legs and propped her feet on top of a pillow. Frustration—for so many different reasons—ate at her. Sexual frustration? Yes. Confusion? Definitely. Sighing, she gripped her notebook and stones to her chest. She didn't want to become one of these lovesick women. Didn't want to lose herself in a man.

And that's what would happen if she gave in to Valerian. Foolishly, that seemed to matter less and less.

A short while later, different warriors began to straggle into the room, collecting their women. They were covered in sweat and sand, even blood. Each time the curtain lifted, she found herself tensing with dread and anticipation. Would it be Valerian?

It never was.

Soon there were only a few females remaining. One was the girl with curly black hair and sad brown eyes, the one who had struggled on the beach and, like Shaye, hadn't wanted to be chosen by a warrior. Shaye watched her for a moment, then gathered her supplies, stood and walked to her.

Normally Shaye didn't approach strangers and strike up conversations. That totally negated her "remain detached" preference. But there was something vulnerable about this girl. Something almost…haunting. She found herself drawn to her, found herself sympathizing with her obvious unhappiness.

"Hi. I'm, uh, Shaye." God, she felt awkward. Without an invite, she sat.

The girl flicked her a nervous glance. "Brenna," she said. Her voice was deep, rough, halting and strained. A smoker?

"I've noticed that you're the only other person who isn't ecstatic to be here. Were you…did the one who picked you…"

Brenna shook her head.

"Good." Shaye sighed with relief. Just in front of her, there was a table piled with food. She leaned over, swiped a handful of bread squares, then handed a few to Brenna. They ate in silence for a bit. "I, uh, also noticed you said you were a healer and that you were put in charge of Joachim's care."

A nod—this one hesitant.

"How's he doing? Will he live?"

Another nod—this one sure. And, Shaye saw, there was a gleam of something…hot in the girl's brown eyes. Oh, oh, oh. What was this? Did Brenna have a crush on her patient? "You like him?" she asked.

Brenna shook her head violently. Protesting too much, in Shaye's estimation. She knew all about that. "Scared," the girl said.

Scared. Yeah, Shaye had experienced her fair share of that emotion. In the beginning, her fear had been of the unknown and of whether or not Valerian meant to hurt her. Now, well, her fear was for an entirely different reason. If she desired Valerian so intensely now, what would happen if she actually knew what it was like to make love with him?

Don't you dare find out, either. Keep fighting the attraction. "I wonder why all the women are slaves to their hormones and we aren't," she mused aloud.

"Smart," Brenna said, and they both laughed.

But Shaye's humor quickly faded. "I don't feel smart."

"Me, either." Brenna sighed dejectedly, her humor gone, too.

Shaye opened her mouth to ask why, but her gaze snagged on the two men who suddenly entered the room. Shivawn and Valerian. Valerian stopped and stood utterly still, watching her. A shiver of awareness swept through her.

Unbidden, she eased to her feet. Her grip tightened on the notebook, but she never removed her eyes from him. He was the most beautiful sight she'd ever beheld, and all she could think about just then was his mouth on hers.

"Come," he said, just as he had earlier that morning.

She did. Without protest. Brenna and everything else forgotten. *Mine,* her mind whispered, all of her possessive instincts resurfacing. He led her through the hallway, and her heart gave a nervous flutter. He looked determined. Hardened.

"Where are we going?" she asked.

"The Outer City, just as I promised."

VALERIAN ESCORTED SHAYE out of the palace and into the afternoon heat. The crystal dome glowed brightly, and birds whistled playfully. They hadn't left yet, but already he had a fierce need to return. So when he reached the stables, he quickly commanded one of the centaurs to prepare for travel. The dark horse-man leapt into action, trotting over to him.

"It will be my pleasure to take you into the city, great one."

Shaye gaped up at him. "Uh, that horse is half *man*," she said, "and you expect me to *ride* him?"

"Yes."

She gulped. Valerian mounted and held out his hand. Tentative, she placed her palm over his. He lifted her up behind him, loving the feel of her pressed so close to him. Much as he loved it, though, it increased his need to hurry this trip along. *You want her to fall in love with the city, remember?*

"Was practice rough?" she asked after the centaur began descending the cliffs. She sounded nervous.

Valerian didn't answer. He'd worked his men and himself until sweat had poured from them. Until exhaustion had set in. He'd needed an outlet for his frustration, but it hadn't worked.

There was only one thing that would work.

Shaye, in his bed. Shaye, joined with him.

He'd never been more determined to win her. "I'm sorry, but we can't stay long."

"I don't care. I'm just happy to visit."

Happy. Just the way he wanted her.

They reached the Outer City in minutes. As usual, there were no females present. Having sensed his arrival, they'd hidden away. Only males—centaurs, minotaurs and formorions—manned the tables and booths, selling their wares, from food to jewelry to clothing.

While they were there, Valerian saw to Shaye's every need. Whenever she wanted to look, he took her. When she was thirsty, he bought her a drink. When she was hungry, he purchased her a snack. Delicious meat pies that seduced the taste buds. As time ticked by, he forgot about his need to return and simply enjoyed her.

At first she was wary of him and treated him coolly, distantly. But as a troupe of siren males passed them on the cobbled street, singing of love and passion, she began to warm, as if she just couldn't help herself. She watched with delight. Griffins charged by them, chasing their tails, and she skipped after them. He'd never seen her so relaxed; he'd never seen her so happy.

Looking at her, light glowing around her like a halo, love swelled inside his chest. *This* was the real Shaye. He knew it, sensed it, and he would bring her here every day if needed. Next time he would even take her to the waterfalls and watch her splash in the pools.

"Is anyone selling oranges, do you think?" she asked him wistfully, slowing to a walk.

"We shall see." But the few stands that sold the fruit were out. Shaye couldn't hide her disappointment, and Valerian vowed to search all of Atlantis if necessary. His mate would have her oranges before the day ended. "Ready to return?"

She cast a wistful glance at her surroundings. "Yes. I can't believe how beautiful this place is," she said as they found and mounted their centaur. "It's paradise."

She was paradise.

"Thank you for taking me."

"My pleasure, love. My pleasure."

She shivered against him.

His lips lifted in a slow smile—thankfully, it was a smile she could not see. Her defenses were down, just as he'd hoped, and her desire for him was making itself known. They reached the palace a few minutes later, and his blood heated. Almost time…

At the stable he dismounted and helped Shaye do the same. She no longer hesitated to touch him, he was pleased to notice. After thanking the centaur for the ride, he led Shaye to his room. Along the way, he sent a few of his men to search for oranges.

"I have a surprise for you," he told Shaye.

"Good or bad?"

Before collecting her for their journey, he'd gone to his own chambers and filled them with food. He'd scented the pool with oil and removed some of the wall sconces for a dimmer atmosphere. He'd also circled a group of satin pillows around a low table nearly spilling over with fruits and desserts.

When she saw what he'd done, her eyes widened. "You're…this is…"

"Sit at the table," he instructed.

For a minute she didn't obey. She glanced from him to the table, from the table to him. She gulped. He expected her to say something in rebuke, but she surprised him by walking to the table and sitting.

He loved the way his shirt and pants draped her slim body, but all he could think about was getting under them.

He removed his armor, unbuckling the links at his shoulders and letting the gold pieces fall to the ground. He washed his face in the basin, splashing cool water over his skin. He should have bathed before collecting her and taking her into the city, but he'd been too eager to see her. And a part of him hoped to bathe *with* her.

"We are going to have a conversation, you and I," he said, striding to the table. He sat across from her and filled two goblets with wine.

"Very well." She sounded reluctant, unsure. At least she hadn't denied him outright.

"I was going to have a few of my former lovers advise you of my wondrous skill, but in the light of day that did not seem so wise."

"No," she said, nearly choking on her wine.

"Instead, I will tell you something about myself. Then you will tell me something about yourself. A conversation, as I said. Do we have a bargain?"

"I hate talking about myself," she said, tracing her fingertip over the bottom of her glass.

"Still, you will do it." Pause. "Please."

She bit her lip again, but nodded.

He sipped his goblet of wine, watching her over the rim. "I will begin." He paused, gathering his thoughts. How did one go about getting to know another person? What bits of his past should he give her? "I…had a brother," he said. It was as good a place as any to start, he supposed, as it was something he rarely spoke of, and never with a woman. The subject was too painful.

"Had?" she asked softly.

Nodding, he pinched a piece of fish between his fingers and popped it into his mouth. He chewed, swallowed. "He was my twin. He was stolen when we were children."

Her eyes widened. "Who took him?"

Familiar rage filled him, but he tamped it down. "The gorgons."

"The gor—what?" She crossed her legs, one over the other, and leaned forward, propping her elbows on the table. He had her full attention. She was interested in what he had to say, and her usual shields were still down.

"Gorgons are a race of women who can turn a man to stone with only a glance. Snakes slither on their heads. They are evil. Pure evil."

Ah. Like Medusa. "Why did they take him?"

Valerian slid a platter of grapes toward her and beckoned her to take one. She did. "They hoped to trade him for my father's aid—which they did not receive," he added darkly. "They killed Verryn for it. He and I shared a mind connection, and when that went dark I knew that he was gone." The last emerged as little more than a whisper. He glanced to Shaye, trying to clear his mind of the hated memories. "Now, it's your turn. Tell me something about yourself."

What should she tell him? Shaye wondered. He'd divulged something personal, something painful. She could do no less. Still, she tried to hold herself back. Tried not to reveal too much. He'd completely enchanted her today, and she feared she would never recover.

"Once I had a stepsister who chopped off all my

hair," she said. "I was sleeping and didn't know it until the next morning." The action had been punishment, in her stepsister's mind, for cutting the hair of her favorite doll—a crime Shaye hadn't committed. That honor went to her stepbrother.

When ten-year-old Shaye ran crying to her mother, she was told to "work it out like a big girl."

Valerian's features darkened. "Your hair is sheer beauty, like moonlight and stars. Anyone who cuts it deserves death."

Pleasure speared her, utterly sweet in its headiness. She wasn't used to receiving compliments, yet Valerian gave them to her so readily. "Thank you."

"Living with the little demon must have been difficult."

"Yes. Thankfully, though, my mom was only married to her father for a year."

"Your mother had more than one mate?"

Shaye nodded. "She's had six."

"Six!"

She nodded again.

"Here a man takes but one mate, and keeps her for eternity."

She frowned as she considered his words. "What if the mated people are miserable with each other?"

"They must perform a blood ritual and offer a sacrifice."

"Oh, ick." She bit her bottom lip, not allowing herself to ask what *type* of sacrifice.

Valerian's gaze caught and lingered on her mouth, making her tingle, making her blood flow hot and achy. Then he shook his head, as if pulling himself from a spell. "What else would you like to know about me?" he asked.

"What about your first time?" she found herself saying. She wanted him, she did, and the more they talked, the weaker her resistance became. Surely hearing about his escapades with other women would strengthen her resolve.

He arched a brow. "Are you sure you want to know?" When she nodded, he said, "It was with my mother's favorite servant. She came into my room to bring me clean clothing, found me in the pool and joined me."

At her disappointed expression, he laughed. "What did you expect? Toys? Orgies?"

"Well, yeah."

His smile grew. "What about you? How was your first time?" The moment he asked the question, he tensed. His eyes darkened with what looked like fury.

Okay. What was he mad about now? "I, uh…" She stumbled over her words, even felt a blush heat her cheeks. "I haven't had a first time yet."

His mouth fell open. "Surely you jest."

"Hardly. Look," she said, defensive. "I never wanted to have to deal with the problems associated with a sexual relationship."

"What problems?" Valerian's shock had yet to fade; it only seemed to intensify. Shaye was virgin. She was untouched.

She was his.

He wanted her more in that moment than ever before. He wanted to be the only man to taste her. Now. Ever.

"Emotional entanglements are messy," she said. "And if I don't get involved, I don't have to worry about getting hurt."

"I will never hurt you, Shaye. I will never lie to you."

He'd meant to learn more about her, to let her learn more about him. But he found himself saying, "I think, perhaps, the only way to convince you of this is to show you. So from this moment on, there will be no more talking. Only doing."

CHAPTER SEVENTEEN

"I AM GLAD YOU RETURNED," Joachim said.

Brenna inched toward his bed. Shivawn had escorted her here and now stood at the doorway behind her, watching and guarding her. She'd allowed it before, and she allowed it now. Usually, however, she could not stand having anyone behind her. That was how the attack had happened. Ethan had come at her from behind, surprising her, before flipping her around and—She cut off the thought.

They'd been together for a while, but his temper had grown blacker and blacker. When she'd tried to end things, he'd snapped. She should have died that day, so badly did he hurt her. So many times since then, she'd *wished* to die.

But today, having someone behind her—having *Shivawn* behind her—didn't scare her. She was coming to like Shivawn and his gentleness. Despite everything and even in such a short amount of time, she was beginning to feel safe with him and had even pictured herself doing…intimate things with him. Him, she assured herself. Not Joachim.

Earlier, when she'd been locked inside that room with the other women and they'd been retelling their sensual exploits, wanton images had bombarded her. She hadn't been able to picture the man's face as he pleasured her in her mind, but she'd known it was Shivawn because she'd felt protected. *He* made her feel that way. Joachim…didn't. He made her feel dizzy and achy and weak, completely out of control.

At one time, she might have welcomed those things. Yeah, she'd once loved sex. She'd once loved men. But that had changed. Or so she'd thought.

It's Shivawn who turns you on. Has to be. Except, she'd been waiting for this moment all day, wanting to see Joachim again, to hear his voice and trace her hands over his body. That, she couldn't deny and it scared her. He was nothing like Shivawn. He wasn't kind, and he wasn't gentle. He was a hard, volatile warlord who wasn't afraid to use his fists. Yet even now, thinking about him made her heart race, and not just with fear.

Stupid, she told herself for the thousandth time. If she ever allowed herself to be intimate with a man again, it would be with someone like Shivawn.

Stop thinking about sex, Johnston. Get to work. Silently she cleaned and rebandaged Joachim's wounds, glad to see he was healing nicely. No sign of infection. He was still too weak to rise, but his strength would return. He would even have full use of his arms and leg, once the tissue reconnected.

Just as she was finishing up, a new man stepped inside the room. He carried a long, menacing sword; she saw it from the corner of her eye and immediately tried to jump toward Shivawn, the only safe haven available, but Joachim latched on to her hand and held tight.

The action terrified her—not only because it was abrupt, but also because it fired her blood in a way it shouldn't. She cried out and was instantly released. She stumbled to her feet, away from all of the men.

"You are needed in the dining hall," the intruder said to Shivawn.

Shivawn looked at her, then Joachim, ignoring the stranger. He frowned fiercely. "Did he hurt you?" he asked her.

She rubbed her wrist and shook her head no.

"Valerian has summoned you," the stranger added impatiently.

Shivawn flicked the man an irritated glance, then stepped forward and gave her shoulder a comforting squeeze. "I hate to leave you, but I must obey the king. Will you be all right without me?"

Panic sprouted wings inside her chest. She didn't want him to go. Truly, he'd become her safety net in this unknown and wild land. But she forced herself to nod. Depending so desperately on one person was foolish.

"Would you like to go with me?" he asked.

Again, she shook her head no. She would stay. She would be brave. And she wouldn't allow Joachim to affect or scare her. *Easier said than done, Johnston.*

Shivawn gave Joachim a brief but dark look, gently caressed Brenna's cheek, and then strode into the hallway, following the messenger. Brenna and Joachim were alone.

You can do this. You can do this. Joachim's too weak to do anything to you. Slowly she turned toward him and eased back onto the bed. She was careful not to look into his eyes, those blue, blue eyes that seemed to cut straight to her soul. Her fingers shook as she finished wrapping the last bandage.

"I am Joachim," he said, breaking the silence.

"I know." Her voice trembled as much as her hands. "Should not have challenged king."

She imagined his nostrils flaring in fury. Still, she forged ahead. "Silly. Strength lies in compassion, not battles."

For a moment the air was so charged she thought he meant to yell at her. But he didn't. He changed the subject, admitting grudgingly, "I thought of you last night." Half pain, half accusation. "And today. I cannot seem to get you out of my mind."

Before she could stop it, her gaze jumped to his. She gasped at what she saw. Desire. White-hot desire. Her hands stilled, poised over his thigh. She had a sheet draped over his middle—to protect her modesty rather than his. The sheet was higher than it had been a moment ago.

"I see fear in your eyes," he said, still speaking low, voice heated. "But I also see interest."

She bit her lip and shook her head. She would not admit to any type of interest. That would only encourage him. But…

"Talk to me, Brenna," he said. "Tell me of yourself."

His quiet beseeching surprised her. She never would have expected it from such a power-hungry warlord. "Wh-what would. You. Like to. Know?" Her throat was constricted, making it harder for her to speak.

"Everything." Joachim tilted his head and regarded Brenna more intently. "I want to know everything about you." Already he knew her smell—violets and the sunshine he'd encountered so briefly on the surface. He knew her voice—scratchy and harsh, eliciting visions of passion and naked bodies.

Now he wanted to know her past. Her likes. Her dislikes. All the things that made her Brenna, the woman who obsessed him more with every second that passed. *Strength lies in compassion,* she'd said. He wanted to snort at that, but couldn't. He didn't know why.

"We will begin with something easy," he said. "What is your favorite color?"

She glanced at the door, as if wondering what she should do. Stay and talk, or run. "Blue," she finally replied.

If she were his woman, he would give her all the sapphires he owned. "Do you have family?" A family she missed? Wished to return to?

She shook her head. "Dead."

He should not have felt relieved, but he did. "How did they die?"

"Car accident."

Car? He was intrigued by a "car" that could kill an entire family, but was more curious about Brenna herself. "I am sorry for your loss, little one."

Features shadowed, she waved a hand through the air. Her hand was shaking, he noticed. "Long time ago," she said in that broken voice.

He wanted to grab her up and kiss her, anything to wipe away those shadows, but he ended up fisting the sheets and keeping his hands at his sides. "Do you like this new world? Atlantis?"

Her gaze drifted away from him, onto the wall behind him. She shook her head.

"Why not?" Disappointment hummed through his

blood. He'd hoped she had already come to love it as he did.

"Scary," she admitted softly. She traced a fingertip over the sheet.

"You are frightened of us?"

She gave no response. Didn't move a muscle.

"I would never hurt you, Brenna," he told her as gently as his fierce timbre would allow. "This I swear to you."

A shiver stole through her. "Might not mean to, but—"

"Never. *Never.*"

"What are you saying to her, Joachim?" Shivawn demanded as he strode back into the room. "You have no right to use that tone with her."

Brenna jolted to her feet, looking between them with fear in her eyes.

"Watch *your* tone, boy," Joachim snapped. "You're scaring her."

Shivawn's features instantly softened. "I'm sorry," he told her. "I was called away to look for oranges, but I'm here now. I'm not angry, I promise you."

Brenna gazed between the two men, a little...aroused and unsure who—or what—was causing that arousal. They were trying to soothe her and it was working. It was working! She was actually standing between two men who despised each other, two men who could attack and kill at any moment, and her fear was dissipating.

How are they doing this to me? she mused, dazed.

Even more shocking, as the fear left her, something else took its place: desire. White-hot, consuming. An image of naked, straining bodies suddenly filled her mind. Once again, she couldn't see the man's face, but the image was so lifelike she even heard the pleasure-moans of the couple. Her nipples tightened; moisture pooled between her legs.

Joachim bared his teeth and hissed in a breath. In fury? "You're aroused. I can smell it on you."

Her cheeks heated to a blazing inferno.

"I can, too," Shivawn said brokenly. "Brenna…"

She heard him take a step toward her, heard the thump of his boot. Again, there was no fear inside her. *What's wrong with me? What's happening to me?* This wasn't like her, not at all.

Joachim eased to a sitting position, and Shivawn continued to move forward.

"You are in need of a man, Brenna," Joachim said, showing no mercy to her embarrassment. "But you are afraid of your desire, yes? You must be, to resist."

"Yes," Shivawn answered for her. "She is."

"Have you ever been with a man?" Joachim asked her.

Breathless, she nodded.

"Did you like it?" Shivawn.

Another nod. She should stop this line of questioning, but a part of her was strangely relieved to have it out in the open.

"The man who hurt you and damaged your voice," Joachim persisted. "Did he make you afraid of sex?"

She hesitated for a long while, finally opting for the truth. "Yes."

Both men growled low in their throats, as if they wanted to kill the man with their bare hands. Still, the fear did not return. "I understand now," Shivawn said. "Once a woman has been forced, she is not the same."

"Yes," Joachim said. "I, too, understand." His voice sounded far away, a little weak.

"Joachim?" she said, sudden concern for him making her forget all else.

He fell back onto the bed, and his head lolled onto the pillow, his skin draining of color.

She hurried to him. "Okay?"

"Dizzy. Weak," he admitted in an enraged snarl. "Shouldn't have sat up."

She could tell the lack of strength did more than anger him; it unnerved him. As much of a fighter as he was, he was probably used to absolute control. Hadn't he told the king, Valerian, that he respected and liked him, but he just didn't want to take orders anymore?

Finally bits of her fear returned. Control. Something she valued, as well. She couldn't relinquish hers, no matter how aroused she became. And to give herself to either of these men was to give up her precious control. How could she have forgotten that, even for a second?

Frowning, she moved toward the door.

Realizing she meant to leave, Joachim uttered an abrupt, "Stay."

There was total command in his voice. Oh, yes, he expected absolute obedience. Shaking her head, she backed up another step. Her eyes were unnaturally wide, she knew they were.

"Brenna," he said. He tried to sit up again, but he didn't have the strength this time. "I will not always be so weak." There was a warning in his tone.

She maneuvered around Shivawn, her gaze again darting between the two men. They were so beautiful, it almost hurt to look at them. And they were offering everything she'd once wanted for herself: love, passion, companionship. *That dream is dead, remember? It's safest that way.*

But a wave of longing swept through her. For a moment she wished one of the men would reach for her. Touch her…kiss her…slip inside her, sinking, gliding erotically. No, not one of the men. Shivawn, she told herself. But it wasn't green eyes she suddenly glimpsed inside her mind, above her, staring down at her. The man's eyes were blue. She scrubbed a hand over her own eyes to block the image.

How could someone like Joachim arouse her like this when no man had been able to do so for many years?

"I won't hurt you," Shivawn said. He held up his hands, all innocence.

"Come to me, Brenna," Joachim intoned.

"No," she told Shivawn and Joachim grinned. "No," she told Joachim, wiping away his smugness. Better to be without both of them.

"I want to know you," Shivawn said. His voice was gentle. "I'll keep you safe. I won't let anyone else hurt you."

"Do not let your need for safety destroy your love of life. I can teach you to conquer your fear and finally live again," Joachim told her.

Shivawn faced Joachim, and the two squared off. "I can teach her to conquer her fear, too."

"Maybe. But you will never truly make her happy," Joachim snapped.

Perhaps neither of them could, and the knowledge filled her with a keen sense of disappointment. For with the return of his anger, Joachim had reminded her of exactly why she would never allow herself to be with him. If he ever directed that anger at her, he would kill her. *Control,* she reminded herself.

For a moment, that one precious moment when the fear had vanished, she'd thought to really *live* again. Now…knowing such a thing was impossible, she ran out of the room before she did something stupid. Like cry.

SHIVAWN DIDN'T FOLLOW her, but remained in the room. For a long while he and Joachim did not speak.

"I want her," Joachim admitted softly.

Shivawn's hands tightened into fists. He'd known that, but hearing the words… "I want her, too, and she is my woman. Who do you think will get her?"

"I will challenge you for her," Joachim gritted out.

"Not accepted. She looked at me with desire, and I find that I need to see that look again."

"That desire was for me, boy. *Me.* Anything you saw was merely a reflection of that."

Shivawn frowned. Yes, she *had* looked at Joachim with desire. More desire than a woman had ever projected at him, and the knowledge did not settle well. But she had wanted him, too. He would swear to that. Frustrated, he tossed his arms in the air. "So where does that leave us?"

"Give her to me."

"No."

Joachim stroked his chin with two fingers. "I will not give up. I will pursue her."

"Is that a threat?"

"Merely a warning. I want her, and I will do all that is in my power to win her."

Shivawn nearly drew his sword, his anger was so great. He felt protective of Brenna, wanted her to be happy, and couldn't stand to think of such a delicate creature with this power-hungry warrior. "If you scare her, I will kill you. Do you understand me? I will kill you."

A dark cloud descended over Joachim's face. "I would never scare her."

"Ha! You scared her with your forcefulness. That's why she ran."

"Do not try and pretend you know her reasons, and do not pretend you know what she needs. You scared her just as badly or she would have given herself to you by now."

"Perhaps she will. Tonight," Shivawn taunted.

Fury blazed in Joachim's eyes. "No. She will not give herself to you. That I know, because you will never understand her the way I do."

"You? How do *you* think to understand her?" Shivawn said through clenched teeth.

"That you have to ask proves my point." Joachim closed his eyes, bringing Brenna's innocent face to the forefront of his mind. Someone had hurt her during sex—someone who would feel the end of Joachim's sword one day soon. If he had to travel to the surface and hunt the bastard down, he would.

He would stake his life on the fact that Brenna had been a woman of passion and vitality once. There was a spark in her eyes she just couldn't hide. Deep inside, no matter how strong her fears, she had to crave that type of life again.

He could win her from Shivawn, he knew he could. She'd looked at him with undiluted passion, and he knew she would not be happy with anyone else. When she'd looked at Shivawn, there had been no passion.

Desire, yes, but it hadn't been sexual. It had been...
fearful, as a child sometimes looked to its mother. For
protection.

Which meant Joachim did indeed scare her. Which
also meant he could not claim her until he had conquered her fears. Forever.

And he would. Whatever was necessary.

More than he wanted his own satisfaction, he wanted
hers. *Strength lies in compassion.* Again her words played
through his mind. Compassion...something she valued.

She needed something special for her first time. Oh,
he knew she wasn't virgin. She'd said as much. After
her torture—for that's what it had been—she'd cut
herself off from men. So her next time *would* be like her
first time. She'd cut herself off from desires and the
sweetest of intimacies. She needed an avalanche of both
to push her out of that staid existence. *Compassion.*

Once he was healed...there would be no stopping him.

"I will have her, Shivawn," he said. "It's me she will
always crave in her bed."

A muscle ticked in Shivawn's jaw. "You're wrong.
She wants safety. To her, *I* am safety. Not you. And
I'll prove it."

POSEIDON HUMMED with the intensity of his relish.
Waves whirled and crashed against him, their cerulean
beauty lethal to mere mortals. He tasted salt in his
mouth, smelled it in his nose, its familiarity increasing
his enjoyment.

No Atlantean was permitted to enter the surface.
Well, that was not entirely true. A Guardian of the portal
was allowed to enter to protect the secrets of the under-

ground city. But none of the nymphs were guardians—
and they had entered anyway, it seemed. It was now
Poseidon's greatest joy to punish them.

"So. You're telling me that you saw the nymphs steal
human women from the surface and bring them into
Atlantis?" he asked, his voice booming across the ocean
floor. Sand jumped, floating high in the water; pink and
white coral vibrated. Colorful fish darted in every direction, desperate to escape his vicinity.

The two mermaids before him bowed their heads.
Both possessed hair as inky black as the night, and
those tresses blended together, floating around their
delicate shoulders.

"Yes," Denae said.

"Yes," Marie agreed.

"Through the portal?" he insisted. He slammed the
end of his trident into the marble base he stood upon,
cracking it from one end to the other. This was the most
excitement he'd experienced in ages.

"Yes," both women said again, in unison.

"Very good." Poseidon's lips lifted slowly as he
stepped from the dais, his white robe dancing around
his ankles. From where he stood, he could see the huge
crystal dome encompassing the cursed city. It radiated
golden rays, sparkling like a mound of glitter. He
whisked himself to it, far away one moment, in front
of it the next. He needed no portal or doorway to let him
inside a world he himself had helped create. He simply
walked through the crystal as if it were not there.

He didn't yet want the citizens to know of his arrival,
so he kept himself hidden in a cloak of invisibility. He
breathed deeply of the pure, salty air. Closed his eyes,

enjoyed. Yes, he had turned his back on this land and its people for far too long. A mistake.

Hundreds of years had passed since he'd last entered, and all seemed quite tranquil. Minotaur children played in mud puddles, centaurs frolicked through thick, dewy grass. Vampires, dragons, griffins, cyclops, gorgons, harpies—they were all present.

These monstrosities were the gods' first attempt at creating Man. But they had grown more powerful than intended. A few of the gods had panicked and had cursed them to live under the sea. To Poseidon, they'd been abominations, ugly, but not a threat. Perhaps Poseidon and his immortal brothers and sisters should have destroyed the lot of them a millennium ago, but they'd thought to use the creatures for…what? Sex? Some of the women of Atlantis *were* pretty. Why had he not known that? For warring? The warriors *were* strong.

He couldn't recall the right answer, though, and didn't really care anymore.

How to punish the nymphs, how to punish the nymphs… Waving his trident, he whisked himself to the palace where Valerian, King of the Nymphs, now resided, maintaining invisibility. Within seconds he found himself in a room occupied by three very human women. They were discussing the various positions in which they'd been taken, the various positions in which they wanted to be taken, and how sad they were that Valerian now had a mate and paid them no attention.

Slowly Poseidon allowed his form to appear, though he took the appearance of a nymph warrior. Dark-haired, vivid blue eyes. Muscled. Tanned. When the women spotted him, they smiled, jumped to their feet and rushed to him.

"Did you come to make love to us?"

"You are the most beautiful man I've ever seen! More beautiful than Valerian, even."

"Silence," he said, the sound booming. Now was not the time for pleasure. Later, though… "Sit down." He motioned to the mound of pillows behind them.

They sat without question, without comment, eyeing him as if he were a delicious platter of chocolate. He settled beside them and allowed them to drape themselves over his legs, stroking him like a prized pet. Hmm, nice. Very nice.

Nymphs needed sex to survive. That was probably why they'd stolen the women. Still, their reasons didn't matter. The law had been created, the law must be obeyed. For Atlanteans to enter the surface world was to destroy it, or so prophecy claimed.

"First you will tell me exactly how you came to be here," he said. He would hear the damning truth firsthand. "Then you will tell me all you know about the nymphs."

One of the women kissed his thigh. Another kissed his shoulder. He closed his eyes, a blissful moan slipping from him. Answers, smanswers.

He cleared his throat. "You may tell me later," he said, and began to kiss them back. Already his venture into Atlantis was doing more for his boredom than a thousand tropical storms.

CHAPTER EIGHTEEN

"I AM DONE WAITING, Shaye."

Shaye jumped to her feet and backed away from Valerian as if he were poison. He still sat on the pillows, watching her, a smile curling the edges of his mouth. He didn't want to talk about his first time anymore—he wanted to give *her* a first time. *Languidly,* her mind added. *Deliciously. Quickly. Roughly. Softly.*

Panic? Yes. Anticipation? Absolutely. The gleam in his eyes…the husky richness of his voice…

"I need to rebandage your arm. Blood is, uh, seeping from it."

"After," he said, a heady entreaty. He stood inch by agonizing inch, unfolding his big, strong body. He never removed his gaze from her. His pants were tight over his muscled legs, but even tighter over his large erection.

Her eyes widened as he stepped closer. She'd wanted him many times since meeting him. Now, faced with the inevitability of it, she was panicky. More so than usual. "Stay where you are, okay. I need time to think about this."

"Thinking about it has gotten us nowhere." Stalking forward, he waved a hand toward the wall. "You will notice that I removed all the weapons."

Her wide gaze scanned the room. Sure enough, all the blades were missing. "Valerian," she said warningly.

"You simply fear what you do not know, Shaye. I realize that now."

"Stop!" She squared her shoulders, refusing to retreat yet again.

"You are my woman, yet you issue orders and expect them to be obeyed. Perhaps I should train and treat you as a warrior, then."

She forced out a laugh, but the sound was completely devoid of humor. "I'm not your woman." Yet. "And I'm not one of your warriors. What, are you going to fight me?"

"Oh, no. I'm going to give you a command and you're going to obey. If you fail to heed the command, I will punish you."

Her nostrils flared. "Don't you dare threaten me."

"Threaten? No, I merely promise." His eyelids dipped to half-mast, giving him a slumberous, I-need-a-bed cast.

"Didn't we discuss this the very first day? I will not accept punishment, and I will not obey you."

"Yes, you will. And you will enjoy it, I assure you."

She stomped her foot because she knew, *knew,* she was about to lose this battle. And a part of her was glad. "If you think I'll sit quietly while you spank me or something, you're wrong."

"What a naughty little mind you have, moon. I meant only to lash you with my tongue. If you prefer I spank you, I will do so. You know how I love to please you."

Evil, evil man. She shivered. "Is that how you punish your warriors? By licking them?"

"You saw how I punish my warriors. As I refuse to

hurt you, special consideration must be taken." Another step.

Her stomach twisted. She wanted to run to him, to take what he offered. True. But too much did she dread what would happen afterward. Would he dismiss her? Would he turn his attentions to another? Would she crave more of him? Fall in love, lose herself? Make a fool of herself for him? Would he ultimately hurt her, as everyone else in her life had?

"I need time, Valerian."

The words dripped between them along with all of her fear, all of her desires. He paused, looking tortured. Then he gave a stiff nod. He didn't want to, she saw it in his eyes, but he caved. Again. Her wish his to grant. "If time is what you desire, time you shall have." With barely a breath, he added, "I am in need of a bath. You may join me, if you wish, or watch me. The choice is yours."

"I…I choose neither." She wasn't going to bathe with him, and she wasn't going to watch him. Water droplets would trickle down his neck, perhaps catch on his nipples before falling to the ridges of muscle on his stomach. His soap-lathered hands would glide over his strength. "I want to go back to my room."

"You'll watch or you'll join. This is a give-and-take between us, Shaye. I give you time, and now you must give me something in return. Choose."

Her lashes nearly fused all the way together, leaving only a tiny line of vision. *He* occupied every inch of it. "What happened to giving me everything that I want?"

"You do not know what you want." He closed the rest of the gap between them, so close his chest brushed hers. Behind him, he left a trail of sand and blood. His wounds had opened. He showed not an ounce of pain, proving just how capable he truly was. A warrior, through and through.

His scent filled her nose, sexual and fierce. Heat curled from him, wrapping her in sultry coils, squeezing so tightly she had trouble dragging in her next breath. A rush of passion flooded her.

He was the kind of man women fantasized about but never actually encountered. And he continually offered himself to her, an all-you-can-eat smorgasbord of erotic delights. Whatever she could consume was hers for the taking.

How tempting it was to take....

He licked his lips and leaned toward her. Her heartbeat drummed in her ears, an eternity passing between each one. *Accept him or reject him, but do it now!*

Gathering her strength, she jerked away from him, nearly tripping on her own feet as she scrambled backward. "No," she said. "No."

A muscle ticked beneath his eyes. "Never has a word sounded more foul," he said between clenched teeth.

She raised her chin. "It's all you're going to hear from me."

"I could push you for more, Shaye. We both know I could. We both know you'd like it."

"No," she said again. This time it was a trembling, wispy entreaty.

Struggling with the force of his need, Valerian paused and studied Shaye. Damn this! He didn't want to force her to acknowledge her desires. He wanted her to accept them—and him—willingly.

When she'd told him she was virgin, he'd simply reacted. Blood and need had traveled through him at lightning speed. His cock had hardened painfully. The need to brand her as his woman had sung in his ears. He'd known, deep down, that she'd waited for him. He only wished he'd waited for her.

He *felt* like a virgin with her, however. Unsure, eager. Excited by the possibilities. In such a short time, she'd become everything to him.

Want me. Come to me.

She didn't. And as the minutes ticked by, her resolve to resist him seemed to intensify. Finally he said, "Yet again I find that I am unable to force you to accept what is inevitable."

"Valerian," she said in that shaky voice.

"Not another word, moon."

"It's not you, okay. Well, maybe it is. A little. I just…can't, okay. I can't let myself want you. Not yet." He looked tortured again, she thought, sad and wistful and rock hard. "I wish I could. I do. But…" Too many things stood in the way. The thought of letting someone so close to her was terrifying.

He stalked from the main room and into the bathing area without another word, leaving her alone. Alone with only her throbbing body, her treacherous thoughts.

Why had he left? He'd said he meant to make her choose.

Doesn't matter, she decided in the next instant. *He isn't the man for you.* He liked sex, and he liked it with multiple women. Shaye wasn't her mother and wouldn't accept the small scraps of affection some man decided to toss her way. She wouldn't fall in love, using the fickle emotion as an excuse to have the good while tolerating too much of the bad.

She liked being alone, was content that way. And her deepest feminine instincts sensed that to make love with Valerian was to fall so deeply in love with the man that she'd give up everything for him. Even herself.

The curtain blocking her view from the bathing pool continued to rustle. The sound of falling clothing echoed, then the splash of water. She gulped. Was he naked? Most likely. Steam was probably wafting around him. His skin probably glistened with moisture. He probably resembled an angel floating through the heavens.

In that instant all the reasons she'd rejected him faded from her thoughts. Desire. So much desire. She'd said she wouldn't watch him bathe, but one peek suddenly didn't seem so bad. One peek… Really, there was no harm in that.

Unbidden, she found her feet moving toward the entrance. He couldn't possibly be as exquisite as she was imagining. Could he? She quietly peeled the curtain to the side—but only a little. Valerian's naked back came into view. Muscles rippled under tawny skin as he cupped and poured water over himself.

Steam did indeed waft around him, making him appear nothing more than a dream, a fantasy, a genie visiting from a lamp, come to grant her every wish. His hair was soaked and dripping down his back. She bit her lip. Maybe it wouldn't hurt to be with him once and finally put her body out of its misery. If she guarded her heart, she could use him and be done with him. Right?

He turned to the side and clamped his hand around a sapphire glass bottle. He poured whatever was inside—more of that orchid oil?—into his other hand. Oh, to be that oil, she thought, watching, throat constricted as he rubbed the oil into his chest. The fragrance joined the steam and floated to her.

"You can still join me, you know," he said, his voice rough.

She yelped and released the curtain. It fell back into place, completely blocking him from view. Her cheeks erupted into flames.

She was saved from having to analyze her thoughts and actions when Brenna burst into the room. The girl was panting; her gaze was wild. Black curls bounced over her face. She stilled when she spotted Shaye and exhaled a huge sigh of relief.

"What's wrong?" Alarmed, Shaye rushed to her side. "Did something happen?"

Behind her, she heard the splash of water, the pound of footsteps, then Valerian was there, standing in the doorway. He was naked. Mouthwateringly naked. He didn't seem surprised to see Brenna with her, even though the girl had made no real noise. "Did something happen?" he echoed.

Shaye's mouth fell open at this first, full-frontal glance of him. He was tall and well muscled, but she'd already seen that. What she hadn't seen was his erection. Until now. It was as long and hard as she'd imagined, rising proudly from between his legs. He wasn't modest and didn't reach for any type of covering. Water droplets cascaded from his hair, down his stomach, and onto his—

Dear God.

Brenna's mouth had fallen open, too, and Shaye had

to tamp the urge to cover the girl's eyes. "We're fine." Shaye gave a jerky point. "Go back to your bath, Valerian. Please! For God's sake, we're just going to have a little girl talk."

With a nod, he stalked off. Damn the man, he looked as good from behind as he did from the front.

Only when the drape blocked him was Shaye able to breathe again.

"Big," Brenna said in that broken voice of hers, her eyes still wide.

Mine, Shaye almost snapped. She frowned. She had no right to him. She'd just turned him down. Again. *Concentrate.* "Did someone hurt you, Brenna? Or threaten you?"

Brenna shook her head. "Problem."

"What kind? With whom?"

"Joachim."

Her frown deepened. "Is he hurt?"

"No."

"Did he hurt you?"

"No."

O-kay. Shaye clasped her friend's hand—was Brenna her friend? she wondered. She'd never really had one before. Assistants, yes. Employees, yes. But had she ever really spent quality personal time with someone else? Well, whatever Brenna was, Shaye led her to the couch. "What's wrong?" she asked again, settling into the cushions.

"Shivawn," Brenna said.

Her brows furrowed together. "Is *he* hurt?"

"No."

"Did he hurt you?"

"No."

Had she ever had a more confusing conversation?

Shaye pushed out a frustrated exhalation. They were getting nowhere this way. "You have to help me understand what's going on."

A rosy blush stained Brenna's cheeks. She bit her bottom lip. "Want. Them."

"You…want them?" Shaye blinked. "As in, sexually?"

The girl's blush intensified, and she looked away. "Maybe. But…think I really want one when I should want the other. Scared. Confused."

"That would scare me, too." She could barely handle her desire for Valerian. She didn't know what she'd do if she should want to be with one of his warriors, instead. "It's that whole duty versus desire thing, huh? Like we see in the movies?"

Brenna gripped her hands, perhaps willing her to understand. "Kind of. Maybe. I don't know!"

"I wish I had an answer for you, and if we were on the surface, I might. But these men, these…nymphs. They cast a spell over everything female and screw with our common sense." Shaye's bitterness seeped through her tone. "I don't like it."

"You once mentioned escape." Brenna mimed the last so Valerian wouldn't hear.

Shaye's body went still; even her heartbeat stopped for several seconds. Escape. What she'd wanted from the beginning. What she wasn't sure she wanted right now, but knew was for the best. *You have a home. A job. Employees who count on your revenue.*

"I haven't found a way out," she admitted softly. Not that she'd looked all that hard. "But there is one *sure* way. Do you remember the portal?"

Brenna nodded.

"Valerian said I couldn't survive it alone. Together, you and I can swim to the surface. We just have to find it."

They stood in unison and glanced to the bathing curtain. "There's no better time than now," Shaye said, speaking past the sudden lump in her throat. She wished she had time to tell Valerian goodbye, wished she could kiss him once more. "Are you ready?"

Again Brenna nodded.

As if he'd heard their entire conversation, Valerian called, "Shaye!"

Her eyes widened, and Brenna gasped. If she didn't leave now, she would lose this opportunity. "Come on." They sprinted past the front door and into the hallway.

"Shaye!" A command now. Water splashed.

She plowed into a couple writhing on the floor and tumbled face-first. Frantic, Brenna helped her up. The couple yelped, but didn't stop their naked dance. Shaye's lungs nearly burst from strain as she dared a backward glance. A naked Valerian was closing in on her. How could she want to run *to* him?

"Move!" she panted. "Faster. Do you know the way?" All she remembered was that the closer they came to the portal, the barer the walls would become. Fewer jewels. Fewer sconces.

"Yes."

They encountered a fork, and Brenna swerved right. Shaye followed. God, she hoped this was the right direction. If Valerian caught her… The walls looked the same to her. Doorways branched in every direction. They raced past other women, other warriors. The men regarded them with curiosity, but didn't try to stop them.

Then, suddenly, steal clamps anchored onto her waist and she was thrown into the air. Her arms flailed. She screamed. Brenna ground to a halt and whipped around just as Shaye's legs kicked out, reaching for a solid foundation. As she fell, she screamed again.

Strong arms caught her, wrapping around her and locking her in place. She was panting and didn't allow herself to meet Valerian's angry gaze. Or look down at his wet, aroused body.

"When a warrior runs from his commander," he said ominously, "he is punished. Are you ready for your punishment, Shaye?"

CHAPTER NINETEEN

VALERIAN ESCORTED BRENNA to Shivawn without a word. The warrior accepted her with a frown and a muttered, "Thank you, great king," and then they were off. Shaye had never been so nervous. This was the first time Valerian had ever projected such bleak fury in her direction.

And yet, she was oddly relieved that she'd failed to escape.

"Go back to your duties," Valerian growled to the soldiers watching in the hallway.

His men jumped into motion, looking anywhere but at his naked form. Looking anywhere but at Shaye, who was carted unceremoniously over his shoulder. "Valer—"

"Do not speak," he snapped at her.

"Valerian," she persisted. "I told you I would try to escape. You can't say I didn't warn you. At least I didn't lie to you. We'll always be honest with each other, remember?"

"I gave you what you wanted, Shaye. I did not press you to make love, and yet you ran from me." Valerian still couldn't believe her daring. He stalked to his room and tossed her onto the bed. She gasped. He stood in place, staring down at her. She didn't try to run again, just watched him warily.

Light as she was, carrying her shouldn't have affected him. But he was panting. His arms fell to his sides, and he realized just how quickly he was losing strength.

He needed sex.

He needed Shaye.

He'd felt her watching him during his bath. Had smelled her desire for him. He'd thought victory was within his grasp. And then she'd run. Run! Was the thought of welcoming him into her body that abhorrent to her?

"The time has come," he said darkly.

She scrambled to the far edge of the bed, as if the spell of motionlessness she'd been under had lifted with his words. He continued to stare down at her. Her overlarge shirt gaped open, revealing succulent hints of her breasts.

"Let's talk about this," she said nervously.

"You tried to escape me. The time for conversation is over."

"Couples should always make time to chat."

One brow winged up. "We are a couple now?"

She kept her gaze on his chest, not daring to look down, where he was thick and ready. He watched a tremble sweep through her. In fear? In desire? Something inside him lurched. He sighed heavily. Would she always tie him in knots? He tried a different approach.

"You look so beautiful on my bed, moon, with your hair draped over your shoulders, your legs stretched in front of you. But…"

"But?" she prompted, frowning.

"But you will look even better on me." He let his knees fall on the mattress, followed by his hands. Slowly he crawled forward.

Eyes wide, she tried to scoot back even farther. The wall blocked any escape. "Stop," she said. She sounded breathless. Eager. "Just stop."

"You feel the connection between us, I know you do."

Her teeth ground together, and a flash of something dark settled over her expression. "So what if I do?" she snapped. "That doesn't mean I want to sleep with you."

"Innocent moonbeam, neither of us will be sleeping." His gaze swept over her, and he suddenly wished he possessed the fire of the dragons so he could burn away her clothing. "I know you have never been with a man, but have you ever engaged in love play?"

Stubborn as always, she pressed her lips together. "That's none of your business."

"I do not smell any man on you, not even the faintest hint."

"I—I lied to you earlier, okay." She studied her nails, yawned with exaggeration. "I've been with lots of men. Thousands."

He paused, his hands on either side of her knees. That she didn't try to kick him was more telling than she probably knew. Some part of her wanted him.

Untouched echoed through his mind. His mate was untouched by any man. He would be her first. Her only. He'd be careful with her. "I like that you are virgin, moon."

She flicked a piece of lint off her shirt. "I *don't* like the fact that you are a male whore, Valerian."

"I am sorry that I do not come to you pure." Nymphs never saved themselves for their mates; they were too sexual, their needs too great. But now he wished to the gods that he'd waited for her. "Perhaps every other woman was merely practice for the day I met you."

She swallowed, bit her lip. Her nipples hardened beneath the shirt, and she could no longer pretend boredom. "That's, like, the corniest line I've ever heard."

"It is true nonetheless." Blood heated to a sizzle inside his veins. Possessiveness and pride stormed him as surely as his army stormed castles. No man had ever sneaked past this woman's cool facade to discover the passion underneath, but he was close. So close to victory. *I will give her so much pleasure she will scream with it.*

He crawled the rest of the way up her body, placing them nose to nose. "Was I right? Is that why you have denied me? Why you've denied yourself?" he asked, placing the softest of kisses on her lush mouth. "Because you have not known a man?"

Her mouth parted on a gasp—perhaps a sigh. "Don't...don't fool yourself." She ran her tongue over her lips. "I want no part of you. That's why I denied you." Again she sounded breathless. Needy.

"I think you want *every* part of me."

"You're delusional."

"Or perhaps I'm more perceptive than you are comfortable with."

Her eyes narrowed, hiding the emotion banked in their depths. "Are we going to talk all day or are you going to get this seduction routine over with?"

As she uttered those last words, he reached out and palmed the fullness of her breast. Her eyes closed, her hips arched slightly. A look of divine pleasure blanketed her expression.

"We can get it over with," he said. "But are you sure you want it to end quickly?"

"I...I don't know," she breathed.

"Tell me to leave you right now, and I will. Tell me."

She opened her mouth but said nothing.

"Tell me to leave, Shaye. I will *not* force you. I will walk away from you."

Again, not a word. Satisfaction speared him. He plucked at her nipple with his fingertips. "Do you hate me when I do this?"

A moan shuddered past her lips. "It feels…it feels terrible."

Gods, he loved seeing her cheeks pinken with arousal. "Just think how much worse it will feel when I suck this hard little morsel into my mouth."

She groaned, a sound so laden with need he responded on a primal level, his muscles clenching, his bones vibrating. When he removed his hand—only for the barest of seconds—her groan became a growl. He slid his fingers under her shirt, gliding over the smooth skin of her stomach, surely the softest, sweetest flesh he'd ever encountered.

Her features clouded with rapture, and she trembled.

"Does this make you shudder in revulsion?" he asked, strained. His fingertip brushed the underside of her breast.

"Utterly," she gasped.

"Me, too. Oh, me, too. See, I'm shaking with the force of my disgust."

"It's the…worst thing…ever," she said, panting. *I should make him stop,* Shaye thought. *Should make him stop…in just a…little while.* His fingers were white-hot, searing, and everywhere they touched, a fire kindled below the surface of her skin. He sank more deeply into her, making her gasp.

His body was like a live wire, she realized, and then her mind went blank, consumed only with pleasure as his hand closed over her bare breast. Instinctively she parted her legs, a silent invitation for him to pin her completely.

He didn't accept. In fact, he lifted slightly.

She almost cursed him.

With his other hand, he inched up the hem of her shirt. "If I cover you, I'll take you," he explained. "I need to see you first."

"Yes," she said, wondering who this passionate creature was. Not Shaye, surely. She wasn't concerned with either of their pasts, wasn't concerned with what would happen once the loving was finished as she lifted her hips to make it easier for him. His bare erection rubbed against her. Absolute pleasure. Total sensation.

He hissed in a breath, and she did the same. Despite the clothing she still wore, it felt as if he touched the core of her. "Mmm, yes," she said. "I like. No, hate. I hate."

Her stomach tightened, quivered. Unable to stop herself, she did it again, purposefully this time, and caressed herself against his cock. Valerian sucked in another breath. He jerked her top over her head, freeing her breasts for his gaze.

"I have to taste them. Have to have those sweet little beads in my mouth."

Shaye shouldn't let things go any further, but curiosity was getting the better of her. At least, she was calling the unquenchable desire to feel him slide and pump and grind inside her *curiosity*. To know and understand how people became slaves to their emotions over this one act.

Valerian closed his fingers over her wrist. "What are you thinking about?"

"Passion," she admitted. "Sex."

"Look at me."

She didn't think to disobey. Her gaze jerked to him, and she stilled, amazed by what she saw. He was drinking in the sight of her breasts as if they were the most beautiful things he'd ever beheld. As if her too-pale skin and her average-size breasts topped his Christmas list.

"I am thinking that I have never seen a more wondrous sight. Your loveliness captivates me," he said, his tone reverent.

"But you've been with a thousand women," she reminded him softly. "A thousand times more beautiful than me."

"None are more beautiful than you, love."

"I'm nothing," she insisted. "I'm—"

"Everything." One of his hands cupped her jaw, and his thumb caressed the side of her face. He forced her to look at him, to *see* him. "I told you that. You are everything to me."

It was too astonishing to believe and yet, it was everything she'd ever wanted to hear. People just didn't say things like that to her. Tears stung her eyes, and she scrubbed them away. She'd always prided herself on her independence, on her lack of need for another's approval. But until this moment, she hadn't realized how incredible approval could actually be. How powerful it could make her feel.

I have to be cold, she reminded herself—how many times would she be forced to issue the reminder to herself? *I have to be heartless.* But as her gaze slid over Valerian, she couldn't force herself to rebuke him.

He was poised above her, his big, hard body illuminated by a golden glow of light. Muscles bunched, strength and arousal exuded from him in mouthwatering waves. His stomach was ripped and hard. His penis stretched toward her center, so thick, so hard, reaching for her. The heavy weight of his testicles was surrounded by a sprinkling of golden hair.

The sight of him, this god of beauty and sex, made her breathless. "You—" she cleared her throat "—aren't bad-looking, either," she said. She'd never given a man a compliment before; she always shoved them out of her life as quickly as they entered.

His lips twitched. "I am glad you do not find me ugly, for you are everything I've ever needed."

Inch by agonizing inch, he lowered his head. A gasp of anticipation caught in her windpipe. His mouth closed over her nipple, surrounding it with moist heat. When his tongue flicked back and forth against the pearled bud, her hand tangled in his hair, holding his head in place. He kneaded her other breast with his hand, and the double sensation had her hips writhing.

"Did I not promise you it would feel terrible?"

"Awful, just awful. Don't stop." Wait. She'd meant to tell him to stop. Things were getting out of hand.

"You make me feel feverish, as if my very life depends on you." He sucked hard, and she groaned at the pleasure/pain of it, then he licked away the sting and she moaned at the heady bliss. "When a nymph makes love, he becomes completely absorbed in the act, ferocious and bestial. Nothing else matters except his woman."

Need him the way he seems to need you, she thought, yearning, and something cracked inside her. Something crumbled. The last vestiges of her resistance? Fear? Doubt? They were suddenly gone, replaced by a need to know him, all of him. In that moment he became more important to her than breathing.

Growling, she wrapped her legs around his waist, locked her ankles and jerked him on top of her. All of his weight—blissful. She savored, reveled in the exquisite press of him. Basked in her first true taste of capitulation. No more denying her needs, no more ignoring her secret wants.

"Shaye?" he said, his voice hoarse. He closed his eyes in sweet surrender, his expression entranced, shocked, awed.

"Valerian."

He nipped at her collarbone, licked up and down her neck. His hand worked at the waist of her pants. His fingers glided past them, under her panties, and through her fine tuft of pubic hair.

She nearly screamed as she arched her hips to urge him further.

"Most women think this is the most pleasure-receptive place on their bodies." His fingers pinched her clitoris lightly. He was sweating, trying to go slowly when she wanted him fast.

With that one touch, she almost reached the gates of paradise. So close to climax…so close… "They'd be right," she managed on a pant.

"No, they are wrong." He slid a finger through her damp folds and into the very heat of her. "Small," he said, strained. "Tight. Wonderful."

Had she thought she'd neared paradise before? Not even close. Her feminine walls clamped around him, holding him captive. In and out he moved. Slowly. Sheer torture. She gasped and gasped and gasped.

"Some women think this rhythm is the cause of their desire."

"Are they…wrong, too?" Holy hell, she was on fire. Her cells were traveling through her bloodstream at full speed, scorching everything in their path.

"Oh, yes. They are wrong."

He continued sliding those fingers into her, and her stomach coiled, tensed; her leg muscles quivered around him. Orgasm teetered on the sweet brink of arrival. "Valerian," she beseeched.

"Oh, how I like my name on your lips." His thumb brushed her clitoris.

Her head thrashed from side to side. She burned, so hot, nearing explosion. "Show me the most pleasure-receptive place on a woman's body." She had to come. Had to…would die…soon…

"For a kiss," he said, wanting to bargain even now. "I'll give you the world for a single kiss."

Without hesitation, she meshed her lips into his. The moment his tongue collided with hers, his taste filled her mouth. The exquisite sensations between her legs intensified. She unlocked her ankles, letting her knees fall apart and onto the bed, spreading her wide open for whatever he might do.

Lost in passion, that was Shaye. She was exactly what she'd feared: a slave to it, desperate for it. But she didn't care. The kiss was hard and hot and only became harder and hotter. Tongues battled, teeth clashed.

Valerian's fingers continued to pump her, as frantic and insatiable as the kiss.

But then, suddenly, he stopped. Stopped the kiss, stopped the motion of his fingers. Her body throbbed, and a sob nearly burst from her lips.

"What are you doing?" she moaned. She tangled her hands in his hair and tried to force his mouth back to hers. Finally she'd allowed herself to enjoy a man, and he stopped?

"Now I will show you where you are most sensitive, where you will verge on climax every time I touch you."

Hmm. Yes. "Hurry."

Sweat continued to trickle from his temples. The lines of tension around his eyes had deepened, bracketing his features. He, too, needed relief, she realized. Did he ache with an almost unquenchable ferocity like she did? Was he desperate, eager? Did he feel like he would blast past the stars if he didn't touch her again?

His lips brushed her softly, once, twice. "Your taste…it's like no one else's. Like nothing I've ever had. It's addictive. I think I would die without it."

Touch me. Make love to me. "Valerian, I'm glad you like how I taste and everything, but you've got a point to prove here and I'm a little disappointed that I have to remind you of that fact."

He uttered a labored chuckle. "You're right. I just need to look at you a moment longer, just need to savor the sight of you. Very soon I *will* strip you completely. Very soon I will slide your pants over your legs."

As he spoke, that image filled her mind. She could see very clearly that he *was* stripping her. He *was* wrapping his hands around her—

"Ankles," he said. "And I bring your foot to my mouth. I lick—"

—the arch, gliding his tongue slowly. She saw it, saw the pictures, more vivid with every second that passed. His mouth moved up her calf, swirling little hearts over her skin before—

"—biting your inner thigh. You pant and writhe, just like you're doing now, and you grow even wetter for me. So wet. I bring your own hand between your legs and watch you touch yourself. You—"

—circle her own finger over her clitoris, watching him all the while. In her mind, his eyes lowered to half-mast and his hand curled around his cock, moving up and down. He told her how much he wanted her mouth to replace his hand, how much he wanted his mouth to replace hers. Then he kissed her but it—

"—wasn't enough. I crave another taste of you, a more intimate taste, and talking about it won't be enough, either. I lower my head between your legs. Your hands grasp my hair, pulling roughly because you're so far gone with need you aren't able to control your reactions."

She couldn't control her reactions *now*. By this time, Shaye was writhing insatiably. She still wore her pants, but it actually felt as if phantom hands were working at her, as if a phantom tongue was licking her. She was gasping, her breath hot in her throat.

"Valerian, Valerian," she chanted. "Valerian, please."

"Please what?" His voice was rough, so rough. Husky, so husky.

"Please finish me."

"But I like savoring you."

"Show me the most erotic place on my body, damn it. You won't live to savor me if you don't hurry."

"I'll die of pleasure either way." His voice broke with arousal. He pinched her clitoris again, and she nearly jumped off the bed. The decadent sensations were acute, almost painful. "I'm going to taste you here before I love you," he said. "And when I love you, you're going to know the most pleasure-receptive place on *my* body."

"Your penis?" she gasped out. She was almost beyond speech. It was too much. He was too much. His words, his actions. His very essence.

"No, my—"

"My king," a voice said urgently.

Valerian stilled. He growled low in his throat, and it was an animal sound. A killing sound.

A moment passed before Shaye realized what was going on. There was a warrior standing at the edge of the bed, his eyes on Valerian, his expression concerned. Losing her passion haze, she screamed and scrambled for the bedcovers. Mortification bombarded her as she covered her bare breasts. Yet still she ached for Valerian.

"Turn around, Broderick," he growled. His teeth bared in a fierce, lethal scowl. "I'm close to killing you already."

Broderick instantly turned.

"Leave us, or I *will* kill you."

"Dragons," Broderick said. He didn't leave as he'd been commanded. "They are approaching, intent on war."

CHAPTER TWENTY

VALERIAN COULDN'T BELIEVE someone had entered his room without his knowledge. Even when he was caught up in the most animalistic of his desires, his warrior instincts did not diminish.

Not so with Shaye. With her, he concentrated only on the loving. Such a thing had never happened before.

At the moment he battled a fierce torrent of rage and desire. He had Shaye where he'd wanted and needed her for so long, and now he had to leave her. But her safety came before her seduction. Always.

Her safety came before his own pleasure.

Perhaps he was trapped inside a nightmare, for this was the worst thing that could have happened to him. "Warn the others," he told Broderick, the words ripped from him. "I want everyone in full armor and in the arena. I will be there shortly."

"Consider it done" was the reply before his second-in-command rushed off.

He rubbed a hand over his face. Gods, he'd known this day would come. Why could it not have come in the morning? "Broderick," he called, and the warrior quickly returned. "Have the women been seen to?"

"They are being hidden even now."

"Excellent. Go, then. You have your orders."

Broderick stalked from the room a second time, his hurried footsteps echoing off the walls.

"I'm sorry, moon," Valerian said, gazing down at Shaye. Color flushed her cheeks; her pale hair splayed over the bed like ribbons of white silk. Her breasts, covered by the violet sheet, were outlined, her nipples pearled. "I must go."

She didn't respond.

He didn't know what else to say. Withdrawing from the bed, from her embrace, was the most difficult thing he'd ever done. He wished there was time, at least, to sate *her* desire and give one of them relief.

As he hurriedly dressed, tugging on his pants and retrieving his chest armor—still stained with blood from today's practice—he realized he was still not at full strength. His grip wasn't as tight, his limbs not as steady. There was no help for it now. He laced up his boots.

"You're going to war?" Finally his woman spoke, but her voice gave no indication of her emotions. It was as blank and cool as if he'd never caressed her. Never moved his fingers inside her.

That angered him as much as Broderick's interruption. "If that is what is required to keep this palace, then yes, I will go to war."

"But…you're injured."

"Yes."

"You shouldn't be fighting. You'll make your wounds worse."

He kept his back to her as he gathered his helmet and shield. The Skull rested inside. "Do not begin doubting me again, moon. I am well able to protect and defend."

"Why don't you just give the dragons back their palace?"

He would not have his army become wanderers again, no real home, no real refuge. "It is mine now, and I keep what is mine. Always." He uttered the words as a warning to her. She was his now, and he would never let her go. "Get dressed."

She glanced down at the sheet she clasped, at her gaping pants. She gasped as if she only then realized she had yet to cover herself completely. Motions stiff, she grabbed the black shirt from the floor and tugged it over her head.

Valerian mourned the loss of her seminakedness. He held out his free hand and motioned her to join him. Surprisingly she did so without protest, anchoring her belt into place as she walked. However, she didn't take his offered hand.

"Where are you taking me?" she asked. Deep concern swam in the dark pools of her eyes. For him? he wondered hopefully. He doubted it was for herself.

"I want you safe, which means I'm going to place you with the other women."

"Where?" she insisted. "The room we were in earlier today?"

"No. I will show you." He knew she would balk if he told her where she would be placed. If he simply took her there, her steps willing, he would save them both time and exertion.

Urgency battered him. He must get Shaye to safety.

He grabbed her hand and tugged her through three separate hallways. Several of his men rushed past him, nodding in acknowledgment as they headed for the arena. That was not his destination. As he continued on, the air became cold, thick with moisture. Mist curled toward the ceiling.

"You're taking me to the portal?" Shaye slapped him on the shoulder. "I thought you said I'd drown if I went back through."

"I am not, nor will I ever send you into the portal. Not for any reason." Cave walls came into view. Rocky. Jagged. Sensual murals painted all around. He bypassed the swirling portal, careful not to touch the dappled liquid separating him and Shaye from the sea.

"I don't understand," Shaye said.

The sound of female voices filled his ears. Twigs and bones—left over from when the dragons owned the palace and killed every human who strayed into Atlantis—snapped under his boots. More than once Valerian had wondered why Atlanteans could not survive upon the surface but humans could come and go as they pleased. Armies had once passed through, which was why the dragons had killed so unmercifully, why this cavern had once been a place of death and destruction.

Still, Valerian thought it was better off in *his* hands. Innocents did not deserve to die. What if Shaye had passed through before his arrival? She would have been slain.

"Are those bones?" Shaye covered her mouth with a shaky hand. "I didn't notice them before."

He explained about the dragons, about the portal. "Humans have tried to destroy the creatures of Atlantis in an attempt to steal their riches. Dragons did what they thought was right to protect the Atlanteans."

Valerian descended a flight of stairs, this one hidden in the narrow crevice between two bloodstained boulders. The portal was exactly why the dragons wanted control of this palace again. They would fight to the death to have it. Darius, King of the Dragons, was Guardian, a slayer of trespassers.

"You never told me the most erotic place on a woman's body," Shaye said. Fear layered her voice, as if she was desperate to think of anything but war and death.

"Nor will I," he replied. The mystery would occupy her mind, keeping her distracted. "Not until I have you in bed again."

"Jerk."

"Beauty."

A pause. A sharp intake of breath. Shaye ground to an abrupt halt. "What is this place?" Her voice echoed around them.

They had reached the bottom of the stairs, had entered a new room. Valerian propped his shield against the wall and slipped a hand around Shaye's waist, urging her to his side—if only to prevent her from running when she spied the prison cell. "Welcome to the dungeon, moon."

The gaggle of voices tapered to quiet a second before happy coos sprang forth. "Valerian, you gorgeous thing! I'm so happy to see you."

"Valerian!"

"Hi, Valerian."

Glowing blue bars came into view, bars that held all of the other women.

"Hell, no," Shaye said, and he knew she'd seen the prison—a prison that could hold an immortal if necessary. She jerked from him, cutting off all contact. "I'm not letting you trap me like that. I will not be helpless!"

Determined, he faced her. She, too, wore an expression of determination. Her dark eyes flashed fire as he backed her into the wall.

"Try and intimidate me all you want." She squared her shoulders and raised her chin, the picture of total defiance. "I'm not staying down here while you war it up, up there."

"This is the safest place for you."

"What if you're killed? Will we be stuck down here forever?"

"That will not happen," he insisted.

"Can you guarantee it with one hundred percent certainty?"

"Yes." He would allow nothing bad to happen to himself because Shaye's life depended on him. That was fact.

She crossed her arms over her chest. "How can you guarantee such a thing? Are you psychic?"

His eye twitched as he jerkily pointed to the group of warriors standing in front of the prison bars. "If anything happens to me, these men will release you. Satisfied?"

"I'm not a little cupcake who will do stupid things while the big, strong he-warrior takes care of her. You don't have to worry about me rushing into the battle. I'll stay in this room, okay. You don't have to lock me up."

"The bars aren't for you. They are for the dragons. If they catch you, they will burn you or ravish you. Perhaps both. Is that the fate you desire for yourself?"

What little color her face held drained away.

He softened his tone. "Try and keep the others calm while I'm gone. Will you do this for me?"

She stared into his eyes, and for a brief moment he caught a glimpse of sheer terror. For him. For his safety. But she frowned and nodded. "Fine. I'll do it. But they aren't upset," she grumbled. "They're freakishly happy to see you."

"We are, Valerian," a brunette said, stepping forward. She gripped the bars. A buttercup-yellow robe draped her lush body. "We're *very* happy to see you."

Shaye pinched the bridge of her nose. "If you don't come back, I swear to God I'll kill you."

Valerian nodded to Terran, who stood sentry at the cell. Terran extended his arm and brushed his fingers against the bars, making them nothing more than mist. Valerian couldn't help himself. He crushed Shaye's lips with his own, his tongue swooping inside for a quick taste, bringing all of his fiercest desires to the surface. She responded violently, brutally, taking everything he could give her.

As he kissed her, he backed her into the cell. When she was ensconced inside, he jerked away from her and the bars solidified in front of her face.

Their eyes locked. Silence sizzled between them for a heartbeat. Her gaze widened in understanding, and she gripped the bars. She gave them a good shake, but they did not even rattle. "You bastard! I said I would willingly stay here. You didn't have to trick me inside."

"I'm sorry." He hated to leave her. Wanted to kiss her again. Wanted to linger. He couldn't. He hefted up his shield and stalked from the enclosure, her curses ringing in his ears. He headed for the dining hall. Broderick met him halfway.

"The men are ready."

He pushed Shaye from his mind, determined to act as a warrior should. Cold, unemotional. Lethal. "Excellent. How far are the dragons from reaching us?"

"They are still in the Outer City."

"Have they any allies with them?"

"No. They come alone."

"Darius leads them?"

"Yes."

Valerian nodded. He and Darius had fought once before, and though Valerian had injured the hulking beast, the end had been a draw, with neither man able to completely conquer the other. "I want our best men on the parapet and a group of soldiers strategically placed in the surrounding forest. I want the dragons' every move tracked. I want to know if they send flyers onto the roof."

"And if they do?"

"Cut them down." All dragons had wings that allowed them to soar through the air. They were also fire-breathers and if they weren't stopped quickly, they could decimate everything in their path. The nymphs' greatest strength lay in their power to seduce. Even men were not immune and could be caught in their spell, slaves to their will. More than that, the nymphs' passion spilled into every area of their lives. Not just sexual passion, but fury.

The dragons would not fall prey to their charms, which meant they would have to rely on their wits, sword skill and potent fury. At least the palace, which had been made for dragons, was fire resistant.

"Do you want traps set?" Broderick asked.

He considered the idea. "No. Let the dragons reach

us without incident. They'll be less likely to rush in to attack, and we can launch a surprise assault of our own in the coming darkness."

Broderick rushed to convey all he'd been ordered.

In the dining hall, Valerian strode to the wall of windows and gazed out. Empty streets greeted him. The citizens who lived in the Outer City must have spied the dragons and run home, fearing for their lives.

War had finally arrived.

Valerian spun on his heel and strode to the arena. Broderick was busy instructing the men. As they received orders, they raced to obey. "May the gods go with you," he told those who passed him.

"And you, my king," he heard uttered numerous times.

Those without assignments formed a line and eyed him expectantly. He paced in front of them, saying, "I want you to circle around the Outer City undetected and remain behind the dragons. I want them flanked by nymphs on every side."

They nodded in unison.

"When you receive my signal, close in on them and let them know you are there. Now go."

Hurried footsteps echoed as the men rushed to obey. Valerian found himself alone. Gripping his sword hilt, he stood there a moment, his thoughts drifting inexorably to Shaye. Had she not been here, he most likely would have led a section of his army into the outskirts of the city and attacked the dragons there. As it was, he wanted all of his forces surrounding the palace. Close at hand. A circle of protection.

All he had to do now was await the dragons' arrival. And kill, of course. Kill each and every one of his enemies.

CHAPTER TWENTY-ONE

SHAYE STUDIED the other women locked inside the cell. Of course, they were the same ones who'd been locked inside the hobby room with her. They didn't seem to mind the current situation, and were, in fact, chatting amicably with each other.

How could they possibly be from the same planet as her? God, what a nightmare. Was Brenna here? Shaye really needed an ally. Someone to share her worries with, someone to keep her calm. "Brenna," she called.

The girl shouldered her way through the thick crowd. "Here."

"Thank God." Shaye pulled her into the nearest corner. "How are you? Did Shivawn punish you for trying to escape?"

"Escape," the one called Tiffany groaned. She leaned against one of the side bars. "Please tell me you two aren't going to try to escape again. At least, not right now. Don't you know you're supposed to wait until everyone is sleeping, *then* run? That's how all the movies do it."

"I still don't understand why you'd want to escape Valerian." The dark-haired girl who'd left Valerian's room that first night stepped toward them, unabashedly joining the conversation. "He's amazing."

Yes, he was, Shaye thought, her hands fisting at her sides as jealousy speared her.

"I still dream about him," the woman added, sighing dreamily. "Does he ever speak of me? I'm Kathleen, by the way."

Shaye's teeth gnashed together as images of Valerian and Kathleen—naked and straining—consumed her mind. This jealousy thing was new to her, and she didn't exactly know how to deal with it. "No. He hasn't mentioned you."

"Oh." Kathleen's shoulders sagged with disappointment. "Hopefully he'll tire of you soon. I really, really, *really* want him back."

"What makes you think he'll tire of me at all?" she snapped. She hated that she possessed that fear herself. How long would Valerian remain interested in her? How long until his eye began to rove in search of someone else? Someone sweeter and more biddable?

Kathleen shrugged. "You tried to escape him. I can't see that such behavior will appeal to him for long. I give you a week, two at most."

Shaye stepped forward, hands clenched, ready to strike. Brenna grabbed her arm, a silent command to stop. "No tools to patch Kathleen," her friend said hoarsely.

Expelling a deep breath, Shaye turned away from the bitch in question. She wanted out of this cell, away from these women. She wanted to go home, to be alone—except the thought left her with a hollow ache in her chest.

The group began chatting about the arrival of a new nymph, one more handsome than any of the others, including Valerian. Apparently this nymph liked to ask questions and could bring women to climax with only a look. After a while Shaye tuned out the prattle. Fury seethed like a ticking bomb in her blood, detonation assured.

If she stayed here, *this* was the life she would have. She would be trapped in a cell every time war threatened. One day, she would be forgotten by Valerian, just another of his conquests. And all the while, she would crave him because he'd awakened desires that she'd thought buried.

What would she do when he got tired of her? He'd said he wouldn't, but he could not predict the future. Another woman might one day catch his eye. He was a nymph, after all, and that was par for the course.

I can't let him dump me.

Everyone she'd ever come to love had either abandoned her or disappointed her. No one stuck around. No one wanted to work at relationships. She knew that. She also knew that if she didn't love, then she didn't hurt when everything crumbled.

Yet here she was, falling for Valerian and giving him more of herself than she'd ever given another.

Her first instincts had been right. She *needed* to leave him.

Determined, she faced Brenna. "This is our best chance for escape," she whispered. The ache that had sprouted in her chest just a little while ago intensified dramatically. Ignoring it, she leaned forward and curled her fingers around the bars. "Are you with me?"

Indecision played over Brenna's features. She nibbled on her bottom lip and wrung her hands together. Finally she nodded, the action hesitant.

The bars were thick and blue, bright, about the width

of a baseball bat, and hot to the touch. Not enough to blister, but enough to burn. She rattled them, or tried to at least. They didn't move.

"Do you know how Valerian turned the bars to mist?" As she spoke, she attempted to shake them again.

Brenna shook her head.

Shaye replayed the goodbye kiss Valerian had given her through her mind. His lips had met hers and he'd backed her into the bars. Only, the bars hadn't been there. They'd—what? Disappeared? Her eyes widened. Maybe they had. Maybe an outside touch was required. Valerian hadn't pushed a button or used a key. His guard had simply touched the glowing bars and they'd vanished.

She had to get one of the guards to reach into the cell. "I've got it!" she told Brenna, then strode over to Kathleen. "You want to get rid of me, then you have to help me." She explained what she wanted the woman to do.

Kathleen's eyes narrowed. "So you plan on leaving Atlantis? Forever?"

Again Shaye's chest throbbed with prickles of pain. "Yes."

"In that case, helping you will be my pleasure." Kathleen sashayed her way to the front of the crowd. She gripped the bars, smiled sweetly, and said, "Terran, you look so handsome today. I could just eat you up."

He grinned over at her, hungry yearning in his eyes.

"You look handsome, too, Dylan," Kathleen added, playing her role perfectly. "Your muscles are so big. Can I feel them?"

Both men trudged toward her as if pulled by an invisible cord, but they didn't reach for her.

Shaye kept her attention divided between the men and the bars, ready to exit at a moment's notice.

Kathleen whispered throatily, "May I lick your neck, Dylan? Please. I have to taste you."

He didn't even think of denying her. "Of course." He gripped the bars and leaned into Kathleen's waiting lips.

In that instant, the entire cell turned to mist.

"I want to lick you, too," Shaye heard other women say.

The girls surged forward, past the mist. They were suddenly crawling all over the two guards, completely claiming their attention. Shaye easily and silently slipped out of the prison, Brenna beside her. She smiled smugly as she tiptoed from that section of the cavern.

"Women, return to the cell. Return to the cell!" Amid the guards' now-frantic pleas, she and Brenna rounded the corner. *Yes! We did it!* Following the curls of fog, they soon came to the portal and approached tentatively. It swirled and churned, its jellylike center beckoning. Shaye shivered from the cold—not from regret, she assured herself—and wrapped her arms around her middle.

"I can't believe how easy that was," she said. But she didn't go another step farther.

Brenna didn't respond.

She tore her attention from the portal and faced her partner in crime—who was twisting her hands, her expression tortured. "What's wrong?"

"Joachim needs me."

Ah, crap. The nymphs had brainwashed another one. She didn't need this now. If Brenna backed out... "He's healing nicely. You said so yourself."

Brenna bit her lip. Probably a nervous action, since she did it a lot. "Shivawn is sweet."

Expelling a sharp breath, Shaye pushed a hand through her hair. "You really want to stay with them?"

At first Brenna said nothing, did nothing, but then she slowly nodded. "I think I do. I thought to leave, but now…"

"What about the little love triangle that scared you so badly?"

Her cheeks colored a rosy pink. "Would rather deal than leave."

Great. Just great. "Fine. Stay." Shaye frowned and whipped to the portal. Before, she'd been afraid to enter it on her own. She'd drown, Valerian had said. The thought of entering with Brenna had given her courage. They would have fought the ocean waves together. Now that she had to enter all by herself…

She reached out, but stopped herself before actually touching it. *I survived once. I'll survive again. I'm a good swimmer. I can kick my way to the surface.* She nodded, drawing on her courage. Fighting her way through the ocean was better than staying here. Right? God, her chest hurt.

Slowly she reached out. Almost…there…she jerked back, stopping before contact yet again. She flicked Brenna an irritated glance. The girl was watching her attentively. "I don't know why I'm hesitating. I've wanted to leave since I got here. Valerian knows that."

Brenna nodded in understanding.

Damn it. Valerian might be injured or killed during the battle with the dragons, and she would never know it. She might never see him again. "If he gets hurt," she said, "will you patch him up?"

Brenna gave another nod.

She should have been overjoyed by that, but she wasn't. She didn't want Brenna touching him, even to doctor him. *What's wrong with me?* Staying here was stupid. She would have Valerian for a while, true, but he would soon pawn her off on one of his men, like he'd done with the others.

"Leaving is for the best." She squared her shoulders, lifted her chin—nervous actions she resorted to a lot, she realized. She gathered her resolve and reached out again. Her hand began to shake, and the vibration of it swept through the rest of her body. Ow, ow, ow. Her chest was throbbing so badly now, it almost doubled her over.

What if he kept you? What if he wanted you forever, like he said? She stilled. *What if he* loved *you?*

Her heart fluttered at the thought. *I don't believe in love,* she reminded herself. Love was for people like her parents who needed an excuse to do foolish, selfish things. Love had no place in her life. Love sucked. Love…

Would be so nice if it came from Valerian.

Shaye raised her hands and dropped her head into her waiting palms. "I'm not ready to leave him," she admitted brokenly.

Brenna patted her shoulder.

She rubbed a hand over her eyes and pushed out a frustrated breath. "You heard Kathleen. I'm just his flavor of the week. I'm so stupid for staying."

"Afraid?"

Of losing him? "Yes."

"Time to conquer your fears. Time for me to do the same."

"Yes." But she comforted herself with the thought that she didn't have to stay here forever. She could allow herself a few more days with Valerian. She could get to know him a little better, perhaps finish what they'd started in his room. If he treated her badly, well, she now knew how to find the portal.

From prisoner to willing guest, she mused. She snorted in disgust and turned away from the fog-laden portal. All of a sudden the ache in her chest died.

"I don't want to go back to the cell," she said. "Do you?"

"No."

"We can't go into the palace, though." Valerian had asked her to stay down here, so stay down here she would. She didn't want to distract him, placing him in unnecessary danger. Nor did she want to accidentally place herself in enemy hands, thereby giving them the advantage.

But the desire to help him, even to protect him, was strong. Ignoring it was damn near impossible.

Sighing, she led Brenna through the cave and into the cavern next to the cell. "We can stay here." The guards wouldn't hear them because the *drip drip* of water was too loud, and they couldn't leave the women to come look for them—if they even noticed she and Brenna were gone. Wouldn't Valerian get a nice surprise when he came to get her and she wasn't in the cell? Thwarting him, however slightly, brought a smile to her lips.

If he survived.

She lost her grin.

As time ticked by with agonizing slowness, she studied the cave walls to distract herself. She traced her fingers over the images there. "Pretty, aren't they?" Something caught her eye and she studied it more closely. When she realized the images told a story, she motioned her friend over. "Brenna, come look at this."

The first picture showed a group of…gods? They were sitting high above an empty world, looking down upon it. The second picture showed a world filled with terrible monsters forming from a sprinkling of blood and a mixture of the four elements. In the third, the creatures were being thrown into a hidden prison. She saw a portal—*the* portal. Two of them, actually.

The pictures went on to show the creatures adapting to their new land. Yet the very next image showed an army stomping through one of the portals and slaying everything in its path.

Humans? They carried swords and guns, an odd combination of past and present. Perhaps two different armies had marched through the land. Several of the monstrous races rose up in retaliation and destroyed the enemy army.

"Scary," Brenna said.

"Yes." What a violent place Atlantis was. Did she really want to stay, even for a little while? Valerian's face swam into her mind, reminding her exactly how he'd looked poised over her, about to enter her. His hair had fallen in disarray over his strong shoulders. His eyes had gleamed with desire.

Yes, she thought, she wanted to stay. Despite the violence, despite the circumstances, she wanted to stay with Valerian.

For a little while, she reminded herself. Only for a little while. Besides, she kind of liked the Outer City.

The corner of her eye snagged on a particular

grouping of rocks on the far wall. "What's that?" she asked, pointing.

Brenna's brow crinkled, and she moved forward.

Shaye kept pace beside her. The closer they came to it, the chillier the air became. A tremor racked her spine. Once they reached it, she realized it was an opening, a doorway. She looked to Brenna. "Should we?"

"Not sure."

Heart racing, Shaye stepped forward and found herself standing on the precipice of another prison. She heard the shuffle of feet and her ears perked. Who did Valerian have inside?

The first day she'd entered this cave, she recalled how he'd discussed "prisoners" with one of his men. Curiosity propelled her farther, and she slowly inched around the corner. Her eyes widened. Several hulking warriors paced inside a cell. They didn't look like nymphs, for they lacked that air of raw sexuality. These warriors were dark and strong, obviously young, and all had golden, glowing eyes.

One of them spotted her, and she jerked backward with a gasp.

"You," the man said. "Let us out of here. *Please.*"

CHAPTER TWENTY-TWO

VALERIAN PACED THE PARAPET. The rhythmic pounding of army footsteps reverberated in his ears. He could see the dragon army at last, hundreds of them, cresting the violet horizon. That they'd chosen to walk to the palace instead of flying in dragon form meant they were not overcome by rage—yet—and did not mean to attack—yet.

Waiting for their arrival was maddening. He was a man of action. More than that, he was a man eager to finish the fight and return to his woman.

He stumbled forward, one boot snagging on a branch. He caught himself with his hands, bracing them on the wall. He drew in a shaky breath. The wait had drained more of his strength. What he needed was sex. With Shaye. His might wasn't at an optimum level, and he was now feeling its absence.

"My king," Broderick said, concerned, suddenly at his side. "Are you well?"

"I'm fine." He straightened. He was not fine, and he knew it. He'd gone two days without sex, without self-pleasuring, and weakness was unfurling insidious fingers through him. He was well enough to fight, he hoped; well enough to lead, he knew; but for how long?

His arm injury had increased the speed and intensity of his weakness. Had he managed to get inside Shaye earlier, he would be completely healed. "If the dragons come within a hundred yards of the palace, shoot them down," he said.

Broderick nodded. "Archers," he called. "Prepare."

The men knelt and pulled their bows tight. Waiting. Waiting. Time ticked by slowly. Surprisingly, Joachim stepped onto the parapet and approached Valerian. The man limped and his features were tight with pain, but he managed to stay upright.

"What are you doing?" Valerian demanded.

"Fighting," was the harsh reply. "There is to be a war, is there not?"

"You have yet to recover."

"That does not mean I should remain in bed while my brothers fight."

Valerian searched his cousin's face, seeing determination, the need to make things right. He nodded in approval. "Very well. Take your place in the lines below."

Joachim turned, ready to do as he'd been commanded. Then he paused. "I will not apologize for challenging you," he said stiffly, "but I will tell you that I respect your skill and your leadership."

The words were unexpected and surprising. But more than that, his cousin's tone was unexpected and surprising. He'd spoken with affection, as if they were the inseparable boys they'd once been. "Thank you," Valerian said and clapped him lightly on the shoulder. He assumed a battle stance at the wall, overlooking the clear field that led to the palace. Ever closer the dragons came. Their armor glinted in the day's light. Trees rattled behind them, the ground visibly shaken. Colorful petals floated from flowers.

His hand curled around the hilt of The Skull as Darius, king of the dragons, claimed the lead position. He, too, clutched a sword, a long, menacing blade stained crimson from his many kills. Yes, Darius was a lethal killer, an unfeeling warrior with no conscience that Valerian knew of. A worthy adversary, to be sure.

The dragon soldiers came to an abrupt halt.

"Hold," Valerian told his men. "Hold until I give the signal." To the dragons, he called, "Welcome to my home, fire-breathers. You will understand if I do not invite you inside."

Darius scowled. "You know very well the palace belongs to me."

He *tsked* under his tongue. "If you wanted to keep it, you should have sent a stronger battalion to guard it."

"What did you do with the dragons inside?"

"I locked them away, of course. They will make powerful bargaining tools."

"I have your word of honor that you did not kill them, then?"

"You have my word of honor that I did not kill *all* of them."

Darius nodded, the action clipped. "My wife has asked that I not slaughter your entire race for daring to steal what is mine. I will heed her wishes—for now— if you do the two things I require of you."

"And what are those?"

"Release my men and leave the palace."

Valerian laughed. "I'm rather fond of it. I think I'll stay."

"You are inviting war, nymph."

His eyes narrowed, and he gave up all pretense of humor. "As are you, dragon."

"Yes, but *you* invite the wrath of the gods, for you know not what to do with the surface travelers. Already you have allowed one human male to slip into Atlantis, a human who captured our Jewel of Dunamis."

Valerian shrugged, unconcerned. The jewel was better off in human hands. When an Atlantean owned it, they became all-powerful, undefeatable.

"Do you know what happens when humans learn of Atlantis, Valerian? They tell others of their kind, and soon armies of humans are marching through our land, trying to kill us all."

"I must disagree. None of my humans have been allowed back to the surface, so they are unable to lead anyone here. They are too busy occupying our beds." Several of his men chuckled.

"So other humans have come through?" Darius growled.

"Did I not just say so?"

The dragon king's eyes glinted sharply. "Tell me you slayed them. Or tell me you at least wiped their memory."

"I did no such thing. I told you, we bedded them."

"You truly do curry the wrath of the gods, Valerian."

"The gods have forgotten us. Surely you know that. Now, we are done with this conversation. I find I am bored."

Smoke curled from Darius's nostrils, the first sign he would soon morph into his dragon form. "You wish to pit your army against mine, then, for I *will* reclaim the palace and I *will* take charge of the humans you so foolishly hold."

"Try," Valerian said, his jaw clenched, "and I will kill you myself. The portal and everyone who has come through it belong to me. They are mine."

Darius paused, as if he hadn't expected such a forceful response. "Why do you want charge of the portal so badly? You cannot survive on the surface."

He opened his mouth to give a flippant reply but stopped. Why not give the truth? "I do not care about the surface. I care about my people, my home." His voice rose with the ferocity of his conviction. "The nymphs have never possessed a home of their own. Since the dawning of our time, we have traveled from one place to the other, living with one race or another, sleeping in their beds, eating their food. We were good only for pleasuring and warring. Our women deserve a home of their own."

"As to that..." Darius's lips curled in a gradual, arrogant smile. "*I* have your women."

Crackles of fury ignited inside him. "What did you say?"

"They were on their way to this palace, and we captured them."

"Have you hurt them?"

"No. They are safe."

"Thank you for that," he allowed. What Valerian really wanted to do was beat the dragon king until his blood flowed, a river of pain. Those women were *his* responsibility.

"I know your men are weak without sex. And since I have the female nymphs, I can guess the lot of you will be easy to destroy. Are you sure you want to war?"

"We are plenty strong, Darius. I told you, the surface dwellers have occupied our beds."

Darius uttered another growl, smug no longer. "How shall we do this, then, to keep it fair?"

A fair fight from a dragon? Inconceivable. And yet, if Darius meant to fight dirty he would have done so already, sneaking in at night for a surprise attack. However, Valerian wouldn't doubt if Darius had an alternate plan of action. "I suggest a battle of sword skill."

"Very well. Shall we meet on the battlefield in the morning?"

"Why wait?" Valerian didn't want Shaye locked away for longer than necessary. He wanted this over and done with as quickly as possible. "We can settle this, you and I. No others need fight."

"I accept." Darius grinned as if that had been his hope all along, his sharp teeth gleaming. He wore no armor, but then, he couldn't. Not if he wanted to transform into a true dragon. "Winner takes the palace and everything inside."

"Agreed."

"But, my king," Broderick said at his side, speaking in a low, whispering tone. "You have not—"

"Worry not, my friend. I will prevail."

Broderick was not convinced. "At least go to Shaye. Let her suck you or welcome you into her body, but do not go down there without—"

"Silence." He held up his hand. He would not have Shaye's first time be nothing more than a quick tumble meant to strengthen him. No, their first time would be slow and tender. She would be mad with desire for him. He would show her the most pleasurable place on her body, then introduce her to his. "I will be down shortly, Darius," he called.

The dragon king nodded.

Valerian turned to Broderick and the men even now circling him.

"This could be a trap." Joachim clutched his sword hilt. "Once you go down, they could close in on you and kill you. That is what I would do."

"Keep the archers in place," Valerian instructed. "If a dragon warrior appears to step out of rank, kill him."

Broderick nodded.

"There is something I must do before I meet the dragons." None of his men said a word as he strode away from them. They knew what he meant to do—at least, they suspected. They were partly right.

He exited the parapet and found an empty corner room. While he would not visit Shaye, neither would he fight the dragon king without first doing *something*. He conjured his mate's pale face in his mind, saw her lips parted, saw desire in her velvety-brown eyes. As he imagined sinking inside her body, he slipped a hand inside his pants and wrapped it around his cock. Up and down he stroked the thick, hard length.

He could almost feel her hot, wet tightness. Could almost hear her breathy moans and eager purrs. He'd increase his tempo because she'd be wild with need and would crave a hard slamming. His testicles would slap her, and even that would be arousing. Wildly so.

When he heard her shout his name in climax, he roared with his own. Seed squirted from him. And with the release of his seed came a wave of strength. Not as intense as if he'd been with Shaye, but enough.

He cleaned himself and stalked back to his men.

"Here is your shield," Joachim said. The change in his attitude was remarkable, and more than Valerian could ever have hoped for. "The Skull is inside."

"Do you require your spear?" Shivawn asked.

Valerian gripped the shield and cast a glance to Darius, who now stood in the center of a half circle, dragons flanking him. Darius held only a sword. Because they'd fought before, Valerian knew that was not the man's only weapon. Darius would use his teeth, his claws and his fire, and Valerian in turn would need every weapon at his disposal.

"Yes," he said. "Spear. I will need a dragon medallion, as well."

Shivawn gathered the items and handed them to him. "May the gods be with you, my king."

Valerian anchored the necklace around his neck and slapped Shivawn on the shoulder. "I finally have something worth fighting for. I will not allow a dragon to keep me from her."

Broderick arched a brow. "Her? Do you not fight for the palace?"

"I fight for Shaye. I fight for all of our women, nymph and human, that they might have a home."

"Half of the men should come down with you," Joachim said. "We can close the circle with *your* allies."

He nodded. "Excellent."

With a troupe of nymphs marching behind him, he sliced down the steps on the edge of the wall and soon stood at the door.

"Open," he said, lifting the necklace. The door instantly obeyed; a crack formed between the white stones, slowly widening.

He and his men filed out, never relaxing their guard. The dragons remained in place, growling. Nymphs snarled in response. Valerian's eyes locked on Darius, the only blue-eyed dragon in existence.

The dragon king had a stern face, harsh and savage. Up close, Valerian could see the scar that slashed down Darius's face—a scar he himself had inflicted. "This is amusing, really," Valerian told him.

Darius arched his brows in a menacing salute. "And why is that?"

"You took a human woman for your mate, and now you scold us for doing the same."

"*You* have taken a mate?" Darius laughed. "Your conquests are legendary."

"As are my victories," he said with a proud tilt of his chin. "I will fight to the death—your death—to keep my woman safe."

Gradually the dragon's amusement faded, and he regarded Valerian with something akin to understanding. "Though they have been absent from us for many years, the gods cannot like such continued defiance. I was ordered, long ago, never to enter the surface and never to bring humans here." He spewed a stream of fire. "I fear you will bring their wrath to us all."

"Me? What of you?" Valerian leapt forward. The fight had begun. He leveled his spear at Darius's middle and stabbed.

Darius jumped out of the way, spraying more fire as he did so. Valerian rolled from its path of destruction, the flames barely missing him. The scent of charred hair filled his nose. He used the momentum of his roll to stab at Darius again.

The spear *whooshed,* hitting only air. Darius's wings expanded, the thick length of opalescent membrane gliding up and down. Valerian popped to his feet. He dodged left, away from another blast of fire, then spun on his heel and pretended to lunge. Instead, he swung his spear behind him and stabbed forward from the opposite side. The tip grazed Darius's thigh while he still hovered in the air.

The other dragons hissed, but Darius gave no outward reaction. He simply opened his mouth, unleashing a terrible inferno. Valerian raised his shield just in time, blocking. But the metal began to burn his hand. He leapt up and swung.

Clang. The vibration from metal against metal stung the wound in his arm. He moved with the impetus, though, and twisted, slicing his spear through the air and forcing Darius to duck. Without pause, Darius charged. Valerian blocked and lunged. Blocked. Stabbed.

"We could do this all day, for I am sure we will once again prove to be an even match," Darius growled.

Valerian gouged his spear at a downward angle, hoping to slice into Darius's other thigh. If he could hobble the dragon, making him rely only on his wings, Valerian could gain the advantage. But Darius jolted up and down quickly, placing the wooden length of the spear under his foot and snapping the weapon in two.

Immediately Valerian slid The Skull from its scabbard on the inside of his shield. He ran two steps, jumped and cut downward. This time Darius did not move quickly enough and the blade sliced into his arm.

Once again the dragons hissed, and once again Darius gave no reaction. It was as if he was impervious to pain. Unfortunately, Valerian was not. His wounded arm throbbed and his legs were growing shaky. If the fight didn't end soon...

Distantly he heard his men cheering for him.

"For Shaye," Broderick shouted. "Shaye. Shaye. Shaye."

Her lovely face flashed before his mind, and he gathered his strength. Rallied himself. He'd been pushed to the brink before. There had been times he'd gone without food and water, his people without a home. He could prevail. Perhaps he should change his battle strategy. Instead of forcing Darius to fly, perhaps he should cut into Darius's wings, grounding him....

The dragon king suddenly slammed into him, knocking him down, hacking his chest armor. He tasted dirt in his mouth, felt warm blood ooze, and kicked backward. Darius soared over him, taking Valerian's shield with him. Valerian didn't bother rising to his feet this time. He spied Darius from the corner of his eye and simply shot out his sword.

It stabbed into Darius's side, between arm and rib.

There was a collective gasp from the dragons, as if they couldn't believe it had happened. There was a cheer from the nymphs. Then Darius hit the sword with his own, proving it had slid through air, not flesh. Valerian anchored his feet and leapt up. He swung behind him. *Clang.* Quickly he pivoted, swinging again. *Clang.*

"Shall we do this all day or will you finally leave the palace?" Darius said, his tone a bit hollow. He spoke between hits.

Clang. "I'd really rather kill you now," Valerian answered, "if it's all the same to you."

"I will let you keep the women." *Clang.*

"And how will we shelter them without the palace?" He drew in a deep breath—and noticed the scents of blood and death had suddenly thickened the air.

"Vampires," a dragon hissed.

The word echoed through the crowd. A curse to dragons, a blessing to nymphs. No one warred more fiercely with the vampires than the dragons.

Darius stilled. Valerian did the same. He could see that the vampires were interspersed with the contingent of men he'd sent to close in the rear.

"You tricked me," Darius snarled. "This was not to be a fair fight, after all. You dared bring the vampires here to aid you."

"I didn't ask them to come, but I certainly won't send them away. They are my allies. We can finish this fight here and now, you and me."

"As if I will trust the vampires not to attack me while I'm distracted. We will leave now, Valerian, but we are not finished with you and yours."

As he spoke, the black-clad vampires closed in. They floated rather than walked, and they were hurling curses at the dragons. The dragons in turn mutated into their bestial forms. Wings sprouted from their backs, ripping every piece of their clothing. Scales consumed their skin, green and black and menacing. Fangs grew in place of their teeth. Tails sprouted from their lower backs.

They didn't engage the vampires or nymphs in any way. No, they sprang into the sky, moving higher and higher, before disappearing from Valerian's line of vision.

They would be back, Valerian knew, and the fight would not be as mild as it had been today. It would not be a battle between two men, but a bloodbath between races.

LAYEL, KING OF THE VAMPIRES, and his army came to an abrupt stop on the field. Seeing the dragons had disappeared, he and his army gave a cheer.

"Good to see you again, my friend," Valerian said when the cheers died down.

"I heard the dragons were marching toward you and decided to help."

Valerian clasped him on the shoulder. "Last time I saw you, you were holding court with the demon queen." He had not forgiven those hideous creatures for what they'd done to his people. "Do you ally yourself with her still?"

Layel smiled slowly. He had white hair, though it wasn't as pale as Shaye's. Ice-blue eyes, strong, mystical features. "I never allied myself with her. I used her, and then I killed her."

Valerian returned the grin. "Then you and yours are welcome inside."

"My king," a female vampire said, approaching Layel's side. She had the same pale shade of hair as Layel, the same blue eyes, except her features were soft, eerily beautiful.

Usually Layel did not allow his females near the nymphs.

"Alyssa," the king acknowledged.

"Do we have your permission to...dally?" Her gaze was locked on Shivawn, and there was lust in her eyes.

Ah. Valerian suddenly understood why she'd been

allowed to come. She wanted Shivawn and had probably asked to join the army just to see him.

Layel looked to Valerian. Valerian, of course, nodded his permission. The woman, Alyssa, grinned seductively and floated to Shivawn.

"Come," Valerian said. He turned on his heel and strode to the palace, taking the dragon medallion from under his shirt and holding it up so the door sensor would allow the entrance to open.

Layel kept pace beside him, the others closing in behind them.

"Did you ever find the Jewel of Dunamis?" Valerian asked him. They entered the main hall. "I know you were on a crusade to unearth it, yet Darius told me a human now has possession."

"Alas, it escaped me. It escaped all of us, really."

"On the surface, as Darius said?"

"Yes."

"Any way to get it back?"

"None, I'm afraid."

Perhaps he could travel to the surface and search for it, Valerian thought suddenly, for it might be the best way to protect Shaye. He would ponder that later. For now, he had a reprieve from battle. He was weak and tired and needed his mate.

"Broderick," he called, "see that guards are stationed around the entire palace, top and bottom, inside and out."

"My men can help," Layel offered.

"You are guests. You will enjoy. Dorian, see to our guests' comfort."

Layel's brows arched. "You are not remaining with us?"

"No. There is a woman I must see to."

His friend grinned, though sadness clung to the edges. He'd lost his love years ago. "I understand. Go. Be on your way. We will be fine without you."

Valerian needed no further urging. He strode down the rest of the hall. His hands itched for Shaye. Finally he would make her his. Completely.

CHAPTER TWENTY-THREE

SHAYE KEPT HER BACK pressed against the far wall of the enclosure, as far away as she could get from the prisoners. She didn't want to accidentally release them. They begged and pleaded relentlessly, and she tried to distract herself by composing anti-cards. Well, not really *anti*. All her ideas were for a new, not-so-anti collection. Things like, *"I'd like to spend more time with you."* And, *"Being with you isn't so bad."*

"Let us out!" one of the prisoners said, cutting into her thoughts.

Beasts, Valerian had once called them. *Killers.*

They didn't look like killers. They looked like handsome men who were tinted blue from cold. Well, not *men* so much. They looked like little more than boys.

"Be careful," she told Brenna.

"Who are they?" her friend asked, a tinge of fear in her voice.

"I don't exactly know."

"Please," the youngest beseeched. "My name is Kendrick. Let us go. We will not hurt you. We would never hurt a woman. Perhaps we can help each other," he rushed on. "I will help free you from the nymphs' spell, and you can let me go. Just touch the bars."

Whether she believed him or not was moot. These boys despised the nymphs. When Kendrick had said the word, he'd sneered with absolute hatred. Because of that, they would remain here. Valerian's safety came first. "Why were you imprisoned?" she asked.

"Because we are dragons. Because this is *our* palace and the nymphs coveted it for their own."

As she'd suspected. Still. "Sorry, boys," she said. She did feel sorry for them. "I can't. However, I will speak to Valerian about setting you free in the wild or something."

They looked to Brenna.

She bit her lip and shook her head no.

"Don't you see?" The most handsome of the group gripped the bars, gazing at them with piercing gold eyes. "You're under Valerian's spell. Fight it or you'll remain his slave for eternity."

Under Valerian's spell…how true those words were. She hadn't been herself since she'd first laid eyes on him. Was it the general allure of the nymph, though, or Valerian the man that enchanted her? She suspected the latter, because none of the other men appealed to her.

"Even still." She squared her shoulders, determined. "I'm leaving you in here. And I feel really bad about that, but—"

"You look like you feel bad," Kendrick said dryly. "Your eyes are sparkling."

The thought of seeing Valerian again did that to her. "Hey." She blinked as a thought occurred to her. "You're speaking English. *My* language."

He shrugged, as if the observation had no importance. "Our king wed a human."

She blinked in surprise. "So there are more humans in the city? How—"

"Where is she?" she heard a man shout. There was terror and fury in his tone.

Valerian.

Her heart kicked into overtime, beating like a silly drum. Heat infused her cells. "Gotta go," she told the boys. "I won't forget you, I promise, and I'll even talk to Valerian about you. Come on, Brenna."

"Shaye!" Valerian shouted, his voice frantic. "Shaye!"

"Don't leave us," Kendrick pleaded. "Fight against his allure."

She gave him a pinky wave and raced from the enclosure, Brenna right behind her. When they emerged from between the rocks, they rounded the corner and stepped directly behind the portal. She heard another, "Shaye," this one more panicked than before.

"I'll return as soon as possible," he said to someone.

He was about to step into the portal, she realized. "I'm here, Valerian. I'm here."

He whipped to face her, reaching out automatically to grab her arm. He tugged her to him, and their gazes locked. Shadows of relief couched his features...followed quickly by fury. He released her and braced his arms over his chest, and it was then she saw what he was holding. She almost cried. He was holding an orange.

A lump filled her throat. He'd found it for her. She had mentioned that she wanted one, and in the midst of war he'd found one.

Her knees shook. Her nerve endings sizzled as she took it from him. "Thank you," she said softly. She drank him in.

302 THE NYMPH KING

His hair was sweat soaked and hanging in sand-coated tangles at his temples. Streaks of blood covered his face and arms, and his turquoise eyes shot sparks at her. Of fury, yes, but also of lust.

She nearly dropped the orange as she noticed the rest of him. A deep gash branded his chest. "You're hurt," she said stupidly.

"I am fine. How did you escape the cell?" The question was uttered in a still, quiet voice, so much more ominous than if he'd shouted. "And I see you took Brenna with you."

Shaye, too, assumed a battle stance. If he wasn't worried about the wound, she wouldn't be, either. "Leave her out of this. I got out with a little thing called ingenuity."

He ran his tongue over his teeth. "How long have you been free?"

"Long enough to go through the portal."

His expression relaxed in gradual degrees. "But you didn't."

"But I didn't." Why were they talking? She wanted his tongue on her. She wanted, finally, to know the most erotic place on her body, and she wanted him to bring her to shuddering climax. Twice. She wanted to drip orange on his skin and lick it up.

Behind her, Dylan and Terran ushered the rest of the women from the cell. "Take this one, as well," Valerian said, motioning to Brenna.

"No," Brenna said. "No touching."

"Take her, but do not touch her," Valerian allowed.

Brenna walked willingly to the group.

Kathleen spotted Shaye and frowned. "I thought you were going to escape."

"Didn't work out," she said, fighting the urge to hang a sign around Valerian's neck that said *Mine*. She faced him. "Listen. I was chatting with the dragons and—" She pressed her mouth together. Maybe that wasn't a good thing to admit.

Valerian's nostrils flared. "I put you in that cell to protect you. Not only do you escape, you visit my enemies, too."

Shaye drew herself to her full height. "That's right. So? I will not tolerate being locked away. I told you that. Where's my thanks for staying down here when I could have gone back to the surface?"

"Your thanks? *Your thanks?*" He pounded a fist into his open palm. "Did the dragons hurt you? Did they touch you in any way?"

"No. And since we're on the subject, I think you should let them go. They're just boys, Valerian."

He smoothed a hand down his face. "They are dragons, Shaye."

"So give them back to the rest of the dragons."

"That is my plan," he said, throwing his arms in the air. "They will make excellent bargaining tools."

"Good."

"Good." He shook his head. "While I like that you are stepping into the role of queen, advising me and issuing orders, you are in dire need of punishment, woman."

His words elicited an erotic response from her. That wasn't what he intended, but that was what he got. Her eyes lowered to half-mast. "Punish me, then. Go ahead, for God's sake. You know how much I hate it."

Instant fire consumed his anger, leaving only white-hot lust. "You hate it? Truly?"

"More than I can ever say," she whispered. Her stomach clenched deliciously, swirling and fluttering with need. It was as if he'd never stopped making love to her. All of her desires returned full force.

She, the woman who prided herself on remaining distant from every situation, couldn't fight Valerian's allure. She, who found comfort in a frosty, utterly cold attitude, quaked with sensation. Was desperate. Needy. Raw and exposed. There was a vulnerability inside her she hadn't known was there, one that cried out for the love and affection she'd never received. Not from anyone.

Except this man.

Slowly, never breaking eye contact, he closed the small gap between them. The closer he came, the hotter the air grew, chasing away any hint of chill. Her nipples beaded painfully, reaching for him, yearning for some type of contact.

"I won't stop this time," he warned. "Not for any reason."

"Good. We agree about something else." *Touch me.* She didn't care that people were just beyond the rock. She only cared about Valerian.

"Run," he said softly.

She blinked, certain she had misheard him. "What?" Was he turning her away?

"Run. To my room. Now."

There was no humor in his tone, no sense that he was through with her. Instead, he projected a fierce lust that went beyond anything he'd ever shown her before. The breath in her throat snagged. She backed away from him, her heart skipping a beat. His expression was intense, savage. Utterly wild.

"Run," he repeated. "Now."

Clutching the orange, she sprang forward, racing around him, careful not to touch him. Her arms pumped at her sides as she pounded up the stairs. Footsteps echoed behind her. She remembered the path to the room and whipped around corners. Warriors roamed the halls, collecting their bed partners. Some hadn't made it to a room and were having sex right there in the hall.

Panting, she barreled past them. Thankfully no one tried to stop her. Valerian's intensity was frightening. And arousing. And startling. And wonderful.

When she reached the outer bathing area, she picked up speed. What was he going to do to her when he caught her? She shot past the white curtain separating the two sections of the room, and it whooshed behind her. A split second later, it whooshed again.

Valerian. Close, so close.

She gulped, was just about to spin around and demand he explain why he'd not picked her up and carried her here, why he'd not let her wrap her legs around his waist and feel every step he took between her legs, when he slammed into her from behind. Together they soared through the air. She screamed, dropped her fruit. Just before she hit the bed, Valerian turned them, absorbing the impact with his own body.

One of his arms flipped her over and banded around her waist. The other pulled at her shirt, stripping her.

"Why…why?" she panted, unable to get any other word out.

"Couldn't wait." Her breasts were suddenly bared. He held her above him and laved one of her nipples into his mouth. Pure heat. She sucked in a gasp of air. Some-where along the way, he'd lost his chest armor. Her hands kneaded him, mindful of his injuries. His nipples were hard and abraded her palms erotically; his nipple ring was cool to the touch yet burned her with its masculinity.

She straddled his waist, anchoring her weight on her knees. This was exactly where she belonged, she mused. Her hair cascaded around her shoulders. Adrenaline from the chase rushed through her blood, blending with desire, making it all the more potent. All the more con-suming. Her skin felt alive with pulses of electricity.

He untied the belt holding her pants in place and flung it aside, causing the pants to gape open. He paused a moment, staring at her with purpose.

"I'm going to kiss you here," he muttered roughly. His fingertip grazed a path along the center of her panties. "Then I'm going to pleasure your body the way I've wanted from the moment I saw you."

"Yes." She loved his raw language, was excited by it. "Pleasure. Do it."

"Nothing will stop me."

"Nothing." She arched her hips slightly forward, sliding over the hard length of his erection. Sensations of utter bliss tore through her, and she moaned.

"You'll love everything I do." His hand clenched on her waist. His eyes closed, and he bit his lower lip. "You'll beg for more."

She slid over him again. They both groaned. "Love it," she promised. "Beg."

He rolled her over, jerking at her pants while he did so. His feet kicked the material the rest of the way down. Her panties quickly followed, yet he didn't have the patience to work them off her so he ripped the seams and discarded the tattered remains.

Completely naked, she reached between them and worked at *his* pants. Her motions were clipped, eager, desperate, but she made no progress. "I can't get them off," she growled. "Help me get them off."

Within seconds he had them peeled away and she was in heaven. Hmm. Skin to skin.

"Soft," he praised. He traced a path along her collarbone, then nipped at her neck, grazing her overly sensitive flesh with his teeth.

She could feel his penis on her belly, as hot as a steel band. She arched against it, needing it inside her. "Now," she said.

His shaft jerked against her. His teeth bit more sharply. "Kiss," he said hoarsely. He licked down her body, exploring her breasts again, lingering at her stomach, flicking her belly button.

"Grip the top of the bed," he demanded.

She'd been reaching down, intent on threading her fingers through his hair. "But—"

"Do it. Grip the bed."

She obeyed. The moment her fingers curled around the ivory base, his tongue glided over her clitoris. Her hips shot up, and she gasped his name.

With one of his hands, he opened her fully. With the other he glided a finger into her, probing, stretching. His tongue never stopped working her. The combination of sensations was shattering. Another coast of his tongue. A pump of his fingers. Then he sucked at her, increasing the tempo. She cried. She sobbed. Oh, the bliss. Her legs locked around him. Her hands clutched the headboard so tightly her knuckles could have snapped.

Her eyelids squeezed shut. In her mind she saw him between her legs, his tawny hair falling onto her thighs. His muscled back clenched tight as he reined in his own need.

"Valerian! I can't take any more."

"By the end of the night, you'll have taken everything I have to give."

"Push me...give me...let me come."

She writhed. On the verge. So close, yet not close enough. He slid another finger into her, and it was a tight fit. Stretching her. Filling her. So. Good. Quickly his tongue flicked over her clitoris, showing no mercy. Not that she wanted any. This was everything she'd dreamed, everything she'd ever needed without knowing she did.

"I'm going to sink my cock into you, Shaye. You're going to spread your legs and welcome me, every stretching inch."

"Yes." Oh, God, yes. The thought of his penis inside her pushed her over the sweet edge. She spasmed around his fingers, clenching them tight. A scream, a sob. Flashing white lights blinked behind her eyes.

He suddenly loomed above her, her legs cradled in the crook of his arms, opening her fully. Exposing her completely. He was poised on the brink of penetration. "Once I'm inside you, you will be mine. Say it."

"Yours. I'll be yours." There was no denying it. She *was* his. Now, this moment, she was his. She reached up and wrapped her fingers around his neck, tangling in his hair. His chest was pressed against hers and she could feel the fine-grained sand that still clung to him from the fight, adding friction, another depth of pleasure. "Kiss," she beseeched.

His head swooped down, and he claimed her mouth. The moment their tongues touched, he slammed inside her. No waiting. No gradually letting her become accustomed. He was simply in her to the hilt. As if he couldn't go another minute without being there.

She cried out in his mouth; he swallowed the sound. She was so aroused, so slick with desire, so prepared for him, there was only a slight sting, then complete pleasure. He stretched her erotically, filled her inexorably.

On and on the kiss continued. She tasted herself on his lips. Tasted him, the heat of him, the passion. In and out his tongue probed in sync with his strong body. In and out. Moving quickly, hurtling them both to the stars.

"Can't…slow…down," he panted.

"Glad."

His testicles slapped at her. The tip of him hit all the way to her womb, the exact spot she needed him. She was already close, ready to explode for the second time. Tension coiled in her stomach, in her blood.

"Shaye!" he roared. He pumped into her, hard, delicious. "Mine."

Mine, she silently repeated. The climax gripped her, more intense than the first, making her shudder against him. Her knees clenched at him, and to the heavens she soared. High, so high.

He joined her there. He spasmed against her, inside her. Gave a final, pounding thrust. His eyes squeezed tight. Bliss consumed his features.

"Mine," he growled. "Mine."

VALERIAN HAD NEVER FELT more powerful. Strength radiated from him, filled him, pulsed and sizzled. He always felt invigorated after sex, but this… Never like this. And with Shaye it had not been sex, he thought. It had been lovemaking. A union. Total and complete. Especially that last time when they'd licked her favorite fruit off each other.

Mine, he thought again.

The word would not leave him. He'd never felt so possessive of another person. Actually, he'd never felt so possessive of anything, including his cherished sword. Including the palace. She'd tasted like no other woman. Erupted like no other woman. Pleased him like no other woman. He was the nymph, yet it was she who wrapped him in her sensual spell. It was she who enslaved him.

She snuggled into his side, her curves nestled against him. He could feel the soft exhalations of her breath. He would die without this woman. Simply perish. Cease to exist. He wanted to give her the world, offer her everything her heart desired.

Never more than now had he been so determined to keep the palace. He would not have his woman homeless, staying in whatever shack he could find for them. Yes, he would keep this place from the dragons.

He would keep Shaye. For eternity.

When he'd returned to the dungeon and she had not been inside the cell, his heart had stopped beating. Panic, dread, fury had consumed him. He'd nearly hacked Dylan and Terran to pieces. Then, when he'd seen Shaye as relaxed and at ease as if she had not a care—while standing next to the portal, for the love of the gods—he'd panicked again.

How close he'd come to losing her.

Then she'd begun issuing orders with bravery and wisdom, acting every bit the queen she was meant to be, and he'd been struck anew with love for her.

Somehow, some way, he'd gain her oath to stay forever. He would never let her go.

CHAPTER TWENTY-FOUR

AFTER HE'D SATED HIMSELF on the women and listened to their tales, Poseidon had whisked himself to the nearest river, a crystal stream of tranquility. Lilies floated on the surface. He now blended himself into the water, flowing with it, absorbing its coolness.

The nymphs had indeed broken the law. He needed to punish them quickly, before others thought to do the same. And he knew just what to do....

When he reached a fork in the river, he stopped. The water itself stilled, no waves, no liquid movement. Only the silent wind above, the patter of nearby animals. Then...the bank on his left suddenly flooded with dragon warriors, their wings flapping as they landed. Still, the water did not ripple.

Poseidon watched them. A long while passed before their dragon forms faded to human. Smooth, though scarred, skin instead of scales. Silky hair. Teeth instead of fangs. No tail. Of course, they were now naked, wearing only dragon medallions and holding their swords.

They began drinking from the stream, their angry chatter echoing between the trees. His gaze found Darius. The leader of the dragons was speaking with several of his men, issuing orders, his expression fierce.

He hadn't liked abandoning the palace, Poseidon knew. His instincts had been to stay and fight the nymphs—Valerian in particular. But Darius, if he recalled correctly, was a warrior who weighed the odds, studied the situation and calculated the percentages. He'd been outnumbered severely and he hadn't wanted his men injured when a sneak attack could work in their favor, evening the odds.

He was a smart man and exactly what Poseidon needed.

Come to me, he commanded Darius, his voice carrying on the wind.

Darius paused and stiffened. His eyes searched the surrounding wooded area, glazed over the river, saw nothing and returned to his men. His shoulders remained stiff, his posture erect and his hands clenched tightly on the hilt of his sword.

Come, Poseidon said again.

Darius's attention whipped to the river for the second time. His eyes narrowed. Poseidon knew the water provided only a reflection of his god-image, a glint in the fading light. Still, Darius obeyed this time, striding to the river's edge. The men he'd been speaking with watched in confusion.

"Is something wrong?" a hulking blond giant asked.

"Rest a while, Brand," the dragon king responded without looking back. When he stood alone, he said, "You called, water god?"

The complete irreverence in his tone annoyed the god. "You know me, then."

"I know *of* you."

Poseidon's jaw clenched, causing a ripple in the

water. "Then you know the consequences of speaking to me thus. You know the suffering I can cause."

Darius gave a clipped nod.

Not the bow of homage Poseidon preferred, but it would do. "I have learned some things since my return, Darius, things that do not please me. Because of this, I have several tasks to ask of you."

A muscle ticked beneath his eyes. "Then I am at your command, of course."

"Good. I wish you to return to the palace."

There was a pause. "That is not my plan."

"No, you wish to gather more men. That will take time, and I want my will obeyed now. This moment."

Darius stood firm. "That will place dragon lives in unnecessary danger, and I can't allow that."

"There will be no danger to you and yours if you sneak inside."

"I do plan to sneak inside. But there *is* danger if I do not have enough men to take the palace once we are within."

Poseidon grinned slowly. "Not if you are able to destroy half of the nymph and vampire forces before you even reach the palace hallways."

Darius's brows arched, and interest sparked in his blue eyes. "Tell me how that is possible."

"There is a doorway, a secret entrance below the portal."

"Where exactly?" He sounded faraway, as if he was already breaching it in his mind.

"Do not worry. I will show you once you get there. You will sneak inside and return the human women to the surface, their memories wiped clean."

"Done."

"Once they are returned, you will destroy the nymphs. They'll be weak without their women and easy for you to take. Every one of them must die for daring to enter the surface world. They are not guardians, which means they have disobeyed the law."

A muscle clenched in Darius's jaw. "Surely you do not mean all of them."

"All."

"Male *and* female?"

"All. You have done such deeds before. This should be no hardship for you, Guardian. If you think to refuse me, I will have your own wife sent back to the surface. You acquired her from there, did you not?"

A blaze of fury lit Darius's face, revealing the merciless killer he had once been. "I will not allow Grace to be taken. She is mine, a daughter of Atlantis now, pregnant with my child."

"Yes, I know," Poseidon said dryly. "The child is the only reason I'm allowing you to keep her. You, Guardian, should never have brought her back here in the first place."

"I'm grateful you have finally decided to take an interest in your people, great god," Darius said, his tone just as dry.

"Is this sarcasm something you acquired from your bride?" Poseidon did not like it. "Watch your tongue, or I will feed it to the vampires. If I wished to amuse myself elsewhere for a little while, that was my right. Go now," he said. "Return to the palace. I will be there waiting, and I will show you the way inside."

"Before you leave," Darius said, irreverence still sparkling in his eyes, "perhaps you could gift us with clothing."

"It will be my pleasure." As a slight punishment for Darius's impertinence today, Poseidon blew his breath upon the dragon army, spraying them with a fine mist of sea and leaving them dressed in women's scarves.

Their hisses of shock rang in his ears long after he left them.

BRENNA'S HANDS TWISTED together. She stood at the edge of the dining hall, watching Shivawn, waiting for him to notice her. She'd been escorted to him after leaving the cave. He was speaking heatedly with a female Brenna hadn't seen before—a white-haired beauty who was caressing her fingertip down his chest.

Brenna watched the interaction with only the slightest hint of…jealousy? She wasn't sure. That was an emotion she hadn't felt in years. Whatever the emotion, she suspected it stemmed from not knowing what would happen to her if Shivawn found another woman. Would she be given to someone else? Joachim, perhaps?

Another question slithered through her mind. Would she be jealous if it had been Joachim talking so heatedly with another woman? She feared the answer.

Just thinking about the man made her shiver. No. No, no, no. It could be Shivawn making her shiver, she rationalized. He was safety, while Joachim was everything she feared: controlling, dominant and violent. So why did she have to desire him at all? Why could she not simply want Shivawn?

She sighed. As she'd stared into the portal today, about to return home, she'd been struck by a wonderfully frightening realization. She wanted to leave the past in the past and embrace her new future. By embracing it, she could finally know true contentment and joy. By embracing it, she could finally *live*.

It had been in that moment that she'd decided to sleep with Shivawn. But then Joachim's image had forced its way into her mind, and well, now she just didn't know. She *was* going to have a relationship: sexual, emotional, intimate. But which man would she pick? Life with Shivawn would be sweet and tender. Life with Joachim would be turbulent and exciting.

As she stood there debating with herself, Shivawn's head jerked to the side. He snarled something to the now-scowling woman, and his eyes met Brenna's. He stopped midsentence and stalked toward her. He didn't speak a word, just grabbed her hand and propelled her from the room.

Her blood heated with thoughts of being with him, of going to his room and tracing her hands all over his body, of feeling *his* hands on *her*. Her nipples even beaded…until she realized it still wasn't Shivawn's face she saw in her mind.

They weren't heading toward his room, she noticed a moment later. "Where?" she asked Shivawn. The walls surrounding his room were in a different state of repair than the ones here. These were… Realization struck her before he said a word, and her eyes widened. Joachim's room. They were going to Joachim's room. She knew because she'd curiously searched for and found it earlier. Menacing weapons had hung on the walls, a blatant reminder of why she couldn't want a man like him. Her stomach twisted with a mixture of apprehension and anticipation.

"Joachim is okay?"

"He is well."

That meant…what? They arrived at the curtain a moment later. Shivawn didn't pause, didn't announce himself, just strode past the scarf barrier. He released her hand and stalked to a side table. He kept his back to her and poured a drink for himself. He downed it.

The first thing she noticed about the room was that the weapons were gone. Not a single sword hung on the wall. Why had they been removed?

Her gaze flicked to Joachim. He sat on the bed, his legs over the side, his elbows resting on his knees. His gaze devoured her. "Brenna," he said, her name a sensual caress.

Instantly her blood heated another degree. Her nipples hardened further. Need pooled between her legs. With only a word, he brought her to readiness. They were going to make her choose, she realized. Last time she'd run from this, from her feelings. She squared her shoulders. Not this time. The other women in the palace were well satisfied. They never stopped grinning, never experienced a single fear. So badly she wanted to be one of them. She *would* be one of them.

No, there would be no more running. But could she risk the safety she was sure to find with Shivawn for the passion she was sure to find with Joachim? There would be no going back once she'd made her choice. They were too possessive, each too determined to be "the one."

Shivawn didn't waste any more time. "You've kept me waiting long enough. You've kept *yourself* waiting long enough. End the agony and give me a chance, Brenna," he said, once again at her side. He gently gripped her shoulders and turned her to face him. "I will never allow another man to hurt you. I will take care of you, pleasure you, make you so happy you'll forget ever being sad."

She bit her lip.

He added, "The man on that bed will never be kind or gentle or any of the things I sense that you need." He turned her again, this time making her face Joachim.

Her eyes met Joachim's once more, and her stomach quivered.

"Look at him," Shivawn said. "Even now there's a wildness about him that you cannot deny. He will never be able to control his temper. He will never be able to destroy the demons that plague you."

Shivawn's words were supposed to comfort her, to assure her that choosing safety over passion was the right decision. But they didn't. Because there was no stronger warrior than Joachim. He did have a temper, and he did appear wild. Yet, if anyone could fight and destroy demons of the past, it was him. He was just so *vital*.

Joachim didn't utter a sound. He simply pulled four strips of cloth from underneath his pillow. He draped them over his knees.

"What are those for?" Shivawn demanded.

"Tie me to the bed, Brenna," Joachim said.

She glanced down at the material in puzzlement…and desire. "What?"

"Tie me to the bed."

Her gaze swiftly returned to Joachim's face. His expression was hard, resolved and aroused. So aroused. Heat blazed in his blue eyes, burning her inside and out. "Why? Don't understand."

"I'm not going to tell you that you'll hate yourself later if you choose Shivawn. You could probably be happy with him, and you'll always feel safe. But he can't fill the void inside you and give you the life I know you've dreamed of having. I can. All you have to do is trust that I'll never hurt you. Never. I would die first. I'll do whatever it takes to prove it."

"Joachim," Shivawn snarled.

"Tie me to the bed, and you will be in control of everything that happens," Joachim explained. A muscle ticked beneath his eye. "I'm giving you complete…power over me. You need to take back your sense of control, so I'm going to help you."

He was talking about bondage. About sex. Her wild gaze darted between the two men. "Shi—Shivawn?" What did he have to say about this?

He was the one to remain silent this time. He was stiff and radiated fury.

"I noticed how you jump every time someone comes up behind you," Joachim said, "so I'm going to show you the pleasure of having a man there. Later. This time I want to show you the pleasure of being in control."

This big, strong warrior was willing to give up control—his precious control—for her. A tremor worked through her. The revelation startled her, *strengthened* her. She'd wanted passion, she'd admitted that to herself already. No one could give her more passion than Joachim. She'd admitted that, too, but she'd been scared of it. Scared of him. And so she'd done her best to fall for Shivawn. She might even have convinced herself of it. For a while. Eventually, she would have realized the truth.

All along, it had been Joachim she'd desired. She simply hadn't wanted to want him. He was taking a chance on her with his willingness to be bound. She could do no less for him. *I'm not going to be scared anymore.*

Eyes filling with tears, she looked at Shivawn. He was so sweet, so kind and giving. But as she looked at him, she realized he was exactly what she didn't need anymore. A bodyguard. She could take care of herself now. She'd been in this palace for days and hadn't been hurt. She'd faced down the warriors and hadn't been attacked.

"You can walk away from both of us," Joachim said, his voice rough. "We won't stop you."

Run, and stay locked in her safe little world. No feeling. No pain. No pleasure. *I'll never run again.* "I'm so sorry, Shivawn," she said, chin trembling. "I wanted it to be you. I did. But…"

"Stop. Please. Just stop." He studied her for a long while, jaw locked tight. Then he slowly turned to Joachim. "She is yours. I relinquish all claim to her."

"Thank you," Joachim said tightly.

Shivawn flicked her one last glance, nodded, and strode from the room, leaving her alone with Joachim. Brenna gulped. Gathering her courage, she faced him.

Her man.

Fear would never rule her life again.

She'd chosen him, and she was only sorry it had taken her so long to realize the depth of this man's honor. He trusted her to chain him; she would trust him not to hurt her.

Ready to finally move on with her life, she walked forward. Her heart raced erratically, but she didn't stop until she was in front of him. Joachim stood, grasping the ties in his fists.

His gaze was hard, unrelenting. "Did your attacker use his hands or a weapon? If he used a weapon, I want you to use the same on me."

At first, she didn't answer, didn't let the memory intrude on this precious time. "Only hands," she managed on a trembling breath.

He nodded and gave her the bonds. Slowly, very slowly, Joachim unfastened his pants and pushed them from his hips. They pooled on the floor and she was given a glimpse of large, aroused male.

"Come here," he commanded, lying on the bed. "Tie me."

Her hands were shaky as she tied his wrists to the posts, then his ankles. Then she stood at the side of the bed, staring down at him. Such magnificence, hers to control.

Joachim didn't utter a word, but he watched her intently. Her knees almost buckled because she knew what he expected, what he wanted. It was her turn to strip. After the attack, she'd stopped working out and had tried to make herself as unattractive as possible. Would Joachim find her body undesirable?

She reached up with shaky fingers and undid her robe's shoulder ties, revealing her breasts. She continued to watch Joachim, gauging his reaction. There was no disappointment in his eyes. Only desire. She lost a little of her uncertainty. Delicious bumps broke out over her skin as his gaze skimmed over her, his nostrils flaring with arousal.

"You are beautiful, Brenna."

When her robe was completely loosed, it fell from her body and joined Joachim's pants on the floor. Finally she was naked, like him. Her cheeks heated as Joachim's eyes raked over her again. At one time, the thought of joining a man on a bed would have paralyzed her. This time, her hormones were too busy rejoicing.

"Close your eyes," he said.

She didn't think to argue.

"Imagine me behind you. Imagine my hands caressing your shoulders and cupping your breasts. Imagine me rolling your nipples between my fingers."

Yes. Yes! She saw it in her mind, just like before, only this time the image was clearer. Her head would fall back onto his shoulder, her hair tickling them both. His fingers would touch every inch of her.

Imagining was almost as good as the real thing. Almost. But thinking about it *did* make her unbearably wet.

"I want to lick you," Joachim said.

"Yes," she said breathlessly.

She climbed onto the bed without hesitation. Soon she straddled Joachim, her knees at his waist, his erection between her legs, touching her intimately but not entering her. She moaned at the utter decadence.

"Lean forward," Joachim urged roughly.

He might be tied, but he was still a warrior. For the first time, a small kernel of fear sprouted. *You're safe. You're protected.* She crawled up him until her breasts were poised over his waiting mouth. Her black curls fell around them like a curtain as he eagerly sucked on her, dissolving her fear, filling her with pleasure. Contact with his hot, hot mouth was like nothing she'd ever experienced. His mouth possessed volts of electricity, and those volts lanced inside her body.

She groaned, the sound broken and rough.

While Joachim sucked her, she continued to imagine. Had his hands been free, he would have traced them over her back, over the ridges of her spine. Over the curve of her bottom. Yes, yes! She saw it happening, somehow felt it. Everywhere his phantom hands touched, his mouth followed, his phantom tongue laving her skin. She couldn't help herself. She writhed against Joachim's penis without actual penetration. She was so wet, she slid up and down with ease.

"You taste like heaven," Joachim said.

In her mind, Joachim's hands circled her and urged her to straighten, then his fingers were sinking past her pubic hair and into her moist, hot center. She gave another groan of absolute pleasure.

Why had she tied him? she mused.

He sucked her nipple with delicious force.

"Yes," she gasped out, unable to say anything else. "Yes."

Her head again fell back.

"Do you want me to lick between your legs?"

"Yes." She didn't try to deny it or play coy. She wanted Joachim's mouth there. She wanted it fiercely. Would have killed for it.

"Come here," Joachim said. Sweat beaded over his skin. His jaw was tense.

She moved forward until she was poised over Joachim's body, the apex of her thighs mere inches from his face.

"Lower," he commanded, a rough snarl.

"Joachim," she said, sinking into him and in the next instant he was loving her with his face. His tongue, his lips, his teeth. He used them all. She screamed at the intense sensation, the heady pleasure. Her hips writhed back and forth.

"Come, Brenna. Come for me," Joachim said, and she obeyed. Her pleasure exploded. Erupted. Her entire body shook and trembled with her climax, propelling her to the gates of paradise. Joachim drank her up until she thought she could take no more.

"Take me," he said. "Put me inside you."

Limbs weak, she straddled Joachim's waist without hesitation. She rose up, placed Joachim's shaft at her entrance and sank down on him, taking him all the way to the hilt. He was big, and it had been so long. He stretched her, but it was a wonderful stretch. Made her feel alive.

Joachim roared.

She panted his name over and over again. "Joachim." She couldn't say it enough. It was in her head, branded on every cell in her body. "Joachim."

She was safe. She was sated—and would soon find release again. Her nerve endings were already sparking with renewed life.

She anchored her hands on Joachim's chest. Their faces were inches apart, his breath a part of her and her breath a part of him.

"Kiss me," he said.

Her mouth meshed against Joachim's. She gasped in pleasure and he swallowed the sound. Hard, hot, gentle, fast, slow, his tongue sparred with hers as she rode him. It was sheer bliss. Total ravishment.

The kiss became savage, and in turn, the loving became savage. Her teeth banged his; her body slammed up and down. She purred, she groaned, she gasped some more.

"That's it," Joachim praised. "Take it all."

"Yes."

"No more fear." Joachim.

"No more," she panted.

"Come for me, sweet." Joachim nipped her collarbone. He strained against his bonds. "Show me how much you like having me inside you."

There was no holding back at that point, no prolonging the pleasure. She erupted for the second time. The orgasm was so intense a black web clouded her vision. She was dying slowly, quickly, unable to breathe, yet so alive she could have stayed exactly where she was forever. "Joachim," she screamed, and for once she didn't care how broken her voice sounded.

"Brenna." Joachim roared loud and long and reared up, sinking deep, deeper than she'd ever thought possible.

She collapsed onto his chest. "Thank you," she panted. "Thank you."

"Untie me," he ordered harshly.

She didn't think to deny him. Blindly she reached up and removed the bonds. His arms instantly wrapped around her, pulling her close and holding her tightly. Cherishing her.

"No more fear," he said again.

"No more," she agreed. She would have agreed with anything he said just then. Marry him—yes. Be his slave—of course. His heat surrounded her, enveloped her, beckoned her.

"Mine," he said.

"Yours," she breathed. "Joachim's." Her eyes closed, her lids growing heavier and heavier with every second that passed. Sleep summoned, a peaceful sleep she'd needed for so long but had been too afraid to take. "Don't let me go."

"Never."

Oblivion claimed her then. She was smiling.

SHIVAWN STOOD IN THE hallway for a long while. He wished Brenna had chosen him, but it had been Joachim her eyes had heated for. Joachim she'd probably wanted all along. He was angry, so very angry. She was beautiful, she was passionate, she was kind. But she wasn't his. He knew that now. No matter how much pleasure Shivawn could have given her, no matter how safe he could have made her feel, she would always have wanted Joachim.

The two were mates, that much was clear now.

And so he ended up alone.

Perhaps one day he would find a woman who loved him like that. Who wanted him above all others.

He blinked when he realized Alyssa had stepped into the hall and now stood a few feet away from him. He scowled at her.

She frowned at him. "You smell like a human," she said flatly. "Have you been with one? Is she your mate?"

"What business is it of yours?" He leapt into a quick stride.

She followed suit, keeping pace beside him. "Is she?"

"No," he snapped.

"I told you I would see to your needs," she snapped back. "You should have come to me."

"And I told you no." Alyssa was beautiful, and Shivawn even felt himself stir for a taste of her, but he would not touch her. He didn't have Valerian's love for the vampires.

Vampires survived on blood and sometimes took more than they should. He'd made the mistake of bedding a vampire only once and had almost died for it. Never again, he'd vowed. Alyssa knew that, but she always sought him out when she came to visit.

"Goodbye, Alyssa," he said, and strode away from her.

She wasn't content to remain behind this time. She rushed after him, even jumped in front of him. Her eyes glowed. "I've always known I would have you one day, Shivawn, and I've decided today is that day."

Her lips slammed into his, her tongue forcing its way into his mouth. The taste of her filled him. Not a taste of blood and death, but of woman. Shivawn found himself responding. He was disgusted with himself but maybe, just maybe, she could help him forget his loneliness.

"One night," he growled. "That's all I'll give you."

Triumph blazed in her eyes, and her red, red lips curled in a sensual smile. "That's all I'm asking for."

CHAPTER TWENTY-FIVE

SHAYE LOUNGED AT THE EDGE of the bathing pool. Warm, steaming water lapped at her sensitized skin. The scent of orchids filled the room, sweetly perfuming the air with a sultry ambiance. She inhaled deeply. Her body was sore, but her spirit was invigorated.

Valerian sat behind her, massaging her shoulders. His magical fingers worked her muscles expertly. He knew exactly where to rub, knew the precise amount of pressure to apply for optimum enjoyment. Her head lolled back, resting on his shoulder. Steam coated their skin and his exhalations chilled the sheen of liquid.

"Thank you for gifting me with your virginity," he said.

"My pleasure." Really. She'd never enjoyed herself more. Never thought losing all control, all sense of her cool facade could be so blissful.

In the pleasure-filled hours they'd just spent together, she'd realized a few things. She'd given Valerian more than her body; she'd given him pieces of herself, just as she'd feared. She hadn't meant to, had tried to guard against it, yet been helpless to do otherwise. But it was going to be okay.

He was a nymph, and nymphs liked sex (and lots of

it), but she would be the one he came to. She was going to trust him. Not love him, she assured herself, still refusing to experience the emotion. But trust.

It would be hard, she didn't doubt that, but to keep him in her life she was willing to try.

"Your wounds healed," she said without turning to face him. She'd noticed when they adjourned to this bath.

"Yes."

"I'm glad."

"Me, too."

"Now you have the strength to tell me the secret spot on a woman's body," she said. "The place that brings maximum pleasure."

"Mmm, well. I will tell you for a kiss." He nuzzled the side of her cheek.

Ah, she loved his bargaining. "I'll kiss you if you tell me what I want to know," she said throatily, grinding against the erection pressed against her lower back.

He hissed in a breath. "I love when you move like that. Keep doing it and I will tell you all my deep, dark secrets."

Up, down she moved.

His hands tightened on her waist. "Close your eyes," he commanded softly.

They'd made love only an hour ago, but it felt like an eternity. She needed him inside her again. Addicting…that's what he was.

"Shaye." He *tsked*. "Close. Your. Eyes."

Her eyelids fluttered shut. Darkness blanketed her mind. His hands glided over her shoulders, caressed her neck, then dipped to her breasts, kneading.

"Picture what I'm doing to you."

"I thought—"

"Do it."

Picture it, he'd said, so she did. In her mind, she could see the thickness of his hands covering the pale mounds of her breasts. Her nipples, pink and pearled, peaked through the crevices of his fingers. Pleasure spiraled through her, hot and needy. Seemingly unquenchable.

Unbidden, her legs spread, silently begging for his attentions. A single touch, a pinch, something. Anything. She ached, oh, she ached.

One of Valerian's hands glided down her stomach. She felt it, yes, just the way she'd wanted it, but more than that she *saw* it in her mind. Another picture of them. Valerian behind her, this time with his hand between her legs, parting her wet folds. But he didn't touch her where she needed him most. Not yet. He stayed poised, inches above her entrance.

"What do you see?" His voice was strained, as if it required all of his strength to remain still.

"You. Me."

"Do you see me licking you here or sliding my fingers into you?"

"F-fingers," she managed.

"Are they moving slowly, savoring or pounding in and out?"

As he spoke, she again pictured it. Again saw it, unable to stop the flood of images. Yet he didn't do it, didn't do what she needed. Her hips moved forward, seeking. Back, seeking. Forward, back. Writhing and arching. "Touch me, Valerian. Please."

"Tell me. What do you see? Slow or fast?"

"Fast. Hard." Water sloshed over the pool's rim. "So hard."

He pinched her nipple, and a lance of desire hit directly between her legs. She cried out at the amazing torment of it.

"Shaye. Moon. Your mind shows you the things your body needs before you actually know you need them."

No more talking, she wanted to shout. *Make love to me.* "I don't understand."

"The most erotic place on a woman's body is her mind. By giving her the right images, a man can increase her pleasure a hundred times." He bit her ear. "Lean forward for me, moon."

She did, and even that served as a stimulant. The water caressed her clitoris, making her shiver.

"Hold on to the ledge," Valerian beseeched.

Angling forward a few more inches, she curled her hands on the ledge. Her breasts and hips were out of the water now and Valerian was granted a full view of her from behind.

A long while passed in silence. She stayed where she was, anticipating the first touch. Wet hair tumbled down her back and shoulders. Some of the ends treaded the water's surface. When would he touch her? She needed him to touch her. "Valerian?"

"You are magnificent," he said, his voice heavy with awe. He traced the tattoo on her lower back.

A shiver danced through her.

"I like this," he said. "A skull with a pretty bow on top. It is a mark that says you are both warrior and woman." His lips brushed the tattoo; the hot wetness of his tongue traced it. He kissed his way up her spine and grazed the back of her neck, smoothing her hair aside to get to her.

"The first time I saw you," she said, "I thought you were a god, rising from the sea."

"And I thought you were the thing I needed most in my life."

His words acted with the heady intoxication of a caress. She licked her lips, then bit into them to tamp down a loud, long scream of pleasure when his cock pressed into her opening.

"So tight," he praised.

"More."

He gave her an inch. "Is that all you want?"

"More."

Another inch. Not enough. "And now?"

"More, more, more."

He pounded all the way in. She gasped. He groaned. But he didn't move, just left them both at the edge. "Do you know the most erotic place on a man's body, moon?"

By this point, she was incapable of speech. She needed him too fiercely. The ache was all consuming. Burning. Yes, she burned fiery hot. Pulses of electricity sparked along her veins, demanding completion.

"His heart," Valerian finally said. "His heart."

His heart… She climaxed, throbbing, throbbing. Screaming, sobbing. The force of it raked her, vibrated and hummed. Valerian slid out and pounded forward. Over and over, driving hard and deep.

"Shaye," he roared, shuddering into her a final time. "Love. You." His hands dug into her hips. Gripping. Bruising deliciously. "Love you," he said again.

"I'M BEING RUDE to my guests," Valerian said a long while later. He lay on the bed, and he held Shaye in his arms. He was loath to let her go. They were both naked, and he was tempted to remain that way for all of eternity.

He loved the way Shaye's curves fit against him. Like the last piece of a puzzle, perfectly matched.

She yawned. "What guests?" she asked, her breath fanning his chest.

"Vampires. They helped us with the dragons and bought us a bit of a reprieve."

"I should run screaming from this room, but I'm too tired to be scared of vampires. Even vampires that are in the same house as me." She chuckled. "Do you mind that you're ignoring them?" Her fingertip slid along the ridges of his stomach.

"It is my greatest pleasure to ignore them," he said roughly, aroused by her touch *and* her words. She was adapting to life here. Maybe even coming to love it as he craved.

Her finger looped through his nipple ring, and she chuckled again.

He liked the sound of that laughter and realized he'd never really heard her amusement before. "How old are you?" he asked, wanting to know everything about her.

"Twenty-five. How old are *you?*"

"A lot older," he said dryly. "Hundreds of years older."

Her mouth fell open. "No way."

"It's true."

"So you're going to, what? Live forever? Never age?"

"I age, just slower than humans."

Her entire body tensed. "What you're telling me is

that if I stay here, I'll grow old while you continue to look like *that?*"

"You are in Atlantis now, love. Your aging process will slow, as well."

"Oh." Little by little, she relaxed. "That's okay, then."

"Do you miss your surface life as you did before?" he found himself asking.

An intense stillness came over her. "That's a hard question to answer."

"Yes or no is all that is required." He didn't want her to miss her old life. He wanted her happy, completely, with him. If she did miss it… What would he do? His two greatest desires would be at war with one another—the desire to keep her with him and the desire to see to her happiness. Always. No matter the cost to himself.

A sigh slipped from her. "I'm not sure if I miss it or not. I mean, I'm not close to my family. I never have been, really, but closure would have been nice."

"Why exactly were you not close with them?" He could not imagine such a thing with his brother if Verryn had lived.

"They wanted me to be something I wasn't," she said.

"What?"

"Sweet."

He snorted. "You *are* sweet. You like to pretend otherwise, but you are most definitely the sweetest morsel I have ever sampled."

Shaye bit him on the shoulder and licked away the sting. This man saw into her soul; he saw the woman she'd always secretly wanted to be. Something her own mother hadn't been able to do.

"How can your family not see how sweet you are? More shame, them."

She raised her head, cupping his cheeks with her palms. "Thank you for that."

Valerian's chest tightened. This woman possessed his heart, of that he had no doubt. Now he wanted hers. "Have you been able to make your anti-cards here?"

"Yes."

"If you were to make one for me, what would it say?"

"Well…let's see." She rested her head on his shoulder. A minute ticked by, then another. "Are you sure you want to know?"

"Yes."

"If I were going to make and send you a card, it would say…" She paused, frowned. "It would say, I'm trusting you not to break my heart. If it gets even a scratch, I'll break your face."

His lips twitched. "Break my face?"

"You heard me."

Break his face if he broke her heart… Her heart. Valerian stilled, the significance of what she'd said finally registering. Even his blood ceased flowing. Breath froze in his lungs. A wave of dizziness hit him as emotion after emotion crashed through him. "You are trusting me with your heart?" He was almost afraid to ask, afraid he'd misunderstood.

He, a warrior who had laughed at danger his entire life, was afraid this tiny, pale woman would not want him.

"Kind of," she said. "I'm not saying I love you or anything like that." A layer of panic coated her words. "But I'm going to trust you not to be with anyone else while you're with me. That means no other women."

"Moon, I desire no other save you."

"Now you don't. But what about later, when the novelty of me wears off?"

As she spoke, he heard her vulnerability. He rolled her to her back and stared down at her. "You are my mate. I have told you that, but I do not think you understand what that means. None arouse me anymore but you. None tempt me. None appeal to me. Only you. When a nymph takes a mate, that is the way of it. Now and always."

Her gaze softened, and he knew she wanted to believe him. "Yeah, well," she said, "we'll see what happens in the coming days."

"So you want to stay with me?"

Radiating vulnerability, she whispered, "Yes."

Joy burst through him, full but not complete. Not yet. "You want to stay with me but you do not love me?"

"Right. Love is complicated and messy."

"I love the way your nipples are pushing into my chest. That is not complicated."

Her lips pursed. "That's not what I meant, and you know it. Loving someone gives them permission to do bad things to you because they know you'll forgive them."

"What kind of bad things have been done to you by those you loved?" The question emerged quietly, lethally. He would slay anyone, man or woman, who dared hurt this woman.

"I've been abandoned, rejected, dismissed and forgotten," she said, and he tensed. "Plus, I saw the way you pushed aside the women who came before me."

"I did not expect you, moon. You were a surprise. I cannot undo what I have done in the past. But you have my vow of honor that I will never tire of you. In time, you will realize this for yourself." He paused, intent. "I know you said you would stay, but I'd like your vow. Promise me you will give me time to prove myself and my intentions toward you."

Her eyes searched his face, probing. Whatever she saw in his expression must have comforted her because she gave him a slow smile and nodded. "You have my vow."

He breathed a sigh of relief and renewed joy. Leaning down, he brushed his lips over hers. His hands searched for and found her own, and he intertwined their fingers before anchoring them above her head. This lifted her chest and meshed her breasts deeper into him. She licked her lips as her eyelids lowered.

"While you have seen only the bad side of love, I have seen the best. My mother and father were mated and completely devoted to each other."

"Where are they, your parents?"

"They died many years ago. My father died in battle and my mother's sadness took her not long after."

My God, Shaye thought. To be so devoted to someone you actually died without them. Simply lost the will to live. It was something out of a movie, yet a part of her she didn't want to acknowledge understood such devotion. She was frightened, and yet for the first time, utterly excited by the prospect.

"I'm sorry you lost them," she said softly.

"Uh-oh. You are showing your sweet side again."

She grinned. "How dare you say such a thing. I'm a hard-core bitch."

"And you hate the things I do to you."

"Hate them," she agreed with a laugh.

His breath tunneled into her ear, followed by his tongue. Her hands tangled in his hair as she trembled.

"Just like you hate me," he breathed.

She couldn't give him the words he wanted so she gave him these instead. "Yes," she whispered. "I hate you so very much."

"Good. Because I'm going to hate you until you can't imagine life without me."

Too late, her mind whispered as he slid into her.

CHAPTER TWENTY-SIX

LEAVING SHAYE ASLEEP in his bed—*their* bed, Valerian amended—was the hardest thing he'd ever done. Her soft, pale tresses tapered over the violet sheets, as ethereal as a dream. Her features were relaxed, the sandy length of her lashes casting shadows over her cheekbones. Her lips were plump and rosy from his kisses.

He'd already dressed, had hastily tugged on a black shirt and pants before he'd lost his resolve to leave. As leader of this palace, it was his duty to see to his guests. But more than that, he wanted to see to the palace's defenses and ensure they were well fortified, strong enough to withstand the most violent of attacks.

This peaceful reprieve the vampires had given them would not last long, he knew. Darius would be back. Valerian only hoped it would be later rather than sooner. The longer he had to solidify his bond with Shaye, the better.

He couldn't resist placing a chaste kiss on the tip of her nose—which proved to be a mistake. She muttered under her breath, an airy gurgling of unintelligible words. One of them might have been his name. He was suddenly rock hard for her, so aroused it was as if he'd never taken her. *Leave. Now. Before you can't.*

Forcing one foot in front of the other required all of his concentration. But he did it, his quick stride widening the distance. Now that Shaye had decided to stay, he knew she would begin to make his home her own, gifting it with little touches of her personality.

Flowers would most likely fill the rooms, and he would take great pleasure in procuring them for her. Paintings, colored stones, beaded pillows. He would take her into the city and purchase everything she wanted, everything she needed. All the things women used to make a home, well, a home. She would want for nothing, her every wish his to grant.

He was grinning as he entered the dining hall. Vampires surrounded the table. Most clutched goblets filled with some type of blood, he was sure. Several nymphs were here, though most were on duty and if not on duty, loving a woman. There were no females present.

Layel, who had claimed the head of the table, spotted him and motioned him over.

"Acting as king of the place, already?" Valerian said with a grin. He plopped onto the now-vacant spot beside his friend.

"Of course." Layel sipped at his goblet. "I don't think you've ever looked so sated, Valerian."

"Mated life agrees with me."

A curtain of sadness flittered over Layel's expression. "I remember it well, mated life."

Layel had lost his mate years ago. She'd been a human, descended from those the gods had banished from the surface and dropped into the city for punishment. A rogue group of dragons had raped and burned her. Not Darius, but a contingent of his tutor's men. It did not matter to Layel that Darius was innocent. The vampire king despised all dragons and wanted them destroyed.

Valerian recalled well the devastation Layel had endured when he'd discovered his lover's charred remains. His grief had been severe and gut-wrenching.

"The dragons have captured a group of nymph females," Valerian said, "and that is something I cannot allow."

"It would be my pleasure to retrieve them for you," the vampire king said with relish.

"No. I will not have your vampires go after them. I would like to send my own men, but if I do so, I will need to make up for the loss here."

"You wish us to remain?"

He nodded. "If you are able."

Layel didn't hesitate. "You need us, we stay. There is nothing more to discuss."

Layel had always been that way. Loyal. Giving of himself and his time. That was why Valerian valued his friendship as he did. There were not many men so willing to help a race other than their own.

Those who earned the vampire king's wrath, however, were enemies for life. Layel lived for their suffering. He never forgot a wrong.

"Thank you, my friend." Valerian clapped him on the back. "If you ever need me, I am here."

Layel's face was as pale as Shaye's, yet a rush of color suffused his cheeks. "You are a cherished friend, Valerian."

"As are you." He stood. "Take what animals you need. If you have need of women, which I'm sure you will, you will have to get them from the Outer City yourself, I'm afraid. They have been hiding from us."

Layel gave a booming laugh. "That means they are smart."

Valerian snorted. He didn't offer the use of the human women, and Layel didn't ask for the honor. A nymph might share his lover with other nymphs, but not with other creatures. The women would then carry that creature's scent and no male liked another creature's smell on his lover. Well, that wasn't entirely true. He could recall several of his men who became excited by that.

"We will talk again soon," he said. "I must now see to the palace."

"I know you, Valerian. You might see to the palace, but your true goal is to get back to your bed."

He grinned wickedly. "Yes, you do know me well."

A HARD, CALLUSED HAND slapped over Shaye's mouth. She came awake instantly, a scream lodged in her throat. It emerged as nothing more than a quiet murmur. She knew the hand did not belong to Valerian. It smelled different, not as erotic, like a storm about to fall. It did not spark awareness inside her.

Vampire, perhaps? Valerian had mentioned the vampires were inside the palace. Panicked, she swung her fist and connected with something solid. Her captor grunted.

"Do not move again, woman. We will not hurt you."

Undeterred, she thrashed and kicked.

"We will not hurt you," that deep, accented voice said. "Please, be still."

We? Her gaze darted throughout the darkness. What she wouldn't have given for a flashlight just then. Scratch that. A stun gun or a knife was what she needed. She wrapped her fingers around the man's wrist and jerked.

"If I must, I will render you unconscious and neither of us will like how I do that."

She stilled, knowing that to be unconscious was to lose this battle completely. If she could break free, she could run and scream and find Valerian.

"Good," the man—vampire?—said. "Now, I'm going to remove my hand. If you draw your lover here, we will kill him without hesitation. Understand?"

One nod in the affirmative. Inside, she screamed and screamed and screamed. No. *No!* Valerian was strong, but he was also flesh and blood. She didn't know how many men were inside the room. She didn't know what weapons they possessed.

She had to warn him without drawing him into an ambush. What could she do? *Think, Shaye, think.*

As promised, the man removed his hold on her mouth. She dragged in a shaky breath. "Who are you? What do you want?"

"We are dragons, and we are going to take you home."

Dragons. The enemy. Dear God. *They will ravish you and burn you,* Valerian had said. She shook her head, tendrils of hair slapping her cheeks. "I *am* home."

"That's what the others said, but it didn't sway us from our purpose."

"You can't take me. I won't let you." *I promised Valerian I'd stay. Valerian!* her mind shouted. Slowly her eyes adjusted to the dark. She counted four silhouettes, each larger than the other. Weapons of all shapes and sizes were strapped to their bodies.

"We can do whatever we want," one of the men said with amusement. "Sit up. Slowly."

She did as instructed, and the sheet tumbled to her waist. Cool air kissed her bare skin. Gasping, she jerked the sheet up. "I'm naked." She hadn't meant to blurt the words aloud, but the realization had shocked her. *Stupid. Idiot! Why don't you just ask them to rape you.*

"Here," another of them said. He was at her left. "Put this on."

A bundle of material was shoved over her head, surprising her. "Why are you doing this?" she demanded, quickly pulling it down. It was a robe, soft and sheer but a covering nonetheless.

"It is the will of the gods," was the calm reply. "Stand. Keep your arms to your side."

She inched from the bed as quietly as possible, hoping they wouldn't sense her exact location. The door was to the left, and she inched one step, then two. Then she broke into a full run. Strong arms anchored around her before she reached the curtain, bringing her to a dead stop.

"Damn you," she muttered, flailing. "Let me go."

"Woman, I warned you."

Knowing he meant to knock her out, Shaye increased her struggles. She slashed with her nails, tugged her captor's hair, and punched him in the stomach. "I'm going to pray your gods curse you!"

"They already have." A heavy sigh. "I'm sorry to do this, but you've given me no choice."

Someone muttered a series of unintelligible words

and a wave of lethargy swept through her. Her eyelids drifted shut, so heavy she could not hold them open. Sleep called to her, as alluring as any nymph. *Help,* she tried to scream, knowing that to fall asleep was to be taken from Valerian. She needed more time with him.

Sleep…sleep…no. She shook her head. *Scream.* She opened her mouth, but no sound emerged. And still sleep called to her, beckoning. Lulling.

"She's a fighter," someone said in awe.

"I've never seen the like."

"She should have dropped by now."

"Sleep, woman. On the morrow, you will not remember any of this."

Strength abandoned her limbs, slowly, quickly. She wasn't sure. Time ceased to exist. Utter darkness crept gnarled fingers inside her mind. *Fight…fight…fi…*

She knew nothing else.

CHAPTER TWENTY-SEVEN

WITH THE NIGHT'S activities complete and morning fast approaching, the palace fortified, his guests seen to, Valerian raced back to his bedroom. Urgency filled him. He wanted Shaye again. He hungered for her. The more time he spent with her, the more he needed her. The more time he spent without her, the more he needed her.

He just needed her.

And he sensed that she needed him. A moment ago, he'd heard her voice in his mind, calling out to him. He quickened his pace, speeding through the hallway, through the curtain blocking him from his room. He'd strip, then crawl into bed beside Shaye and awaken her with his mouth between her legs. She'd scream his name, the sound echoing between—

He stopped abruptly. He stood at the edge of the bed, golden rays of light streaming over its emptiness. Only rumpled sheets remained. "Shaye," he called.

When silence greeted him, he spun, searching. She had not been in the bathing pool; he would have seen her when he passed. "Shaye?"

Again, only silence. Thick, frightening silence. Where had she gone? He didn't want her roaming the halls alone. He wanted nothing taken for granted where Shaye's safety was concerned. He didn't allow himself to panic—yet. Her scent covered the walls, permeating his senses. But there was another scent…his nose crinkled and he frowned, hoping he simply smelled the ones who'd lived here before him.

He stepped into the bathing room, then into the hallway. For twenty minutes he searched the main areas: the dining hall—receiving curious glances—the training room, the weapons room in case she'd gotten lost. He'd been remiss in his duty toward her. He should have taught her the layout of the palace.

Everyone he encountered, he demanded to know if they'd seen her. No one had. In fact, several warriors were looking for their women, as well.

"I cannot find Brenna," Joachim said, worry thick in his voice.

So, Joachim had taken Brenna from Shivawn—or maybe Shivawn had given her to the man. Valerian didn't know and at the moment he didn't care. All that mattered was Shaye.

"I cannot find my bed partner," another said.

"I cannot find mine." Still another.

Hearing this, Valerian finally allowed his panic free rein. He sprinted to the cave. Surely Shaye hadn't left him, hadn't led all the women into the portal. She'd promised to stay. She'd told him she desired time with him. She had been so close to giving him her love. Had she changed her mind?

Had she lied?

Sweat trickled from his skin. Tension thrummed and pulsed. What if she had tricked him? Had gained his trust so he would leave her alone, without a guard, so she could gather the other humans and—

No, he told himself. No. She would not have left him willingly. She hadn't lied. Last time he'd seen her, she'd worn a soft, sated expression. Vulnerability had glinted in her eyes as she vowed to trust him. She'd said she craved fidelity from him and those were not the words of a woman intent on leaving.

He pounded his fist into the wall. When he'd held her in his arms, there had been truth between them.

That meant only one thing. She had to have been taken. But where? And by whom? He'd smelled dragon in his room. Had his enemy returned more quickly than he'd anticipated? If so, why had they taken the women and not killed a single nymph?

Damn this! What in Hades had happened? He swung around and backtracked to the top floor, leaving the coldness of the cave behind. He ran into Broderick.

"Where are the women?" Broderick asked. "I am in need of a lover."

"They have been taken. It happened within the last few hours, so there is a good chance they are still here. Keep searching." Yet there was nowhere else to look and he knew it. He'd been through the palace top to bottom.

He stalked into the dining hall. Layel still sat at the table, staring into emptiness, sadness consuming his features. Valerian's teeth ground together. If the women had been taken out of the palace and into the Outer City… It was not a place for unarmed females. Demons would eat anything, for they survived on fear and carnage. They would view the women as succulent treats.

"Layel," he said. He did not think the vampire or his

people responsible. Blood would have stained the floor, the beds, something. "I need your help."

His friend jolted upright. "It is yours."

"Can you and your people withstand the light?"

"Most of us."

"You can scent humans as no one else. Take your vampires through the forest and into the city and search for our women. Someone has taken them."

In a movement so fluid it was almost undetectable, Layel stood. "I will do as you've asked. Do you stay or do you go?"

Valerian didn't know what to do. If he stayed and Shaye was in the city, she would not know Layel and would fight him, perhaps getting hurt in the process. But if Valerian left, and she was still inside the palace, perhaps being hidden and held against her will, he would never forgive himself for leaving her.

Indecision and frustration ate at him. Fear and hope slicked through him. Go? Stay? "I will go," he finally said. "Ready your men."

Layel nodded and rushed off.

Valerian raced into his room and gathered the dragon medallion he'd tossed aside when making love with Shaye. He stuffed it in his pocket before hunting down Broderick, who had a small contingent of armed warriors stomping through every room, questioning other nymphs and vampires. "I am going into the city. Send a messenger if they are found…whatever you find," he added starkly.

Broderick nodded.

Alone, Valerian dropped to his knees and prayed. For the first time in his life, he prayed. He beseeched the gods, begging them to surround Shaye in a hedge of protection, to bring her back to him, healthy and whole. "I will trade my own life for her. Gladly," he said to the heavens.

Still torn apart inside, still raw and frantic, he stood and raced outside. The vampires possessed an unnatural speed. They would move much faster without him, and as much as he wanted to reach Shaye first, he would not hinder them.

At the outer gates, the vampires gathered, preparing for the search. "Do not let me slow you down," he told Layel. "Move as quickly as you can, and I will make my own way. Gather any human females you find."

Layel's eyes glowed bright, vivid blue. "We will find her, Valerian."

Valerian turned away before he broke down, just fell to his knees and sobbed. Loss was not new to him, but this loss would kill him. "Go." The single word was hoarse, scratching his burning throat. "Go."

The vampires leapt into action; one moment they were there, the next moment they weren't. Valerian entered the stable and mounted the same centaur that had taken Shaye and him to the city only a day ago. They raced around trees and quicksand, as he continually shouted Shaye's name. Pausing, listening for any sign of her.

She was not in the forest.

She was not in the Outer City, either. None of the humans were. He spent all day looking, until dusk fell once again. Seething emotions pulsed through him. Fear. So much fear. Where was she? She was not…dead. He could barely even think the hated word. He would feel it. As her mate, he would know. Just as he'd known when his twin had died, all those years ago. Wouldn't he?

He left Layel and his army in the city with instructions to continue the hunt, then he returned to the palace. When he reached the gates, he dismounted and ran inside without a word. As he ran, he withdrew the dragon medallion from his pocket. The crystal door split apart and closed behind him.

The palace was eerily silent, none of his men anywhere to be seen. "Broderick," he called. "Joachim. Shivawn." He ground to a halt. The fine hairs on the back of his neck stood at attention, and he encountered the same faint scent he'd smelled in his room. He quickly withdrew his sword from the sheath at his side.

"Your men are otherwise occupied," a voice said above him.

A dragon voice. Darius's voice.

Lips thinning in a fierce scowl, Valerian looked up. There, circling him from the second floor, was the entire dragon army. "What did you do with my woman?"

"We sent her home, nymph. We sent her home."

CHAPTER TWENTY-EIGHT

"WAKE UP, SHAYE." Shake. "Wake up."

Shaye heard the voice from a long, dark tunnel. *Yes,* she thought. *Must. Wake. Up.* Trouble was nearby. Trouble for her, for Valerian. Gradually consciousness worked through her mind, chasing away the darkness.

"Wake up."

Slowly she cracked open her eyelids. Sunlight glared down at her and orange-gold spots danced before her vision. Dry cotton filled her mouth. Sand and salt coated her entire body. Her clothes were stiff, as if they'd soaked and dried right on her. The sound of lulling waves greeted her ears, soothing, familiar. Yet…wrong. The smells weren't right, either. Yes, she smelled salt, but not orchids. Not Valerian.

"Valerian," she said. Her throat felt raw, scratchy. "Valerian."

"No. It's me."

Her attention veered to the speaker. Her… "Mom?" She rubbed at her eyes. "What are you doing here?"

"I've been haunting the beach since you were taken. Are you—" her mother gulped "—okay? Did they hurt you?"

"I'm fine." From the corner of her eye, she saw

Kathleen pass her, dark hair hanging in tangles around her sandy face. "What's going on?" Shaye demanded of her.

"We were brought back to the surface," she said, never slowing.

Brought back... Understanding clicked. Yes. The dragons had invaded Valerian's room, had threatened to take her to the surface, then rendered her unconscious. She shoved to her feet. Her equilibrium was off balance, and she swayed. Her mom wrapped an arm around her waist.

"Are you sure you're okay?"

"Yes. I'll be fine," Shaye said, massaging her temples to ward off the dizziness. When the world righted itself, she catalogued her surroundings. White-gold sand stretched as far as the eyes could see. Waves crested to the beach, leaving sea foam in their wake. The sun shone brightly, no hint of crystal.

There was a group of scuba-clad men sitting nearby, reminiscent of the time Valerian came to the surface. They were gazing around the beach in confusion.

"I wasn't here when they arrived," her mom explained, realizing the direction of her gaze. "But I questioned them when they awoke. They can't recall their names, why they're here, or even how they got here."

Had the dragons wiped their memories, too? *Sleep, woman,* they'd told her. *On the morrow, you will not remember any of this.* But she did remember. Everything. Kathleen, too, had seemed to remember.

"There's even a boat docked over there." Her mom pointed to the right. "The men inside don't know anything, either, but I saw the initials OBI on some papers, whatever that means."

"I still don't understand why you're here," Shaye said, pinning her with a frown.

Tamara's expression became tortured. "After you disappeared, the police arrived at the tent. They didn't believe us when we told them what had happened. They laughed at us, said you girls had probably gotten bored and taken off. All I could think was that you were gone, I'd never see you again, and the last words between us had been harsh."

"I—" didn't know what to say, Shaye realized. Her mother had never shown her such a vulnerable, repentant side.

"I haven't been the best mother. I know that," the distressed woman rushed on. "And I know things will probably never be comfortable between us. I'm just glad you're okay."

Tears burned Shaye's eyes as she wrapped her arms around her mom. "Thank you for that." She'd wanted closure, and she'd gotten it.

Tamara hugged her back, expelling a shaky breath.

"So you're happy?" Shaye asked her.

"Yes." Her mom drew back and wiped at her own tears with the back of her wrist. "I think Conner truly is the love of my life, and Preston seems to like me. They're at opposite ends of the beach, passing out fliers with your picture and asking if anyone's seen you."

Wow. For the first time in her life, Shaye felt like she had an actual family. An honest-to-God family. But… "I have to go back, Mom." She wanted—needed— Valerian. He probably thought she'd left him on purpose. If he wasn't— No! She wouldn't think of him as dead. He was strong, the strongest man she'd ever encountered. He would have gathered his army and defeated the dragons.

"I have to go back," she repeated.

"Go back where, exactly?"

She didn't have time to explain. "Just…find Conner and Preston and tell them I'm okay. Tell Preston I'm sorry for the way I acted at the wedding. I'll return if I can. If not, know that I'm happy and that I've found the man of my dreams, too."

"But—"

"Trust me. Please." Shaye gave her mom one last hug and moved toward the water. All around her, women in Atlantean robes were awakening. Any beach-goers probably assumed they'd come from a costume party, and had drunk and swum afterward.

"Are you going back?" Kathleen asked, suddenly at her side.

"Yes."

"I want to go with you."

The whole world could come if they wanted. She didn't care, as long as she could go back herself. She loved Valerian. There, she'd admitted it. She did. She loved him with all of her heart, a heart she'd once thought too cold to care for anyone. But she couldn't deny her feelings any longer.

Fear had made her do so, she realized that now. When faced with the choice to live without Valerian…there was no greater fear than that. He loved her, too. She wouldn't doubt him any longer. He loved her for exactly who she was; he didn't want her to change.

Water lapped at her ankles, sand squished between her toes. Rising, rising, the cool liquid soon hit her calves, her thighs. If those dragons hurt her man in any way, she'd hunt them down and destroy them.

She swam as far as she could, all the women with her, then dove under the water. When she didn't see the portal, she came back up for air. Hours passed, but they didn't give up their search. Shaye's body tired, her lungs burned.

"Why are we doing this?" Kathleen panted as she treaded water beside her. "I...I can't remember."

"Atlantis." Shaye swallowed a mouthful of salty liquid. "The nymphs."

"The who?" Kathleen's face scrunched in confusion. So did everyone else's—except Brenna's. She possessed an aura of determination, just like Shaye.

"I hate to swim," one of the women said. "I'm going home."

"Me, too."

"This is stupid."

"I don't even know how I got here. Wasn't I at a wedding?" On and on they muttered as they swam back to the beach.

They were forgetting, just as the dragons had promised, and Shaye was suddenly afraid of the same happening to herself. Already Valerian's face was blurred in her mind. "I won't forget," she said between labored breaths.

"We have to get back," Brenna wheezed.

They swam under and up for an hour longer. By then Shaye was shaking with fatigue. Tears streamed down her cheeks, tears of frustration and fury. If she didn't go back to shore, she would drown here. Brenna, too. The need to get back to...what was his name?

I will not forget. Valerian. Yes! That was it. His name

was Valerian, and she loved him. "One more dive," she told Brenna.

Brenna was gasping for breath, but she nodded. "Need. Joachim."

If they failed to find the portal this time, they would swim back to shore and try again tomorrow. Try every day until they succeeded. When Shaye went under, the salt stung her eyes. But she pushed herself farther than ever before, Brenna at her side.

The ocean's bottom remained out of sight.

Shaye's arms and legs shook violently. Fish brushed against her. *Damn this,* she mentally cried. Brenna stopped moving, her hands and feet stilling, and Shaye grabbed on to her. She switched directions, angling upward. But it was too late. She'd pushed herself too far and didn't have the strength to swim the rest of the way up.

At first she panicked, flailing, opening her mouth, desperate to fill her burning lungs with oxygen. She swallowed more water instead. Still she retained a grip on her friend, trying to get them both to the top.

A strange blackness, thicker than any other darkness she'd ever encountered, began to weave through her mind. Then a flash of light sparked in her line of vision. A bubble floated in front of her, growing, growing, until it completely surrounded her and Brenna.

She spit out a mouthful of water and gasped for breath. Miraculously, she sucked in actual air. Wet hair clung to her face, but she didn't brush it aside. Couldn't. Was she dreaming? Dead? She dropped to her knees in front of Brenna, who lay unconscious. She'd never performed CPR, but she'd seen it done and mimicked the motions.

"Come on," she panted. "Come on."

After a long while of pumping and breathing for her friend, Brenna coughed. Her eyes remained closed, but she, too, sucked in a breath of air. Depleted, Shaye sagged beside her.

"Foolish human," a deep, thunderous voice growled. "Why are you doing this? You nearly died, both of you. And for what?"

Her exhausted gaze circled the bubble. Water churned around it, but she couldn't see a person—inside or out. "Where are you? *Who* are you?"

"I am Poseidon, God of the Sea."

A god. A freaking god. "Take me to Valerian," she demanded.

He laughed. "A command from a human. Your sense of humor pleases me. Unfortunately, your lover is already dead."

"No." Fierce despair tried to sink sharp claws inside of her. "No. He can't be."

Colorful sparks appeared just in front of her, solidifying into a male form. He was beautiful, more so than even Valerian. White hair framed an utterly masculine face. His eyes were as blue as the ocean, a liquid crystal, utterly hypnotic. They were almost neon, glowing, pulsing with energy and power.

"Valerian disobeyed the laws of Atlantis. He brought humans into the city."

"He doesn't deserve to die for that," she snarled at him, trying to gather the strength to rise. She could only lie there.

Poseidon smiled at her, an amused twitching of his sensual lips. "I had forgotten how fierce you humans can be when someone you love is threatened. It is quite entertaining."

"Take me to Valerian. Right now!"

He quickly lost his smile. "Do you wish to die? With your every word, you are begging me to slay you."

"Please." She nearly curled into a sobbing heap. "I just want Valerian."

Poseidon studied her face for a long while, then studied Brenna's. His expression never softened. "I told you, he is already dead."

"No. I won't believe you until you show him to me. I would know if he was dead. I would feel it."

Silence. Even the water refused to make noise.

Then, "What would you give me if I allowed you to see him? To go to him?"

"Anything. Everything." A huge black-and-white whale swam past her side, its majestic body consuming the area. She watched in amazement as it lowered its head to Poseidon.

"Your own life?" the god asked.

"Yes."

He blinked in surprise.

"Have you never been in love?" she asked. "Have you never craved another person so much you would rather die without them?"

"No," he admitted. "The concept is laughable at best." Slowly he circled her, his hair like a curtain, ribboning in the air. His body was fluid, rippling like waves.

She maintained eye contact.

"I am not an evil god, but to send you back into Atlantis and allow the nymphs to live will make me appear soft. My people will continue to break the law."

Joy thrummed through her because, with his words, he'd confirmed the nymphs were not yet dead, that there was still time. "Or," she said, "they'll think you merciful and sing your praises and be happy to obey your every whim."

His eyes narrowed, but not before she saw sparks of pleasure flickering in their depths. "You think you are clever, don't you?"

"I just want to be with my man."

There was a long pause. "Watching one such as you battle with the nymph king *could* be amusing," he said absently.

He wanted to be amused, did he? "I'll give him nothing but trouble," she promised. "I'll turn his life upside down. I'll create absolute havoc."

As she spoke, the god's expression became more and more excited. Visions of the coming trouble were rolling through his mind; she could see it in his eyes. "Very well," he said, and there was relish in his tone. "I will allow you to reenter Atlantis."

Her joy tripled, an avalanche of incomparable force. "Thank you, thank you so much. Brenna, too, right?"

"I suppose." He sighed.

"You will not regret this, I promise you."

"However," he continued as if she hadn't spoken, "I will not stop the course I have set. I will allow the Fates to decide what befalls the nymphs. The dragons even now have them at their mercy—a mercy they do not possess."

The bubble burst in the next instant, and water suddenly barraged her. She reached for Brenna but couldn't find her. Water shot inside her nostrils, her mouth, her lungs. A dark void closed around her, spinning her in every direction. Stars winked in and out. Then the water was sucked away, leaving only a tunnel.

She coughed and sputtered as she fell, tumbling headlong into an abyss. She wasn't frightened, though. She knew Valerian awaited her on the other end. Valerian. Her love, her life.

Suddenly her feet hit a solid foundation, jarring her all the way to her bones. She swayed, righted herself. Cracked open her eyes. Never had she seen a more welcome sight. The stark walls of the cave closed around her, crimson-stained, decorated with those beautiful murals. Cool air slithered from every corner.

Home. She was home.

She heard a female moan and glanced down. Brenna was sprawled out and just opening her eyes. "We did it," Shaye told her. She couldn't stop grinning. "We did it."

Eyes lighting, Brenna eased to her feet.

The sound of angry, *familiar* male voices bombarded her ears, and she whipped around. The nymphs must have been placed in the cells. She motioned to Brenna to be quiet, and her friend nodded.

Just in case dragons were guarding the area, she sneaked along the walls. Brenna tiptoed behind her. They remained in the shadows. Leaning forward, she peeked at the cell. It was overcrowded, positively bursting with nymphs. She looked for Valerian, but didn't see him. Still, she didn't allow herself to become upset. He was here and he was alive. She knew it.

There was a single dragon guard, probably because the fewer men outside the cell, the fewer who could open it. She picked up the largest rock she could find and mouthed for Brenna to run for the cell and free the men.

Eagerness danced through her as she silently held up her fingers. *One. Two. Three.* They burst inside. Shaye surprised the guard and smashed his temple with her rock.

He roared, but didn't fall. At the same time, Brenna touched the bars. They misted and the nymphs spilled out, toppling the guard.

"Brenna!" a male voice shouted.

Brenna squealed happily and rushed forward. Joachim wrapped his big arms around her. Shaye searched for Valerian. *He's here, he's here, he's here.* The crowd of nymphs was parting, but she didn't see him. "Valerian? Valerian!"

Where was he?

CHAPTER TWENTY-NINE

"VALERIAN!"

He heard his name being called, and his stomach clenched. Shaye's voice. His head shot up; his mouth fell open. "Shaye? Where are you?" Before the last word left him, he spotted her in front of the cell. He stood and their gazes locked.

A grin split her entire face, jubilant. Radiant.

"You came back." He pushed forward, past his men. He felt tears burn his eyes—not that he'd ever admit such a thing aloud. He thought perhaps Broderick went to free the nymphs from the other cell, but he wasn't sure. He cared only about reaching Shaye.

She met him halfway.

He grabbed her, kissing her and nipping at her face. "I thought you were lost to me," he said, and his voice shook.

His arms banded around her, lifting her feet off the ground. She wound her legs around his waist, kissing him with the same welcoming, relieved intensity he'd bestowed on her.

"I promised to stay, didn't I?" she said.

Valerian breathed deeply of her scent, letting it fill him, strengthen him. "I'd planned to come for you. I was going to help my men retake the palace then go to you. Live with you up there. One day with you is better than a lifetime without."

"I love you so much."

"Thank the gods." His arms tightened around her. "I love you so much, my sweet moonbeam. I can't believe you came back to me."

"Always."

"What of the others?" Broderick asked her. He stood just off to the side. "Did they return, as well?"

"No. Only Brenna and me," Shaye told him, apologetic. "I'm sorry."

Broderick shrugged. "Oh, well. Their presence would have been nice since we are about to go to battle."

Valerian turned to his men, but didn't release Shaye. He wasn't ready to let her go, couldn't stop touching her.

"It's time we reclaimed the palace," Shaye said before he could speak. Several of the warriors smiled at her.

Valerian flicked her a grin of his own. "That's right. The dragons have the female nymphs, so you will not go without a woman for long, Broderick." He placed a kiss on Shaye's soft lips, lingered far longer than he should have, savoring her taste, then sighed.

"You're going to kick dragon ass, right?" she asked.

"Absolutely." He grinned. Despite his humor, grim determination churned inside him.

"Where are the vampires? They could help us."

"I sent them into the city. By the time they returned, the dragons had already regained control and barred them from entering." His stare became hard, penetrating. "I want to leave you down here."

"No," she said.

"Shaye."

"Valerian."

"She is queen," Broderick said, clearly entertained. "You will not be able to command her."

Valerian sighed. "Promise me you will duck and hide when the fighting begins."

"Promise," she said.

His hand closed around hers. Gods, he loved the feel of her. "Men, we go in hard and we go in fast."

"Like Broderick does with his women," someone joked.

Male chuckles abounded.

"Where is Shivawn?" Brenna asked.

"No one has seen him," Joachim replied, hugging Brenna close. "He probably left the palace before the dragons arrived and is sleeping off the night's excess."

"Lucky bastard," Broderick muttered, but he was smiling. Everyone was happy to be out of the cells.

"Try not to kill the dragons," Shaye said. "They could have killed us—and you—but they placed us on the surface unharmed and only locked you away. You owe them the same consideration."

"My mate is very wise," Valerian said. "Listen to her." After confining them inside the cells, Darius had looked him in the eyes and said, "I have been ordered by the gods to execute every nymph ever created. Perhaps I bring the gods' wrath upon my own head, but I do not think your race deserves annihilation. You will remain here until I decide what to do with you."

An honorable man such as that did not deserve to die.

As quietly as possible, he crept up the stairs, Shaye behind him, the army behind her. They were without weapons, yet they were determined. This was their home, and they weren't giving it up.

"Split," Valerian uttered softly when they reached the top.

The men branched in every direction. Joachim had kept Brenna with him, as well, Valerian noticed. Surprise was their biggest advantage right now. Their footsteps sounded lightly, barely echoing from the walls. Torches glowed, heating the air, lighting their path.

"This way." Valerian led his contingent into the dining hall. A group of dragons came into view. They stood at the table, discussing their best course of action.

"Kill them and be done with it," one of them growled. "I do not wish Poseidon's wrath upon my family."

"If we let Poseidon's threats affect us, we give him complete control of our lives," Darius said. "What if he wishes us to kill our own women tomorrow?"

"If we disobey him, we may not live long enough to know."

"There is a reason the gods have never slain us, a reason why they sent us back into this palace instead of destroying the nymphs themselves." Darius again.

"What reason?"

"I do not know, yet knowing there *is* a reason gives us a bit of power. All I am saying is that if we do this, we become servants and we put our own race in danger. If the gods destroy one, what is to keep them destroying another?"

"Nothing," Valerian answered. His signal.

Weaponless, the nymphs swarmed forward. Valerian wished to the gods he held The Skull, but he could not postpone this fight. Streams of fire spewed from the dragons the moment they realized they were under attack. Valerian shoved Shaye behind a small side table and leapt forward. He and Darius met midair. That the dragon king retained his human form meant he was not enraged. Yet.

They grappled to the ground. Valerian landed a hard punch into his opponent's face. Blood trickled from Darius's mouth, yet the cut healed quickly. Dragons possessed accelerated healing, which made them difficult to slow. He gave another punch and rolled, then kicked out his leg, hitting Darius's stomach.

Darius was flung backward, but immediately righted himself. He spun. His tail had sprouted and that tail slashed at Valerian's face, cutting deep. He felt the sting of it, but didn't let it affect him.

All around him nymphs and dragons warred. Their grunts permeated the air.

"I agree with what you said about the gods." Valerian lunged, punched. Contact.

"Then you are not as foolish as I thought." Darius kicked again, and his foot slammed into Valerian's side.

Spinning continuously, he lashed out at Darius. He landed four successive blows. "I will not give up this palace. It belongs to us. *You* already have a home."

"For the safety of Atlantis, the portal must be guarded. How can I trust you to do this? To not use it for your own gain?"

Valerian paused.

Darius did the same.

They stared each other down, both panting. "When we win the nymph females back from you, we will have no more need of the surface world."

Around them, the battle still raged. Valerian ducked

as a stream of fire propelled toward him. The heat of it burned, singed, even though none of the flames touched him.

Darius said, "Poseidon said that according to the laws, only Guardians were to use the portals to travel to the surface, that any other deserved punishment. If you were a Guardian…"

"I would do my duty." Valerian studied Darius's face. That scar slashed from eyebrow to chin. His eyes were swirling blue, determined to kill if he must, but hoping to find another way.

"The portal I guard leads to a jungle on the surface. The portal here leads to an ocean on the surface, as I'm sure you know. If you stay here," Darius said, "human travelers will come through. Most often they simply swim too deeply, are innocent, but they will be yours to destroy. The Outer City will be yours to guard. I am ready to relinquish this duty as it was never meant to be mine. I have enough handling the Inner City."

"I will protect it with my life," Valerian vowed. "This is the only home we have ever known."

"Then kneel."

Valerian knelt without hesitation. He stared up at Darius, who sliced a thin cut down the center of his chest, and offered a blood oath to always guard the portal, to keep the city safe.

Around them, the men finally stopped fighting to listen and watch. Shaye approached Valerian's side, and he stood. He linked their fingers. He should have scolded her for leaving the safety of the table, but he liked her where she was too much.

Darius's gaze flicked to her and widened with surprise.

"I told you I wouldn't leave him," she said with a proud tilt of her chin.

His lips twitched. "My Grace would have done the same."

"Shall we trust each other, dragon?" Valerian waited impatiently for the answer. Everything he'd ever wanted hovered within his grasp.

Darius's gaze became piercing. "Yes," he finally said. "We shall trust each other. And battle the gods together if we must."

Valerian held out his hand. Darius eyed it for several seconds before clasping it with his own. The truce was sealed, and Valerian did not know how he would explain this to Layel. "Let us hope we live long enough to regret this." He turned to Shaye and gathered her in his arms, where she belonged. Where he planned to keep her for all of eternity.

"This is the most unhappy I've ever been," she said, grinning. "I just hate you so much."

Softly he kissed her lips. "Not nearly as much as I hate you."

Oh, but they were going to have a long, happy life together.

EPILOGUE

"HOW MUCH IS THIS ONE?"

"That one will cost you a kiss. A big wet one. Probably a ten-second Frencher."

Valerian pushed away the basket of oranges he always kept in his room and studied the card Shaye had made. "Without you, I'm nothing," it read. With each day that passed, her cards became more and more poetic. Which was a good thing, since his men needed the cards to lure the female nymphs from their pique. Seemed they weren't too happy about being left with the dragons for so long.

But the sweet cards also meant that Shaye herself was being lured from her past hurts. She was adapting to life here admirably, amusing herself by making and selling cards to him and his men and the residents of the Outer City, where she'd set up shop. Always guarded from demons and other forces, of course. Even the dragons bought them when they came to visit— Darius had needed one for his pregnant wife. The vampires, too, bought them, though they did not visit often. Layel was upset by the alliance between nymphs and dragons. Valerian was determined to unite the two races.

So far Poseidon and the other gods had not returned. Or rather, had not made themselves known. Maybe they would soon, maybe they wouldn't. Valerian had Shaye, and that was all that mattered. He could handle everything else that happened. He'd even promised Shaye he would find a way to take her to see her mother. And he would. What Shaye wanted, Shaye would receive.

Life, at the moment, was all that he'd ever dreamed. Joachim was mated to Brenna and the little woman had become the army's best healer. She patched the men after every training session and battle, and she did it with a smile, followed by a lecture about "acting like babies" when the fearless warriors whimpered at the sight of a needle.

Shivawn was his only reason for upset. The man's mood grew blacker and blacker, and he was spending more and more time in the vampire camp, most likely sleeping with Alyssa (even though he had many nymph females to choose from) and not liking that he was driven to do so. Oh, well. The warrior would find his way. Of that Valerian was sure.

"Well, do you like it?" Shaye asked, pointing to the card in Valerian's hand.

"I love it. But a kiss is too low a price, moon." She sat behind a table and he leaned over it, placing them nose-to-nose. "You should demand sex and nothing less."

She chuckled. "Your men would buy more if I did so, I'm willing to bet."

"I will pay my men's debts," he growled with mock ferocity. "In fact, I owe you for several Joachim purchased and it's time I paid up."

Her arms wound around his neck. "Take me to bed, Valerian."

"That will be my pleasure."

"And mine, love. And mine."

* * * * *